Critical Acclaim for

THE STEEL ALBATROSS

"CARPENTER PUTS THE IMPORTANCE OF INDIVIDUAL INGENUITY IN THE FOREFRONT . . . A GUNG-HO TALE. . . . *THE STEEL ALBATROSS'* STRENGTHS ARE IN THE GADGETRY AND THE AUTHOR'S SOLEMN RESPECT FOR THE MILITARY VIRTUES OF TRAINING AND COMMAND."

—*Philadelphia Inquirer*

"*THE STEEL ALBATROSS* [SHOWS] COMPREHENSIVE KNOWLEDGE OF NAVAL ROUTINE, AS SEEN FROM THE VANTAGE POINTS OF THE LOWEST SEAMEN AND THE HIGHEST PENTAGON OFFICIALS. . . . IF YOU THINK THAT MARINE TRAINING IS HARD, WAIT UNTIL YOU READ THIS BOOK."

—*The New York Times Book Review*

"MR. CARPENTER SPRINKLES FASCINATING UNDERWATER SCENES AND DETAILS ABOUT DEEP-SEA DIVING THROUGH A SKILLFULLY UNFOLDING PLOT."

—*Washington Times*

An Alternate Selection of the Literary Guild

(more . . .)

"*THE STEEL ALBATROSS* IS AS HIGH-TECH AS THEY COME. . . . A FAST . . . ENTERTAINING READ, *ALBATROSS* SHOULD SATISFY YOU."

—*Denver Post*

"THE LATEST IN TECHNO-THRILLERS COMES FROM A FIRST-HAND SOURCE. . . . Carpenter's technological experience lends a certain authority . . . and he tackles the job at hand—well-paced adventure—very well."

—*Baton Rouge Advocate*

"SUPERB. . . . HIGH-TECH THRILLS FROM AN EXPERT. . . . A GREAT READ. . . ."

—*Newport News Daily Press* (Virginia)

"Scott Carpenter has now blossomed out as a novelist, and a good one at that! . . . Both Russians and Americans are intelligent, dedicated, and of course courageous."

—*West Coast Review of Books*

"FAST-MOVING. . . . The details in this page-turner are so plausible. . . . Carpenter calls on his extensive undersea experience with the Navy SEALAB program."

—*Publishers Weekly*

"The ultimate conflict . . . a bang-bang ending. . . . CARPENTER DOES A MAGNIFICENT JOB. . . ."

—*Orlando Sentinel*

"A new method of breathing liquid, similar to how fish extract oxygen from the water, is so vivid it will have readers gasping for breath. . . . HIGH EXCITEMENT. . . ."

—*Grand Rapids Press*

"A steady flow of Navy humor provides *THE STEEL ALBATROSS* with an insouciant tongue-in-cheek charm which adds another layer of enjoyment . . . a successful first foray into the adventure thriller form. . . . ENTERTAINING. . . ."

Winnipeg Free Press

"*THE STEEL ALBATROSS* JOINS SUCH BOOKS AS *THE HUNT FOR RED OCTOBER* FOR ARMCHAIR-GRIPPING UNDERWATER EXCITEMENT."

—*Everett Herald* (Washington)

". . . CARRIES THE READER IN A HEADLONG RUSH TO THE CLIFFHANGER ENDING."

—*Calgary Herald*

"A MODERN-DAY THRILLER . . . SURE TO SEND SHIVERS THROUGH THE ESPIONAGE WORLD. . . . CARPENTER DELIVERS EVERYTHING A READER COULD WANT IN EXCITEMENT. . . . SUPERBLY WRITTEN."

—*Ocala Star-Banner* (Florida)

THE STEEL ALBATROSS

SCOTT CARPENTER

POCKET STAR BOOKS
New York London Toronto Sydney Tokyo Singapore

This book is a work of fiction. Names, characters, places and incidents are either products of the author's imagination or are used fictitiously. Any resemblance to actual events or locales or persons, living or dead, is entirely coincidental.

A Pocket Star Book published by
POCKET BOOKS, a division of Simon & Schuster Inc.
1230 Avenue of the Americas, New York, NY 10020

ISBN: 0-671-67314-9

First Pocket Books paperback printing April 1992

10 9 8 7 6 5 4 3 2 1

Printed in the U.S.A.

To my underwater mentors, George Bond and Bob Barth, and to those other unsung heroes—Navy and civilian divers—who work, always in peril, in the deep waters of the world.

Acknowledgments

Major contributors during this effort are WordStar, a Packard Bell Laptop, and Dr. John Heilborn, who rendered invaluable technical support and word processor expertise. Significant editorial help was given by Jane Chelius and Doug Grad, to whom, along with Jeanne Drewsen, who inspired it all, I extend deep gratitude.

PART I

RUMBLINGS

BC*Iran Courts Soviets, Bjt, 500*FL*

Welcome for Soviet Minister Seen as Move Toward Renewed Ties

EDS: Moved in advance for SUNDAY; Note embargo 06/15

BY: Ernest J. Kean*FC*
AP Mideast Correspondent

TEHRAN (AP)—By standards of the former monarchy, it wasn't much of a ceremony.

No bands.

No braid.

No cheering throng, no expansive oratory.

But there was nonetheless a sense of history, marking at least a 90-degree change in direction Wednesday as Iranian officials stood solemnly in the heat and dust of summer outside the new

VIP terminal of Mehrabad International Airport to welcome the first high-level official visitor from the Soviet Union in nearly a decade.

Dimitri F. Petchukocov, Soviet Minister of Agriculture and one-time chief ideologist of the Politburo, had come to confer with his opposite number in the Iranian government on problems common to farmers of the Turkmen S.S.R. and the neighboring Khurasan region of Iran.

The exact nature of those problems—and the chances of successful Soviet-Iranian cooperation in confronting them—were not spelled out in the Iranian government's tersely worded bulletin announcing Petchukocov's visit.

And the Soviets' selection of an emissary could hardly be seen as an augury of success, at least in the business of handling farm difficulties.

Petchukocov is no agriculturist.

A former political officer in the Soviet armed forces, he was for seven years chief director of the GRU—army intelligence—before ascending to the inner circle of the Politburo during the Brezhnev era.

More recently, he appeared to have been downgraded in the Soviet hierarchy following a major power struggle between backers and opponents of glasnost.

Indeed, Petchukocov's appearance in the Iranian capital came as a considerable surprise to some observers, who had speculated that the aging bureaucrat either had been forcibly retired from public life or was, in fact, dead.

One of the few Westerners invited to attend the bare-bones welcoming ceremonies at Mehrabad Airport said Petchukocov appeared to be in good health, however, and actually smiled—a rare display of emotion for him—in response to a brief address by the Ayatollah Bani Bazargan calling his visit a "glimmering of light in darkness."

The smile, indeed, would have been hard to repress.

Bazargan, known locally as Ayatollah Margh (Ayatollah Death), had until that moment been one of the Iranian regime's best-known Russia-haters, publicly characterizing the Soviet Union as "the great serpent of our time" and "the author of lies, for whose destruction I pray hourly."

(End part 1 of 3 parts)
AP-BC-6-11 07:44 ejk*FC

The Persian Gulf

Thursday, June 12
10:26 A.M.

The sudden burst of shellfire ruined Rick Tallman's whole morning. A Marine shavetail from Indiana named Jinx Rafferty had already contributed twenty dollars to the Richard Biddle Tallman Shore Leave and General Welfare Fund in their first two games of acey-deucy. Rick speculated that the Defense Department might cut a good chunk off its budget by just paying the jarheads and then giving the Navy a chance to play acey-deucy with them. But the third game went unfinished.

Those who knew about such things say that a man never forgets the first shot fired at him, and Rick decided this was probably true. The weapon fired in his direction was a three-inch gun, and the first round had landed close aboard.

"Jee . . . zus!"

He and Jinx had been lazing away the morning, flaked out on cargo pallets jammed into the after well deck of the old LCU that was carrying them across the Persian Gulf. For some reason Jinx's idea of fun wasn't running barefoot over a searing-hot deck—jarheads were just born that way—and Rick was a full step ahead going up the ladder to the pint-size bridge.

The foreign ship closing on their port quarter was a surprise. Not because of the Iranian colors—who else would be firing on an American warship in the Persian Gulf? But Rick had expected to see one of the Ayatollah's wave-hoppers; those lightly armed motor launches the Iranians used to make a nuisance of themselves. Their antagonist, however, was a brand-new jet gunship. It was one of the 40-knot, aluminum-hulled types, equipped with a pair of small diesel engines for maneuvering and two big J-57 jet engines as its main power plant, complete with fore and aft torpedo tubes, and a three-inch naval rifle mounted in a turret on its foredeck.

The first round from the cannon had gone past the LCU's bow—the time-honored signal to stop—and Rick thought the second shot might really have been intended to deliver the same message. But if so, the Iranian gun-pointer was a poor shot. The gunship was wearing to port, backing a little on its diesel-driven screws and trying to hold station about three hundred yards ahead. There was an apologetic puff of smoke from the muzzle of the three-inch gun, followed by an ear-numbing explosion a scant five feet aft of the LCU's bow ramp. It bit a chunk out of the rusty side, spraying shrapnel across the forward well deck (and the side of a missile-firing Bradley tank parked in the open there), throwing at least one stray, buzzing bit of metal so close to Rick's ear that his stomach wanted to jump overboard without bothering to wait for the rest of his body.

The party was getting rough, and Rick wondered what useful purpose he and Jinx were serving, crowding into the exposed area of the bridge.

Screw it. He and Jinx were passengers—part of the cargo, like the tank, or the chain-link fencing stowed aft. The Navy has a subtle way of letting its minions know how they rate with the hierarchy. Stay in her good graces and you travel first class—jet transport and official helicopter from one duty assignment to another. Screw the pooch, and you wind up crossing the Persian Gulf in an LCU, which is a kind of rectangular steel box that moves through the water at a stately flank speed of six knots, its cargo space open to the sky in the fore and aft well decks, and equipped with a bow ramp that can be lowered to allow motorized equipment to move ashore under its own power. Strictly economy class.

Jinx Rafferty didn't mind, because he was assigned to babysit the guided-missile tank and its crew. They were his people and his property. But Rick was en route to a tour of duty as air intelligence officer in the most godforsaken billet that could be found by someone in the Navy Bureau of Personnel. Perhaps they considered his removal from flight status and drop out of the Top Gun program at Miramar a punishable offense.

Rick was turning to climb down from the bridge when someone at the base of the ladder said three words that made all the difference in the world as far as he was concerned.

"Christ! The skipper!"

Rick froze and swiveled his head toward the speaker. The captain of *LCU 1609* was Lt. Lewis "Bubba" Cannon, a classmate at Annapolis and a good friend. Bubba couldn't be hurt. Steel head and iron constitution. Bubba was going to be an admiral before he was forty.

Bubba Cannon had been en route to the bridge when he was hit. The rating who had shouted was holding him now, and there was a lot of blood. The LCU's captain was unconscious and looked as though he might stay that way for a while.

"Shit," Rick said. Then he forced himself to look away, meeting Jinx's eyes and telling the Marine everything he needed to know. He then fixed his gaze on the man now officially in command of the ship.

He was a chief boatswain called Petro—short for Petropoulos—with whom Rick had exchanged about a dozen words since coming aboard the day before.

LCUs of the 1600 class normally carry a complement of two officers and a dozen enlisted men, including various specialist ratings, but before they shoved off Bubba had explained that his executive officer was ashore for a little R and R. No replacement was immediately available, and the captain would have been justified in refusing to sail without a second watchstanding officer. But the only real danger on the haul to Bahrain, now that Iran and Iraq had declared a reluctant armistice, was supposed to be terminal boredom.

Rick looked at the chief now, but the chief wasn't looking at him. His eyes were on the Iranian gunship, and Rick could see him quickly coming to a decision no one on board the LCU was going to like.

"Break out small arms," the chief boomed in a voice that didn't need a bullhorn, "and prepare to repel boarding party! Lookouts, man the fifties."

Rick drew a harsh breath and glanced again at Jinx. The Marine didn't like the odds, either.

"Gillespie!" the chief shouted.

A wide-eyed face popped into view above the armored front of the tank on the foredeck. "Yo!"

"The captain's down. Get your ass back here with the medical kit. On the double."

Ever since the spy vessel USS *Pueblo* was captured and its crew held for ransom by North Korea in 1968, the Navy had set down a "no surrender, no hostage" policy. The chief seemed to be following its dictates to the letter. But it was bullshit, Rick knew. Especially in this case. The Navy—and all other services—had violated the "no hostage" part of the doctrine over and over again. Surrender, in hopeless circumstances after all means of resistance have been exhausted and in order to save the lives of your crew, was still a necessary part of sane thinking. However, the situation of *LCU 1609* was far from hopeless.

Rick looked at the tank in the forward well deck and then back at Jinx, who seemed to read Rick's thoughts—and favored him with a sudden, delighted grin.

"Betcher ass!" he said, and jumped for the ladder.

But the chief had noticed none of this. Cool and determined, he was preparing to do battle with an adversary whose vessel was roughly five times as fast as his own and mounted with ten times the firepower. The two lookouts had already armed the .50-caliber machine guns spiked at either side of the bridge, and down below, Rick could see someone serving out .45 pistols and a pair of old Thompson submachine guns.

Gutsy, Rick admitted, but suicidal. He was sure they could do better. He had been carrying a little notebook to keep track of his acey-deucy winnings, and now he used a page of it to write out two sentences that he realized were clear grounds for a general court-martial. When he was done, he tapped the chief on the shoulder, handed him the scribbled note, and waited for reaction.

The chief read the lines, blinked, and read them again.

"This—" he began.

"—is an absolutely illegal order, amounting to mutiny," Rick said, nodding, cutting him off. "But I'm putting it in writing to make sure they hang the right person later. As senior officer present afloat, I relieve you of command of this ship, Chief. Questions?"

There were several hundred of them, but no time to ask them, and they both knew it. There was only a moment of hesitation before the chief came to attention, saluted, and started to back away from the command position just abaft the ship's helm.

"Belay that!" Rick said, giving no time for second thoughts. "You have the conn, Chief. But get those guys away from the damn guns before they get us all killed."

The chief wondered if he had made a mistake. The shirtless fly-boy who had just relieved him could be a hysteric or an out-and-out coward who wanted to surrender without a fight. But he had already taken the biggest step, and he followed it now by passing Rick's orders.

"All engines stop!"

No hesitation this time as the chief rang the order, but Rick could see the man's eyes sliding sideways to take in a sudden burst of activity on the open foredeck below. Out of sight from the Iranian vessel because of the LCU's high bow-ramp, Jinx Rafferty's Marines had the top hatch of their Bradley tank open, and four of them were running back and forth carrying heavy objects from a red-painted ammunition container.

"Tell me, Chief," Rick said, distracting him, "how quickly do you think you can get the bow ramp down? In an emergency, I mean."

The chief's mind shifted gears. "Here? At sea?"

"I know it can be done; it's exactly what an LCU's built to do. That's why the bow rides so high. But . . . how fast?"

The chief looked at the bow ramp, glanced back at the tank, and suddenly made the connection. "Holy shit!" he said.

"Yeah. But the bow ramp: How quick?"

"Bang—like that! A second or two."

"Good," Rick said. "Because that's how much time we'll have. Get someone in position, ready to drop the ramp, on my order."

"Yes, sir!"

The chief was grinning now, and Rick grinned back, enjoying the adrenaline rush.

The Iranian gunship had taken the LCU's sudden slackening of speed, and the sight of its crew backing away from the .50-caliber machine guns, as a willingness to bow to superior force and firepower. The Iranian captain had shut down his jet engines, ready to maneuver on diesel power, and Rick could see a boarding party on the starboard rail. Let the towelheads go right on thinking that way.

But the Marines were still working frantically on the tank, and the chief was busy getting his men out of the way. Rick picked up a loud-hailer, to stall for time.

"Ahoy, the gunship," he called. "We are in international waters. Who are you, and what are your intentions?"

At that range, still a little more than a tenth of a mile, Rick could pick out the beard who seemed to be in command of the Iranian ship. He didn't understand Rick's words, and another beard—probably an interpreter—explained. And when the explanation was done, he didn't like it.

Turning on the interpreter, the captain loosed a torrent of fury. Then the second beard used his own bullhorn to declare that his ship was flying the flag of the Glorious Islamic Republic, and to demand that the Americans prepare to receive boarders.

Rick brought the loud-hailer up and mumbled something that wasn't really words but could be mistaken for a further question.

It seemed to agitate the Iranians, and while they were trying to frame an answer, Rick talked over his shoulder to Chief Petropoulos. He moved his mouth and chin as little as possible against the chance that someone on the other ship might have binoculars and some experience in lip-reading.

"Use our engines," he said, "just enough to keep our bow pointed in their direction."

LCUs are awkward and slow, but their twin screws enable them to maneuver right or left without using the rudder, backing one engine while going forward with the other. The chief nodded and moved to transmit the message, keeping his eyes front to avoid giving away any clue.

"Say again," the Iranian interpreter called across the water.

Rick offered him another wordless mumble, bracing his legs as the LCU moved in response to the chief's orders to the engine room. At that moment Jinx turned away from what he was doing with another big smile and a thumbs-up gesture.

"All right, then . . . let's boogie!"

But now the Iranian ship commander was out of patience.

Cursing in Farsi at the interpreter, he seized the bullhorn and turned it up to full power to make sure everyone heard what may have been the only words he knew in English.

"Give up, Yankee fooker!"

Fair enough, Rick thought. Fook him, too . . . and the camel he rode in on.

"Down ramp!" Rick yelled—and down it came.

The missile rig mounted on the Bradley tank chassis was called TOW because it fired a "tube-launched, optically tracked, wire-guided" missile designed for close tactical engagements on land. But it was especially handy in the present circumstances because the double-charge rocket propellant—one small charge to push the missile out of the tube and move it the first twenty feet; a much larger one set to ignite at that point and drive the missile the rest of the way to the target—minimizes retro-blast effect, which might make problems for the gunner and those behind him.

The sudden appearance of the tank seemed to impress the Iranians mightily. Although they ducked for cover, the three-inch gun on their foredeck came to life again. Which forced Rick to give the next order: "Main battery . . . fire!"

One notable characteristic of a TOW missile is the slowness of its flight—especially during the first two or three seconds after launch. It gathers speed as it moves, but remains under control of the gunner all the way to the target. Other missiles go ballistic at one point or another, or they are controlled by "smart" on-board computers. But the TOW can fly for two miles, unreeling a thin wire behind it to maintain contact with the gunner, who tracks its progress visually and can alter its course or altitude as required.

The Iranian captain had been standing still, like a mouse hypnotized by a cobra. But he sprang to life when he saw the TOW missile coming straight at him. "*Allah akh bar!*" he screamed into the bullhorn, and tried to jump over the side from the wing of his bridge, misjudging the distance badly enough to tumble headfirst into his own port scuppers.

The TOW missile, guided by Jinx, found its target, scoring a direct hit on the deck mounts of the three-inch gun.

"Hot damn!"

Petro approved of the Marine officer's shooting—and choice of target—as the three-inch gun cracked loose from its mountings and toppled over the side of the gunship.

"Main battery, cease fire!"

Jinx already had another TOW rocket in the tube and seemed ready to proclaim Armageddon to the unforgiven, but the Iranians had changed their minds. An argument broke out on the bridge of the gunship, but it was quickly resolved with the bearded interpreter in control. Angry-sounding voices shouted orders in Farsi, and Iranian crewmen crawled from their hidey-holes to execute them.

Rick kept the bow ramp of the LCU down and his own crew—including Jinx's Marines—at general quarters. Then the gunship was under way, using its diesel engines to come about, then galloping for the horizon when the J-57s cut in, but Rick didn't give the order to secure until he was sure the Iranians were out of torpedo range and not just beating a strategic retreat.

Watching them go left him with mixed feelings. Life, he knew, is full of temptations, and it would have been satisfying to have Jinx toss one more TOW into their wake, just for old times' sake. But there would be enough shit flying around as it was when their contact report hit Fleet Operations. Rick turned to Petro.

"The skipper . . . ?"

Chief Petropoulos, who had left the bridge as soon as the threat from the gunship appeared to be under control, gave his report with a grim face. "Shrapnel hole in his chest and a cracked skull," he said, "and Gillespie tells me he's lost a hell of a lot of blood. But a rescue chopper's on the way. And so's a flight of F-14s—in case some ayatollah didn't get the word."

Rick managed a smile for the chief and a "Well done" for the crew before he climbed down to have a personal look at his classmate and friend.

Bubba Cannon was still unconscious, and Gillespie, the pharmacist's mate who acted as medic on board the LCU, didn't look happy when Rick stuck his head into the mess compartment that had been turned into a temporary sick bay.

"Any sign of the chopper, sir?" Gillespie asked anxiously.

"No. But the chief says there's one on its way."

"Wish they'd hurry."

So did Rick. If old Bubba bought the farm now, he thought, he was going to have one hell of a time trying to explain to himself why he'd ceased firing without sinking the bastards.

Jinx Rafferty showed up, looking worried. "Bad?"

"Not good. He's still out cold and the hole in his chest looks like forty miles of bad road."

Jinx followed Rick back up the ladder to the bridge, where they stood in silence for a moment, looking at the cargo pallets where the remains of their acey-deucy game were scattered.

"You, uh, suppose . . . ?" Jinx began.

Rick just stared at him. "Ahhhh, what the hell."

Manama, Bahrain

Friday, June 13
9:33 A.M.

As Rick had figured, no one offered anyone from *LCU 1609* the Navy Cross. But the storm clouds gathered between the time the old rust-bucket dropped anchor in Manama harbor and the moment, hours later, when debriefing officers had wrung every minute detail of the gunship confrontation from all available parties.

The LCU was then dispatched to a port outside the Persian Gulf, its one-striper executive officer hastily snatched back from leave and spiked into command, while Rick, Jinx, and Chief Petropoulos were brought ashore under guard.

Nobody mentioned the word *arrest*. Nobody suggested that they weren't free to go anywhere they liked, or that there was anything unusual about the Shore Patrol "escort" who followed each of them, even into the head. But the escort was always there, and when the other shoe finally dropped, nobody was surprised. Except Rick, and only when he heard the name of the admiral to whose office they were to report at 1600 sharp.

"Carter?"

Jinx nodded. "Wasn't there an astronaut named Carter who flew the shuttle a time or two, then went back to the Navy?"

Rick nodded. "Carter, R. B.," he said. "Rear admiral, USN.

Nickname, Fang. And that, old buddy, is not a Phyllis Diller joke."

Jinx took the information in, digested it, and sighed.

"Well, sir," he said, "if the old guy is in a mood to kick some ass, we are in deep shit. You game for a little more acey-deucy while we wait?"

Rick wondered if it was something the Corps put in its coffee. "How can you possibly have any money left?"

The admiral lived up to advance billing. At 1600 the trio—Chief Petropoulos in the lead, followed by Jinx, with Rick bringing up the rear—filed into his office and heard the yeoman close the door behind them. They reported, then stood silently at attention for a full five minutes while the admiral read through a sheaf of papers on his desk, pausing from time to time to check something in a thick tome. Rick recognized it at once as The Book: Navy Regulations—Rocks and Shoals, unabridged.

When the admiral was finally done, he stacked the papers, put them back in a manila folder, closed The Book . . . and slammed an oversize hand down on it.

"Mutiny!" he roared.

No one breathed.

"Or piracy," the admiral went on after a moment, warming to the subject. "For the life of me I can't decide which it was out there. But the legal beagles will be able to come up with a satisfactory answer."

"Sir . . ."

Chief Petropoulos had spoken, and Rick was on the wrong end of the line to kick him. He hoped Jinx would. But it was already too late; the admiral had turned to focus on the chief, and Rick could see a full set of petty-officer stripes beginning to melt.

"You . . . spoke?"

"Yes, sir," Petropoulos said, unintimidated. "I was in command of that ship, *LCU 1609*, at all times after Mr. Cannon—the captain—was incapacitated."

"I see. Go on."

"Anything that happened," the chief said, "happened either with my permission or by my order. The responsibility is entirely mine."

The admiral did not snort, or interrupt. He just waited.

"That's not true, sir."

Rick could not believe it was really his own voice he heard. But he went on. "I gave Chief Petropoulos a written order, assuming command as senior officer present afloat, as soon as I saw the captain was out of action. Any orders issued subsequent to that time came entirely from me. Sir."

The voice trailed off, not because he had nothing more to say but because he'd never been much good at talking when this particular admiral was around. The admiral went on looking at him expectantly for a moment. And then it was Jinx Rafferty's turn.

"Lieutenant? Surely you have something to contribute?"

Jinx took a deep breath and let it all out in two declarative sentences and one snort, eyes front and body braced at attention.

"Firing-of-the-TOW-weapon-was-entirely-on-my-own-initiative. I-alone-am-fully-accountable. Sir!"

The admiral waited again, but that was all Jinx had to say. The Marine Corps did not mess around.

"Well, now." The admiral leaned back in his swivel chair and let his eyes run search patterns across the three faces. "Well, now—that was as fine and manly a performance as I would hope to see outside a Gomer Pyle rerun. Congratulations!"

"Sir. If I may interrupt," Petropoulos started to say, but the admiral wasn't having any.

"Shut . . . your . . . beak."

The chief did and stood mute with the others.

"All right, then," the admiral said finally, in a voice that was back to normal pitch and volume but still edged with sharp icicles. "Since you're in such an all-fired hurry to talk, Chief, let's start with you. How many years have you been in the Navy?"

"Sixteen years. Sir!"

"And an interesting sixteen years they've been." His fingers tapped a pile of folders on the left side of the desktop, and Rick recognized them as Navy record jackets. Personnel files. Three of them. "You know, Petropoulos, I'd expect a bunch of sea-lawyer hogwash from the other two. They're too young to think, and too stupid to read. But a man like you—with your experience!"

The chief didn't seem to have any rebuttal to offer.

"You are aware," the admiral went on, "that the officer relieving you was an aviator—a brown-shoe fly-boy, with no experience or qualification whatever in command of a surface ship?"

That called for a reply, and the chief did not hesitate. "Yes, sir!"

"You were also aware that as a passenger on board your ship, this officer—senior though he might be—had absolutely no place in the chain of command?"

A little hesitation this time. "Yes, sir!"

"I see." The admiral paused, as though drawing breath for a real blast. But when he spoke, his tone was surprisingly mild.

"Then what," he said, "by all that's holy, what caused you even to consider handing over your ship to him?"

The chief licked his lips, and Rick wished for some way to send him a message to keep silent. It was the only thing that ever worked with the admiral.

"Mr. Tallman did the right thing," the chief said. "The thinking and tactics may have been a little unorthodox, but they worked—and I was fresh out of ideas and alternatives."

Rick groaned inwardly and braced himself for the shock wave. But when the admiral spoke again, it was in the same restrained voice.

"And you, Lieutenant," he said, turning to Jinx. "Have you anything to add to the chief's testimonial?"

"Sir! Mr. Tallman's decision to use the tank's armament to engage the Iranian vessel was both correct and justified, given the circumstances of their having fired twice on us, wounding the captain, and having threatened to fire again—at extreme hazard to the ship and its crew."

It was an unaccustomed mouthful for Jinx, and Rick found himself admiring the jarhead's fortitude and choice of phrasing, suicidal though it may have been.

The admiral digested the words and studied Jinx like a scientist inspecting a particularly interesting and unusual lower life-form. Then he leaned back in his chair and let his eyes focus on the middle distance.

He seemed pointedly to avoid looking at Rick again, and his next remarks were addressed to the other two men. But Rick knew he wasn't being slighted. His turn would come.

"The action you are defending," he said, speaking now with the detached air of a Naval Institute lecturer, "consists of two specific parts, to wit: the act of mutiny, and the act of war. Let us consider them separately.

"First, the act of mutiny. The written order by which Mr. Tallman assumed command of *LCU 1609* has a certain fascination all its own because, while it did not and could not protect you, Chief, from charges of aiding and abetting mutiny—specifically, permitting an unqualified officer illegally to gain command of a vessel in your charge—it is prima facie evidence of his own guilt, thus condemning you both instead of leaving some room, however meager, for doubt. And as for you, Rafferty, your compliance with and acceptance of the situation is also damning. You are, all of you, mutineers . . . which, in wartime, could earn you a trip to the hangman's dock—and even now is worth about twenty years in federal prison. Plus a dishonorable discharge."

He paused for a moment to let that sink in.

"The act of war, however, complicates matters to a degree," he continued. "This is for two reasons. One, while not a direct violation of policy—you were, indeed, under orders to fire if fired upon—the use of a powerful and sophisticated weapons system such as TOW in response to a three-inch popgun is a little like swatting a fly with a flatiron."

Rick held his breath, waiting for someone to remind the admiral that the TOW had been their only effective on-board weapon, and how the Iranians had attacked only because they thought they possessed superior force. But to his relief they held their peace.

"And two, it disclosed the presence of the weapon in this theater of operations—a presence we were not at all anxious to advertise at this time, since it is intended for engagement between land vehicles and its deployment here might be . . . misinterpreted."

More sinking-in time. Rick hadn't considered that, and he was fairly sure it hadn't occurred to the others, either. He wondered if there were career counselors on staff at Norfolk

Naval Prison. Not that it would matter for the next decade or so.

"Fortunately," the admiral continued, "the Iranians have a few problems of their own. They opened fire on a ship of the United States Navy in international waters, with serious harm to a member of the crew—the captain, by God—and with visible intent of abduction. So they can hardly speak from a platform of injured innocence, no matter how many lies their lunatic holy men try to invent."

Rick felt the muscles at the back of his neck relax ever so slightly. Though he hadn't actually said so, the admiral had just told him that someone had taken a fix on the LCU when it transmitted its action report. And offered to verify the ship's position.

"In fact," the admiral said, "after a day of screaming to high heaven about a Yankee warship attacking a peaceful Islamic patrol craft inside their coastal waters, they have now switched to a flat denial that any such contact ever took place."

The admiral wasn't quite ready to quit, though.

"So you two"—the number was not lost on Rick—"got lucky this time. No charges will be filed, no permanent record of the incident will be retained, and there will be no notation, favorable or otherwise, in your personnel records."

Jinx was almost smiling. Though at attention and thus unable to look in the Marine's direction, Rick thought he could feel the grin-spasm working its way irresistibly toward the surface of the Hoosier's face.

"Before telling you to get the hell out of my sight, however," the admiral said, "I want to issue one small word of caution. You will not . . . ever . . . discuss this matter, or anything connected with it, with anyone outside this room. Do you understand?" This time he was waiting for an answer.

"Yes, sir!" Two voices; a single thought.

"Dismissed!"

Jinx and Chief Petropoulos executed a simultaneous about-face that Rick longed to join. A moment later, he was alone with the admiral.

But the older man surprised him. Intercom orders to his yeoman—"You can start setting up the phone link now, and make sure we're not disturbed"—were crisply impersonal, and there was no change in the aggressive set of the admiral's shoulders. But the blue-gray eyes that had been so hard a moment earlier were merely old—and tired—when he told Rick to be at ease and draw up one of the chairs ranked along the wall.

Rick did it and watched impassively as the admiral dragged his personnel file to the center of the desk.

"Your naval career, Lieutenant," he said, "has not been a parade to glory."

Rick followed longstanding personal policy in all matters involving Rear Adm. R. B. Carter, USN, and sat still with his mouth closed, trying to look intelligent. He knew it probably wouldn't help. He'd never found anything that did.

"On the other hand," the admiral continued, "it has the virtue of being unusual. I looked it over again this morning—not that I really needed to—and was struck by the remarkable contrasts." He flipped open the cover of the file and tapped the first stapled sheaf of papers. "You were near the head of your class scholastically and athletically during your first two years at Annapolis?"

Rick didn't reply. The admiral knew the answer.

"You failed to graduate, however. Bilged," the admiral said, "on disciplinary grounds. Too many demerits. Almost a new record, I understand." He picked up the folder and held it for a moment as though he were going to throw it at Rick's head.

"Bilging out of the Academy isn't the end of the world, as better men than you have discovered. Acceptance to Princeton does not come in a box of Cracker Jacks, and your marks there were excellent. But you failed to graduate . . . quit, before the start of your senior year."

To join the Navy—go through pilot training as a cadet. But Rick didn't say so.

"In flight training," the admiral continued, "things seemed to be looking up. Excellent record, all the way to graduation. Top fitness reports afterward, good enough to rate a regular commission. And then assignment to advanced fighter-weapons training at Miramar, after a tour of carrier duty."

Here it comes, and Rick was surprised to discover that he really didn't care. The hell with it. What could the old bastard say that he hadn't already said to himself?

"You were doing well at Top Gun. Neck 'n' neck for the top scoring trophy. And then, like Annapolis and Princeton, you were out. Physically disqualified due to injuries sustained off duty. Driving a goddamn motorcycle into a tree. While drunk!"

Rick was sure that the admiral knew that wasn't true. He'd had a drink or two, sure. But the California Highway Patrol had insisted on a blood-alcohol test after the crackup, and the concentration in his blood had registered under .03 percent. Sober. The fact was in his record jacket, so it was a cheap shot, and the hell with him. Thank God the admiral didn't know that Rick's passenger that night was the new wife of Top Gun's chief instructor. And that her arms hadn't been wrapped tightly around Rick's waist just to keep herself from falling off the motorcycle.

"The injury to your arm," the admiral said in a voice that was almost civil, "can it be repaired?"

Rick straightened his left arm as much as he could, then rotated it through the limited arc it was still capable of describing. The injury had restricted it to a little more than thirty degrees.

"Two doctors said no way," he said. "The main damage was to the elbow, which is as complicated as the knee, and they said they'd just be spinning their wheels."

"But . . . ?"

"One Navy bone-chopper. A surgeon named Sam Deane—I never met him—looked at the X rays and the rest of the stuff and said it could be done. But only with extensive therapy afterward."

"So when's the operation?"

The admiral seemed genuinely interested, and suddenly Rick realized the older man didn't have the full picture after all. BuPers was behind; the doctor's official response wasn't in the file yet.

"Never," he said flatly. "Apparently this Sam Deane saw my records—and decided I'd be a bad surgical risk because I wouldn't have the personal discipline to handle the follow-up therapy."

The old eyes blinked; that was the admiral's only outward response. Give the old son of a bitch this much, Rick told himself: You sure wouldn't want to play poker against him.

"So you're grounded."

"I could get back on flight status," Rick said. "Qualify in patrol aircraft. With a medical waiver."

"But the restricted arm motion would keep you out of fighters."

"Yes, sir."

"I see." The eyes got a little older, and—if such a thing were possible—a little colder. But he hadn't expected the man to offer him a cigar.

"Well," the admiral said. "You can't stay here." At last Carter might be ready to tell him what was on his mind.

"Iranian denial of the incident notwithstanding, I've had new orders cut for Chief Petropoulos and Lieutenant Rafferty, taking them out of this theater. You present a whole different set of problems."

And always had, Rick thought.

"As I see it, you have three options," the admiral said, leaning back in the padded chair, "and it's time you faced up to them. The assignment here, to air intelligence, was really just a stopgap. Or perhaps some smartass in BuPers's notion of a joke. The way it stands, I have the option of ordering you back to the States for reassignment to a patrol squadron, after retraining as a multiengine pilot—"

Forget that, Rick thought.

"—or endorse a request for separation from the service on partial—very damn partial—disability—"

That, too.

"—or scratch around for some other kind of duty, perhaps better suited to your, ah, more obvious talents and proclivities."

Laundry officer in Alaska? Rick had come up with the same three choices himself, chugging across the gulf in the old LCU. You've got to play the hand you're dealt.

"Your decision, mister?"

"The third alternative, sir, seems to offer the best prospect."

The admiral nodded thoughtfully. "Perhaps," he said. "In any case, we'll know soon enough."

"Sir?"

He seemed to come back from some far place. The eyes snapped into focus, boring into Rick again.

"Your friend Lewis Cannon—Bubba—is in sick bay here. They've done what they could, but he's headed for a hospital stateside and you'll be returning, too, on the same plane. I'm told he's conscious, so I suppose you'll want to see him now."

"Yes, sir!"

The admiral nodded again. "Very well. I'll make my decision as quickly as possible. Your orders will either be cut and delivered to you before takeoff, or transmitted to you in flight. Satisfactory?"

"Yes, sir!" Rick stood up again.

"Sure you want to leave the choice of assignment to me?"

"Yes, sir."

"Very well. Dismissed."

Rick came to attention, executed a stiff, parade-ground about-face, and had reached the door when the admiral stopped him again.

"Richard," he said in a quiet voice Rick hadn't heard for a long time. Rick halted and turned back to face the older man.

"Sir?"

"Your mother."

"Yes, sir?"

"She's waiting in Palm Beach. I had the yeoman get a stateside telephone uplink. Talk to her and let her know you're all right."

"Yes, sir."

"And Richard . . . please give her my regards as well."

"Yes, Father."

Manama, Bahrain

Saturday, June 14
2:33 P.M.

An admiral, Rick Tallman told himself as he took his seat on board the MedEvac 707 jetliner and buckled his seat belt, was not the easiest kind of father to have. But then, he'd never been the easiest kind of son.

Rick's orders still hadn't arrived by the time the plane was ready for boarding, but he wasn't worried as he mounted the portable stairway and found his way to the aft compartment. Bubba Cannon was being strapped into a hospital bunk.

Bubba almost blew a fuse when Rick described the chewing-out he and the others had received over their handling of the confrontation with the Iranian gunship.

"You'd a-done anything else," he declared, "I'd a-kicked your skinny butt from here to Bancroft Hall! Look now—I was in command of that rust-bucket, and I say every damn thing happened out there was on my order and nobody else's, and I will put it in writing—for Fang fucking Carter or any other son of a bitch who's interested!"

"Yeah"—Rick grinned at him—"and you'll sleep good, too, if you drink Ovaltine!"

"Listen, Rick. . . ."

"Back off, Bubba. All right?"

"All right, it's your ass! Those mothers were asking for it, messing with a ship they thought couldn't fight back. All you did—"

"—was usurp a surface command for which I was not, and am not, qualified. Not to mention order the firing of a weapon that was not a part of the ship's authorized armament. End of story. I got no complaint, man. So lighten up."

But Bubba seethed. "Well, what the fuck they want you to do, surrender?"

Rick grinned at him again. "Of course not! The Navy knows damn well I did the right thing at the right time with that weapon."

"No shit."

"Look at it from the Pentagon's viewpoint, Bubba. The action we took headed off another *Pueblo* incident. But now the Iranians say it never happened, and no way is anyone going to contradict them."

"But. . . ."

"But what?"

"But . . . goddamn it . . . he's your father!"

And God help both of us, Rick thought as he headed for his seat. The Military Air Transport Service, or MATS plane, gathered speed and climbed into the cloudless Middle Eastern sky. As always happened when Rick was a passenger and not flying the plane himself, he got drowsy. The dull, steady drone of the jet engines worked on him like a lullaby on a baby. Boeing—Brahms, they both start with *B*. And before the 707 had even reached cruising altitude, Rick's seat was all the way back, his mouth was open, and his eyes were shut.

The F-5 Talon jinked right, trying to get Rick to follow, before rolling into the hard left turn that would have given him a chance to lock on for a tail shot. It was the same tactic that had worked for him—almost to the point of a kill—two minutes earlier. But this time Rick was on to the maneuver and followed, turning his Tomcat inside the F-5's arc and then tightening while the radar intercept officer in the backseat called off the numbers.

Classic!

The ultimate in 1V1 (the logbook entry for 1 vs. 1) aerial combat: Adrenaline was running, and Rick could feel the lift as he completed the turn, ranging in right on the Talon's six, and recognized the bloodred stripe at the top of the rudder. It was the Marine; Lt. Col. "Richtofen" Reich, chief inspector and top dog at Top Gun. In another moment, he'd have a lock on the old bastard and remind him that fighter tactics are for young dudes, not for . . .

Huh?

Suddenly the F-5 was gone, simply removed from the sky. "Lose sight, lose the fight." Reich's voice was loud and clear in Rick's headphones. "I see you. How come you don't see me, sonny?"

The old geezer had outfoxed him; a second before Rick was ready to shoot, he'd rolled his wings level, dropped the nose for a moment, and then reefed the Talon into a vertical climb that let him pull away—right out of sight—while the 'Cat's wings were still racked forward, out of the glove, slowing down for the shot.

"Shit." No chance to get nose-up on the bastard. No energy. Not from this position.

Rick hammerheaded the F-14 over, spent a second or two looking head-on at the blue Pacific, then craned his neck trying to eyeball Reich's red-finned F-5. But it was gone again.

"Ne'mine," came the soft Tennessee drawl of his backseat RIO, "Mush" Mussbergh, who offered whatever comfort was

possible in the circumstances. "Ne'mine, boy. Mothah be dropping in on us bim-bi."

Pulling out to honor the 10,000-foot "hard deck" low-altitude limit imposed by safety rules, Rick found Reich again—up sun, of course, almost on top of him—and kicked the F-14 into a hairy bat-turn, going full macho Zone V burner and snap-rolling 180 degrees toward the Talon to be sure of keeping it in sight. But Reich had been expecting that, too.

"Idle and boards," Mush called from the backseat, meaning the senior instructor had cut his throttles and popped his speed brakes, digging his Talon into a six-G, nose-low turn, hanging in the sky like a free balloon. In just a few seconds, Reich had put himself at Rick's eight-o'clock, about 2,500 feet away; a near-perfect gun solution.

"Shit." This time, Rick and Mush had spoken the word—the fighter pilot's prayer—in unison. But there was no time for philosophy, time only to screw up the old bastard's shot.

Rick stomped in left rudder, and the violence of the resulting yaw banged his helmet into the right canopy as they dropped into a high-G roll.

Reich was right with them. Rick caught a momentary glimpse of the red rudder, solid above the power-bright afterburners, and knew the instructor had the hammer down, going for knots. But he lost sight of him again almost at once as he slammed the Tomcat into another six-G turn, trying to manhandle the heavy airplane into Fox Two parameters: a Sidewinder shot into the afterburners of Reich's F-5.

It was against accepted doctrine, and something they'd been warned against. The maneuver was a violation of the Tomcat's published limits—and doubly dangerous because they were now down close to the 10,000-foot "hard deck" again. Lots of space between you and disaster if you were flying a Cessna 152; no space at all for something as fast and heavy as the 'Cat.

But suddenly . . . there it was: Reich's F-5 appeared dead ahead, and Mush locked on for the intercept. Dead meat. Mort! The turn, and Rick's willingness to push the 'Cat to the ragged edge of its envelope, had paid off; they were locked on the stack of the senior instructor's F-5.

"Tomcat on Fox Two," Rick called off the kill on squadron

frequency, and waited for confirmation, while Mush burbled happily in the backseat, savoring the victory.

"Fox Two," Reich said. "Rrrrrrog."

That was confirmation; he and Reich each had one kill on the board for the morning, and it was coming up fast on bingo fuel; time to head for the barn. Rick joined Reich and two other aircraft in a tight wing for the trip back to Miramar. But the elation he had felt earlier was dying, as was the adrenal tingle in his hands and feet. Something was wrong.

Lt. Col. "Richtofen" Reich, USMC, was a tough competitor, but a fair man. Always quick with a compliment for the good tactical solution. But no cigar this time. There'd been an odd kind of flatness in his voice when he'd confirmed Rick's kill position.

Rick wondered about it, picking at the problem with the back of his mind while he brought his F-14 home to Top Gun. What was biting the old bastard, anyway?

"Too low!" Mush's voice was drowned out by the raucous clangor of the Tomcat's ground-proximity alarm, and Rick suddenly found himself beset by sight and sound. The alarm was deafening, going off in a series of two-second bursts, and he'd never heard a ground-prox alarm do that before. He pulled back hard on the stick to get the Tomcat above 10,000 feet, and the shoulder harness bit into his shoulders from the force of the extra G's. He squirmed to get comfortable, and now only his left shoulder was in the belt's grip. If he could get his left shoulder free, he and Mush would be okay, but the strap wouldn't let go.

"Mr. Tallman?"

A rating who wore the chevrons of a hospitalman first class broke into Rick's reverie, shaking him awake by the shoulder.

"This came for you, sir," the sailor said. "From Bahrain."

Rick thanked him and accepted the message, but waited a moment before unfolding the radiogram.

Where, he wondered, had the Navy—and his father—decided to hide him?

One thing for sure; he wouldn't be going back to flight duty. He'd ruled out patrol planes, and Dr. Sam Deane's decision not to repair the arm would keep him out of fighters.

Deck officer? It would be an unusual career shift for an aviator, but not entirely unheard of. He was still junior enough to find a slot somewhere that would let him qualify. But he really couldn't see himself following a career track like Bubba Cannon's. With such a late start, he wasn't likely to rate a command of his own until he was in his forties, which would put him a long way behind in the Flag Rank Sweepstakes.

Couldn't be multiengine pilot. "Patrol planes and transports," he had told a BuPers counselor after the motorcycle accident, "are interesting and complicated and there is a real sense of power for the man in the left seat. But in the end, it's just the ultimate truck. You load it up with cargo or bombs or mines and get it airborne and punch data into the autopilot and George flies the damn thing, while you sit still and talk about women and sports and women and politics and women and retirement plans and women—and worry about getting in some handball to try and cut down on the gut you've started pushing around in front of you.

"But a fighter jock's ass is on the line every moment he's in the air. It's real! It keeps the blood circulating, and you're alive in the only way that really counts." Which was a nice, civilized way of phrasing the dirty little secret he'd been carrying around since long before he had been able to spell it out for himself.

I'm an adrenaline freak, he admitted, a thrill junkie. Colors are brighter, smiles are sharper, and the reflexes stand right up at attention when you're betting it all on the next card.

It can be addictive, and Rick had found out about it when he was just six years old, on the beach at his home in Florida. His mother had looked away for a moment, and by pure luck he'd caught the curl of a big, well-shaped wave just right to bodysurf in on it. Young as he was, he'd realized that he could be injured; the surge and thrum of power under him told him so. If he was going to get through the next minute without major damage, he would have to do everything exactly right.

And that was when he'd started to laugh. Not out loud. Inside. Laughing and twisting and bending over the monster wave, trying to keep himself going, to keep on feeling the wonderful tingling in fingers and toes; the waves—not of water, but of elation—that made him ten feet tall.

When the wave finally broke and dropped him on the sand,

his mother had screamed and come running. She grabbed him and dragged him back up the beach while he fought her like a pint-size fury, trying to get back to where the action was.

Even when his mother had picked him up and carried him, still kicking and screaming, into the big house and put him in bed, he had kept trying to escape. She even called his stepfather at work, who had her call a doctor to check him out against the possibility that he'd knocked a screw loose riding that wave.

The doctor said Rick was all right. Just overtired, perhaps, and maybe suffering from a bit too much sun. Keep him quiet. A good night's rest was all the boy needed. But by that time Rick had begun to think (one thing about wanting to get back to the surf, it had forced him to actually use his brain) so he didn't argue, but simply pretended to drift off to lullaby land.

His mother had stayed around for a while, poking at the covers and feeling his forehead. But at last she went to see about the dinner party she was giving that night, leaving him free to sneak out the window and get back to the Fun Zone.

In a way, he told himself, he'd been doing the same thing ever since.

Rick took a deep breath and settled back to read the radiogram. The heading was standard:

TO: TALLMAN, RICHARD B., LTJG, USN
FROM: BUREAU OF NAVAL PERSONNEL
SUBJECT: REASSIGNMENT

But the rest might as well have been Sanskrit for all he could make of it on first reading:

1. PURSUANT TO VOLUNTARY APPLICATION FOR SEA AIR LAND TEAM TRAINING . . .

Voluntary?
Application?

2. SUBJECT OFFICER WILL REPORT TO COMMANDING OFFICER, NAVAL SPECIAL WARFARE CENTER, CORONADO . . .

Special Warfare Center?

Sea Air Land Team . . . !

Rick read the rest of the printout through once, and then again, slowly, looking for the snapper. The exit line. The joker. But it wasn't there.

Suddenly, Rick found himself fighting desperately to contain the storm of lunatic laughter that he could feel gathering force in his chest.

That bastard! That crazy old son of a bitch! Fang fucking Carter, his own father, had shipped his ass—volunteered him, no less—into the meanest, toughest, most anonymous duty the Navy had to offer. Underwater demolition: hard labor with the threat of drowning. He was en route "by first available air transport" to the SEALs.

Seawater was wet, salty, cold, dangerous, and the opposite direction from the way he wanted to go. He was a fighter jock, damn it, not a fish.

On the other hand, Tallman, he told himself before he was engulfed by another wave of laughter, you did leave yourself wide open, didn't you? Told him to make the decision? Practically issued the maniac an engraved invitation to your funeral? Can't really blame him, then, for using it.

And besides—you know a man shouldn't join the Navy if he can't take a joke.

PART II

BUREAUCRACY

La Jolla, California

Monday, June 16
5:33 A.M.

The first thing Rick Tallman did when he got back to California was telephone Capt. Will Ward. And the second was to rent a car in order to pay him a visit.

He didn't yet have a hotel room for the night—or even a billet at one of the Navy's bachelor officers' quarters. And his luggage was still in the transient-terminal baggage locker at Miramar Naval Air Station, where a MATS flight from Washington had dropped him on a quick stop before turning north toward China Lake. But Rick needed to see a friendly face.

He hadn't seen the captain for a while. Not, in fact, since the day he'd gotten the news that the fly-boy career of LTJG Richard Biddle Tallman, USN, had gone permanently into the dumper. But Captain Ward—always ready to listen—hadn't let him brood, had encouraged him to go to the air intelligence school and accept whatever assignment he was given. Tough it out for at least a year before making any permanent career decisions. Good advice, no matter how things had turned out.

On the telephone he had seemed eager to see Rick again, even on short notice.

Abruptly, Rick gunned the rented Mustang convertible and jinked left to pass a line of traffic stuck behind three 18-wheelers, swinging back in time to make the turn into Torrey

Pines Road. He drove around the backside of Revelle College, and then left onto La Jolla Shores Drive, where a series of switchbacks brought him to the little stone monument that marked the entrance to the Scripps Institution of Oceanography. He began to search for a parking slot not specifically reserved for faculty or staff (no minor problem, even at five-thirty in the morning) that was also within walking distance of his destination.

Discovering one at last, and easing the car into it, Rick found himself responding to the idyllic setting. Solid and California-stately amid live oaks, torrey pines, and royal palms, the Scripps Institution of Oceanography sat on a green cliff leaning down toward the rim of the Pacific. A separate campus and research complex of the University of California, San Diego—it is the West Coast counterpart to Woods Hole in Massachusetts—its various buildings are a stern reflection of a compound planned by engineers and scientists for their own austere purposes.

Supported by private and public monies, Scripps operates a fleet of oceanographic research vessels—many of them equipped with classrooms for on-site teaching. An array of shore-based programs probes every phase of biological, chemical, geological, and physical oceanography as well. Scientists come to Scripps to study everything from the nature of the atmosphere to the cause of earthquakes or the influence of the oceans upon weather. Textbooks, learned tomes, and scientific papers come trooping off the Scripps campus in lockstep like the marching Chinese, and foundations allocate support funds for programs there almost as a matter of course. Doctorates abound.

And the government is ready with research grants of its own . . . some of them requiring security classifications to Q and above just to say the name of the project.

But all the somber weight of learning was powerless against the sheer physical beauty of the place, dominated and carried away by the eternal restlessness of the ocean—and flavored by the scent of salt and seaweed borne in by the onshore breeze.

It was this duality that accounted, Rick believed, for the peculiar stratification of Scripps' insular society. The pure eggheads never seemed to know what time it was, and the aesthetes just didn't care.

The man Rick had come to see, however, did not fit into either category. Like the campus itself, he was one of a kind. The first thing anyone ever seemed to notice about Capt. Wilson W. Ward, USN (Ret.), was that he resembled a fireplug: short, solid, and made of cast iron. Built to last. And all Navy.

The slacks and aloha shirt he wore in retirement might cause the casual viewer to speculate about an explosion in a paint factory, but somehow as worn by Captain Ward they took on the appearance of a uniform, an impression strongly affirmed by the ramrod posture that made him seem to be always at attention.

Ward was his father's oldest friend; roommate during their plebe year at Annapolis and friendly rival during the junior-officer vicissitudes after graduation. Rick's father, Admiral Carter, had become a fighter pilot and later flew in space, while his erstwhile roommate volunteered for the submarine service and later moved on into the exotic world of deep-submergence systems.

Godfather at Rick's baptism, Will Ward had presided over fishing trips and scuba excursions in the years that followed, persisting in his godfatherly function after his parents' divorce and Rick's adoption by his stepfather. But he hated when Rick teased him by calling him Uncle Will. He'd retort, "That would make me a relative of your father's, and I'll be damned before you pin that on me."

There was nothing soft about Captain Ward. His face showed the seams of three decades at sea. His piercing blue eyes lanced out from beneath a bramble of untrimmed black brow. And he had an armor-piercing voice shaped by half a lifetime of shouting orders into a high wind and years of diving with mixed-gas gear.

"God damn it, Ricky," the older man roared, wasting no time in preliminaries as his godson entered the room, "get your butt up here and give me a hand!"

Rick grinned and bounded up the metal stairway two steps at a time. The captain was atop a superstructure, probing the bottom of a room-size tank with a long steel grappling rod. He was having trouble making contact with something shiny and metallic lying in a far corner. Rick moved along to a vantage point where he could offer directions and advice.

"A little to the left . . . now forward . . . okay. Right there. Now . . . close the claws."

The water seemed murky, and even when the captain made contact with the grapple and began to lift the object toward him, Rick was unable to see it clearly. And the captain, citing possible "security problems," had not offered much in the way of information during their telephone conversation, except to say that he had "a new toy" he wanted to show off.

"Little motherfucker," Captain Ward growled, toweling the shiny object with tenderness, then cradling it in his arms. "Works well enough by radio control in there, but the damn thing leaks like a cheap pen, and every time it makes a dive I have to get out the grabber and fish it off the bottom."

He clambered down the ladder, followed by Rick, and moved to a wooden worktable, where he set his burden down and stood back, regarding it with the air of a proud parent.

"Ugly, ain't it?"

Rick looked the object over at close range. Out of the water and lying on its side, he thought, the captain's brainchild resembled a factory-reject model airplane, fabricated from stainless steel. A child's plaything gone grotesquely wrong.

Stubby wings, oddly rounded and equipped with what seemed to be a system of spoilers, flaps, and ailerons, protruded from a slim fuselage on either side of the streamlined canopy faired into its top (or at any rate, Rick decided it probably was the top—though with the thing lying inert on its side it was not possible to be absolutely sure).

The tail section seemed wrong, too. It consisted of a single tall, unarticulated dorsal-fin rudder (hinged at the center so that the whole thing would move; the through-hull fitting, if it had one, might be the source of the leak the captain had mentioned) with elevators drooping at an angle to either side of the boat—their action apparently balanced or augmented by what looked like dive fins, pitch-attitude control surfaces of the canard type, at the bow.

But something was lacking. Puzzled, Rick scanned the glistening little model again. The boat had no jets, screws, or other visible means of propulsion.

"What do you call her?" he inquired, carefully avoiding any direct opinion.

"You mean the name?"

"Uh . . . yes."

"Well, it doesn't really have one. Just a designation: On the books, she's the SA-1a. *S* as in 'submersible.' *A* as in 'aquaplane.' And the little sub-*a* at the end is because it's just a model. But a full-scale version of the boat is being built—got almost all the money we need to build it, by God. By the time the big one's ready to go into the water, I guess we'll need a real name. For the christening. Any ideas?"

Rick looked at the model and thought of several, offhand. But none that his godfather would like.

The idea that someone was spending good money to construct a life-size replica of Captain Ward's self-destructive little tub toy struck him as so outrageous that he couldn't help asking a question that seemed tactless, to say the least.

"What does it do?" he inquired.

But Captain Ward seemed only a little surprised. "I didn't tell you?" he said, glancing up from the notes he was making on some papers at the far end of the worktable. "No, Christ, I guess I didn't, so how the hell would you know? Okay, then. Rick, boy, what you're looking at there is a one-twenty-fifth-scale working model—well, working sometimes, anyway—of what I think will be a whole new generation of submersible stealth vehicles.

"You noticed it doesn't have a screw or anything else visible—or audible—to move it through the water? Well, that's the whole gimmick right there. No engine noise. No propeller cavitation, no sound at all to register on anyone's damn hydrophones, no matter how sensitive they are.

"Because, son, this little sucker is a glider! Although she has some very clever auxiliary thrusters, she's the world's one and only true underwater sailplane. A genuine first! Now, lemme alone a minute, okay? I got to think."

Rick stood silent for a moment, sorting out the captain's words, then noted that the appearance of the SA-1a seemed suddenly to have improved.

Penguins and ostriches, he reminded himself, seemed grotesque if you think of them as birds, as life-forms intended for flight through the air. Think of a penguin as an animal that "flies" underwater, or the ostrich as a creature designed to move swiftly over the ground, and they don't look so strange after all. Well, penguins, anyway.

Suddenly the stubby little wings and peculiar tail assembly began to make sense. And the boat itself didn't seem quite so ugly anymore.

"Flood the ballast tanks to achieve negative buoyancy," Rick said, thinking aloud, "and you can use gravity—use its energy, expressed as speed of descent—to produce horizontal thrust. The control surfaces maneuver the boat underwater the same way a sailplane's control surfaces maneuver it in the air. And when you're as low as you want to go—"

"—you reverse the process," the captain said, nodding, giving his godson a froglike smile that illuminated the whole room. "Blow the tanks to get positive buoyancy and use ascent energy to 'fly' the boat upward the same way you 'flew' it down. Yeah, boy. You got it."

Rick's eyes were fixed on the little steel model. "So . . . simple," he said. "So damn simple."

"Yeah, Ricky, sometimes I think of all the weird shit I've been involved with over the years—bizarre stuff like a water-breathing project with human guinea pigs, an experimental undersea lab where guys lived for months at a time, to name a couple. They were all complicated and some never panned out, but you're right about this one. It's so damn simple that we overlooked it for more than a century, by God! And it beats the shit outta me why. Submarines—the regular kind, with regular propulsion systems, I mean—have used a version of what the SA-1a does since, well, since the beginning. Submariners know they can use the forward dive planes and after control surfaces to give the boat added forward motion every time they make a sudden change in depth. You remember the early gliders?"

Rick grinned at his godfather. "No," he said. "Do you? But I think I know what you mean: the kind they had back in the twenties—that could only slide downhill?"

"Yeah. Them." Captain Ward picked up the SA-1a and

shook it gently, holding the little boat close to his ear, trying to determine whether there was any water left inside. "The lift-to-drag ratio on those old kites was so low they could only go about six feet forward for every foot of descent. Not near good enough. Finding updrafts, thermal or contour, didn't really help because you couldn't gain enough altitude to make any real difference. So glider flights had to be pretty short . . . unless you could find someone with a car to tow you across the countryside. Or put an auxiliary engine on board, the way some did."

"Or went gliding off a cliff," Rick chimed in. "But then someone invented a better wing."

"There you go! That's what happened, the first true sailplanes, with those long, tapered wings that could give you twenty feet forward for each foot of descent; they changed the whole picture. Suddenly, a pilot who really knew his stuff could fly all day without an engine by finding a heated column of air that was going up, getting into it, and letting it take him upstairs."

Rick looked back at the SA-1a, started to speak, but hesitated.

"Go on," Captain Ward prodded.

"Uh . . . the wings . . ."

"Don't look a hell of a lot like the ones on a regular sailplane, do they?" The captain started to replace the drain plug in the bottom of the model, but instead gave it a final shake and blew forcefully into the hole. "No. They don't. But that kind of wing—the one you're thinking about—is designed for use in the air. Wouldn't work worth a shit underwater. On a sub."

He set the plug back in place, giving it an extra shove, then held the model up for further inspection.

"Boats and airplanes both use propellers to shove them along, but an airplane propeller's no use if you put it underwater, and the kind designed for a boat would look pretty silly hooked onto the nose of a Cessna. You got to take the medium into account. You know, the medium sends a message."

Rick thought it over and voiced another question, harking back to the captain's earlier theme.

"Updrafts?" he said. "In the ocean?"

"Of course updrafts," Captain Ward said with a trace of

impatience. "Okay, hell—you're a fly-boy. A brown-shoe. And what the hell would someone who goes pooting around the sky with his tail on fire know about the ocean? I used to have that argument about once a day with your dad. But you had some time at the Academy, and you've got a good mind when you use it, so you ought to know there are updrafts and downdrafts under the surface of the ocean. And for that matter, underwater rivers—currents of different speed, temperature, salinity, and direction—running every damn whichway. Slower than air currents, sure. Everything down there is slower. But it's there, and the SA-1a . . . aw, hell, lemme show you."

Still cradling the SA-1a in his arms, he remounted the stairs to the catwalk and gently set the little boat back in the water. It floated there while he climbed down again and seated himself at an improvised remote control console.

"Just breadboarding, a lot of this," the captain said, confirming Rick's guess, as his hands moved over the complex of switches and relays. "It works, sort of, and that's all you can say for it. But the control system we're building for the full-size boat—well, no sense trying to explain. Just call it advanced state-of-the-art."

Lights came on inside the test tank, and he ran through some kind of predive checklist attached to the clipboard at his side, muttering to himself in total absorption.

"Okay," he said at last. "Green board. Ready to dive." He looked at Rick. "Watch close, now," he said, and pressed a red button in the center of a small control panel.

A few bubbles skittered to the surface from the forward and after sections of the hull. And then the boat submerged, nose first.

Captain Ward had abetted the move somewhat by trimming the forward control surface—the dive-plane canards—to a sharp down-angle just before the moment began, but trimmed them flat again almost at once, and the SA-1a began swift forward movement . . . under full control.

The tank was large, but not limitless, so the first maneuvers had to be a series of descending curves—S turns—to avoid crashing into the sides. The boat banked through the maneuvers with the aplomb of a hungry shark, then switched to a descending spiral that slowed as it approached the bottom.

Nodding absently to himself, Captain Ward touched another control on the panel, and the SA-1a's motion slowed almost to a stop.

"Blowing a little more air into her," the captain explained, not taking his eyes from the tank. "Deballasting, to cut the rate of descent—which slows forward motion, too. And that, of course, reduces control."

For a moment, the SA-1a seemed almost to hang suspended in the water, still sinking a little, but not enough to give her control surfaces any real bite. The nose turned slowly to the left as a line of bubbles trailed from what Rick belatedly recognized as a tiny thrust-port on the starboard bow. It was one of the auxiliary thrusters Ward had mentioned.

The nose of the model rose sharply as it gathered speed and began to ascend, repeating the series of S curves it had demonstrated on the way down, and throwing in a figure eight or two for good measure. The captain slowed the boat's progress again a foot or two below the surface.

"This test tank," he said, "has got a lot of built-in goodies. Air jets and water jets to simulate underwater explosions and suchlike."

A huge bubble erupted suddenly from the bottom of the tank and hurled itself upward to explode on the surface.

"But most of the gizmos are just high-speed water circulators. To give us the effect of those underwater rivers and upwelling currents I was telling you about."

Turning to a computer keyboard that was connected to the control console, he punched in a combination, touched the entry key, and suddenly the SA-1a was in trouble.

"See that?"

Captain Ward's expression was rapt as his model submarine yawed violently to starboard and then took on a list that increased to fifty degrees. She gradually began to right herself in the strong underwater current that moved her effortlessly across the tank . . . and then thrust her up to the surface when she reached the side.

"Not too damn realistic," the captain went on. "No test-tank sides in the ocean, unless you want to talk about seamounts—peaks in the floor of the ocean—or maybe the continental shelf."

The current that had been shoving the surfaced SA-1a slowly into a corner of the tank subsided as Captain Ward punched new commands into the computer, and he turned back to the main console to resume remote control, flooding the boat's tanks again and holding it this time in a tight descending spiral until she was almost on the bottom.

"Upwellings," he continued, "occur in the ocean for the same reason as updrafts in the atmosphere. The medium is reacting to differences in density and temperature. Now I'm going to stabilize the boat—hold it steady in the water for a moment, like so—and then let you see what even a minor upwelling can do."

Leaning briefly toward the computer keyboard, he typed in another combination, entered it, and then moved quickly back to the controls of the SA-1a.

An aerial sailplane, using an updraft to gain altitude, keeps its nose down in order to maintain control speed and avoid stalling. And that, Rick told himself, was one place where the captain's analogy was less than exact—because the SA-1a could hang almost motionless in the water, using its attitude jets to maintain a more-or-less even keel, while a heavier-than-air craft could not.

In that single respect, it was more like a blimp or dirigible than a sailplane. But blimps and dirigibles both needed motorized propulsion systems to move themselves from place to place, which the SA-1a did not.

Rick abandoned the effort to find an exact analogy as he watched and admired the precision with which Captain Ward managed the boat's ascent. He maneuvered it in the upwelling, maintaining a degree or two of nose-down attitude as it rose.

"Again, that's not entirely realistic," the captain admitted when the SA-1a finally broke the surface. "Upwellings aren't usually as strong as all that. Or as localized. And you can't be sure of their dimension or duration. You got to kind of feel for it—the way you do with a sailplane. But you get the picture."

Rick did, and he spent a moment admiring it. But what he had seen so far raised more questions than it answered.

"Nose down, with negative buoyancy and given a strong upwelling," the captain went on, as if reading his mind, "the boat can maneuver for hours . . . in what amounts to total silence."

"And even without finding an updraft . . . an upwelling, excuse me . . . the only real noise you'd make would be when you're flooding the tanks."

"Or blowing the water back out. Right."

Rick thought it over for a moment and found what looked like a flaw.

"Sonar could still find you."

Captain Ward nodded. "Yeah, it could—though we think we've found a pretty good answer for that, too, on the full-scale job. Show it to you, maybe, if you're still in this part of the world when the big one's finished. But the thing is, you don't go pinging around down there, making an active sonar search, unless you got a good reason."

"Pinging gives away the pinger's own position."

"Damn right. Even Soviet attack boats don't ping all the time . . . much less their missile subs. The boomers."

"What about passive sensors?"

The captain favored him with another froglike smile.

"The best passive gear anyone's come up with so far," he said, "is the polar glass transducer hydrophones we carry on our own 688 boats—the Los Angeles–class attack subs. And lucky me, I just happen to have a set of them right here."

He jerked a thumb in the direction of a headphone-and-cathode-ray-tube combination Rick hadn't noticed before, at the far end of the SA-1a's control console. Rick examined the rig with interest.

"Just happen to have?" he said.

Captain Ward shrugged, but didn't reply.

"I suppose," Rick said conversationally, "that I could always claim I thought you had this gear legally. With someone's permission. And they might even believe me. But if the Naval Investigative Service catches you with it, they'll slam your tail into the brig so hard you'll bounce for half an hour after the cell door's locked."

Another shrug. "Look, I just borrowed the damn things," the captain said. "And I'm gonna give 'em back when I'm done." He turned to meet his godson's gaze, and after a moment Rick groaned and looked away.

"So . . . what else is new?" he said to no one in particular.

Captain Ward picked up the phones and handed them to Rick.

"Put 'em on. And listen."

At first there seemed to be nothing—only the seashell-noise vibrations of his own eardrums getting accustomed to their new environment. And then a minor explosion, amplified to sound like a noisy toilet flush. He looked at the captain.

"Hear anything?"

"Nah," Rick replied, "your shirt's too loud."

"Turn the gain up a little," Captain Ward said, ignoring Rick's remark. Rick turned a lever below the video display a few notches up the scale and paused again to listen.

The SA-1a was moving forward and descending, and he realized, belatedly, that the sound he'd heard before was probably the audible evidence of her ballast tanks releasing air to bring the boat to a state of negative buoyancy. Captain Ward hadn't been joking about the sensitivity of the hydrophones. He started to move the volume control again, but thought better of it and stood still, listening to the sound of the model's progress through the water.

But there was really nothing to hear. Once in a while the sensor would track a bubble breaking free from the air-vent hole in the bottom of the tank. Rick knew it had to be that because each time he heard a noise a little air-balloon went kiting to the surface. And there was also an occasional whisper of sound he decided was probably made by the upsurge and ocean-river generating equipment.

But Captain Ward was listening on a second set of phones, and the second or third time it happened, he gave Rick the true explanation.

"Control surfaces," he said, nodding toward the SA-1a, which was now nearing the bottom of the tank. "The rudder and dive-planes squeak a little when they move, and these phones are sensitive enough to pick up the noise. But that's just because this is a model instead of the real thing. The full-size boat won't squeak—and even if it did, the ambient noise of the ocean . . . aw, shit!"

The last came in response to a mishap that rattled Rick's brain when its amplified sound pattern hit his eardrums. The SA-1a had hit bottom.

"Leaking again," Captain Ward explained. "Sorry, Ricky. Didn't mean to bring it down so hard."

Rick took off the headset, making a mental note to put it on again only under duress. He got up to take a closer look at the model.

"Can't you just push the water back out of the hull by blowing air in from the tanks or something?"

Captain Ward shook his head. "Just so much capacity in the little carbon dioxide bottles we're using on the model—and it's not near enough to bring her up twice when you've had a load of water in where it shouldn't be." He stood up and took off his own headphones. "Now I got to go fish her out again."

"No other way to come up?"

The captain stopped halfway up the ladder to the catwalk and returned to the console, grinning sourly. "Oh, hell, yes," he said. "Always more than one way to do the job. Redundancy—the first principle of marine architecture."

Rick had noticed one switch, at the bottom of the control console, was covered by a red guard-cap. Now Captain Ward snapped the guard out of the way and pushed the button it had shielded. This produced a small but clearly audible click from the SA-1a. Abruptly, the model submarine was moving swiftly toward the surface . . . where it promptly rolled over on its side and floated like a dead goldfish.

"If nothing else works," Captain Ward said, "you can always bring the boat up in a hurry by dropping the keel—the solid ballast on the bottom of the hull that keeps the boat right side up in the water. But if you do that, anyone on board better be ready for one hell of a hairy ride."

The captain climbed back up to the catwalk and leaned over to scoop the working model of his invention out of the water, then picked up the grapple to probe for the abandoned keel. Rick joined him on the catwalk to act again as observer, but his mind was working at full speed.

One of the chief attractions of a naval career, he reminded

himself, was the chance to play with the very latest technological gadgetry, and it was easy to become jaded. But the more he thought about Wilson Ward's silent-running submarine, the more it excited him.

"You know," he said casually, watching as the grapple made another unsuccessful pass at the discarded keel, "you're really going to need a name for the full-size boat. I just got an idea that might be good."

"That a fact?" Captain Ward's mouth tightened and twisted to the side as he maneuvered the pole for another try.

"That's the fact, Jack. You want to hear it?"

"No, damn it! But you're gonna tell me anyway, aren't you?"

"Well—it seems just right, based on what I've seen here today. And the name even matches the official initials."

"Matches the 'SA' designation?"

"Yep."

"Okay, then. I still got a feeling I'm gonna regret this. But let's hear it, anyway."

Rick grinned. "How about calling your baby the *Steel Albatross?*" he said.

"Thanks a fat lot."

"Don't thank me right now. Wait, and turn it over in your mind."

"Shoulda drowned you on one of the damn fishing trips."

But Captain Ward was grinning, too, and further conversation died as the grapple finally made contact and the claws seized the errant keel. The captain withdrew the rod, bringing the keel to the surface, and wiped it carefully before reattaching it to the body of the SA-1a.

"*Steel Albatross,*" he grumbled, running his hand fondly over the gleaming surface of the model.

"How long before the full-size boat will be ready?" Rick inquired.

Captain Ward shook his head, minutely examining the through-hull fittings for the little boat's control surfaces. "Anybody's guess," he said. "The big one's ninety percent ready right now, and we could be ready for initial testing—hell, maybe even the first couple of dives, just to see if she goes up and down—in a month or so. If someone would give us the damn money."

"You mean," Rick said, "the Navy's so short of dough that the Bureau of Ships can't fund a project as important as yours? I know the government wants to cut back military spending, but that's ridiculous. Someone in BuShips must be crazy!"

The captain stopped examining his model boat and turned to give Rick the full azure force of eyes that were suddenly ablaze with the resurgent energy of long-banked rage.

"Navy?" he grated. "Navy? Navy, my hairy ass! Every bit of the financing for this boat—and maybe *Steel Albatross* might be a good name for it, at that, by God, now that I think of it—every damn bit has come from private industry. With a little help, now and again, from one foundation or another. Hell's fire, boy, why do you think I'm doing all the work here at Scripps instead of some naval shipyard? Or maybe one of BuWeps fancy-Dan research labs? There ain't a cryin' dime of the Navy's money in this thing. We offered it to the bastards . . . and they pissed on it!"

Manama, Bahrain

Tuesday, June 17
1:55 A.M.

The admiral's quarters in the American compound at Manama were well guarded, and it took the Marine lieutenant colonel nearly forty minutes to get through the outer shield to the duty officer to the aide who actually made the decision to wake the Old Man.

After that, the pace quickened. In just three minutes, Lt. Col. Stanley Leppard, USMC, was face-to-face with a fully roused (and crisply uniformed) Rear Adm. R. B. "Fang" Carter, USN. Aides and Marine sentries had been told to make themselves scarce.

Carter gave his visitor one of the slow, up-and-down inspections permitted senior officers whose sleep has been interrupted by those of lesser rank. "The card you sent in," the admiral said, "identifies you as a liaison officer for Joint Chiefs."

"Yes, sir," Leppard replied neutrally.

Carter nodded, still eyeing the colonel.

"Bullshit," he said.

"Yes, sir," Leppard said.

"You're DIA—or some other kind of spook."

The colonel did not reply.

"And you're here, goddammit, because of that letter I got from Yuri Narmonov."

Still no denial.

Carter shrugged and gestured toward one of the easy chairs drawn up before the uncluttered desk.

"Take a load off," he said, moving behind the desk and picking up a heavy carafe that emitted an exclamation point of steam when he tilted the lid.

"Coffee?"

"Yes, thanks."

"Hope you drink it black. Damn cows hereabouts all got something wrong with them. Milk'll give you the nine-day trembles. And I hate the ersatz stuff."

He poured two cups and carried them both back to the visitors' side of the desk, where he handed one to the Marine before lowering himself into the other easy chair.

"Now, then," he said after a deep swallow of the black brew, "just what the hell is it about the letter that brings you across half the world to this hellhole . . . and can't wait till morning?"

The colonel grinned. "If you're pissed, I can only welcome you to the club. Less than twelve hours ago, I was on the third tee at Burning Tree, ready to trim three of the clumsiest divot-diggers in the Pentagon at ten dollars per, Nassau. Been bringing them along for three months."

The admiral sighed. "War is hell, Colonel."

"Ain't it a fact, Admiral." The Marine swallowed some of the coffee, carefully suppressed a grimace, and put down the cup.

"The Russkies just lofted another recon bird," he said in a tone that might have been conversational, but wasn't. "A Cosmos 2100. One-fifty-, two-hundred-mile orbit. Digital return."

Admiral Carter nodded, his expression noncommittal. "Read about it in yesterday's official digest," he said.

"And?"

"And what? It's a new sky-spy. Follow-on to the 2030 series;

longer lived and more sophisticated. Probably the telemetry's one result of the warm-up in our relations with the Russkies. We let them buy a few of our better computer chips. Now they're using them."

"Uh-huh. Using them . . . just the way your old buddy Yuri Narmonov said they would. He had the series number right and the orbit right and the delivery system right . . ."

"So, of course, everything else in the letter was straight goods, too. Right?"

The colonel shrugged. "That's what I'm here to talk about."

Admiral Carter sighed again. "I was afraid of that."

"Yes, sir." Colonel Leppard had entered the room carrying a slim leather dispatch case. Now he opened it, drew out a sheaf of papers, and set them on the desk. "Narmonov says the new satellite's a killer," he began without further preamble. "Centerpiece of something he called Temnota, which I understand is Russian for 'darkness' or 'oblivion' or somesuch."

The admiral glanced at the papers and then back at the Marine officer without comment.

"What I got here," Leppard continued, "is copies of the original letter itself—the one you forwarded to intelligence—and of the official translation, plus interpreter's notes on possible nuances of key words, plus an evaluation by specialists at NSA and CIA."

The admiral blinked. "Hell of a lot of trouble," he said, "over a little three-page letter."

"Maybe," Leppard said. "Maybe not. Depends."

"On whether or not we can trust him?"

Leppard shrugged. "The Russkies are telling everyone he's nuts, you know. Narmonov, I mean. Last we heard, they had him locked up in a special fool-farm they keep for special political cases. At Gorky. That's where he was, in fact, when he wrote to you. In the loony bin."

"Uh-huh."

"So, with that in mind—"

"So with that in mind," the admiral broke in, "what you want to know is, do I think the guy's really fool-farm material. Or is it just another political incarceration, like so many others?"

"Something like that."

Admiral Carter let the words lie there between them for a long moment, then shook his head.

"Something more," he said. "You didn't come halfway around the world and get me out of bed in the middle of the night just to ask if I trust Yuri Narmonov. You could have handled that by phone."

Colonel Leppard smiled, but there was no warmth in it. The emotion never reached as far north as the eyes.

"Sometimes it helps," he said, "to be in the same room with a man. Get a feel for what he's feeling when he speaks."

"Decide whether he's a liar."

"Yes." Leppard nodded. "Or a damn fool. Or in your own case, figure out whether your evaluation is, or could be, colored by feelings of friendship."

"For Narmonov?"

"Who else?"

"But—hell—we only met each other a couple of times."

Leppard nodded. "The first time," he said, eyes fixed on infinity as if he were reading information from a printed page, "was when you were in the astronaut program and were assigned to escort him and three other Russian cosmonauts on a tour of NASA facilities in Texas and Florida."

"And then again," Carter chimed in, "a couple of years later, after I was back in the Navy, when the State Department set up that joint tour of Europe for astronauts and cosmonauts."

Leppard smiled thinly, looking at the admiral, and after a moment or two Carter smiled back.

"Oh, well, Christ," he said deprecatingly. "Sure—the press made such a hell of a thing about it."

Leppard went on smiling, but did not interrupt.

"So Yuri and I . . . kind of got lost from the group for a while, there in Vienna."

"That. Yes."

"Big deal! One afternoon away from the watchdogs. Just a little tourist excursion—"

"—that wound up with every KGB and CIA man in the vicinity combing the city, figuring the two of you had been either kidnapped by terrorists or had defected to West Hollywood."

"We told everyone all about it later."

"You lied."

"We—"

"You told everyone you spent the afternoon at the little mezzanine bar of the Imperial Hotel, across from the opera house."

"And that's where we were!"

"Balls." The colonel's voice was flat, defying contradiction. "That's where you were when the hounds finally caught up with you. But earlier in the day—from thirteen oh two to nineteen thirty-three, to be exact—you were completely out of pocket, breaking the speed limit on the way out of town to visit your old buddy, and former Annapolis roommate, Freddie Auster."

Admiral Carter started to object again, but stopped with his mouth still wrapped silently around the first word.

"Right so far, Admiral?" Colonel Leppard prompted.

"How the . . . hell . . . ?"

The Marine officer grinned and took another sip of the coffee, not bothering to grimace this time.

"Like to take credit," he said. "But I just don't have the guts. No. We got it all later—from GRU. Soviet military intelligence. I said the CIA and KGB were busy looking for you. GRU wasn't. You never got out of their sight."

"But . . ."

"Never mind," Leppard advised. "You don't need to know the answer to the question you were about to ask, and besides, I don't know it myself. The important thing is that you and Narmonov seemed to like each other well enough, and had enough in common, to spend the afternoon together at Freddie's—and even go flying together, from the private Auster airstrip."

"Jesus Christ!"

"Him"—Leppard nodded—"and all his relatives couldn't have helped you if anything'd gone wrong. But it didn't. You strapped Freddie's little Citabria to your asses and went flat-hatting out over the countryside, under bridges and between trees and every other illegal, damn-fool thing either one of you could think of for more than an hour, and then landed just in time for nightfall to hide you from the Austrian Luftpolizei, who would have put the both of you away until hell froze over."

The admiral snorted. "If they could have caught us."

"If they could have caught you," Leppard conceded. "But the point of the exercise, Admiral, is that you and Narmonov seemed, somehow, to forge a special kind of relationship that day. Never mind that you only met each other twice. There was something . . ."

Carter picked up his coffee, started to sip it, but then put the cup down and allowed himself to relax into the chair.

"Something," he admitted. "Yes. To this day, I don't know exactly what it was. Not just space flight. More than that, I mean—we had that in common, yes. But the thing was, we were alike in other ways that didn't have anything to do with space."

"Such as?"

"Women."

"Women?"

"Well . . . wives, anyway. Both of us had marriages that had gone sour. Yuri was a widower, but I found out he and his wife hadn't had much to say to each other for a long time before her death. And he didn't know why that had happened any more than I ever knew what it was . . . well . . . there was that, anyway. And then, we were both fathers. One child apiece."

"And both were boys," Leppard said.

"Both boys. Yes. His son, Andrey, a year or so younger than Ricky. My son. He . . . uh . . . doesn't go by my name."

Leppard nodded. "Tallman, his father's name. Legally adopted. But still, I gather, in contact with you."

Admiral Carter's shoulders shifted uncomfortably. "Well—"

The marine cut him off with a shake of the head. "I know about the dustup with the Iranian gunboat out there in the Gulf," he said. "Read the whole report before I left Washington."

"Oh."

"In fact," Leppard continued, "I suppose you could say that was one of the reasons I came out in person. I wanted a personal—not official—evaluation."

"Personal?"

"As officer in command here, you're bound to take the objective view. Even if it's your own son. But to me, it seemed like just a little too much of a coincidence: The admiral's son gets put in a position where he could screw up big or even become a hostage . . . right under papa's nose. What do you think?"

"By God!"

Leppard looked at the older man searchingly.

"Surely," he said, "it must have occurred to you. I mean—first the letter from old buddy Yuri, apparently smuggled out of the Gorky nuthouse and full of warnings about a Soviet super space weapon. Then a couple of weeks later your kid turns up out here, and presto, suddenly he's in the middle of what could have been a very nasty international incident. One that could have been seriously compromising for you, if it hadn't worked out just the way it did."

Carter thought it over. And then slowly shook his head.

"No," he said. "Truthfully, I never thought of that at all. I think you've been in the spy business too long, and you're starting to connect incidents that just aren't related."

"Well, think of it now. And then kindly tell me again what you think of Yuri Narmonov, and the information in that letter that he sent to you."

Admiral Carter's eyes closed. But he was not asleep.

Leppard waited with a patience that seemed infinite.

And at length, the eyes opened again.

"I trust Yuri," Carter said. "But I don't trust the mental hospital at Gorky."

Leppard nodded neutrally. "Which means . . . ?"

"Which means, Yuri and I got pretty well acquainted, and I like him. I don't think he'd lie to me. But a place like Gorky can make a man do damn near anything. So, the new space launch notwithstanding, I think I'd still handle anything in the letter with kid gloves. Especially if it meant taking any kind of overt action."

"Overt action?"

"Don't play games with me, Colonel. If what Yuri Narmonov said about the new Russian bird is anything like true, it's a major threat—or will be, soon as they get it fully operational.

The time to stop it would be now. Right now. Before it can start doing what it was intended to do."

"You think a satellite could actually have such potential? Such . . . power?"

Carter's eyes focused on the Marine officer, and for the first time his voice betrayed some of the anger and impatience carefully concealed beneath the surface.

"I fly 'em," he said coldly. "I don't build 'em."

"But—"

"But nothing. You want to know what the bird could do—ask one of the geniuses at Houston. Or the Cape. Or NORAD."

Leppard subsided and began to gather his papers and file them back into the dispatch case.

"You don't think your son's little—uh—problem had anything to do with this, then?"

"No, I don't."

"But the possibility does exist?"

"I suppose so."

"Is he—the boy, I mean—still here. In Bahrain?"

"No."

Leppard closed the case, but did not stand up at once.

"You reassigned him?"

"Yes."

Leppard seemed on the point of asking yet another question, but thought better of it.

"I sent him back to the States," Admiral Carter said, answering anyway. "I, uh, volunteered him for the SEALs. I think the discipline they dish out will do him some good, and besides that, an old friend of mine—who's Rick's godfather—lives out there. Putters round at the Scripps Institute now. Old Navy man—maybe you've heard of him—Will Ward?"

"Sure I know the old submariner. Doesn't everybody?" Leppard said.

"Everybody that's been in it as long as we have, yeah. Well, things have gone wrong for Rick lately, and I hope Ward can help straighten him out."

Leppard grinned, coming easily to his feet. "Well, he's your son."

Carter nodded. "He damn sure is."

The Marine turned to go, but stopped at the door and looked back at the admiral, who was still seated.

"That Citabria," he said. "The airplane you borrowed from Auster . . . ?"

"Yes?"

"I don't fly, myself."

"No?"

"No. But I've often thought I'd like to learn. So, personally—not for the record—I'd like to ask: You risked a lot, the two of you, to go flying around the countryside together for an hour. A hell of a lot."

"Yes. We did."

Leppard nodded. "Uh-huh. So . . . was it worth it? Was it really that much fun?"

This time the admiral's grin was wide and sincere.

"Son," he said, "that kind of flying is just exactly the most fun you can possibly have with your clothes on."

Gorky, U.S.S.R.

Tuesday, June 17
6 P.M.

"Well, Comrade Doctor," General Viktor I. Tregorin said, "how soon do you think the patient will be ready?"

The doctor, a member of the Institute staff, stirred uneasily in his chair and wished he could look away. Tregorin had appeared that morning with a suggestion that they spend the day observing Yuri Narmonov on one of his aimless summertime rambles through the town.

Narmonov had been sent to the Institute—a state clinic entirely funded and operated by the GRU, the Soviet military intelligence apparat—for specific purposes.

Let the modernists of the KGB employ their "psychological treatment centers" as warehouses for political prisoners too famous to be eligible for the gulag. And let the foreign press gloat as the entire apparat slowly crumbled to dust in the noonday sun of glasnost and democracy. The GRU had only one mental hospital, and its objective was both simpler and infinitely more ambitious: "We change the mind."

That was the phrase (first enunciated by the Lysenkoist brain surgeon who had founded the Institute) that had pervaded and guided its activities even after the founder's record of bizarre "experimental" operations finally brought him to the firing squad wall in the early days of the Khrushchev regime. And it ruled the Institute no less today.

"As you are aware," the doctor began, trying to frame his reply with infinite caution, "the case in question is a delicate one. Orders from the Central Directorate—"

"Yes, yes! They don't want him damaged." The general's tone was brusque. "At least not where it might show. We've been over all this before. We are interested, now, in results. Is he responding to your treatment? If not, other means, other persuasions, should be attempted."

The doctor drew a deep breath. He had hoped to avoid this. He had planned to parry General Tregorin's questions with other questions, to fill the air with such a smoke screen of "standard recovery rates" and "estimates of progressive reality-acceptance" as to bore the man to sleep—as he had been able to do with the other military officers over the past two years. But this was now clearly impossible. The general wanted real answers.

"Therapy methods employed to this date," the doctor said carefully, "have been of an orthodox nature and results, as you saw today, have been minimal. Narmonov exhibits certain conditioned inhibitions with regard to time and scope of travel. He buys only approved newspapers and drinks tea in preference to the vodka he has always preferred, although vodka is readily available."

"He will perform assigned tasks?"

"Yes."

"Even if they conflict with his . . . original orientation?"

"Oh, yes." The doctor allowed himself to relax a little. "You are asking me about things like the letter—the one he was asked to write to a friend in the West."

The general nodded.

"As you know, the letter was written."

"And he did this without making difficulty?"

"Yes."

"Yet you say there has been no true change of attitude."

"No, Comrade General. He is, essentially, the same man who came to us a year ago. Conditioned, perhaps, by aversion therapy to avoid certain lines of conduct and adopt others, but otherwise intact. And manipulated at times by the fact that his son . . . well . . . never mind. As I said, his mind is basically unchanged."

"Son?" the general said. "What about the son?"

"The boy is now undergoing SPETSNAZ training at Kronstadt. We have found it helpful to offer—or withhold—news of his son's progress. As an auxiliary means of encouraging approved behavior."

Tregorin nodded. "Then what do you suggest?" he prodded.

The doctor shrugged. "Within the scope of the original directive, there is nothing."

"And outside it?"

"Outside it, the Institute has a number of programs—physical, chemical, and mixed media—whose results can be guaranteed."

"Guaranteed, comrade? Guaranteed?"

"Guaranteed," the doctor said, "as far as guarantees may be applied to anything in the real world."

"What about time?" Tregorin said. "How quickly could we expect results?"

"That would depend on the technique employed. If we could take a full year, for instance . . ."

"Three months."

The doctor caught himself just short of repeating the general's words and instead stared at the man in silence.

"In three months," Tregorin went on, "we intend either to display Narmonov publicly—and that means we will allow the foreign press to interview him, under uncontrolled conditions, without apparent restriction—or if that is not possible, announce his death. With great regret, of course."

"There is a technique," the doctor said, not looking at Tregorin, "one that offers such results as you require—and within a very short time span, too. You have heard of total sensory deprivation?" the doctor inquired.

"The nothing tank," Tregorin said, nodding. "Fit the subject with breathing devices, warm the water to body temperature, plug his ears and blindfold him, and set him afloat . . . the ultimate solitary confinement."

"Utter negation of external stimuli," the doctor said. "The primary effect, of course, is to distort time; an eternity can be lived in moments because there is no external referent."

"And reality becomes malleable."

The doctor nodded. "This process has been well-known for more than two decades. But of late, various experimenters—here at the Institute, and also in China, we believe—have begun augmenting its effects chemically. The breakdown of the original personality is intensified and speeded up by making minor changes in the neurohormone serotonin, thus altering the functioning of the brain's serotoninergic pathways, which, with the cholinergic and nonadrenergic pathways, are largely responsible for the brain's ability to store and transmit information."

"Yes, yes! I have read the literature. Including several articles written by you, Comrade Doctor. Get on with it!"

"You know then," the doctor said, stifling an uneasy suspicion that if the general had read the articles he might also be reading his mind, "all I can tell you at this time. Spectacular results can sometimes be accomplished—"

"—but there are more failures than successes."

"And the failures are quite as spectacular as the successes. You may achieve a totally reintegrated personality, possessing all the memories and most—but not all—of the attitudes and foibles of the original. Or you may get a vegetable that will need spoon-feeding and diapering for the rest of its life. Or perhaps a suicidal time bomb, walking around waiting for the impulse to be triggered. Our current success rate is less than thirty percent . . . and we do not yet know exactly what factors determine the difference between negative and positive result. Which is why no such measures have been applied to this subject."

"Until now."

The doctor hesitated, then decided to go the extra mile and say the words in his mind.

"It seems . . . a pity," he said.

The general looked at him with nothing at all visible in his face.

"He was a cosmonaut," the doctor continued. "A man of accomplishment. A person valuable to Mother Russia, the Rodina."

The general nodded equably. "And he is still of value. Comrade Narmonov will still make a contribution. No matter how your little experiment turns out."

Kronstadt, U.S.S.R.

Tuesday, June 17

6:12 A.M.

The order to report to Comrade Colonel Sergetov after morning calisthenics came as no surprise to Trooper Andrey Narmonov. He had been expecting it ever since the old Whisky II–class diesel submarine picked them up and returned them to the Kronstadt base at the end of the Karlskrona operation.

His failure to kill the Swedish sentry had been reported.

Well, what had he thought would happen?

That was the duty of the *michman* (whose rank was similar to the U.S. Navy's warrant officer), to make sure that everyone did his job as ordered. And now they would expel him from SPETSNAZ. And that would be the end.

Volunteering for the special force had been an idiotic gesture at best, a final effort to wash away the stigma that had attached itself to him and his family when his father turned traitor. Thirty long years Yuri Narmonov had served the motherland, as a fighter pilot deployed against the most difficult ground targets in Angola, as a cosmonaut in charge of the most exacting and delicate space operations—and at last as second-in-command of the entire cosmonaut program, just at the time the Soviet space program was finally beginning to overhaul and exceed the Yankee legend that had begun with the first walk on the moon.

And then . . . demonstrations against government policy and

protests—organized efforts at outright subversion to which Andrey's father had lent his name.

It had changed the entire course of Andrey's life. Expelled from the elite Technikon School (for "lack of mathematical aptitude" when he had taken nothing but honors in that field since he was a small child!) and conscripted into military service like any peasant, he had seen in his assignment to naval infantry training a final opportunity to redeem himself.

SPETSNAZ was the key. Universal military service, a policy in the Rodina since the Great Patriotic War, meant that all troops were conscripts. But some specific assignments were for volunteers only, and SPETSNAZ was one of these—especially in the case of the superspecialized naval SPETSNAZ units, for which only the upper one percent were eligible.

Volunteering was almost a formality. Everyone did that. But acceptance, when it came, had seemed an overwhelming stroke of good fortune . . . until the training had actually begun. Then he discovered that he was to be singled out for special attention because of his father. Because of the traitor now confined to a military asylum at Gorky.

Well, in any event, he had come this far. And if the comrade colonel kicked him out now, at least he had given it his best effort.

Suddenly, despite standing orders (trainees at Kronstadt were never permitted to walk, or even stand still unless commanded to do so; trainees were required to run at all times) Narmonov stopped running toward battalion headquarters and stood statue-still in his tracks.

The SPETSNAZ combat-swimmer battalion to which he was assigned for training was commanded by Comrade Colonel Chernyavin, and he alone had the power to expel a trainee. But the summons had come from Colonel Sergetov, the *zampolit*—the battalion political officer.

Thoughtfully, Narmonov put himself back in motion, but this time at a jog. The *zampolit*? But his crime—and failure to kill an enemy as ordered was classed as a felony—had not been political. Why, then, should Colonel Sergetov wish to see him?

He managed to hold that thought, using it to keep his blood

pressure down and his skin from sweating, all the way to the *zampolit*'s office, through the brief waiting period, and all the way into the colonel's inner sanctum. But there assurance deserted him. Especially when the colonel told him to sit down.

Zampolits are military officers only by courtesy; they are forbidden to hold or exercise any command function. But their power is enormous. The *zampolit* alone is empowered to depose the commanding officer.

But now Colonel Sergetov appeared to be in a good mood. Genial. Almost smiling. "You have done well here, Andrey Yureivich," he said, addressing Narmonov with the familiar form of his name, as though they were old friends.

"Thank you, Comrade Colonel," Narmonov responded, restricting himself to the more formal address despite the political officer's apparent friendliness. "I have tried to do my duty."

"And you have succeeded." Sergetov had been holding a manila folder in his hands. Now he dropped it back on the desk, making no effort to conceal the fact that it was Narmonov's own personnel dossier.

"Succeeded," the political officer continued, "and excelled. You know that you are at the very top of your training class? It is true. And you acquitted yourself well on the final training exercise—the mission to Karlskrona."

Narmonov fought to keep his face from showing the astonishment that he felt. So the *michman* had not reported him. Maybe he too had realized that there was no need to waste a human life when the training mission could be accomplished without killing the Swede. But in that case, what could possibly be the purpose of this interview? Colonel Sergetov did not keep him in suspense.

"It is our policy," he said, speaking quietly but fixing his eyes upon Narmonov's face with a peculiar intensity, "in cases such as yours, to offer personal congratulations—"

Narmonov flushed and started to respond. But the colonel was still speaking.

"—and to offer a further opportunity to serve the motherland—in the area of her greatest need."

Narmonov blinked. For a moment, he had begun to suspect

that this interview was no more than a formality, a rite of congratulation. But now there seemed to be something more, and at once he was on guard.

"You have been a member of Komsomol since you were a small boy, I think?"

Narmonov nodded dumbly. Like most children, he had joined the Party youth organization. It was expected, and he did not wish to be different from his friends. But he was not, in fact, a Party member—and did not expect to become one. Party membership was a career in itself; he had other plans. Or once had.

"It is for this reason, and because of the excellence of your record," the *zampolit* continued, "that I am now empowered to make this offer. Listen closely, for it will be made only once—and the answer you give now will be final."

Narmonov surrendered and allowed his face to do what it would.

"There is within the naval SPETSNAZ apparat," Colonel Sergetov said, "a very small central cadre of which most people are entirely ignorant. It is known as the Temnota Corps. You have heard of it?"

Narmonov shook his head. "No, Comrade Colonel."

The colonel smiled indulgently. "If you had said yes and been able to make me believe it, I tell you without exaggeration that someone, somewhere, would have died for it."

Narmonov nodded dumbly.

"SPETSNAZ is an elite unit as you know," Sergetov said, "and recruitment is entirely voluntary. But the Temnota Corps is something else again; its membership is by invitation only. And this invitation is being extended, now, to you."

Narmonov swallowed painfully. "What . . . what . . . ah . . . are the requirements? I mean—there would be additional training?"

Sergetov nodded solemnly. "Additional training, and an additional personal commitment. This is, and I would not disguise the fact from you, a lifetime vocation. Not merely the three years of universal conscription, but an entire career. You understand this?"

Narmonov nodded again. "There is no more that you can

tell me?" he said, looking inquiringly at the political officer and trying to assess what little reaction he could detect.

Sergetov shook his head. "No. Except, perhaps, this: That service to Temnota means sacrifice for the motherland, at the highest human level."

That much Narmonov had already guessed.

"And that it could be beneficial—very, very beneficial indeed—to a family that was, shall we say, under some small political disability."

The bastard.

Narmonov could feel himself coloring, blushing furiously. And was surprised by the sudden rush of hatred he felt for the quiet, patronizing official seated behind the desk. But there it was: the carrot—and the stick. Nothing hidden. Nothing sugarcoated. Simply realpolitik. With a vengeance. There could be no doubt about his response.

"Thank you, Comrade Colonel," he heard himself saying. "Thank you for your frankness. It is deeply appreciated."

"And your answer?"

"You wish to hear it now?"

"Yes. I am sorry. But you understand—as I said, it is an offer made only once. And the decision must be made without hesitation."

"I see."

For a moment, the two men sat facing each other. Young man. Old man. Mouse. Cat.

And then Narmonov broke the silence the only way that he could, with the only reply possible to him. Just as the colonel had known he must.

"I accept," he said. "With thanks."

Coronado, California

Wednesday, June 18
1:03 A.M.

Sweating and shallow-breathing almost to the point of hyperventilation, Rick sat up in bed and tried to look around him.

The darkness was real enough. And so was the ringing. It wasn't the ground-prox alarm, but the telephone. He was having that damn dream again. Seemed he couldn't sleep these last few days without his bed becoming a fighter cockpit.

Groping, unable for the moment to remember where the phone was, Rick rolled out of bed and promptly barked his shin on a heavy chair ranged against the bulkhead.

Right. He was in the visiting officers' quarters on the amphibious base, just across the road from SEAL headquarters. In a room, presumably equipped with electric lighting, if only he could find the switch.

Five steps (and another banged shin) later, he had found the switch. The room flooded with light. He had his hand on the telephone—when it stopped ringing.

What the hell, he wondered, ever became of the old beat-up VOQs of reverent memory: the drafty, scrungy, institutional-gray, pay-phone-at-the-end-of-the-hall barracks of yore? The New Navy had its upside, to be sure. But there was something to be said for a simpler time when whoever was nearest the phone answered when it rang, and then either yelled out a name or came to get you.

Now there was a phone in every bay.

Christ. And not enough light leaking under the hatch to let a man see where the noise was coming from.

But his hand was still on the receiver of the telephone, so only a kind of reflex action was required to pick it up when it rang again.

"Tallman."

"Darling! Are you all right?"

Rick grinned at the wall in spite of himself, and part of the emotion she always evoked—the everlasting love, and sometime amusement—was in his voice when he replied.

"Of course I am, Mama. I told you so when I called from Bahrain."

"Really?"

"Would I lie to you?"

"Only when your lips move, Richard. Only when your lips move."

Rick sighed inwardly. It was an old, old routine between them, rehearsed over the years and second nature now as a beginning of all new conversations. But she seemed to enjoy it, and be reassured by it. So . . .

". . . awfulest time tracking you down, there in Coronado. I thought, of course, you'd be at the hotel."

Rick smiled again. She meant, of course, the ancient and rotund wooden elegance of the old Del Coronado—her home away from home during the few months she'd stayed here during her marriage to his father. No other real hotels were in the vicinity way back then, before the bridge was built and you still had to get to the place by ferry from San Diego—or by bumpy road round the peninsula via Imperial Beach.

"No," he said. "They were . . . uh . . . filled up. For the season. No room at the inn."

"Nonsense!"

"Mama . . ."

"Nonsense, I tell you! I know the management there. Tomorrow, first thing, you have them give me a call and I'll set them straight in half a moment."

"Mama . . ."

"Imagine telling you they had no room—"

"Mama!"

Sudden silence. Rick let it go on for a full second, then picked up the ball.

"Mama—it's okay. I lied to you just now; I never even tried to check in at the Del Coronado. I'm here at the visiting officers' quarters for a night or two; I'll get an apartment or something in town after I check in with the SEALs."

"But darling, there's no need! I know where the SEAL base is; I asked the nice man at Central Locator while he was trying to find you. He says it's only a little walk from the Del Coronado; you could easily live there, and—"

"Mama."

"—have all your wants taken care of, and besides, you know what a wonderful place it is to entertain. They do everything with such an air! And I've already talked to old friends of mine who still live around there. Or in La Jolla. Several of them have daughters you really ought to meet—"

"Mama, for Chrissake!"

She hated it when he used language she considered vulgar, and for that reason he tried to hold it to a mild roar when he was around her. But sometimes there was just no other way to get her attention.

"Mama . . . I don't doubt for a moment that your friends' daughters are just exactly who I ought to meet. But some other time. I'm going to be busy. The SEALs—"

"Oh, yes! I wanted to tell you."

"Mama."

"Avery's brother, the younger one who got into Congress. You remember? Well, I talked to him after I talked to you, and he says it's ridiculous for someone like you to be wasting yourself on something like that. He looked into it and said the duty is hard and dangerous and a career officer like yourself, since you insist on being one, would be much better off in something safe and comfortable right there in Washington. Service liaison with one of his committees, perhaps; he could get you—"

"Mama, goddammit!"

Another silence. This one was full of shock waves. Rick drew another deep lungful of air and let it out.

"Mama, I don't want to date your friends' daughters. I don't want to be a politician. I don't even want to stay at the Del Coronado. The place I'm in is fine."

"Fine, indeed! You forget I was in the service—well, married to it anyway—for a year or two. I know what those places are like. They—"

"It's all changed. This is the New Navy, Mama. Honest! Just like a hotel."

"Well, be that as it may." Rick could hear her shifting gears, somewhere in the dawn's early light of Palm Beach. "Be that as it may, I still want you to live a more rounded life."

"A what?"

"A more rounded life. Social life. And don't tell me you don't know what I mean, either. You're not monastery material and you're not gay, so it's downright unhealthy for you to—"

"Mama!"

"Mama what? You're a grown man, and I'm anxious to see my grandchildren before I have to do it from an iron lung or an Alzheimer's center."

Rick laughed. He couldn't help it.

"Mama," he said. "I love you. I really do. You are not one

of a kind—not by a hell of a shot—but I will have to say you define the genre. Grandchildren! So that's what it's all about. Hot damn!"

"Don't swear, dear. It's common."

"Well, no one's ever going to say that about you, mother of mine. Look, you want me to cat around, maybe sire a few assorted bastards for you to dandle on your knee, why didn't you say so? I'll get right on it—"

"Richard."

"—starting with your friends' daughters. Wait a minute while I get a pencil and paper, so I don't miss any good ones. And you might throw in a description of each. You know I like to—"

"Richard!"

Rick stopped talking and counted off five seconds while they got their breaths. But that was as much silence as his mother could stand.

"Richard, you very well know I did not mean anything of the kind."

"Yes, Mama."

"It's just that, well, ever since you broke up with Teri Jansson—such a nice girl, I'll never be able to understand why—"

"Mama!" Do you have any idea what time it is here?"

"Yes, Richard. I'm sorry. I love you, Richard."

"I know, Mama. And I love you, too. But I'm doing what I want to do, in the place I want to do it. And everything's going to be fine."

More dead-air time. Then: "I know, Richard. I just . . . I know. Really." Rick started to speak, but thought better of it and waited for his mother to go on. "I'm a selfish old woman," she said with something like real contrition in her voice. "My God, I just looked out the window and the sky's not even a little bit light over in the east. So—oh, Lord—it's really the very middle of the night there in California, isn't it? And I woke you out of a sound sleep just because I was up early and started worrying."

"I love you, Mama. And I also love to sleep."

"Richard, I'm so—"

"Mama."

More silence.

"G'night, Mama. I love you."

"Me, too. Good night . . ."

Rick waited, letting the connection be broken at the Palm Beach end, then hung up his own receiver and snapped off the light before rolling back into the narrow bed.

Squeaky and middle-saggy and equipped with regulation lumpy mattress, the bed was a holdover from the Old Navy. New Navy should do something about its beds. And someone should have strangled Alexander Graham Bell in his cradle. My dream, Rick thought. Got to get back in the cockpit and finish off ol' Richtofen Reich.

"Fight's on!"

The bloodred rudder-stripe of Reich's Talon flashed past at a combined closure speed of 1,100 knots. He jammed the thrust levers into max A/B and pulled up to vertical—G suit constricting automatically and urgently, easing suddenly to zero G and then going negative as they arched over the top upside down. Quick half-roll and everything was right side up again; heading down, now, to the set-up altitude, needle slipping past Mach 1; quick glance at the sky to both sides, and . . .

What the hell?

Instead of the wings of the F-14 Tomcat he'd been flying a moment ago, Rick found himself looking in astonishment at the foreshortened stubs that served as the "wings" of Captain Will Ward's SA-1a. Somehow, he had managed to get himself inside the little submarine sailplane.

Optical illusion, of course, but blinking didn't seem to make it go away, and now he realized they were not in the air. Not flying at all. He was underwater; down in the test tank, with Captain Ward looking in at him, grinning that froglike grin. How'd you get me to do a fool thing like this? I bet my old man was in on it. If you don't go up into space, you go down into the sea. Down where it's dark and cold.

But what became of Richtofen Reich? Didn't I hear him say "Fight's on" a moment ago? Or was that his voice? No. No, by God!

Whose voice was it?

"Your ass, Ricky!"

Turning his head halfway around to look directly behind

him—to his own six—he could see Reich's F-5 coming up fast, its progress unimpeded by the watery medium in which they now were operating.

"Fox Two on the Steel Albatross!"

Whose voice?

Familiar. But . . .

"Fox Two on the Steel Albatross, Ricky. Your ass, old buddy!"

Oh, shit!

Teri Jansson. She was down here, grab-assing in Reich's Talon; and probably flipping him off besides.

Well, mate, here is a little 1V1 nobody is going to mind. Who said flying fighters is the most fun you can have with your clothes on? This was even better.

PART III

PROCUREMENT

Gorky, U.S.S.R.

Wednesday, June 18
7:03 P.M.

The pages had been photocopied, and Yuri Narmonov thought that in itself was probably significant.

Despite the primary effects of glasnost and perestroika, copying machines are not generally available in the Soviet Union; identified as a kind of printing press—and therefore dangerous in the wrong hands—the number of duplicating machines, including even the crudest thermocopiers, is strictly limited and access is restricted to those who can prove a definite public need for such services.

But the doctor had gone to the trouble of getting these sheets reproduced by the most technically advanced methods.

"There is a document you might wish to see, comrade," the doctor was saying.

Yuri looked at the man and tried to remember if he had ever seen him before. Lately, he had noticed that it was hard to remember details like that. No. The face did not seem familiar.

"Here. See for yourself."

The doctor extended his hand, obviously expecting Yuri to take the photocopied papers and read them. But for a moment, Yuri did not respond.

In the time he had been a patient at this hospital, he had never been permitted to read or even look at anything as important as a legal document or a newspaper or even a letter. And now this doctor he had never seen before wanted him to read something so important that it had to be copied.

Yuri looked at the duplicated papers and almost turned away without permitting his mind to register their nature. But at the last instant, a single word—a name—caught his eye, leaping out at him from the top page:

"Andrey."

He spoke the name aloud without realizing he had done so, and he was totally unable to prevent his hand from reaching out to take the document.

This was an order transferring Trooper Andrey Narmonov, at his own request, from regular naval infantry training to the elite, highly secret naval section of Special Forces.

"SPETSNAZ . . ."

Again, he had spoken without being aware of it. Now Yuri was reading the second duplicated paper. The one that recorded the young man's performance in SPETSNAZ training. Good.

"Karlskrona . . ."

The doctor's eyes narrowed as he tried to penetrate the careful, blank facade of Yuri Narmonov's features. What was going on behind there? What was the man feeling now? How was he taking the instructors' comments about the boy's failure to kill a Swedish sentry during a training raid? How was he dealing with the decision to let Andrey Narmonov believe his dereliction had gone unnoticed? Now he was moving on to the third document.

"Temnota!"

Ah . . . so the facade was not stamped in marble after all! The man could still feel, still understand that there were things to fear and things to hope for in this world. The paper attesting to SPETSNAZ Trooper Andrey Narmonov's willingness to volunteer for duty with Temnota, and for the surgical procedures such duty would entail, had been as effective as he had hoped.

"Temnota . . . No!"

The face Yuri Narmonov turned toward the doctor was contorted, twisted, and battered in a contest between anguish and blind rage. Berserkers of the Viking age had looked like that. Foaming madmen who ripped out the sleeves of their straitjackets sometimes approached such peaks of passion. But never before had the doctor seen a man go from passive, stoic acceptance to such a state in so short a time.

And then Yuri Narmonov was on him, fingers clawing and grasping for the throat, for the eyes, for a patch of skin that could be grasped, tortured, ripped from the body.

"Guards! Emergency!"

Arms high, trying to protect his face, the doctor allowed himself to be thrown to the floor, where he curled into a fetal-defense posture while awaiting the arrival of the thugs who were supposed to restrain such outbursts.

But even as he felt the former cosmonaut's fingernails scraping channels on his forearms, winced as the handful of hair was torn away, the doctor could feel a sense of relief—even of elation—beginning to replace the tension that had been building in the back of his mind ever since the conversation with Comrade General Tregorin.

"No!" Narmonov was shouting. "No, damn them. Not Andrey—not him. Not my little Andrey. No, God . . . No!"

The guards were on all sides of them now, peeling Yuri Narmonov's arms away, forcing him up and back against the wall. But the man was still screaming and writhing, totally deranged.

"Little Andrey! No! Not him. Not to . . . that! No!"

One of the guards had a tranquilizer shot ready, and he slammed it into Narmonov's leg, driving the plunger in without regard to possible tissue damage. The doctor hoped it was not too much. No sense killing their latest and best guinea pig. Especially since Comrade General Tregorin was so interested.

Coronado, California

Wednesday, June 18
9:23 A.M.

Rick's welcome to the SEALs was exactly what he'd expected, but that didn't mean he had to like it. For the first hour after finding the base, far out on the peninsula and across the road from the Navy's amphibious complex, he couldn't get past the lobby. All he had to keep him company was a life-size statue of the Creature from the Black Lagoon, holding a sign that read "So You Want to Be a SEAL?"

A copy of Rick's orders had arrived before he did—trust Adm. Fang Carter to make sure of that—but it still didn't get him inside. A blank-faced yeoman assigned to the reception desk and switchboard explained it to him in passionless detail: The next two-week course—mandatory physical and psychological indoctrination before he would be permitted to begin the actual twenty-three weeks of basic SEAL training—would not start until Monday. No one was expected before then.

Rick was about to make himself scarce when two men emerged from the door next to the yeoman's desk. They were both in their midthirties and were wearing summer white uniforms with pistol-and-trident badges pinned on the left side of their shirts. The taller man had a double row of ribbons beneath his badge. Both were talking animatedly, two old buddies saying their good-byes.

"Well, Mac," the short one bellowed, "you take care, you ol' web-footed son of a hawah!" The New England accent dissolved into a deep, growling rumble of a laugh.

"Yes, sir!" the taller one called Mac bellowed in return. He backed off a pace and snapped rigidly to attention. "Chief Petty Officer Sonofawhore, if it's all the same to you. Sir!"

It's frustrating, Rick thought, to eavesdrop on a conversation when you don't know what the people are talking about. Like hearing adults discuss sex when you're six years old. You know you're missing something, but you don't know what it is, and you don't know how to ask.

But the two men paid no attention to Rick. The short one, a powerful little barrel of a man, was shaking his head.

"I still can't believe it," he said, "no jeezly way."

"That's the Navy for you, sir," Mac said. "Sooner or later you meet everybody in it . . . twice!"

"Shawah enough!" said the short one, grinning. "And don't you think I'm not going to enjoy this! I'll see you bright and early on Monday then."

"Yes, sir!"

They saluted each other crisply, and the short one disappeared through the door behind the yeoman. With this diversion, Rick decided to give the yeoman another try. As he approached the reception desk, the tall fellow named Mac came up to Rick.

"Got a light?" he asked, patting his pockets.

"Sorry," Rick said.

"Got to give up these damn things come Monday, when training starts."

"You're going through basic here?" Rick asked, wondering what some guy ten years his senior would be doing going through SEAL training.

"Why do you ask?"

"'Cause I start basic on Monday, too." Rick stuck out his hand (the hell with the formalities of Navy custom) and said, "Name's Tallman. Rick Tallman."

"Hiya, Rick, my name's MacDougall." He wasn't a stickler for the Navy's ritual of salutes either. "But everybody calls me Mac. Never could figure out why, though," he said with a mock-ironical grin. "Ah," he said, finding an old matchbook in his back pocket and lighting the cigarette.

"Yeah, I've been assigned to go through training with the next class . . . if I survive the preconditioning. I've been out so long—not swimming nearly enough, not running enough, hardly even breathing—and the rules say you got to requalify if you want to get back into the Teams. And I do."

"So you've already been a SEAL?" Rick asked.

"Oh, yeah," MacDougall said. "I did a tour as a webfoot, in the Teams, 'bout a million years ago. Ancient history, now."

Rick didn't really understand, but was drawn into what MacDougall was saying. The man had an air of easy authority about him—not forced at all, but very strong. This was a natural leader, Rick decided.

"Actually," MacDougall continued, "I started with the Teams 'bout a dozen years ago, just after the SEALs absorbed what was left of the old Underwater Demolition Teams and Frogman units. Things were a little different then—a lot different, really—and I went into a research and development program that was later discontinued. Guess I got caught in the crunch of one of the Navy's 'technological upgrades.' Nothing new. Same sort of thing happened to the foretopmen and sail-makers of the old wind-powered Navy when the service switched over to steam."

The chief petty officer's grin was infectious, the freckles that dotted his nose dancing with each smile. Rick returned the grin. So far, this was only the second friendly face he'd seen since arriving in California.

"Well, it was nice meeting you, Mr. Tallman. I just got back to California myself, and I've got a ton of errands to run today. Not the least of which is doing a little food shopping. Gotta keep the strength up. SEAL training isn't exactly tiddlywinks. Besides, gotta smoke all these damn things up just to get rid of 'em!"

"See you Monday, Mac," Rick said. They executed a couple of highly exaggerated salutes, and Mac exited, laughing.

The yeoman at the desk watched him go—an expression of awe on his face. "One of the legends," he said to no one in particular.

"Huh?" Rick said.

"Mac MacDougall," the yeoman said. "The chief. Or maybe I should say Commander MacDougall. He still is one, way I hear it, in the reserves."

"The chief . . . ?" Rick asked, absorbing the idea.

"Yep." The yeoman's nod was definite. "Was a lieutenant—two-striper—when he served on the Teams. And got another half stripe before they dumped the program he was in. So he kept that rank in the reserve, even though he had to take a bust to chief to stay in the regular Navy. Christ," the yeoman went on, "I been hearing stories about him and the stuff he'd done—equipment he invented himself, and some of the weird things he figured out to do with it—ever since the day I joined the Teams. Sorta like meeting Santa Claus, you know? Or Bigfoot."

There might have been more, but at that moment the phone rang. The yeoman picked it up, barked a "Yes, sir" into it, and hung up. The yeoman snapped back into the blank-eyed mode.

"Mr. Tallman?"

"That's me."

"Mr. Kraus!"

Rick looked around, but they were for the moment alone in

the reception bay. So he stood still and waited for the man to tell him what was on his mind.

"Mr. Kraus wants to see you," the yeoman said. "Now, sir."

Rick nodded, but still didn't move, and after a moment the yeoman broke down and added another hint.

"In his office," he said. But that seemed to be as much as the man was willing to offer on his own. So finally Rick prompted:

"Where?"

"Inside," the yeoman said, nodding in the direction of the portal that MacDougall and the other officer had emerged from. "Second door on your left. Sir."

"Thank you."

"Yes, sir." The yeoman almost smiled, but caught himself at the last possible moment and managed to retain his air of solemn composure while pushing a button that opened the door to the inner corridor before Rick's hand could find the knob.

Rick wondered whether the yeoman had been born that way or learned it in the SEALs.

But he didn't have to wonder for long. The second door to the left in the corridor led to an office that contained a pair of desks. Only the one on the right was occupied, and it was the same officer that had been joking around with Mac a few minutes before. He didn't notice Rick's existence for one full minute. Rick knew, because he counted the seconds off in his head—one gorilla, two gorilla, three gorilla—and had just reached fifty-nine gorillas when the officer put down the file of papers he'd been pretending to read and leaned back in his chair.

Rick awarded him the sixtieth gorilla on points. The guy had earned it.

"You Tallman," the officer said, making it a statement rather than a question.

Rick considered hitting a brace and reeling off the reporting-for-duty routine. But the railroad tracks on the officer's collar told him this was not the commanding officer, and the little black sign at the corner of the desk identified him only as LT. K. W. KRAUS, USN. He wasn't even wearing a duty-officer brassard.

So he stood still and waited for Lt. K. W. Kraus to call the signals in his own good time and on his own chosen terms. Which he did, almost at once.

"You," he said coldly, in that slightly nasal accent that Rick had tentatively identified as down east, "are surer'n God in the wrong place."

That was tempting. Rick found himself toying with the idea of offering immediate agreement and catching the next MATS flight back to Washington. This little Maine squirt was clearly about to serve him a heaping helping of shit, and he didn't really need any more just now. But for some reason he stood still. And remained silent.

"This here is the SEALs," Kraus went on when Rick didn't respond. "The Teams. For by-Jesus pro-fessionals only. For men. No room for amateurs. No room for Rambos. And surer'n hell no room for rich little fly-boys all dressed up in their daddy's admiral suit."

Say this for the son of a bitch, Rick thought, he'd done his homework.

"And no room either, for drunk and disorderly fuckups. You read me, Mr. Tallman?"

Rick was beginning to. It was, he reminded himself, an old and honored service custom—the fright-night lecture for fresh-caught trainees. He'd heard a version of it on arriving at Annapolis, gotten another dose with incoming cadets at preflight, swallowed a third helping when he got to Corpus Christi . . . and yet another when he reported to Top Gun. Enlisted SEAL candidates would probably get theirs later, in a group; he was an officer and so rated this special, private session. So all right, then. No sweat. No surprises.

But Kraus wasn't done. "You some kind of famous, you know," he said, standing up and closing the door. "I mean, you are some well-known: Annapolis; the Fighter Weapons School; even that little set-to with the Iranian Navy that got you kicked out of the Persian Gulf. So now—lucky us—you looking to take your jeezly feather-merchant act on the road. And we get all the benefit. What a shaw-'nough honor! I got to tell you, we are real underwhelmed."

Kraus was back behind the desk now and seated. The voice had neither risen nor lost its overriding nasality. But Kraus's eyes, depthless black and deep set in his skull, held a malevolence that Rick found surprisingly lively. And personal.

"This unit," Kraus said, "is for volunteers. Did you volunteer, Mr. Tallman?"

Rick sighed inwardly.

But, he thought, the hell with it. And the hell, also, with Lt. K. W. Kraus, USN.

"Yes, I did. Sir!" he replied, keeping his eyes front and his face innocent of expression.

Kraus shook his head unbelievingly. "For a fact," he said. "And would you like to tell me—not for the record, just between us—what in Christ's Kingdom made you do a thing like that?"

"Well, sir," Rick replied reasonably, "I heard on a television revival show that God is going to give the world an enema sometime before the end of summer, and I figure the hose has got to go in either here or at Calcutta. So I thought, considering the odds, maybe I'd better brush up on my swimming."

It wasn't his ultimate effort, but the best he could come up with on the spur of the moment. The SEAL officer's reaction, however, was beyond anything he could have hoped. His face paled, etching a pattern of freckles across his cheeks and nose. Tiny points of fire were suddenly visible in the depths of the black eyes, and the rockbound coast of Maine echoed ever more clearly as he spoke.

"Well, son of a hawah," he said. "If we don't have us a comedian heah!"

Rick did not reply and tried his damnedest to keep from smiling.

"The Teams," Kraus was saying, "don't have room, not a single space, for comedians. None a-tall! So tell me, funny man, do you have any idea how many people either flunk out during training, are found medically unfit, or are dropped at their own request . . . what the percentages are?

"Of the men who report for training in each and every new class," Kraus went on, "only one in three will ever wear the pistol-and-trident."

He paused there for the tiniest of glances toward the left side of his own chest, where he wore a complicated gold badge that was somewhat larger than the wings-and-anchor Naval

Aviator insignia that occupied a similar spot on Rick's uniform.

Looking at it, Rick recalled that MacDougall, and the yeoman in the lobby, had been wearing a similar device—gold eagle with spread wings, holding a trident, flintlock pistol, and anchor. He'd never even realized that the SEALs had their own distinctive insignia.

"And I can by Jesus guarantee you, Tallman, that your face will not be seen among the survivors in the next class. Because I love this outfit and intend to spend the rest of my service career in it, and I will do whatever I have to do to make sure you are never a part of it."

It was a long speech, and Kraus paused at the end for breath, giving Rick another opportunity to speak up—and resign—if he wanted to. But once again, something seemed to hold him back. Besides, Kraus seemed to be on his favorite subject, and it seemed a shame to interfere.

"The first rule, and the most important one for this unit, carried over from its beginnings in the Underwater Demolition Teams of World War II and continuing right up to the present day," he said, "is teamwork. The Team—and the mission—take precedence over other considerations. In the whole history of the SEALs there is not one recorded instance of a Team member being abandoned by his buddy, and not one time when a Team failed to complete its mission when that was even remotely possible.

"The Teams have got no room for failure. No room for the kind of record you left behind at the Academy, at Princeton, at Top Gun, and in the Persian Gulf. No room for fuckups or quitters. No room for pampered playboys.

"In short, we got no room a-tall for you . . . rich boy."

Rick had begun to wonder, as the moments passed, whether the lecture he was getting was really just a standard item served up to all incoming officers, or if there might be something more personal involved. He found himself feeling grateful to Kraus for giving him the answer to his question without having to ask. It put the whole thing in perspective. Made him glad he hadn't acted on the impulse to resign.

"Training a SEAL is some expensive," Kraus was saying now. "Runs about eighty thousand dollars, give or take a few thousand, to bring a man all the way to graduation. Dropouts are a total loss on the books. So we've been under a little pressure here lately to cut what they call our trainee-attrition rate.

"Part of that effort is a big brass bell lashed to a post in the main courtyard of the training compound. To quit, a man has got to go ring that bell three times—and then toss his helmet-liner down on the deck under it.

"That's humiliating. An open admission of failure. And it's intended to make trainees think one last time before actually dropping out. Real bad news, you know? So because I'm not really a mean guy, Tallman, I would like to spare you such an experience."

Kraus sat still, eyes blazing up at Rick. But the corners of his mouth had twitched themselves into what might have been a smile, if it had been on another face.

"The order transferring you here," Kraus said, "arrived yesterday. But the rest of your files haven't showed up as yet, so I shouldn't wondah that it would be some easy turning things around. If you agree, I will just dump the whole unholy mess back into BuPers's lap with a notation that some kind of clerical error got made, and the subject officer never actually volunteered for this training. How about it?"

Smarmy little bastard. The bureaucratic sidestep Kraus had proposed was, Rick realized, the easiest way out of the situation, and it had been in the back of Rick's mind ever since the orders had caught up with him on board the hospital flight. But the words just wouldn't come, and he realized suddenly that the argument he'd been having with himself was over. A decision had been reached. And the warmth of his welcome from Lt. K. W. Kraus, USN, had been a real factor in reaching it.

"No, sir!" he said. "That would not be possible. Sir."

Kraus seemed astonished. "Why not?"

"Because I volunteered for SEAL training. And intend to complete the course, sir!"

The smile-rictus that had lifted the bottom of Kraus's face faded, and he sat perfectly still for a long moment. Then he relaxed. But the eyes didn't change.

"All right, then," Kraus said in a voice that was, if anything, even quieter and more deadly than before. "If you want it that way, finest kind. Nothing more to be said. Except maybe this: The decision you made just now was the wrong one. And you going to find out just how wrong it was during the next few weeks, because I am sure-God going to see to it that you do. I will have plenty of opportunity because, in case no one's given you The Word yet, I'm senior instructor here—and I am going to make it my personal business to run your rich-boy ass right out of the Teams before you ever start training!

"Now get the hell out of my sight."

Kraus went back to his paperwork, taking no further account of Rick's presence, but Rick waited a full minute (more gorilla counting) before executing the right-face, forward march that got him out of there and headed back down the corridor.

Rich or poor, he told himself, it's always nice to feel wanted.

Moscow, U.S.S.R.

Monday, July 7
11:17 A.M.

"Comrade General," the Party Secretary said, shifting the deceptively mild focus of his pale blue eyes to the older man sitting opposite him, "are we keeping you from your rest?"

Rocket General Viktor I. Tregorin straightened in his chair, stifled yet another yawn that had been forming in his throat, and forced himself to smile at the upstart whom he planned to destroy.

"Forgive me, Comrade General Secretary," he said. "I think it is the air down here. It always puts me to sleep."

Which was exactly the kind of amiable, sleepy-bear response—an artful blend of truth and evasion—that had made Viktor Tregorin a member of the Politburo inner circle that governed his nation.

But the General Secretary, who was also the President of the Union of Soviet Socialist Republics, seemed to accept the words at face value. And in truth, the windowless meeting room two hundred feet below the Kremlin—connected to it only by heavily guarded elevator shafts—had always depressed him. He suspected that the reason might be the ventilation system, which had been defective for all of the half century that the bunker (actually a branch of the Moscow subway system) had served its dual role as strategic redoubt and executive meeting room for the Central Committee.

"We were discussing arrangements for the Western nuclear inspection teams," the Party Secretary said, "and Comrade Admiral Bukharin had, I think, certain reservations."

Tregorin stiffened, feeling a new surge of the inner tension that was the true cause of his apparent drowsiness, as attention shifted to his old friend and coconspirator. Was Grigoriy Alexandrovich feeling the pressure, too? And if not, what was wrong with him?

But Admiral Bukharin seemed in no mood to temporize. "Comrade General Secretary," he said, "the situation is exactly the one that I and several others here in this room predicted when the arrangements for on-site inspection of our facilities were first discussed. The military officers sent among us are, without exception, espionage agents—spies—and should be treated as such. Coddling them, offering them cooperation of any kind, is tantamount to aiding them in their effort to destroy the Rodina."

Bukharin's voice had risen as he spoke, and Tregorin was sure that the diatribe was only beginning. But the General Secretary cut it off at the root.

"Your objections, Comrade Admiral," he said, breaking into the flow of words with an authority that could not be questioned, "are noted in the record. There is no need to go over this ground again."

The General Secretary paused briefly and looked around the table as if inviting further dissidence. But none appeared, as he had known it would not.

"The Western inspecting officers," he said when it was certain that no other voice would be raised, "are, indeed, spies. What else should they be? Spying is, after all, their specific mission. They are to spy on us, to see if we are keeping our side of the disarmament bargains, as our own people are spying in the West to see that they keep theirs. What of that?

"Comrades, we do not propose to take them into the councils of our military directorate, or to compromise security in other matters that are none of their business! Care is being taken to see that members of the teams carry out the duties of their inspection assignments, and nothing more!

"But let there be no mistake: This is a new day! A new era in the history of our revolution and of the world. It now becomes our task to make sure that everyone—our own people no less than those of other, perhaps presently hostile, nations—comes at last to realize that the changes are real and that they are not merely a passing fad or fancy.

"Some, I realize, take a different view . . ."

The General Secretary paused again, and there was no doubt about which of the men at the table he meant. But no one was singled out, and no one seemed to want to pursue the matter.

". . . to the point of working actively to sabotage the program."

This time the pause was longer, the silence infinitely more deadly. The General Secretary had chosen his words with care. "Sabotage" was, historically, the language of the purge trials of the Stalinist era, the specific charge on which thousands—perhaps millions—of Party dissidents, and those suspected of nonconformist sympathies, had been sent to the wall. Its use, here and now, by the anointed leader of Party and nation, was sufficient to bring even the sleepiest member to full attention.

"One of us," the General Secretary went on when he was sure he had their full attention, "a comrade who has sat among us at this table, has seen fit to make policy without consulting the wishes of those whose business it is to be consulted . . . to enter into negotiations and make promises to a foreign power as if acting in our joint behalf.

"You are all aware," he began, "of recent changes in the Persian military stance."

His use of the ancient name, Tregorin thought, was significant. The General Secretary, no friend of the mullahs and ayatollahs, equated all Iranian governments with the traditional Persian adversaries of the Rodina.

"We send Comrade Petchukocov to Tehran as an agricultural envoy, surely the most innocuous of missions," he continued, "and what is the result? Within days, the entire region threatens to burst again into flames! Can any foreign ministry, even those most friendly to the Rodina, forget that Petchukocov was once a professional soldier? How can they possibly see the subsequent events as mere coincidence? No matter what we say, regardless of how loudly we proclaim our innocence, who will believe us?

"No one, comrades. No one!

"After we have finally been able to withdraw our military forces from Afghanistan—cauterizing the wound that had been bleeding the motherland for a decade of insanity—Petchukocov is at the mullahs' ears, telling them that the hour has come for their Afghan guerrilla puppets, the mujahedin, to strike against the government we left in power!

"Telling them we will not interfere, that we will even support them . . . so long as they make common cause with us against the Great Satan of America!"

"Impossible!" Bukharin burst out, leaping to his feet, his eyes wide. "Impossible! Comrade General Secretary, I have known Comrade Petchukocov for a lifetime." Admiral Bukharin moved closer, his bulk towering above the General Secretary. The others shifted uneasily in their seats. Bukharin spoke softly, but firmly. "He could not have done such a thing."

"But he has." The General Secretary's voice was flat. "The Persian diplomatic office confirms it."

"Treason!" One of the Secretary's own people uttered the word that was in everyone's mind.

"No!" Bukharin shouted, his huge fist pounding the table.

Time to cast oil upon the waters. "Comrade General Secretary," Tregorin said, "perhaps there is some explanation, something that we do not know as yet. Perhaps . . . ?"

"Perhaps. Yes."

The General Secretary's response was thoughtful, betraying none of the irritation that might have been expected. "Your point is well taken, Comrade General," he continued, nodding. "And the measures now contemplated for dealing with the problem do, indeed, include offering Comrade Petchukocov an opportunity to explain his actions, yes."

Tregorin nodded and fell silent.

All was well. An "opportunity to explain." That meant Petchukocov would be summoned here, in person. As planned.

But what on earth was wrong with Bukharin? What had possessed him to speak as he did?

Now, of all times—with Temnota finally making real progress and most of the hardware finally in place—was this a time to rattle the cage of the very man at whose granite head Operation Darkness was actually aimed?

On his own, the weak fool would never have the courage to act, to take the first necessary step toward total, unassailable world domination, no matter how tempting the opportunity. Therefore, he must be assisted.

He must be placed in a position where he would be unable to resist. That was why Temnota had been devised.

Meanwhile, let him sleep the sleep of the just and the idiotic.

Overconfidence had sent as many men of power to their deaths as excessive timidity. The stroke they were planning—aside from its possible international ramifications if it succeeded—was just the thing to touch off a Party purge like those of the 1930s if it failed. And fail it might if the General Secretary or any of his damned clique caught so much as a hint.

Silence was the key, as always. Silence and sleepy smiles and easy compliance. Give Temnota a chance to do its work. And save the arguments for afterward. When they could be backed with cold steel.

Coronado, California

Monday, July 7
0533

Half an hour into the first day of training, the bodies of the forty-two men of second platoon, Basic Underwater Demolition/SEAL (BUDS) Class 1033, were dripping with sweat despite the cool mist blowing in from the sea.

Pounding along the loose sand on the outward-bound leg of their second "warm-up" two-mile run of the day ("A little exercise before breakfast to he'p you work up an appetite," the instructors had explained. "Don't want to hurt them cooks' feelings!"), they counted cadence in a series of deep-lunged gasps:

> "When I los' my blon' Norwegian,
> Hup one; hup two!
> Went an' joined th' Foreign Legion
> Hup three; hup fo'."

But Rick's attention—via peripheral vision—was fixed on Lieutenant Kraus.

The little lobsterman fascinated him.

All the other instructors had begun the day in standard work uniform: blue staff T-shirts over OD athletic shorts. But Kraus, as chief instructor, had selected his own first-day uniform, and Rick thought it typical: crisp, clean suntans ironed to razor-sharp military press.

But that was where reality ended. For Kraus had started out leading the prebreakfast calisthenics, and now he was at the head of the column as it plowed along, in the hard going along Silver Strand. But his uniform looked no different from the way it had looked at reveille. No wrinkling. No bending. No creasing. And most astonishing of all, no sweat stains—not even a meager half-circle under the arms!

Rick had felt sure of his own physical ability to survive the SEAL training course. Despite the stereotypical fly-boy image of physical sloth, he had kept himself in condition by running three miles a day even when his arm had been in a cast, and as a result the two-week SEAL indoctrination/conditioning course had been a snap for him.

The regimen of running, swimming, running, calisthenics, running, rifle practice, running, gymnastics—plus a lot more running, running, and running—had served only to build his confidence.

But watching Kraus's performance this morning was a real morale-bender.

How did he do it?

Unconsciously, Rick increased his own pace to draw closer in the hope of spotting just one little bead of perspiration on the chief instructor's forehead. But there was none.

And his minor breach of discipline, in moving out of assigned position, did not go unnoticed.

"Tallman . . . go get wet!"

Kraus could not have seen him. Not even with the best peripheral vision. But the order he barked (not at all breathlessly; the bastard wasn't even panting) over his shoulder gave Rick unique status in the training unit as the first SEAL candidate to rate administrative discipline.

Ground rules had been set forth clearly during the first five minutes of the day. "Get wet" was a punishment order—for even the most minor infraction.

It meant the trainee must go to the surf line, throw himself into the water while fully clad, and then get back to the unit and complete his duties wearing the water-heavy uniform and squishy boondockers.

Well, hell . . .

Someone had to be first. And say this for Kraus, he hadn't made any secret of his intention to see that Rick got the full benefit of the SEAL training routines.

And anyway, Rick thought as he turned back from the ocean sopping wet (no walking for trainees; all duties to be performed at a dead run) and tried to catch up with the fleeing platoon, he'd always said a man shouldn't join the Navy if he can't take a joke.

Kronstadt, U.S.S.R.

Monday, July 7
1601

The chemicals seemed to work well enough.

Turning on his back to rest for a moment before switching from the breaststroke to the crawl (the only strokes permitted for Temnota trainees), Trooper Andrey Narmonov could see ice floes in the distance. Plenty of them here in the Gulf of Finland, even in summertime.

Water temperature had to be close to zero, Celsius.

But he felt only a pleasant warmth; a kind of glow from the exercise of swimming ten miles—and no anxiety whatever about the miles he still must swim before returning to Kotlin Island for the evening meal.

If this was all their highly touted Temnota conditioning amounted to . . .

He knew it was not, though he had never been told; none of them had been told anything so far, and he was sure they would be told nothing in the future—at least until it became absolutely necessary. That was the way of things in the Rodina, and always had been, even in the time of the czars.

But it was frustrating, all the same, to have chemicals pumped into your body as though it were the Grand Canal of Venice, without being given a hint as to their real nature or purpose . . . unless, of course, you believed the comrade chief medical officer's explanation that the shots were intended to "do for you what layers of blubber do for the whale."

The inoculations had made them almost immune to the extremes of temperature. A week ago, Andrey knew, he could not have survived in near freezing seawater for as much as six minutes, even wearing the best and warmest wet suit ever made. Now he was doing it stark naked.

Today's exercise was intended as a convincer; something to make them aware of their new immunity and to build morale.

Andrey took a deep breath and swept his bare body through a half-turn and began to do the crawl toward Kotlin, just visible on the horizon ahead.

Another hour of swimming, no more than that. They would be just in time for the evening meal. Not that food was any special treat for the Temnota unit.

From the first meal of the first day in their training, they had been fed on paps—milk, enriched by various vitamins and roughage. "Space food," they'd been told; someone had tried to raise their spirits by explaining that this was the same kind of pureed, homogenized stuff cosmonauts ate during their space voyages. No one had been impressed. Least of all Andrey, for whom it only unlocked unhappy memories. But the "space food" had continued to be their whole menu, even on holidays, and by now it almost tasted good. Especially when he was very hungry.

Andrey ducked his head into a wave and allowed himself to tread water for a moment while he looked around. An evening breeze had sprung up, and the gulf was getting choppy. He searched for the rest of the training cadre and spotted them, one by one, a ragged line on either side of him.

Well, at least he was not alone, and at least he was impervious now to the cold, and if necessary he could swim all night. Or float. Or whatever the situation demanded.

He knew they were watching him, waiting for some excuse, waiting for the chance to expel him from the program and send him back to the Naval Infantry with an "unsatisfactory material" stamp on his record dossier.

Let them watch. Andrey Narmonov was not Yuri Narmonov. Andrey Narmonov was a soldier of the motherland. Andrey Narmonov was no traitor.

Gorky, U.S.S.R.

Sunday, July 27
12:16 P.M.

Preparation of the subject had taken longer than expected.

For more than a week after seeing the papers that committed his son to the Temnota project, Yuri Narmonov had been subject to alternate incidents of maniacal rage and suicidal depression.

The doctor had hoped for some kind of reaction—something to indicate a survival of spirit and will behind the facade of placid acceptance that had characterized the patient's behavior since his arrival at the hospital. But the intensity of the backlash had come as a surprise and a revelation.

This was a man of real character and spirit, one who could hide and wait and plan, deep within himself, without ever betraying his true emotional state. Except in response to an immediate threat to his son.

It had only cost the doctor a little blood (they said the scarring from those fingernail tracks on his arm would be permanent), and a brief moment of real fear, to be sure the essential Yuri Narmonov was still alive and well somewhere down under the insulation. But stabilizing his condition enough for him to be a suitable subject for the null tank had turned into a long and slow process.

All drugs had been withdrawn a week ago, and there had been no new incidents of violent behavior. But it was like cooking eggs over a volcano.

The tank was ready now, filled with water warmed to precisely the temperature of Narmonov's own body. He would be immersed in it, below the surface, clad in a wetsuit with elastic tethers for arms, legs, body, even for fingers and toes, and fed automatically through tubes paralleling those that furnished a demand regulator with air (also carefully warmed to body temperature). There was also an exhaust for exhalation.

Narmonov would wear a close, comfortable mask for the eyes, and plugs for the ears.

No possibility of outside stimulus remained, only the well of utter isolation, unrelieved and unrelievable even by pain. It was the ultimate solitary confinement.

When the brain waves finally calmed, when the deltas and alphas finally began to indicate total submergence of the personality, reconditioning could begin.

The earplugs would begin to offer music, followed by persuasion. Then they would see . . .

Yuri Narmonov might be a good subject; he might be the brittle—and ultimately frangible/restructurable—personality General Tregorin hoped. He might become the useful propaganda vehicle Tregorin wanted to show to the West: the "free" spokesman whose words would be believed even when he was merely parroting the latest instructions from the Information Ministry.

Or he might emerge from the tank a blank-brained vegetable, incontinent and hopeless.

Or—least likely of all, but still possible—Narmonov might find some means of resistance, of retaining some shred of his true self despite the tank. In which case the "sad accident" of which the general had spoken would surely come to pass.

"Is he ready, Comrade Doctor?"

The doctor nodded slowly. "Yes. I think so. As ready, at any rate, as we can make him in the time allotted. I believe we can begin tonight. A little dose of Nembutal at midnight and then, without wakening him, into the tank. Call me before he is immersed. I want to be on hand to monitor him for the first hour or so."

"Yes, Comrade Doctor."

Tregorin would be satisfied with nothing less than total effort: total success or total failure.

Narmonov must leave here smiling and joking, ready and able to fulfill his role.

Or, in a casket.

Coronado, California

Monday, July 28
0003

The toughest week of Rick Tallman's life began just after midnight, with a burst of automatic weapons fire and the smell of smoke.

Lights in the training barracks flashed on and off once or twice—and then stayed on, as noisy M-60 flash-bangs exploded outside the windows and instructors raced through the building shouting unintelligible (and deliberately contradictory) orders, while overturning any bunk still occupied.

Rick hit the deck running.

There was fire (smoky but relatively harmless) in the bottom of a crate of toilet paper at the back of the head, and he took charge of the fire-fighting effort while fending off a rapid sequence of orders to "hit the deck" and "hit a brace" and "get wet" and "fall in outside in boondockers and jockstrap."

He had expected all of it.

SEAL training is intended to bring the student along at maximum speed by offering the kind of challenge that will stretch his natural capacities . . . without actually exceeding them.

But the five-day ordeal known as hell week is an exception to all rules.

Since the mid-1980s, when the Defense Department decided to increase the number of SEAL units, with an eye to the expanding role of unconventional warfare in the world, there had been pressure to increase the graduation rate for the Basic Underwater Demolition/SEAL (BUDS) course. Instructors who had once openly competed to see who could chalk up the greatest number of dropouts were now constrained to take a more positive view: "You can do it—and we're here to show you *how* you can do it."

Hell week, however, was still old style. For five days—120 hours—BUDS students swim, run the obstacle course, navigate inflatable boats at sea and on dry land, crawl in the sand, flop in the mud, run up and down the beaches, and are subjected to a general barrage of insult, confusion, and harassment that is intended to increase stress to a point likely to eliminate any candidate who might crack under actual combat conditions.

Kraus, who had wangled reassignment to regular instructor duty after failing to eliminate Rick as promised during the indoctrination period, put it clearly in a little speech he made at the last formation of the previous week's training.

"If you pussies," he said, "can hack the next five days, then more power to you! Because you can probably go the distance. Hell week—the third week of your training—is incorporated in the SEAL curriculum for three reasons: to make you quit, to make you quit, and to make you quit!

"Before this, we've taken it easy on you. The bell's been up there, tied to a post in the main courtyard, and you had to go all that way to ring it and declare yourself out of the program.

"But during hell week, we're gonna take that mother down and carry it with us wherever we go, just so none of you little fairies will hesitate. Anytime you get to feeling sorry for yourself; anytime you think you're too dirty, too wet, too cold, too tired, or too sleepy to go on, all you got to do is reach out a hand—the bell will be right there, and right behind it is a truck to take your asses back to the barracks for a nice, warm shower."

It was a nice little pep talk, and Rick thought it might even have gotten Kraus a round of applause if anyone had for a moment thought that he was kidding. But he wasn't, and he confirmed it in a final, private word he had for his favorite trainee.

"Don't dast think I've forgotten about you, Tallman," he said with one of his cold skeleton-grins. "And don't dast think I changed my mind about anything just because I couldn't run your rich-boy ass into the ground during the last three weeks.

You gonna quit, Sweet Pea, and thank me for the opportunity."

But he was out of sight before Rick could find the proper words to thank him.

Weekend leaves had been shortened. There had been no chance to get over to the Scripps campus for an update on Captain Ward's *Steel Albatross* project (the name Rick suggested had stuck; the captain actually seemed rather proud of it).

No time, even, to become better acquainted with Mac—who had breezed through the first phase of training with an ease that gave the lie to his concerns about being too old and out of condition for the work. Two of the first dropouts from the training class—one at the end of a particularly poor performance on the obstacle course and the other for medical reasons involving a weak ankle—had been the other two commissioned officers, so Mac was now in command of one of the two platoons into which the class was divided.

Rick, commanding the other platoon, had found himself deeply impressed by the way his friend handled the added responsibility while sweating through the training schedule with the kids.

At thirty-seven, the chief was still a young man by most standards, but he was the oldest trainee in the class by nearly a decade. Even with the obvious advantage of having done it all before, the extra years should have been a considerable handicap. The official cutoff for trainees going through the course for the first time was twenty-eight.

But Mac had made it look easy, and watching him do twenty one-hand push-ups now—at the order of an instructor who must have been playing tag in grade school when Mac had gone through the course the first time—was enough to break a younger man's heart. Or even soften an instructor's.

Rick had wondered at first if they might take it easy on Mac and grandfather the older man through the course out of respect. But it hadn't happened. Off duty, Mac might still inspire the kind of awe he'd seen in the eyes of the lobby yeoman the day they'd arrived at the base. But during training hours he was just another grunt at the mercy of those who seemed determined to push him beyond the limit of human endurance.

And they were doing it right now, at 0300, to the accompaniment of unpredictable hand-grenade detonations and a continuing farrago of shouted commands:

"Fall in . . . on the fuckin' bounce, goddamn it. . . . Fall in! Right fuckin' now . . . now . . . now!"

The training company fell in, in various stages of undress, and stood at rigid attention while Lieutenant Kraus and his cohorts strolled down their line with white gloves and flashlights, handing out push-ups and orders to hit the surf for any small infraction or shortcoming, past or present.

Most of the trainees were so bleary that they did their first fifty or sixty push-ups before their eyes were fully open, and the rest in a blue haze of indignation over the sleep they had missed. But the harassment had only begun. The instructors saw to it that the pace remained frantic and rest periods few for the rest of the morning.

Log drill had started during the first week of the training cycle, and it was a killer. The logs were creosote-dipped telephone poles, and each seven-man boat crew (the basic SEAL administrative unit) was expected to lift one, working together as a team, by the numbers:

One—bend and grasp the pole's underside.

Two—lift the pole to waist level.

Three—hoist it to the shoulder.

Four—military-press it overhead, with the whole crew in line below.

Three-two-one reversed the procedure, bringing the log back to earth. But the commands didn't have to be issued in that order, and before dawn the whole thing became a series of quick spasms, straining the body to its limit. But no one dropped out or fainted or died while it was going on.

"One two three four, three four, three four, three four, three four," Kraus counted, smiling and happy on a little camp chair while the crews fought the logs and each other to remain in cadence.

"Three four, three four, three four, three," he counted.

And then a single word: "Four."

The logs halted above the trainees' heads and they stood waiting for the next command. But it didn't come. Kraus seemed suddenly distracted by other matters and left them there, with the logs in the air, while Rick began a slow count of the seconds.

He broke it off after reaching one hundred gorillas.

"Quit."

Kraus said the word quietly the first time, and then again, shouting.

"Quit!"

The trainees stood silent; the logs remained in the air.

"Quit! Give up, you assholes. Go on, ring the bell—it's right over there. We wouldn't hold out on a bunch of old pussies like you. Just ring that little brass bell three times, and it's all ovah. Quit, goddammit!"

It was an attractive offer, made at an attractive time.

Why soak up all the crap when he would almost certainly be bucking for a transfer, or resigning, as soon as the training course was done?

"Quit!"

Kraus was grinning, now, looking squarely at him, and Rick read the SEAL officer's mind. And Kraus read his.

So . . . fuck him!

Rick's shoulders firmed under the load, and he stood there waiting—log held high—until Kraus finally gave up and called out the three-two-one sequence that brought it back to earth.

"You'll never make it," he said. "Not one of you. Quit!"

No one spoke.

"Quit!"

No one moved.

"Quit!"

Still no response.

"Quit!"

Nothing.

So log drill began again . . . this time from the supine position.

Rick decided he was grateful for the change.

A man could get bored.

Odessa, Ukrainian S.S.R.

Monday, July 28
1940

The worst of it, Andrey Narmonov told himself, was the darkness. If you could handle the darkness, you could handle anything. Only, he had always been afraid of the dark.

"Stand up!" yelled the *starshina*, the petty officer assigned to their squad. He had never seen the man. That was part of the training, to learn to identify people and places and objects by senses other than sight.

"Check your equipment!"

The first time he had been told to check equipment in total darkness, he had almost disgraced himself by asking how he was to check what he could not see. But someone else had said it before him, and been disciplined for it. And now it had all become . . . routine.

He knew the world around him was still filled with light. They were in Odessa, the Black Sea port where army SPETSNAZ units went through basic training—not that they had been permitted to come into contact with them. Nonetheless, summer days here were long and warm and he could feel the sun on his arms and chest when they marched or ran in the open air. The headgear they wore—the leather helmets fitted with eye covers in which they ate, slept, and worked—made sure that it remained only a tactile suggestion. The whole purpose of the training was to accustom them to function in total darkness.

But the touch of sunlight on the skin was such a temptation!

The blinder helmets were not, after all, bolted to their skulls. Remove the helmet, and nothing would happen at all. Except that you would be out, no longer a part of Temnota. And it was rumored, out of SPETSNAZ as well—just as though you had failed to complete basic training.

"Narmonov!"

"Da!"

"What are you dreaming of? Stand at attention!"

His mind had been wandering, daydreaming in ranks, like some green recruit's. Well, the *starshina* would see that it didn't happen again.

"Down!"

Andrey dropped to the deck.

"One hundred press-ups. Now!"

His knuckles touched the splintery wood, and he began.

One . . .

Two . . .

Three . . .

At least it was no worse.

Four . . .

Five . . .

Six . . .

One hundred was a lot, but they would never break him. Never make him throw in his helmet. Never make him quit.

Seven . . .

Eight . . .

Nine . . .

He could take this. All day and all night. But—damn—how he wished he were not doing it all in the dark.

Coronado, California

Tuesday, July 29

1513

"Tallman! Hit the deck."

Rick did it the way he'd been taught in the first weeks of training, snapping the legs out smartly behind and dropping to the prone position, breaking his fall with his hands.

"On your feet!"

He was up and at rigid attention on a two count.

"Hit the deck!"

"On your feet!"

"Hit the deck!"

"All right. Lean and rest!"

That was a muscle twister; body horizontal in push-up position, elbows locked, head up, back straight. Rick snapped into it and waited for the command to begin push-ups. But the order didn't come.

Instead, the instructor—Lieutenant Kraus—strolled a few paces toward Rick. He didn't look in Rick's direction once, but was careful to stay in his line of sight (all part of the treatment, Rick decided) while examining a boat and later, when he seated himself on its side and took a knife from his boot to clean his nails. When they were done to his satisfaction, he put the knife back and stood up, looking placidly out to sea and whistling a tune, off-key.

Rick's shoulder and back muscles felt as if they were coming apart. The backs of the thighs went first, just behind the knee, and then the muscles just above the buttocks, where the kidneys are. Rick couldn't see his watch, so he began a one-gorilla, two-gorilla count of the seconds, and he was past six hundred when Kraus finally seemed to notice him once more.

"Ready to quit?" Kraus inquired.

"No, sir!"

Kraus smiled and stood there, looking down at him, while the rest of the class formed up and followed other instructors back to the beach for yet another go at boat drill. Rick kept counting. His legs finally gave out—about the time the gorilla count reached a thousand.

"Hit the deck!"

This time, he almost didn't make it. The knees didn't want to bend, and when they finally did bend, they didn't want to straighten up again. But they did it, in response to clear emergency-override orders Rick gave them, and he was able to hit a brace just short of the normal cadence. Tears formed at the outer corners of his eyes, and he could feel them running down his cheeks.

"Ready to quit yet, Sweet Pea?"

"No, sir!"

Kraus looked him up and down for a moment in silence. But this time without a smile.

"You will, rich boy. You will."

Coronado, California

Wednesday, July 30
0214

"Mac, the guys are beginning to come apart."

"Christ Jesus . . . tell me about it!"

The third day of hell week had begun while they were on a 25-lap swim in the unlighted pool, and now, two hours later, they were supposed to be catching as much sleep as possible before the next rude awakening. But Rick was still wide-eyed, in whispered conversation with Mac in the head reserved for training-platoon commanders.

"That damn bell," Mac muttered.

Rick didn't reply at once, but he knew what the chief meant. The fact that the bell was always with them—not up on a pole in the courtyard, but dismounted and following the class around—made it a constant temptation, one that was hard to resist when the alternative was another rubber-legged tour of the obstacle course or a brisk session with the logs.

"All right, then. Fuck it!" Rick said, sitting down and unlacing his boondockers.

Mac stared at him.

"I got an idea."

Bootless, Rick stood up and rubbed his back. It hurt. But so did everything else, and it wasn't going to get better soon.

"They been giving us an hour or so between night drills," he said. "Hang on to the boots for me, okay? I'll be back."

"Look, Rick . . . I mean . . . Mr. Tallman . . ."

Rick managed a grin. "Make it Rick, anytime we're off duty. Okay, bro? And cool it. Don't worry, I'll be back before they miss me." Barefoot and silent, he stepped to the window, opened it, and began to climb out. "But if for any reason I'm not back," he said, throwing his legs outside and sitting for a moment on the sill, "for God's sake don't try to cover for me. No sense giving the mothers a chance to bilge both of us."

And then he was gone.

Coronado, California

Wednesday, July 30
0913

No one missed the bell until dawn.

Kraus's second-in-command was in charge of it but had delegated the responsibility to another instructor . . . who had simply been too busy running the class through a night problem on the obstacle course to notice that it was not where he had left it when they secured from the 25-lap night swim.

Now it was gone.

And hell was raised. Kraus threatened to flunk the whole class if the guilty party didn't confess—and return the bell—forthwith. But no one did, and after a while he gave up shouting and took what satisfaction he could out of running the whole company for ten miles in loose sand.

But Kraus had been looking straight at Rick when he demanded that the culprit turn himself in. So it came as no particular surprise when orders arrived for Rick to report to SEAL headquarters, on the double.

Well, then, all right. They know I took the damn thing and they know why I did it and they know I hid it somewhere. But they can't prove it. So tough titty. He set off at a smart jog, mentally preparing himself for an interesting hour or so.

And that was what he got. But it wasn't what he'd expected. The summons had not been issued by the SEAL training office itself, but by the unit's chief medical officer. Nobody mentioned the missing bell.

He was ushered into an examination room. Told to sit down on a stool in the corner. And left in solitude to consider his sins.

The examination room was bare, but someone had left an old copy of *All Hands*, the Navy house organ, under the instrument table, and Rick was reading a critique of the Department of Defense senior-level task force on sexual harassment in the military—while wondering just how badly a senior-level officer would have to screw up in order to be assigned to it—when a woman in navy uniform entered, carrying a folder of papers and a clipboard.

"Good morning, Lieutenant," she said in a tone that might have been brisk, but somehow wasn't.

Rick looked up from the magazine, started to smile . . . and stopped with his mouth at full flap.

The woman, who wore the railroad-track collar insignia of a full lieutenant, was of medium height, with orange-red hair and a sprinkling of freckles. Her cheekbones were high, in counterpoint to the little snip of an upturned nose and wide mouth; the features somehow composed and compounded into something that an artist or studio photographer might have identified as carefully understated beauty.

But the central attraction was The Eyes. Their color reminded Rick of Florida—of the green flash that sometimes lights the top of the sun at the final moment of subtropical sunset. Those who have never witnessed it usually dismiss the phenomenon as a kind of local in-joke, something for the tourists. But Rick had seen it several times during childhood and adolescence when visiting friends on the west coast of the state and had never failed to be impressed by the deep-turquoise intensity of the color . . . which he had always assumed was unique to that time and place, because he had encountered it nowhere else. Until now.

He wanted to smile and introduce himself and say something witty and charming that would make her smile back and stay and let him go on looking at The Eyes. He wanted to find out her name and address and phone number and marital status and what she was doing for dinner the night after hell week was over.

But instead, he merely stood and stared until she broke the silence.

"Good morning," she repeated. "My name is Deane—Dr. Samantha Deane—and my specialty is sport and occupational orthopedics. Which is why BuPers assigned me to the SEAL medical team."

Rick went on staring. She was a doctor—not a nurse? Well, big deal! But there was something else; something stirring in one of the middle filing cabinets of memory.

"I apologize for taking you away from hell week, Lieutenant," the doctor continued, apparently oblivious to Rick's prolonged stare. "I should have seen you as soon as you arrived, but I was on leave. So it was only today that I started going over records and came across your name."

Samantha Deane?

Dr. Sam Deane.

Orthopedics.

"Jesus . . . Christ!" Rick said.

Dr. Samantha Deane stopped talking and looked at him. "Lieutenant?"

"You're Dr. Sam Deane," he said.

"Yes. And your name sounded familiar. So I pulled the records to make sure. You're the fighter pilot . . ."

Rick swallowed almost painfully, looking into The Eyes again. "The one whose arm you wouldn't fix," he said. "That one."

She nodded equably. "That one."

The Eyes continued to look at Rick for a moment, and he found himself obscurely pleased to note that they seemed to have a little trouble breaking away. Nice to know that she had feelings. But the rest, he decided, was all Navy sawbones.

"I take it," she said, moving to the window and sorting through one of the folders she was carrying, "that no corrective surgery was, in fact, attempted in your case."

"No."

"Show me the arm, please."

Dr. Deane put the records and clipboard down, and Rick raised his left arm into plain view, rotating it as well as he could. It didn't seem to please her much, and after a moment she moved to another position to get a better look at the elbow.

"Pain?" she inquired.

Rick shook his head. "Nothing to speak of. Not from motion, anyway—or using the arm. It's just that it won't go as far around in a circle as it used to, that's all."

The doctor nodded, put her hands on the elbow, and pressed, hard, on the cartilage. "Anything?"

Rick shook his head again, and she let go and moved back to the window.

"BUDS training, and SEALs duty," she said in a professionally neutral voice, "are both physically taxing, and the physical requirements for entry and retention in the program are quite as stringent as those for flight training. You were accepted here on a waiver—"

Rick started to interrupt.

"—which I would have had to sign, had I been here instead of on leave."

He shut up and sat still, thinking.

There it was, if he wanted it. The perfect easy out. Records would show that he had tried and been beaten by regulations. He could spend a day or two back in Washington, talking to old friends in BuPers about career options, and who knows, maybe come up with something really outstanding.

Any way you sliced it, it was still a better deal than Kraus had offered him. So . . . why did he hear himself hedging?

"The arm's okay," he said.

"For ordinary purposes, perhaps, yes. But not for flying fighters—and maybe not for underwater demolition, either."

"You don't twist your arm that much, swimming."

"Swimming's just a small part of the job; you've been in training long enough to know that."

"Yeager broke the sound barrier—bored a hole through it with the X-1, no sweat—with an arm in such bad shape he couldn't even close his own hatch without the busted end of a broomstick."

"The Air Force will stand for anything."

"I can hack it, Doctor."

Samantha Deane blinked. And so did Rick, because his words were as much a surprise to him as they seemed to be for her. Nothing of the kind had been in his mind; it was like standing off in a corner somewhere, listening to someone else talk.

"Kiwi Kraus doesn't think you'll make it through hell week."

Everyone in the Navy seemed to have a nickname. Rick wondered, irrelevantly, where and how Kraus had acquired that one. The initials K. W. maybe?

"I know what he thinks," Rick said.

"And my mind hasn't changed, either."

So there it was. The reason she'd called him in there. A few months back, Samantha Deane had rejected him as a surgical risk because she didn't believe he would be able to handle the follow-up therapy needed to make the elbow operation a success. And now she was ready to edge him out of SEAL training as well.

"What seems to be the problem?" he inquired. "I mean . . . ordinarily, I'd just think it was my personality. I rub some people the wrong way; maybe you're one of them. But you seem to object to me on general principles."

"On the contrary . . ."

Dr. Deane had started to pick up the files, but now she put them down again and faced Rick.

"You've never seen your own psychological profile," she said.

"Of course I haven't. Regulations make it illegal to see that part of my own personal file." (But Rick had seen it. A hacker friend had helped him break into the BuPers computer for a private look two months earlier.)

"I realize some of what I say is going to be a little hard for you to accept," she said. "But my decision was based on that profile, reinforced by your records at Annapolis and Top Gun."

She said it calmly, then waited to see how he would handle it.

"I believe," Rick said, doing his best to maintain his cool in the face of what seemed to be an obvious attempt to get him to blow his stack, "that if I can hack this training with my arm the way it is, that's proof positive that the arm is not disqualifying for SEAL duty."

"Maybe so, but you could get hurt," she said.

"I've been hurt. I didn't like it. But I survived."

"I meant the arm. The elbow. Any further damage—before the existing condition has been surgically repaired—could make the condition permanent. Irreversible."

"Then you've changed your mind?" he said, not bothering to hide the disbelief in his voice. "You'll operate?"

"Uh . . . no."

"Well, then?"

"Kiwi Kraus knows I wouldn't have signed the waiver if I'd been here," she said. "But he asked me to overlook the whole thing. For now."

"What?" Rick said, caught off guard. "Kiwi . . . ?"

"He said he wanted the fun of making you quit . . . personally."

"Look," Rick said, trying to make it sound like something other than an outright plea, but realizing with a sudden sense of shock just how much he wanted to do what he'd been determined not to do only a few weeks earlier. "Look, just . . . let it drift for a while. Okay?"

"It's wrong."

"I can take care of myself, really."

She still didn't like it, and for a minute she wasn't going to do it. Rick saw the "No" forming behind her face. But then The Eyes wavered and she picked up what he realized, suddenly, must be the personality profile he said he'd never seen, reread something there, and put it back down and closed the cover of the personnel file.

"All right, Lieutenant," she said, all brisk medical efficiency once more. "All right—go back to hell week. Let's see what happens."

He stood up, executed a parade-ground about-face, and got out of there, while the getting was good.

Odessa, Ukrainian S.S.R.

Thursday, July 31
0500

The pressure in the chamber was eye-poppingly high—120 atmospheres and rising, according to the pressure gauge overhead—but at least they could see again.

And that, Andrey Narmonov told himself, was everything.

Not that the pressure seemed to matter anyway. His squad was inside what they had been told was a specially constructed decompression chamber, one built to accommodate unusually large numbers of men at unusually high pressure.

But Andrey didn't really care why. Not as long as he never had to put on one of the blinder helmets again.

"Attention!"

The petty officer, or *starshina*, who had been leaning at ease against the pressure chamber bulkhead just outside the observation window, barked the command into the communicator microphone and snapped to a rigid brace as the men in the tank tried to do the same.

It was hard work for a few of the trainees, though; trembling was no part of the position of attention, and some of them seemed unable to stop.

"I am Dr. Mikoyan."

A dark-haired woman, wearing the uniform of a naval officer, strolled to the chamber and looked in at them through the observation port, without expression.

"Some of you are cold?" she inquired. No one answered.

"You," she said, pointing to one of the tremblers. "Are you cold?"

The man hesitated, looking to either side as if uncertain that he had been singled out for attention, then tried to shake his head. But it was a miserable, almost entirely unsuccessful effort. He simply couldn't seem to control the muscles.

"N-n-n . . . ," he quavered.

The doctor regarded him silently and without compassion.

"N-n-no," the man finally managed to say. "N-n-not . . . cold."

"Quite correct," the doctor said. "You are not cold. But nonetheless, you are trembling. Do you know why? Of course not. Remember—you did not tremble when you swam in the Gulf of Finland? No," the doctor continued, "you did not. The chemicals in your system kept you from feeling the cold. But now you tremble, and it is because of the pressure in the tank rather than from cold. This is a problem known to medicine, and expected. It is called high-pressure nervous syndrome. You have heard of it?"

Unconsciously, Andrey wagged his head negatively along with his trembling teammate.

"No? None of you? No matter." The doctor shrugged, dismissing the question. "High-pressure nervous syndrome—HPNS—is an involuntary trembling caused by the effect of high pressure on the body's nervous system. It also has an effect upon the thought processes, slowing them and causing them to become jumbled and unreliable."

She paused, surveying the men in the tank, visibly separating those who were trembling from those who were not.

"The chemical conditioning you have undergone," she went on, "is also intended to make you immune to HPNS. But individual differences persist. Not everyone reacts to the chemical conditioning in the same way—"

Andrey remembered the men who had developed skin rashes, and the one who had gone foaming mad.

"—and not everyone derives full benefit, either. Some of you seem to be tolerating the hyperbaric situations—the high pressure—well enough. Others, not so. This is because of these individual differences. It is not something that can be controlled, or overcome. Therefore, do not concern yourselves with it."

The dark woman strolled away from the tank, apparently losing all interest in it and its human cargo, and went to an enamel-topped table near the door, where she twirled the dial of a combination lock attached to the front of a small cabinet, opened the door, and brought out a box of vials, which she laid aside.

"The roster," she said to the *starshina*. "You have the roster?"

"Yes, Comrade Doctor."

Mechanically, moving like a kind of oversize windup toy, the *starshina* swiveled to his right, plucked a clipboard from its place on the wall, and marched to the table, where he offered it to the doctor. She glanced at it but did not take it from his hand.

"The ones you see shaking in the chamber," she said passionlessly, "you will note their names, and when you have returned them all to sea-level pressure, you will take the tremblers aside and inform them that they have been eliminated from the program."

"*Da*, Comrade Doctor."

"Tell them the Rodina is grateful for their efforts, and they are to be returned to regular duty with the Naval Infantry. They will be sent orders," the doctor said, "which will make very sure, comrade, that the regular duty to which they return is in some remote place—where they will not be disturbed by outsiders, at least for a while."

"They are to be isolated? Confined?"

The doctor smiled thinly. "Certainly not. We are not jailers, after all. But contact with anyone not already acquainted with the Temnota project is to be avoided. At all costs! Do I make myself clear?"

"*Da*, Comrade Doctor."

"See to it. Now, as to the others . . ."

She opened a supply cabinet and brought out a boxful of disposable hypodermic syringes, which she proceeded to load from the vials.

"For the ones who did not tremble," she said, speaking over her shoulder as she worked, "when they are out of the tank and no longer in contact with the tremblers, each is to have a single shot—forty cc's, as you see here, no more, no less—intramuscularly. This is the booster for the chemical conditioning they have already received; it will reinforce their immunities for approximately a year. We withheld it until now, to be sure that it went only to those who could benefit. Is that clear?"

"Uh . . . *da*, Comrade Doctor."

The doctor glanced at the *starshina*, whose records indicated that he was a qualified medical technician as well as a SPETSNAZ veteran, and nodded in her usual abrupt fashion.

"Make it so," she said, striding away.

Coronado, California

Thursday, July 31
0500

On the fourth day of hell week, Kiwi Kraus changed tactics.

He stopped screaming at Rick and began to use psychology.

After calisthenics (sit-ups, slap-ups, camels, back push-ups, and jumping jacks) the shrinking number of trainees were ordered to pick up their 11-man boats and carry them on their heads to the swimming pool . . . with the instructors on board as passengers.

It might have been possible, just barely; but once hoisted into the air, the instructors insisted on jumping up and down, high-stepping back and forth inside the boat, and generally trying to unbalance the load, turning the trainees' heads and necks into a kind of human trampoline.

And laughing.

Moreover, when the boats at last came tumbling down, passengers and all, the instructors came up sputtering and raving about "deliberate mistreatment of government property" and put the crews to work doing slap-ups in the sand "until we tell you to stop."

But the real trouble began when they finally arrived at the swimming pool, where Kraus was waiting with a three-gallon bucket at his feet and one of his death's-head grins spread across the lower half of his face.

"This," he said conversationally, "is an easy one. And to prove it, I'll show you how it goes."

He jumped into the water, grabbed the bucket from the side, filled it with water, positioned it between his legs. Then, with both hands on the handle, he turned on his back to swim, effortlessly, from one end of the pool to the other, using only a lazy frog-kick.

"Now you," Kiwi said, climbing out of the pool and handing the bucket to the smallest man in Rick's crew, a fireman second from St. Louis whose name was Durant.

Durant froze. And Rick couldn't blame him. He was one of the "sinkers" in the group, a hard-muscled rooster who had barely managed to pass the basic swimming tests. Full of water, the bucket would act as a true sea-anchor; no way was the little man going to be able to carry it anywhere without using his arms to swim. He knew Kraus must be aware of that—and must know, too, that a man like Durant would never give up, short of actually drowning.

Rick looked at Durant, then at Kiwi, and back at Durant, realizing suddenly that both men were looking at him. Durant was blank faced, but clearly hoping his platoon commander would find some way of taking him off the hook. And Kiwi, not so blank, was also waiting.

And then Rick understood. Deliberately striking an instructor except in disarmed-combat drill was an automatic bilge; no trial, no questions. Just a quick out. Kiwi had casually positioned himself in range of any punch Rick might care to throw, waiting for him to take the one action that would assure his elimination from the course. And Rick very much wanted to oblige. The fingers of his right hand curled in anticipation, and he could feel his left heel screwing itself into the earth. But the blow never landed; instead, Rick sneezed.

It was a loud one, and it had just the effect Rick had hoped: Kiwi turned toward him, lungs sucking in air to fire a blast in Rick's direction, and took a single step that brought him a full foot closer than he had been—which was when Rick sneezed for the second time. Kraus went down for the count.

The force of the second sneeze had bent Rick double at just the right moment to allow the hardest point of his forehead to collide with the vulnerable spot just above Kraus's nose.

The chief instructor went down suddenly, but got up slowly. He was in the sick bay for two hours . . . and when he returned, although he said the actual damage appeared to be minimal, the nose still showed signs of bleeding at the smallest excuse.

Which saddened Rick. He'd really intended to flatten it permanently.

Coronado, California

Friday, August 1
2350

By the end of the fifth day of hell week the trainees were cattle, responding to orders because they had forgotten how to do anything else.

Cold and fatigue and lack of sleep had reduced judgment to zero, and even memory was unreliable, so the final hours seemed to go by in a rush—boat-crew races through the mud flats east of the base, with satchel charges going off here and there just to keep everyone encouraged, followed by a cable slide over dirty water that no one in the history of BUDS training had ever completed successfully, followed by boat relays that had to be run while wearing face masks and snorkels, and platoon competition on the obstacle course—with instructors chanting "Quit! Quit! Quit!" every inch of the way.

Seven more men went to sick bay; three of them rolled back

to later classes, the others never to return. But no one quit voluntarily.

At midnight, it was over. "BUDS class . . . secure from hell week!" There were a few cheers, some laughter, and a few of the survivors even cried. They had been standing side by side, arms linked, waist deep in murky water beside the seawall, and some discovered that they couldn't even get back on dry land unassisted. But they had made it.

Odessa, Ukrainian S.S.R.

Saturday, August 2
1622

Only six of them were left, and Andrey Narmonov could hardly believe he was one of them.

The days of blindness to which his original 21-man platoon had been subjected, the *starshina* told them now—and the cold-water swimming and the pressure chamber and the sleeplessness and the endurance exercises and the deliberate mental torture—had been mere "calibration," intended to assess their physical capacity to absorb the kind of indoctrination they were to undergo as candidates for the Temnota unit, and as operational members of the unit afterward.

And the testing had served its purpose.

Four men had discovered that they could not endure prolonged darkness—and for a while, Andrey had thought he was going to go that way, too. At first he had hidden his own fear out of shame. Only small children, he believed, were really afraid of the dark. He went on controlling the almost overpowering urge to scream on a moment-by-moment basis until the *starshina* told him that the tests were over . . . and he had passed.

Three of the candidates had been dropped when they exhibited strong allergic reaction to the shots Dr. Mikoyan had given them. (Eventually, she told them, the developers hoped to find a way to eliminate these side effects. But for the moment such results had to be accepted. Some people simply couldn't tolerate the chemicals.)

Everyone had come through the cold-water testing with flying colors. (Which apparently surprised the doctor a bit; the *starshina* told them she had expected to eliminate one or two more candidates there.)

But the pressure chamber had been another story; seven more men were dropped when they exhibited symptoms of HPNS.

And then one final elimination: the suicide.

Shortly before dawn one of the men, a closemouthed former bicycle mechanic from Leningrad who had come through all the testing with flying colors, had somehow managed to steal an old Makarov TT-33 pistol from the desk of the old clerk in the orderly room, then used it to shoot himself through the head while sitting on the seat of one of the toilets at the end of the Temnota barracks.

Ironic.

But SPETSNAZ was SPETSNAZ, and nothing more was made of the incident; the body was removed while they were at breakfast, and the death was not referred to as they prepared for the day's work.

Today they would run one hundred kilometers, in ten-kilometer stretches up and down the warm sand, while waiting for the plane that would take them north to the unidentified base where, the *starshina* said, the "real training" would begin.

Wonderful.

But after all, what did it matter?

They had made it.

Gorky, U.S.S.R.

Sunday, August 3
10:55 A.M.

"He is brain-dead."

"He is alive—and ready for us. Now."

The biotechnician shook her head, tapping a forefinger on the electroencephalograph printout. "It is a flat line, Comrade Doctor," she said. "Nothing . . ."

"He is ready. We will begin."

She had not been trained for this.

She was an experimental scientist, not a medieval rack-torturer, and what was happening here was wrong.

The doctor checked the dial of his wristwatch. "The stimulant has had time to reach the entire system now. And there is no reaction—none whatever—on the EEG?"

"No activity, Comrade Doctor."

"Good."

The technician blinked. Good? What could be good about a brain-dead subject?

"You are alive."

The doctor's voice was low and soothing—persuasive, with the barest hint of command. He was holding the TANK/TALK button down, trying to communicate now with the mindless being he had created. The technician looked away and tried to concentrate on the EEG monitors.

"You are alive. My voice is real, and you understand my words."

The EEG lines did not move.

"You are alive."

Still no movement.

"You are alive."

6:30 P.M.

As at all times since the beginning of the treatment, the EEG lines were flat.

No response from the man floating in the isolation chamber.

"You are alive."

The female biotechnician who had been watching the vital-sign monitors had begged off after six hours, pleading headache, her place taken by a dour-faced man who offered no comment as he scanned the readouts.

"You are alive."

The doctor checked his wristwatch again. The problem was

simply one of time versus chemical effect; there was no way to estimate just when the hypnotics would wear themselves out and leave the patient awake and aware in the nothingness of the tank.

Soviet psychology, like all other sciences in the motherland, was still paying the price of Lysenkoism—and of the stagnation that had prevailed during the final years of the Brezhnev era. Even the Chinese knew more about sensory-deprivation therapy than the greatest specialist in the Soviet Union.

The doctor forced his mind back to the work at hand.

"You are alive. You are aware of my voice and can respond to it, and you wish to respond because you wish to exist."

The hand had moved.

He was sure of it.

The hand had moved, and that meant there had been a ripple—only a ripple, but all important—in the EEG monitor. He glanced at the biotechnician, but the man seemed to be looking elsewhere, checking circuit readings instead of the EEG screen.

But the printouts would show a ripple. He was sure of it.

"You are alive!"

Gorky, U.S.S.R.

Tuesday, August 5
7:30 P.M.

His name was Yuri. He was sure of it. It was important somehow, and he clung desperately to the thought as he floated, smoky and intangible, in the universe of darkness that had surrounded him for centuries.

His name was Yuri, and he had had a father once whose name was . . . what? Alexei? No. Not Alexei.

Abruptly, the effort to remember became too much to bear, overwhelming, and thought itself dissolved into fragments, disjointed particles of information unrelated one to the other, which floated away in the lightless universe where Yuri hung suspended.

Yuri . . . Alexandrovich. His father's name had been Alexander, and so he was Alexandrovich, son of Alexander—Yuri Alexandrovich.

Wait!

He must forget. Remembering was what had brought him here, to this nothingness. He was not Yuri.

He would be good and he would please them and do as They wished him to do and They would come for him and rescue him and let him be born again into the world of the Others.

There were Others in the universe, powerful Others who knew and saw and understood and could punish. They had put him here.

When? How long had Yuri been here? There was no way of knowing, and it was not important anymore.

But They had done this to him. The Others.

The entity that was Yuri stirred and swelled and knew a moment of brightness, a single, victorious moment of self.

And Yuri would not forget. He would make Them think he had forgotten and he would do as They said and he would obey and be as They wished him to be, because if he did not, he would float here alone and in darkness forever and ever. And never see his little son again.

His son . . . Andrey!

He could remember, now.

And no matter what, he would never forget. Somehow, someway Yuri would remember—would hold on to this knowledge, no matter what They did to him—somehow . . . Yuri would punish Them.

PART IV

STATE OF THE ART

La Jolla, California

Saturday, August 9
8:30 A.M.

Rick parked his rented Mustang on the Scripps campus, locked the door, and took a deep breath of summer-morning air.

His legs hurt. His arms ached. His back felt as though someone had spent the night kicking him in the kidneys, and there were traces of residual stiffness in shoulders, knees, wrists, neck, and hips.

Even after a full week of recuperation, he and everyone else in his training class were still suffering from hell-week hangover.

The Navy had played fair. The moment the ordeal was over the survivors (seventy-one men left, out of the original class of nearly one hundred; thirty-three of them in his own platoon) found thick-cut steaks waiting to be cooked for them in the mess—and brand-new, green T-shirts were handed out to replace their old white ones, a signal that the class had made it over the hump. Moreover, the class was informed that their instructors had "volunteered" to take over all weekend duty slots, so there would be weekend leave for anyone who wanted it.

Rick tried to contact his godfather, Capt. Will Ward, to see how the SA-1a project was coming. But the last time he'd tried—a few hours before the start of hell week—he had found himself blocked by what he suspected were new and more stringent security measures at the Scripps laboratory. The friendly graduate student who had previously acted as combination receptionist/secretary had been replaced by an older woman who informed him that Captain Ward was not free to come to the phone just then, but would return his call as soon as possible. Further inquiries had firmly been rebuffed, and he had put the whole matter on the back burner.

Then he trudged to the training barracks and walked fully clothed into a hot shower, where he stood for a full ten minutes before turning it off, disrobing, and falling into the rack across the room from Mac . . . who had already gone to sleep, still wearing his boondockers.

He awoke at 1900 Saturday, discovered that the galley was still in business, and ordered and consumed a huge bologna-and-Swiss-on-white-with-lettuce-and-tomato. And went right back to sleep.

By Sunday, he was able to stay awake longer and tried again to contact Captain Ward. But he got the same answer and gave up, returning to the barracks for another dose of horizontal therapy. And on Monday, training began once more.

The week that followed was easier, but no free ride, with no change in Kiwi Kraus's attitude (even when his swollen nose had returned to normal).

"Now," Kraus said in a briefing just before the week began in earnest, "comes the hard work of mastering those functions that define the role of the SEAL in modern unconventional warfare."

He paused and grinned sourly.

"Anyway," he said, "that's the way it reads in the manual. But lemme translate for you sonsahawahs. Now you in some kine shape, we really going to teach you your job . . . an' you damn sure better learn!"

Rick used peripheral vision to glance in Mac's direction and thought he detected the faintest trace of a smile. He couldn't be sure. But the chief's handling of his platoon during hell week had left Rick convinced that the Navy was making a serious error in failing to retain the man in commissioned status. Mac was a born leader—the steady, utterly reliable sort that no amount of formal training can hope to produce without the right material to work with. The kind he'd like to be himself, and a hell of a guy besides.

So when he finally made contact with Captain Ward on Wednesday, he'd intended to wangle an invitation for Mac to come with him to the laboratory for a look at the *Steel Albatross*. But before he could speak, the captain apologized for his earlier unavailability and said, "I thought you might come over here to Scripps. Something I want to show you. Oh, yeah . . . and bring Mac MacDougall with you, if the ole webfoot is free."

Rick found himself doing a mental double take at the captain's offhand reference to MacDougall.

Mac, to whom he forwarded the invitation before the start of training the following day, had seemed pleased. But not surprised.

"Oh, yeah," he said offhandedly. "Captain Ward—the skipper—he and I go way back . . . to almost before they invented the wheel. In fact, he was the one first got me interested in saturation diving. Way back when the Navy was still interested in things like that."

But MacDougall had been called out of formation about an hour before the training class was dismissed on Friday and hadn't been seen since, according to the yeoman in charge of duty rosters—who volunteered the information that he had also been ordered to take Mac off the schedule, until further notice.

"I don't know what's going on, either," Rick admitted, explaining the situation to Captain Ward when he had finally managed to find his way through the increased security system that had been erected to bar the way to the SA-1a laboratory since his last visit. "Nobody seems to want to talk about it, and I got no answer from the number Mac gave me for the house where he lives with his sister, in Point Loma."

"Sister?" the captain inquired absently.

"Uh . . . yes. He said something about spending his weekends with her and her little boy. I got the idea she's in the Navy, too. Or maybe married to some Navy guy."

The captain nodded, still working his way through a pile of papers that had been on his desk when the new secretary let Rick into the office adjoining the laboratory/test-tank. "I wouldn't worry too much about what Mac's doing right now, if I were you, Ricky."

"Oh?" Rick looked at his godfather and grinned. "Know something about that, too, do you?"

"Retirement," he said with a shrug, "doesn't really cut you off from The Word, you know. Not if you don't want to be cut. You still hear things. Maybe not as quick as you would if you were still on active duty—scuttlebutt and bullshit always seem to travel at Mach one and better—but eventually, The Word filters down, even to old pelicans like me."

Rick's grin widened. "Especially," he said, "if the old pelican's retirement job suddenly rates some really tight-ass security of its own. Right?"

Captain Ward snorted, waving a dismissive hand in the direction of the door and all that was outside it, but he steered the conversation back to MacDougall rather than addressing Rick's obvious curiosity.

"All that happened to Mac," he said, "is that the Navy's getting real interested in saturation diving again—working with divers in an exotic mixed-gas environment—and a thing like that would naturally involve someone like Mac."

The captain looked at Rick as though expecting immediate comprehension and agreement, then seemed somewhat taken aback when he didn't get them.

"Didn't Mac ever tell you what he used to do in the service?"

Rick shook his head. "I know he was a SEAL before, and that he was an officer. Commanded one of the Teams. But aside from that . . ."

This time it was the captain's turn to grin. "That's Mac. Sort of like the sea itself: big smile and no complications on the outside, everything in the world happening under the surface. Hell, saturation diving was how he happened to leave the SEALs in the first place! Got assigned—or wangled it, more likely—to take charge of a deep-submergence diving program that involved some pretty advanced mixed-gas experimentation. Had me a piece of that action myself. Uh . . . well . . . fact is, he was my executive officer. And we both got caught in the riptide when one of the experiments went wrong. No fault of his. Nor mine, neither; what happened couldn't have been foreseen or prevented. But Mac was there and in charge, and . . . well . . . you know how the Navy does things."

Rick knew.

"The hell of it was," Captain Ward went on, "I think Mac maybe took it into his head to blame himself. Never mind the facts—someone died, and he was in charge. So, of course . . ."

He paused for a moment, off somewhere in a world where men accepted responsibilities instead of trying to evade them—a world long vanished in the mists of management-by-seminar and situational ethics.

"Anyway," he said, "that's what Mac is doing this weekend. Bet on it. So meanwhile, how'd you like to give me a hand on a test dive of the *Steel Albatross*?"

Rick agreed readily, assuming that the captain wanted him to lend a hand once again with the test-tank model he'd seen on his last visit. Something had been said then, he recalled, about a new control system, and he was eager to see it.

But once out of the office, Captain Ward led him right through the test-tank room without pausing, then out of the building and across a quadrangle to a cliffside helipad where a man in civilian clothes was dozing in the pilot's seat of a Long Ranger jet helicopter.

"Yo, Sleeping Beauty!"

The pilot's eyes opened in response to the captain's hail, and he nodded cordially at Rick but asked no questions as they piled into the chopper and strapped themselves into seats while he put the engine through the whining labor of start-up.

"One thing about bossing a civilian project," Captain Ward said as they waited for the blades to come up to speed, "is that it doesn't take an act of Congress to get someone a security clearance when you want one. Just turn in the name, and it all gets done."

Rick wanted to ask a question, but didn't because of the noise—blade whop combined with jet whine—that filled the cabin of the Long Ranger. And the captain answered anyway, without being asked.

"Oh, hell, yes," he said, nodding, when they were airborne and heading seaward. "The spook chasers vetted you, a clean sweep fore and aft, before the first time you ever came to the lab. And again, by God, when we goosed up the security to a higher level a couple of weeks ago. You'll see why soon as we land."

Leaving the Scripps campus, the helicopter lifted them south across Mission Bay and Point Loma, then west as the pilot switched frequencies to contact Navy radio, and finally made course corrections that brought them into the Air Defense Identification Zone surrounding the rocky and desolate pile of rock and brown dirt that Rick recognized from his days at Miramar as San Clemente Island.

Their destination, however, was not the island itself or even the Navy airstrip there, but a helicopter landing platform mounted on the foredeck of a sizable ship—big and beamy, moored about a thousand yards offshore.

Black block letters on the stern identified her as the M/V BERKONE, of San Diego.

Once the helicopter touched down at the exact center of the *Berkone*'s landing pad, Captain Ward wasted neither time nor ceremony on the business of debarking, and Rick was content to keep his eyes open and follow along as his godfather made his way down a ladder to the main deck, and then aft to a central superstructure that turned out to be considerably taller than it had seemed from the air.

At least three decks, Rick decided, glancing upward before following Captain Ward up a ladder and through a hatch to the interior . . . where he paused for a moment to gaze in awe.

A gantry crane was mounted overhead, with rails stretching the length of the enclosed space. But it was the center of the bay that held his interest.

It was a moon-pool; the ship was some kind of double-hull aft, its stern section left open to the sea in order to act as a three-sided floating dock for a black—and somehow formless—floating object moored there.

Everything the captain had said this morning seemed to indicate that they had come here to see the full-size version of his invention, the "underwater sailplane" now officially dubbed *Steel Albatross*. Yet Rick found that he had trouble identifying the black object in the water with the shiny little model he'd played with, back in the test tank.

In fact, he found himself having trouble seeing the thing at all.

California's ocean is colder and murkier than the Florida waters where Rick had been reared. But here in the lee of San Clemente Island the sea was clearer than in most places, and the angle of the morning sunlight should have helped him to pick out the general outline of Captain Ward's *Steel Albatross*, despite the fact that almost everything save the little boat's topside observation port and main hatch—a blister faired into the boat's dorsal curve—was submerged.

But the line of the hull seemed simply to disappear less than a foot below the water's surface, and Rick realized with a minor sense of shock that the reason for this was something more than the light-devouring blackness of the paint job.

The hull didn't seem to want to stay in focus. Puzzled, he glanced at his godfather. But the captain apparently wanted him to work out the problem himself, so Rick dropped to his knees and stretched out a hand to touch the side of the boat just below the hatch. And drew the hand back at once. The boat's surface also seemed to play games with his tactile sense as well. It seemed almost alive. . . .

A second, more lingering, touch indicated that the entire surface of the *Steel Albatross* was pleated—not grossly, like an accordion, but in tiny folds less than an eighth of an inch apart, with the striations molded to follow the shape of the vessel. Looking down through the water from a point directly above and tilting his head to outmaneuver water-surface reflections, Rick was able to see that the boat's control surfaces were also ribbed and contoured, though those lines appeared to be somewhat more widely spaced than the ones on the side, and curved to repeat the blunt lines of the wings, elevators, and canards.

The basic idea behind the sculpturing was clear enough, at least to Rick, who had until recently lived on the leading edge of aeronautical technology. Skins of the Stealth fighter and bomber aircraft were designed for similar purposes—to confuse radar. The idea was to bounce probing signals off at random angles, dispersing and diffusing the echo to keep it from registering as a target on the monitor screen.

The skin sculpturing on Captain Ward's invention might be different from the antiradar design of the aircraft, but its effect on sonar screens could be about the same: no return.

And because the whole thing seemed to have been painted a flat, nonreflecting black, the pleated skin would also tend to diffuse and/or absorb light rays—which was why he'd had trouble focusing his eyes on the little submarine.

But that didn't explain the odd—almost spongy—resilience of the surface. He inclined his head to get a better look.

"Kevlar," Captain Ward said. "Or something pretty much like it. Never mind the trade name; it's classified anyway. And the why," his godfather continued, "is a real breakthrough. Serendipity, you might call it. Something we just stumbled upon in the process of applying the antisonar skin outside the pressure hull."

Rick grinned. "Well, anyway, I got the first part right. I figured the riblet effect on the surface was something intended to fox the sonar."

Captain Ward grinned back. "And it does, believe me. To get the ribbed, pleated effect," he said, "we built this skin outside the pressure hull—using a metallized form of Kevlar to save weight—and once it was in place, discovered a bonus. Feel that stuff, Ricky; I mean, hard!"

Rick pressed a hand against the side of the little boat, then dug his fingers into it.

"That's right. Like that. Now, what you feel there is a kind of flexible, cushioning substance that turns out to be a lot like the outer skin of a porpoise or a whale."

Rick nodded.

"So it does the sonar-scattering job it was intended to do," the captain went on. "But it does something more, too. Rick, in some way we don't entirely understand just yet—though you can by-God bet we've got a whole team of people trying to figure it out—this spongy metallized Kevlar reduces hydrodynamic drag on the boat in just the same way the skin of a whale or porpoise reduces his drag to let him go through the water so fast, with so little expenditure of energy."

Despite Rick's own recent exposure to practical hydrodynamics—in the form of daily swimming and aquatic sports—he had never really thought much about sea mammals or the way they moved through the water. But now it did seem to him that they all seemed to go a long way in a big hurry without much effort.

"But . . ."

"Ricky—if you reduce drag on an airplane, what happens?"

"You go faster."

"Uh-huh. Right. But what else; I mean, what would be the effect, say, on a glider. A sailplane?"

"Well," Rick said cautiously, "for one thing, the lift–drag ratio would be effected. It would . . . oh, shit!"

Captain Ward grinned at him. "Right," he said, nodding. "Now you got it. The lift–drag ratio—expressed as the number of feet you go forward for every foot of descent—would be improved—"

"—so, of course, the same thing happens when you apply the principle to an underwater sailplane. Such as the *Steel Albatross*."

"Such as the *Steel Albatross*."

Rick stood up carefully, looking at the little boat and noticing once again its tendency to slip out of visual focus. And suddenly he was seized with an urge that was shockingly familiar. An impulse to climb aboard and try the boat to its limits; find out just exactly what they were. And then try to exceed them. The same feeling, he realized, that he had felt on getting his first up-close look at an F-14 Tomcat.

Yet, one major question remained. . . . Captain Ward had told him the *Steel Albatross* was strictly a civilian enterprise; he hadn't been able to sell the idea to the Navy, even as an experimental vessel, and its only civilian application—so far as Rick knew—was supposed to be low-impact exploration of the undersea environment. Some marine animals, he knew, were believed to navigate by some built-in form of sonar, and he was willing to admit the bare possibility that the corrugated skin was for their benefit. But on balance, he just didn't believe that was the whole story.

"Spook money," Captain Ward said, nodding, when Rick's face told him he was ready to hear an explanation. "The Navy's not the only government agency that might be interested in a silent submarine. And if something's going to be silent, then it might as well be invisible, too.

"And they offered to pay part of the tab. All with the agreement of my civilian backers, mind you. They okayed it. And they also agreed that the test results remain classified. At least for now."

"And you agreed."

Rick hadn't said the words accusingly and hadn't intended them that way. If anything, he thought the idea of letting one or another of the national intelligence services provide funding for the project made good, practical sense. And he was not surprised to find Captain Ward a bit touchy on the subject. Line officers of the regular Navy tended to look down their noses at anything remotely connected with the half-world of espionage, and his godfather was no exception to the rule.

"I agreed," the captain said. "And their interest in the project is legitimate."

Rick grinned at the older man. "But?"

The captain nodded. "But."

He didn't finish the sentence. The captain had wanted to complete work on his underwater sailplane very badly indeed.

The men at work on the boat seemed to have finished whatever it was they had been doing, and they exchanged a paragraph or so of technical jargon with the captain. Rick listened, but didn't comprehend more than one word in three and waited patiently until it was done, after which Captain Ward moved away briskly, motioning for him to follow.

"Yo! Let's go!"

His godfather's bellow brought several men on the run, moving purposefully toward the moon-pool and the little sub riding there while the captain removed his shoes, socks, jacket, and shirt, and indicated that Rick should do the same.

A locker bolted to the deck turned out to be packed with specialized gear that he later discovered had been tailored especially to the needs of potential *Steel Albatross* crewmen—with himself at the head of the list.

He was surprised to discover that various items seemed to fit him as he and the captain replaced their regular clothing with blouses that resembled wet suits. In place of the discarded shoes, they were helped into light, down-lined boots with double Velcro fittings that extended almost to the knee.

"The *Albatross* is warm enough, really," Captain Ward explained as they turned to go aboard. "But sometimes the feet can get kinda cold."

He opened the hatch, and one of the divers held it as he led the way into the belly of the beast.

"Actually," he said, "the boots and the rest of the gear's not really necessary, especially since we won't be going too deep. But I wanted you to get the feel of the boat. I'm sorta proud of her."

There were two seats in the cockpit of the *Albatross*, arranged in tandem. The captain had entered the boat first and settled himself in the rear position, leaving the forward one for Rick, who dropped into the cushioned supports and was surprised to feel it move of its own volition to conform to the contours of his body.

Captain Ward noted his reaction and chuckled. "Like your perch? The cushions are segmented and oil filled, and they're pressure sensitive. That's to keep you from growing bedsores on your butt during a long dive. Ought to be standard in airplane cockpits—or anywhere else where some poor bastard has to sit still for more than an hour."

"Nice," Rick agreed. "But are we going to be down long enough to make seat comfort a major factor?"

The captain shook his head and grunted negatively. "Not on the schedule for today. But once you're under the surface, you're in an environment as hostile to man as outer space, and just as unexplored. You never know."

Rick nodded thoughtfully, accepting the cautionary note, but Captain Ward moved at once to alleviate any possible uneasiness by explaining that today's dive was programmed for less than an hour and for a depth of no more than a hundred meters—which put matters back into perspective for Rick. In SEAL training he had already made dives to twenty meters, without scuba gear. And the minisubmarine was not totally unfamiliar.

Small undersea transport vehicles called wet subs ("swimmer delivery vehicles" in official naval nomenclature) were no novelty to him. You wore a wet suit and a scuba tank and hung on for the ride. Such devices had been around ever since people learned to carry their air supply with them underwater, and he had used various models himself when diving with friends in the Florida Keys.

The world of the known and commonplace, however, came to an abrupt end when the hatch came down to seal them in.

Rick had never before been in a "dry sub"—the term used to describe small submersibles in which the operators are locked into a bubble of air contained by a pressure hull—not even as a passenger on board a Navy submarine, and this sensation gave him an initial moment of acute discomfort: a salesman-sample taste of claustrophobia. It surprised him and left him wondering if he was about to make a depressing discovery about himself. But before he could pursue the line of thought, he found a major distraction in the boat's control system.

Some parts were achingly familiar, such as the airplanelike joystick (presumably to control the vessel's pitch and roll), apparently interconnected with the boat's rudder to make yaw corrections despite the absence of rudder pedals.

But instrumentation was something else entirely. In fact, at first glance there didn't seem to be any. Instead, a 21-inch cathode-ray tube—similar to an ordinary television screen, but round and somewhat larger—was sealed into the space normally occupied by an instrument panel. It seemed to be turned off.

"Touch it," Captain Ward said.

Rick twisted his head around to look at his godfather, but the captain seemed to be busy with some kind of checklist, so he turned back to the tube and followed the suggestion, gingerly applying the tip of his index finger to the center of the tube.

The screen came to life, showing Rick a deep-red background with text in white:

SA-1
COMMAND MENU

Do you require instruction?
Yes No Cancel

" 'SA' is for 'submersible aquaplane,' " Captain Ward said, speaking over Rick's shoulder. "I told you that's the official designation for the *Albatross.* Tell it no, you don't need the on-screen tutorial program. I'll handle basic training myself."

Rick pressed the NO area with his finger. Which gave him a new display:

SA-1
COMMAND MENU

Do you want the predive checklist?
Yes No Cancel

"You want one," Captain Ward said.

Rick pressed YES.

SA-1
CONTROL OPTIONS

Descend Ascend
Monitor Cancel

"Try MONITOR."

All right . . .

MONITOR ARRAY

This time, the screen showed him a drawing of a simple instrument panel—compass, radio frequency and volume, depth gauge, rate of ascent/descent, turn-and-bank, clinometer, even an artificial horizon.

At the bottom, set apart from the rest of the display by a lighter shade of red, a set of further options was offered:

Descend Ascend
Aux. Inst. Cancel

"What auxiliary instruments do we have?" Rick inquired.

"Check it out for yourself."

Rick pressed the AUX. INST. option, and the lower display changed at once:

Ext. Press.	Gas Mixture
Ext. Temp.	Dive Clock

Several other options were also listed, but Rick didn't have time to read them before the display snapped back to its "Descend-Ascend" mode. Surprised, he was about to press AUX. INST. again when Captain Ward interrupted.

"Let it go for now," he said. "I'll check you out on the rest of the goodies after we're done with our first dive. For now, though, I think you better get your head up and look around."

Rick tore his eyes away from the red glow of the cathode-ray tube (CRT) and decided the captain was right.

Fascination with the boat's computerized instrument panel had caused him to violate the fighter pilot's first law of survival: Thou shalt look around at all times. And in doing so, he had missed their departure from their mother ship.

Mooring lines had been cast off, and the *Steel Albatross* was afloat in the center of the moon-pool, moving aft and connected to the ship only by diver-tended lines.

"Sierra Alfa One under way, departing *Berkone* at zero niner four niner. Switching to two four seven decimal seven. Over."

The captain's tone was flat, and a glance aft gave Rick confirmation that the older man was now wearing one of those headsets with earphones that double as microphones. The bone-conducting mikes minimize distortion and cut out background noise completely. He looked around for his own, found it on a hook arranged out of harm's way under the starboard cockpit coaming, and noted, tardily, that the radio frequency readout had begun to blink as the numbers were changed.

It stopped after a moment, and another over-the-shoulder glance got Rick a grin from Captain Ward.

"Just running through the predive checklist," he said. "Relax. Watch your own screen."

Rick did, and occupied a spare moment wondering if the *Steel Albatross* was intended to be "flown" solo and, if so, from which seat. The boat cleared the mother ship and the divers cast off the lines.

"Check our status," Captain Ward said, and Rick's computer screen switched suddenly to a color display with items such as MAIN HATCH and INDUCTION PORTS and STABILIZER TRIM presented in red or green letters on a white background.

Most of the lettering was green, and as he watched, the final red items—the ones for RADIO PORT and BALLAST TRIM—changed to match.

"Status green!" Captain Ward said. "Sierra Alfa One is ready to dive. Your boat, Mr. Tallman. Take her down!"

Captain Ward's suggestion that he actually take the controls of the *Steel Albatross* caught Rick entirely by surprise, and for a moment he thought the older man had to be joking. Although the captain was serious, was he really ready for this?

He'd been ready enough to take a demonstration ride in the captain's nice new toy. But actually piloting the little monster was a whole different proposition, and suddenly he found himself remembering the time when he was nine years old and his father had ordered him (never much for suggesting things, the admiral) to lend a hand on the controls of the Cessna 172 he was using to ferry Rick back to Palm Beach after a weekend in Norfolk, Virginia.

The admiral had meant it as a compliment—a gesture to show his son that he thought he was old enough to begin learning to fly. And Rick had followed the order without protest. But he'd had bad dreams about it for a month afterward, and now he found himself running through the same complex of feelings, there in the forward seat of the *Steel Albatross*. But his hand moved, almost of its own volition, to the stick, and he forced his left forefinger out to touch the word DESCEND on the screen.

SA-1
DESCEND CHECKLIST

1. Ballast blowers: On
Next Item Cancel

That seemed right, and the captain didn't object, so he touched NEXT ITEM and the screen changed again.

Silently, system by system, the computer led him through

the sequence that would ready the boat for submerged operation, offering the option of canceling the whole evolution at each step. But he hesitated again when the checklist was finally completed.

SA-1
PARAMETERS CHECKLIST

Rate of Descent: 10 mpm
Increase Decrease
Select Cancel

"If this were your ordinary submersible," Captain Ward said, breaking into Rick's train of thought, "we might take it easy on your first dive. Sort of ease her down. But the *Albatross* isn't built to let you do that."

Rick nodded, understanding. "She'll stall."

"Right. Control, here, depends on motion—vertical in this case. Your rate of descent. The water's not especially deep here; bottom's fairly flat until you get to the shelf, which is only about a thousand yards west of here. That's why we selected this site for the initial tests. So for this first run, I'd suggest a descent rate of about twenty-five meters per minute. And I'd also suggest you begin the dive with your trim slightly nose-down—it's the pickle switch right under your thumb; the aft trim's an inch lower on the stick—and be ready to meet the ship's motion, to level out for your landing on the bottom."

Rick was startled. "Landing?"

"Oh, yeah," the captain said. "Sure! The tank model you saw didn't have any kind of landing gear. Hadn't really thought about it at the time the little gizmo was built. But this boat's got one. Nothing fancy; just flat runners sort of like the skis on a plane or a chopper, not to trundle you along on the bottom but hooked to a set of servos that can bring the boat level after touchdown . . . within limits."

"What kind of limits?"

"Well, you got to help a little, see. Find a spot that's not too steep or rocky. It's a machine, not your fairy fucking godmother."

"Uh-huh. What about visibility?"

"The *Albatross* has lights—front and side arrays. The switches are in the third block down, middle row, on the panel to your right. And besides that, we have a real slick bottom-profiling sonar. I'll be monitoring our passive sensors back here—we won't use the active ones this time. I guess you could just think of me as your . . . what do you call it? Weapons officer? Yeah . . . I'm your weapons officer."

The captain stopped talking then, and Rick went back to the electronic checklist.

SA-1

READY TO DIVE

Begin Descent   Recheck
Cancel

"System's ready to dive."

"Permission to begin descent."

"Permission granted."

Rick had expected a final instant of hesitation when he reached out to touch the BEGIN DESCENT command, but was pleasantly surprised to find that there was none. And a moment later, the descent protocol began.

Intakes opened with a discreet slurp, and air flushed out of the ballast tanks in a foaming rush. But the boat itself didn't respond for a moment or two. And then they were underwater.

The nose dropped, and by instinct Rick moved the stick forward to meet the dive and control it, using left aileron to correct a minor deviation to the right. He began to get the "feel" of the vessel, while straining his eyes against the limited visibility afforded by the *Albatross*'s forward lighting array.

Vertical-speed numbers increased and flashed red on the panel, warning that they had begun the dive by exceeding the preselected rate of descent. The boat was sinking at a hundred feet per minute instead of the eighty he had punched into the computer, but the color returned to normal as the nose came up, and the vertical-speed numbers began to decrease . . . as the vessel edged toward a stall. Rick eased the stick forward again to gain speed, reminding himself—with a touch of exasperation—that while everything was bound to work more slowly underwater than it did in the air, he was still supposed to be controlling the *Albatross*, not merely reacting to its whims.

All right, then . . . let's do it!

Rick jockeyed the controls a little as he would have done in an unfamiliar airplane, measuring response times and becoming accustomed to feedback pressures, while computing the amount of control effort needed to achieve a specific result—and made a welcome discovery. Even though the vehicle was strange to him, and the environment was, too, the boat's controls were beginning to feel friendly. The descent rate settled into its assigned neighborhood, and confidence began to build as he allowed himself a deep breath, relaxing the muscles of his upper arm.

A guy could get used to this. . . .

"Prepare for landing!"

Captain Ward had held his peace during Rick's clumsy initial movements and refrained from the kind of kibitzing that might have been expected as his brainchild was generally abused. But now the older man's voice recalled Rick from never-never land and caused him to focus his eyes on something other than the instrument panel.

Abruptly, a new display appeared in the upper-right quadrant of his screen; a little pull-down labeled HEIGHT ABOVE BOTTOM, with digital display in red: 9 METERS.

The *Albatross*'s forward lights had begun to pick out various kinds of plant life, rocks, and mud on the bottom. Rick eased the stick back, slowing descent and forward speed.

Forward and vertical speed bled off swiftly, and though there was no preliminary shudder to warn him, Rick knew the *Albatross* was again approaching a stall. He eased back-pressure on the stick, and his free hand moved, almost without volition, toward the ASCEND option on the control screen. But before he could touch it, the bottom—slightly uneven, but with no major obstacles and a little westward tilt—came floating up to meet the boat.

A single bump; full back-pressure on the stick . . . and they were down.

On solid ground once more, 313 feet beneath the surface of the Pacific Ocean.

Rick inhaled deeply and permitted himself a sour grin. If the landing had been safe and the selection of landing site a good one, it was no thanks to him and he knew it. But why complain? At least he hadn't wrecked the damn thing.

The clinometer said the *Albatross* had settled into a four-degree nose-down attitude, and the artificial horizon indicated that they were listing a bit to port. But within seconds the servos Captain Ward had mentioned brought the boat back to a level attitude, and a quick check of the panels showed all readings within acceptable limits.

"If we had tractor treads instead of skids," Captain Ward said conversationally, "we could move along the bottom now, taking our time and looking things over. Maybe we'll install something like that later."

"But for now," Rick said, "we're pretty much a fixed object until we decide to take off again, right?"

"Well . . . almost."

The display on Rick's screen changed (Captain Ward's doing, he assumed) to show him a slightly different set of options, with a new command menu.

SA-1
ATTITUDE JET OPTIONS

X Axis	Y Axis
Z Axis	Cancel

"Try one."

Rick touched X AXIS. And got a stiff rebuke from the computer.

He had, it seemed, selected an option that was unavailable so long as the landing gear servos were engaged (which he decided must mean anytime the boat was sitting on its skids), and also involved use of a DEVICE NOT PRESENT.

"Not present yet, anyway," the captain said, filling in the words left unsaid by the on-screen message. "The attitude jets are actually in place now. But they're not hooked up or tested yet; I just wanted you to get an idea of how the *Albatross* might be maneuvered—not actually on the bottom, but in tight places where you're at low speed or no speed at all."

"But if it doesn't work when you're on the bottom . . . ?"

"It's still plenty useful, in the same way that attitude-control jets on a space vehicle are useful. And we're still working on various ways to let us get around a little after landing."

"Don't the jets make noise, though?"

"No, they don't. That's the major breakthrough. But the little bastards use up oxygen. Though MacDougall, by God, has come up with a notion or two that might be helpful there. You know . . . that gill of his . . ."

"Gill? MacDougall? What are you talking about?"

"Uh, Gil McDougald, Yankee infielder. Hit a grand slam in the '51 Series."

"Nice try, Uncle Will," Rick said, knowing that would get his goat.

There was a sudden silence that Rick interpreted as tension and self-reproach.

"Maybe," the captain said somberly when the moment had passed, "I really am getting too old."

"Look, skipper . . ."

"You're going to say you'll forget what I said about Mac and his ideas, and we won't mention it again, because you know I've talked out of turn and feel like a damn fool. But that doesn't call the words back . . . and besides, everything we say down here, and every movement of the controls, is recorded. 'For later evaluation' according to the official wording—but more like 'to find out where you made your mistake' if we really screw up. So it's all beside the point."

"Security's really that tight?"

"About the *Albatross*, no. Well, anyway, not so tight I can't take someone for a trial run after he's passed a background check. But the other . . . what I talked out of turn about . . . yes. In fact, hell, yes! Strictly need-to-know. So I'll report my security breach as soon as we get back to the barge. And take my lumps."

"But . . ."

"No buts. Let's go home now." The captain's voice was crisp as he guided Rick through the pre-ascent checklist, but the brusque manner could not conceal his continued irritation with himself.

Rick was sorry about that. And curious about the "gill" (whatever that might be) and its connection to Mac's disappearance from the SEAL base, and how it could be connected to Captain Ward's project.

But the business of "flying" the *Steel Albatross* back to the surface momentarily crowded all else from his consciousness.

Control movements were much the same as on the trip down. As soon as the checklist was completed, Rick initiated the maneuver—on Captain Ward's order—by touching his finger to the ASCEND command on the screen, hearing the barely perceptible high-speed sound of pumps exhausting seawater from the ballast tanks.

With a short assist from the computer-controlled auxiliary power, the boat began to rise almost immediately, and the joystick control firmed in Rick's hand; he used the trim pickle-switch to ease the *Albatross* into a nose-up attitude conforming to the thirty-meters-per-minute ascent rate the captain had suggested—slightly faster than their rate of descent—and was moderately surprised to discover that the boat was more responsive going up than she had been going down.

Rick settled into the accommodating contour of the high-tech seat and let the pilot's instincts he hadn't really exercised for six months reassert themselves, controlling the boat almost automatically while he kept his head up, scanning the world outside and making only the occasional scan of the instrument panel that he would have performed by habit in an airplane.

It was exhilarating and he found himself enjoying the experience immensely. Captain Ward ordered a course change that would bring them up closer to shore, and Rick was able to make the turn with precision, easing off at the right moment to bring the boat to its new heading without drifting through it and having to make a comeback correction.

He was still feeling good about that—and coming to the conclusion that the *Steel Albatross*, for all its unlovely appearance, might turn out to be a real friend—when Captain Ward's voice broke in.

"Wanna try a straight-in approach?"

Rick straightened in his seat. "Say again?"

"We got an option, Ricky: You can try to surface there, close in behind the moon-pool of the mother ship, the *Berkone*. Pop up right in the middle of things. Or you can do it the safe-and-easy way: Bring her up alongside the ship; let the gantry crane pick up the *Albatross* and put it down in the pool. So . . . what's your pleasure?"

The answer the captain wanted (and the one Rick wanted to give him) was to try the straight-in.

Bring it off, and it would be like icing your very first carrier landing; a reason to stand ten feet tall.

But mess it up—bring the *Steel Albatross* up just a few feet to one side or the other, under one of the twin hulls of the *Berkone*—and you'd be risking damage to both the *Albatross* and the mother ship, for no better reason than your own weakness for cowboying around in expensive hardware.

Grow up, Tallman. Be smart. Play it safe. . . .

"Let's go for it!"

"That's m'boy."

"Got a vector for us?"

Riding the backseat, untroubled by the work of controlling the boat, Captain Ward was in a better position than Rick for spotting their objective and estimating a proper course.

"Come right . . . uh . . . three degrees."

Rick edged the boat to the new heading, noting again the slowness of her rudder response and hoping there would be no need for sudden, last-minute corrections. But the captain seemed entirely confident.

"Right another degree or so. More drift'n I'd figgered."

Rick did it, holding just a touch of pressure on the stick as the double hull of the *Berkone* became visible above . . . and then it was done.

In what seemed an instant, the canopy broached the surface in a stream of water that cleared to show the moon-pool area of the mother ship *Berkone*. Dead ahead!

Give that man a ci-gar.

"Sierra Alfa One, on the surface, one zero two five. Awaiting tow. Over."

Rick removed his hand from the stick and looked over his shoulder to find the captain grinning at him, but before he could fully savor the moment of self-congratulation, there was something else to occupy his mind.

Wet-suited frogs were in the water, bringing lines to the *Albatross*—but his attention was captured and held by a familiar figure standing at the gangway where he and Captain Ward had boarded the little submarine half an hour earlier.

And something new had well and truly been added.

Say this for Mac: The guy was full of surprises.

Station "O"

Saturday, August 9
8:30 P.M., Moscow Time

The operator on watch stirred and reached out a hand to readjust the sonar controls.

The screen was blank as usual.

Boredom could make you see things, manufacture emergencies from pure imagination.

When he had first volunteered for this duty—the day after he had signed for a second tour with SPETSNAZ—it had seemed the fulfillment of a dream. Excitement, and a chance to serve the Rodina, combined with a real place in history. A chance to pioneer.

Even the medical aspect, the necessary surgery and the fact that the operation would have to be performed again, in reverse, when the work was done, hadn't seemed so terrible. But they hadn't warned him he would be bored and lonely.

The operator sighed—or would have sighed, if such a thing had still physically been possible—and turned his thoughts and attention back to the control panel before him.

Boredom and loneliness notwithstanding, the output of the reactors still had to be checked. In his sleep, the operator could have recited most of the data pertinent to his work: Control rods regulate reaction, and at best those rods were capable of absorbing about one percent of the neutron flux. Just enough to permit or prevent reaction.

Coax the rods. Adjust them. Nurse them—one hand on the

emergency cooling control, the other never more than inches from the SCRAM lever—as though nursing the very stuff of life itself. For the simple reason . . . no reactor . . . no electric power. No power . . . no habitat. No habitat . . . no anything.

The operator scanned the dials and cathode-ray tubes again, unconsciously following the pattern he had been taught during training. And found himself staring once again at the sonar screen. The screen was clear again now, but there had been a ripple. Not exactly a target and not a blip, but some sort of ripple. And he had never seen a ripple before.

A whale entering the area could cause a disturbance like that. But if so, it must have been moving very rapidly; the return had been there for less than a quarter-sweep before it disappeared.

Perhaps the whale, if that was what had made the ripple, had been at the very limit of the sonar resolution. And near the surface. That much, at least was certain: The disturbance was much nearer the surface than Station "O."

Probably no more than one hundred meters deep.

Perhaps it was that big double-hull that had pulled in four sleep periods ago, near the island at the extreme edge of the sweep-radius. Maybe it had decided to pull up its hooks and go away. No. There it was, faint but unmistakable, just where it had been. Submarine? He knew the signatures of everything the Ami navy was operating in these waters (and also the one or two little wet subs used by abalone divers and salvors), and it was nothing like any of them.

It had to be a whale, or his imagination. He would double-check later and try to match it against the patterns he already knew by heart. But already he knew what he would find. Nothing. Because that was what was out there.

La Jolla, California

Saturday, August 9
10:32 A.M.

Mac MacDougall, in the brand-new uniform of a full commander, USN, did his level best to appear nonchalant. But no one on board *Berkone* could have missed the face-splitting grins he exchanged with Rick and Captain Ward as they climbed out of the cockpit of the *Steel Albatross* and shook his hand.

There were questions to be asked and congratulations to be offered—and all of it had to wait until the three men were alone. So conversation remained at a minimum as they boarded the Long Ranger for the trip back to the Scripps heliport, and it continued to languish until the three were on the ground and walking back toward the laboratory.

Once there, and beyond the range of civilian curiosity, however, Rick had a complaint.

"Five bucks," he mourned. "Shot to hell . . . just because I'm not in uniform."

Mac grinned, but shook his head. "You'd have been too late anyway. I got my first salute—and paid the five bucks—to what looked like the world's youngest and scaredest seaman second, just two steps outside naval district headquarters down in San Diego this morning."

Ward's eyebrows raised. "It wasn't official until then? I heard you . . ."

Mac's grin widened. "I just bet you did. You probably knew all of this was in the works before I did."

Ward didn't deny it. "Scuttlebutt," he said diffidently. "Just scuttlebutt."

"And the only one who doesn't get The Word," Mac said, nodding, "is the poor son of a bitch they're talking about. Still, you couldn't have been too far ahead; the final decisions—about reactivating my old project—really weren't made until a couple of days ago."

Captain Ward started to reply, but changed his mind and glanced pointedly in Rick's direction instead.

"Oh, don't mind me," Rick said. "I just discovered I don't speak the language."

"The hell you say!"

Rick had intended his remark as social noise, a means of easing their conversation out of the security corner into which it seemed headed. But neither man smiled.

"If that were strictly true," Mac said pleasantly, "you

wouldn't be the man Captain Ward chose to begin training today as the first qualified pilot of the SA-1."

Rick blinked, astonished.

"So cut the crap, sonny," said the captain. "We know ya— and you speak the language just fine."

It was a calm statement of fact, and Rick took his time absorbing it. Mac and the captain waited him out.

"Well," he said finally, "maybe a couple of words."

The captain snorted and Mac feinted a jab at Rick's midsection, which Rick slipped neatly, allowing the motion to flow into one of the hook kicks they had been practicing in SEAL training that week.

It missed by a country mile.

Point Loma, California

Saturday, August 9
4:15 P.M.

The problem with getting the Navy to accept the *Steel Albatross*, Mac said, was not so much that it was ahead of its time— or behind or whatever it was—but more that Captain Ward was an original thinker. A maverick.

"And the peacetime Navy," Mac declared, "just doesn't go in for original thinking. Or mavericks."

Which got a laugh from Rick.

The captain had installed a working duplicate of the *Steel Albatross*'s cockpit and computer instrumentation system beside the test tank in his campus laboratory, thus converting the model into a kind of operational simulator, and they spent a pleasant afternoon running the toy boat through various maneuvers while familiarizing themselves with its controls. It was absorbing work, and Rick felt real regret when the captain terminated the session, saying he had "an appointment with some people, about the boat" scheduled for the rest of the afternoon and evening.

He offered no further explanation, and none was asked. But Rick was quick to provide one—and comment sourly on it— as soon as he and Mac were away from the campus and en route, in the Mustang convertible, to the house Mac shared with his sister in Point Loma. "The idea of the skipper's having to beg money from a bunch of spooks drives me up the wall. It's like . . . telling the Wright brothers there was no future in that box kite of theirs!"

This time it was Mac's turn to laugh.

"What's so damn funny?" Rick demanded.

Mac shook his head, and Rick was momentarily distracted as he took evasive action to get out of the way of a teenage hotrock who seemed to have mistaken the street for a drag strip. But they weren't ready to drop the subject.

"In answer to your question," Mac said, "I guess there's really nothing funny at all about what I was thinking. And I guess maybe I laughed to keep myself from crying. You'll do a lot of that if you stay in the Navy long enough.

"The Wright brothers," Mac went on, "flew their first successful airplane in 1903. But by the time World War I began, most of the airplanes in the world were being built in other countries. And in fact, most American aviators who got into that war did their flying in French-built planes."

He leaned back in the seat, not facing Rick, but not looking at the passing scenery either.

"Eugene Ely," he said, "made the world's first landings and takeoffs from a ship—a U.S. Navy cruiser fitted with a temporary flight deck—in 1910. But if the battleship admirals had had their way, the United States would have gone into World War II without a single flattop in the water.

"You've served on modern carriers," Mac said. "Real fancy: angled decks. Automated landing systems. Steam catapults. And did you know not a damn one of those things was developed by us? The Brits invented them all. We took 'em over, after they'd done the work.

"And then there's the carriers themselves. Never mind the fact that the Soviets have at least one attack sub shadowing every one of them, three hundred and sixty-five days a year. And also never mind the war-game computer studies, using just about any scenario you can imagine, that estimate the life expectancy of any carrier in a modern global war at something less than seventeen minutes.

"The easy explanation," Mac said, "is that carrier admirals

are running the Navy. Optimists, and there are still a few of them around, say just be patient because that's all bound to change. But it's wishful thinking, because submariners are actually a big power-bloc in the Pentagon nowadays—and no major changes have been made.

"The problem is more basic than that."

Mac smiled, still not looking directly at Rick. "Hold still while I do a little flag-waving. Okay? Look, America is the freest society in the world, not just because there isn't much of what you might call police control in it, but also because more Americans—people like Captain Will Ward, for instance—are willing to spend time totally rethinking the things that they do, and how they do them.

"It creates a hell of a lot of problems. But it's got the advantage of producing a kind of free-floating creativity and inventiveness. And that's the big plus that has made the difference for us all along the line, and especially in World War II. Neither of us was around for that one—don't look at me like that, damn it, I'm not *that* old—but we've seen plenty of newsreel footage from that war, and even in the dullest film you see things like tank destroyers, tank transporters, swimming tanks, plywood fighter-bombers, armored personnel carriers, bazookas . . . every blessed one of them improvised, almost overnight, to meet some tactical problem. Improvised by people who were willing to try something absolutely new.

"No superman stuff there. No magic. Just general creativity by people who were free from bureaucratic control.

"So it sounds like I'm making some kind of sick joke when I say it has required really monumental effort on the part of other Americans—the bureaucrats who always feel threatened by innovation—to find ways of strangling this ability to produce original solutions. But it's no more than the plain truth, and they've been at it so long that now they've almost succeeded.

"The Navy spends the most money where ideas are the least original. Because when you agree to try a brand-new idea, you run a hell of a chance of finding out later that the idea was wrong. So the safe thing to do is to avoid the original and the innovative, and put your money behind itsy-bitsy improvements in weapons and weapons systems that have been around for a long time. That way, nobody can criticize you and the boat doesn't get rocked and you wind up with a fitness report that'll be a big help when you come up for promotion.

"But the hell of it is that by doing it this way, you also lose all the advantages of free thought and imagination!

"You want to come up with something really workable, something that could stop a potential enemy in his tracks and make him run for cover? Fine, then turn the problem over to some of the little companies up in Silicon Valley. Or one of the two-man engineering shops. Or hell, even the one-man machine shops you'll find in any of the little flyover or whiz-through towns from Oregon to Rhode Island.

"Or go ask some half-crazy old bastard like Captain Will Ward."

"Yeah—particularly someone like him," Rick said.

"Sure, some of the ideas they'd come up with would be crapola. But somewhere in there you'd also find pure gold and diamonds. Christ knows what their ideas would look like. But one thing for sure, they would not look one little bit like anything the Pentagon has on the shelf or on the drawing board."

"Okay, then," Rick said, as they turned right off Nimitz Boulevard and began threading their way south through Fleetridge and Roseville. "Say all that is true. Everything you've said—everything I've heard today, in fact—sounds to me like just one more really first-class argument for my getting the hell out of the Navy while I'm still young enough, and sane enough, to do something else."

It was the first time he'd ever openly admitted the possibility of actually quitting the Navy, and Rick was surprised to discover that he could say it without the rush of guilt he'd expected to feel. Instead, he felt as though he'd put down a heavy load.

"This thing today," he continued. "Captain Ward and the *Steel Albatross* and the way the Navy's handled it . . . that's all part of the same thing, isn't it? And the skipper himself. He's retired, right? But it wasn't a voluntary retirement. The man's a born lifer. Anyone could see that. He'd have stayed on, one way or another. If they'd let him. But they wouldn't let him. Would they?"

"Turn left here," Mac said, apparently ignoring the question. "It's the third house from the corner. On this side."

Rick followed the directions and brought the car to a stop in front of a small ranch-style dwelling with a tricycle lying on its side in the driveway. But Mac made no immediate move to get out.

"The captain's okay," he said evenly. "Don't worry about him."

"I don't. Frankly, I think he's a hundred times better off out of the Navy and doing his own thing. But I know he doesn't feel that way about it. And I don't think you see it that way, either."

It was an obvious gambit, an effort to get Mac to talk about his own service career and problems. And Mac hesitated only a moment before accepting the offer.

"No," he said, "I don't. But the two situations, mine and Captain Ward's, aren't really comparable. And this thing today—my being back on duty in commissioned status, even with an extra half-stripe, plus a nice warm handshake from the admiral—is nice enough. But don't get too impressed, Rick. This is still temporary duty. I'm still just a reserve officer, not a regular. So don't make too big a thing of it."

He got out of the car, heading for the front door of the house, and Rick followed, still absorbed in their subject and intrigued, too, at Mac's apparently casual attitude toward rank and career advancement . . . a point of view wildly at odds with that of any naval officer he had ever known.

"Oh, sure," Mac continued, "the decision, back then, was mine and mine alone. I switched from the SEALs, from the Teams, into deep-submergence systems, because I thought it was the coming thing. The next logical combat arena . . . after space."

He paused for a moment, the suggestion of a smile tugging at the corners of his mouth.

"Remember when space was going to be strictly peaceful?" he asked. "Nonmilitary? Everybody was just sure it would be that way. After all, we had a tacit agreement with the Soviets: no weapons in orbit."

The smile withered. "But somehow, something went wrong along the way, and now more than half the hardware that goes up there is classified stuff—weapons, or add-ons to weapons systems—and everyone's shitting bullets wondering what the other guy will put up there next.

"The point is that human beings will fight in any environment they can get to. Man carries his sword always. Everywhere. Not the fault of one single nation or another; it's all of us. Just human nature. . . . Anyway, I got hard-nosed about it when some Pentagon cost accountant decided the ocean depths were an exception to the rule, and instead of going back to the Teams, which I could have done without penalty right then, I dug my heels in . . . and wound up serving in the surface Navy. As a chief."

There was more to the story than that, Rick was sure.

But before he could frame a question, Mac's key opened the lock on the front door of the little house, and Rick stepped through . . . just in time to intercept a small, high-velocity human projectile that collided with the exact center of his stomach, carrying him backward and down two porch steps to the lawn, where reflexes and recent SEAL training combined to preserve life and limb. He hit the ground in a tuck, rolling backward to protect his head, arms wrapped protectively around the pint-size ballistic missile.

"Billy . . . damn it!"

A woman's voice, controlled but carrying the unmistakable ring of authority, produced instant response from the bundle in Rick's arms. It squirmed, wriggled free, and resolved itself into a small, freckle-faced child—unmistakably male and bearing a notable resemblance to MacDougall.

"Oh," it said. "You're not Uncle Mac."

"Uh, no."

"Oh . . . damn!"

The little boy, who appeared to be about five years old, seemed to have run out of conversation for the moment, so Mac performed the introductions, trying like hell to keep from laughing.

"This item," he said, "is my nephew, William. Also known as Billy. Also known as Billy the Goat. Whose manners—and vocabulary, I might add—seem to be in need of immediate attention!"

Billy the Goat grinned at him, then at Rick, not visibly intimidated.

"And this," Mac continued, "is Billy's mother. Rick, I'd like you to meet my sister, Samantha—also known as Sam—who I'm just sure is going to suggest that we both come in for a cup of coffee or maybe a can or two of good Mexican beer."

Rick turned, preparing a standard, mechanical/social response to the introduction. And stood tongue-tied.

The freckles and cheekbones were as he remembered; the hair somehow looser around the face. And redder. But as before, it was The Eyes that held him speechless, unable to catch the breath he needed for audible sound.

"Sam," Mac was saying, "this is the friend I said I might bring to dinner tonight—if I could catch him. Say hello to Rick Tallman. Rick, my sister, Samantha Deane."

But Samantha Deane, her complexion suddenly the same bright color as her hair, did not reply. It was Rick who broke the sudden deafening silence.

"The doctor and I," he said with a smile, "have met. In fact, you might say we're old friends. Or something."

Murmansk, U.S.S.R.

Sunday, August 10
4:15 A.M.

It was the deepest dive he had ever made, and now he understood why they had wanted to know whether he could handle himself in total darkness. At fifty meters, he couldn't see his hand before his face, and they were still going down.

His fingers tightened on the steel supports of the cage and he shifted his feet, more to reassure himself that the feet still existed and were attached to his ankles than for any actual need to widen his stance. His boots were weighted—more than seven kilograms each—and unlikely to slip.

But the equipment was unfamiliar. Training with the "dry suit" (hardhat) diving rig had begun the day they arrived, and this descent was supposed to be a kind of graduation exercise.

Andrey hoped it was so, as he did not enjoy this kind of

diving, and still did not like being in the dark—even though the instructors had assured him and his teammates that there would be "plenty of light" when they arrived at their destination.

The aura of mystery surrounding Temnota had deepened with every step they took. Informed that they were being moved here from Odessa, he and the others had assumed that they would be stationed at the Northern Fleet base of Polyarnyy, near the head of Kola Fjord. But their tightly guarded barracks were actually on the fjord itself—and carefully insulated from any contact with the base or its personnel. Insulated, in fact, from human contact in any form. No telephone calls were allowed, on duty or off. And letters, restricted to family and/or close friends, were censored.

Not that he had anyone he wanted to talk or write to.

Andrey's mother was long dead, he had never had a real sweetheart, and his father had not attempted to communicate with him since their last, strained meeting just before he was arrested and sent to the madhouse at Gorky.

As a SPETSNAZ candidate at Kronstadt, in addition to intensive physical conditioning and exercises with small arms and explosives, Andrey had been trained as a parachutist and frogman; he had learned to jump fully armed from an airplane into the ocean, to rid himself of the parachute, and then continue his journey to the target underwater. Use of scuba gear had virtually become second nature. He found that he had a kind of natural aptitude for underwater swimming, and a real affinity for the gear that made it possible.

Scuba diving on pure oxygen below ten meters is fatal. But most SPETSNAZ operations are conducted at depths less than that. Basic doctrine regarded the sea simply as a medium for transportation and/or concealment. A way of getting to the target. And naval SPETSNAZ targets were either on dry land or in the shallow waters just offshore.

So hardhat diving, intended for deeper descents, was something entirely new. Modern hardhat, or "dry suit" diving apparatus, he learned, consists of seven parts: air pump, helmet and breastplate, waterproof diving suit, flexible air tube with metal couplings at either end, weighted boots, lifeline, and lead weights for breast and back.

Constructed of two layers of twill cloth with a layer of pure rubber between, the waterproof suit is made to encase the body from foot to neck, with vulcanized rubber cuffs on each sleeve to make a waterproof joint at the diver's wrists. The suit is also fitted with a rubberized collar to which the breastplate (also called a corselet) is secured by a watertight joint.

The helmet, provided with a nonreturn inlet valve to which the air hose is attached, is secured to the breastplate by segmented neck rings that make it possible to connect the two by one-eighth of a turn.

Air is supplied by a pump on the surface, through a hose, and the diver's buoyancy can be controlled by means of an air-outlet valve also attached to the helmet. Left open, the valve allows excess air to escape, deflating the suit; closed, it retains the air and increases buoyancy to a point where the diver will achieve positive buoyancy and pop to the surface at once if not otherwise restrained.

Communication with the surface is via a telephone built into the helmet. Its receiver is located in the crown, with the transmitter between the front glass port and left side-glass. In an emergency, a system of coded tugs on the lifeline also functions as a last-ditch method of communication.

They had tried out all the equipment, including telephones and lifeline, on practical descents.

But on this dive, they had been ordered to stay off the phone except for an emergency.

And as usual, there was no explanation. . . .

Now the darkness was total.

The load on the surface pumps supplying the divers with air was increasing with each foot of depth. At the surface, they needed only one and a half cubic feet of air per minute per diver; at seventy meters this increased to nearly twelve cubic feet. He hoped there would be no failure.

Shifting his feet yet again, Andrey forced his left hand to release its grip on the screen of the diving cage and brought the wrist up to his eyes. They had been in the water for only ten minutes. Had it not been for the chemical conditioning injections that gave them their relative immunity to the effects of high pressure, low temperature, and prolonged water immersion, their descent would have been much slower.

Standard doctrine requires short stops every twenty or thirty feet to accustom the average diver to the increase of pressure. But the *starshina* said they wouldn't require such tender treatment—just one or two stops along the way, more to check reactions than in any real expectation of ill effects from the dive.

Restless once again, Andrey reached out to regrasp the side of the cage . . . but stopped with his left hand still inches from its goal.

There was light below. Dim. Watery-flickering. But real, not an illusion. The instructors had not lied!

The cage was still going down, and Andrey could feel himself taking deeper and deeper breaths—in itself, a violation of doctrine, but let them hang him if they would—as a knot of tension that had formed, unsuspected, in the middle of his back began gradually to relax. The light grew brighter with every foot of descent, and Andrey found his inner confidence returning. As long as he had light, he could handle anything.

And then, suddenly, they were on the bottom. The cage settled into about a twenty-degree list, but Andrey hardly noticed as he strained his eyes into the murk. Seen from this angle, the light source appeared to be rectangular—taller than it was wide—and quite bright. Looking at it, Andrey realized suddenly that it was probably a portal of some kind. A door, perhaps leading to some kind of work station or habitat here at the bottom of the fjord. This must be the Temnota—or some part of it. And its inhabitants . . .

Someone was outside. Fumbling with the entrance of the cage. Little as he liked to admit it, Andrey knew that he was anxious to move closer to that source of light. To the underwater habitat. He turned to assist the person outside. And screamed.

PART V

TESTING

Gorky, U.S.S.R.

Saturday, September 13
3:05 A.M.

The prisoner's face was pale and he was perspiring, but his answers to the interrogator's questions were unhesitating and—within expected parameters—accurate.

"Your name?"

"Narmonov, Yuri Alexandrovich."

"Occupation?"

"Military aviator."

"Rank?"

"Colonel, senior."

"You are a line officer?"

"I was."

"That is not responsive, Comrade Colonel. Are you presently a line officer?"

"I am at present on detached duty . . . ah . . . your clearance, please?"

"You will answer the question, Comrade Colonel. At once!"

The prisoner's respiration rate, closely monitored by the two men observing him from the dark side of the room's one-way mirror, increased almost to the point of hyperventilation. But he sat in silence, staring at the man across from him until the interrogator reached inside his tunic to produce the GRU documents that set forth his qualification to hear the answer to the question.

The two observers—Rocket Forces Gen. V. I. Tregorin and the doctor who had been in charge of Narmonov's null-tank "reorientation"—were pleased. Despite everything, that elementary bit of security discipline had not been forgotten.

Perhaps, Tregorin told himself, the rat trainers were right after all. Perhaps a personality could, in fact, be entirely shattered and then reassembled without loss of peripheral programming.

"I am at present assigned as executive officer—deputy commander—for the Baikonur cosmonaut unit."

Another positive reaction. That had been the prisoner's former assignment, before his reliability came into question.

"You have been a cosmonaut yourself?"

"That is true."

"And you have gone into space?"

"I have."

"You are somewhat well-known, I believe?"

The prisoner's mouth moved as if to form a reply, but no sound came. In the room behind the one-way glass, bodies shifted minutely, and heads turned to a listening attitude.

"Come, come, Comrade Colonel! We are not bashful children here. Fact is only fact; it has no subjective value, and you are, in fact, a celebrity of international stature. Is it not so?"

"I . . . yes."

"Yes, what?"

"Yes, I was—at one time—somewhat well-known, here in the Rodina. And abroad as well."

"Why was this?"

"Because of . . ."

Narmonov's voice trailed off; beads of sweat appeared at the top of his forehead, and his mouth ceased to move.

"Yes, comrade. Go on."

"Because of certain unauthorized actions I took during my last flight into space. And also because of things I said later. To newspaper and television reporters."

"What things?"

"About the . . . the . . . space program of the Rodina."

"You criticized it?"

No answer. Narmonov's face looked as though a clamp had been applied to his lips. They were visibly locked in a spasm of silence and denial.

"Come, Comrade Colonel. You are a soldier. Speak! You criticized the socialist space program, criticized the Rodina, the motherland, to outsiders."

"No! I did not criticize the Rodina. Never! I would not do that."

"But you did imply that the mission of your space shuttle, the *Titov II*, had been imperiled because of faulty and obsolete equipment both on board and in the ground support center."

"I . . ."

"And you did this," the interrogator continued remorselessly, "in an effort to rationalize your deliberate and arrogant insubordination in altering the carefully conceived plan of the space shuttle's mission."

Narmonov was silent.

"Come, comrade cosmonaut. Speak. Tell me that what I have said is not so."

Narmonov drew breath as if actually to voice such a denial, but expelled it soundlessly.

"It . . . is true," he said softly.

"Speak up, please, comrade. I cannot hear you."

"It . . . is . . . true."

"Ah! You admit this. And you admit, also, publicly calling your own comrades—your fellow officers—liars?"

"No. No! I said only that the inspection teams, the ones sent here from the West to see that we lived up to arms treaties, that they might be misled. That they were not being shown some . . . potential weapons . . . that were to be sent into space."

"Then you admit it!"

"I only—"

"—only said officers of the armed forces would lie to them! Would act in an underhanded way."

"I only meant—"

"You dishonored the Rodina! And the Party! And yourself! The Party says you are a traitor and a rebel."

"The Party is mistaken."

"The Party cannot be mistaken."

"The Party—"

Narmonov's voice faltered, and he stopped speaking.

"Yes, comrade? The Party . . . ?"

Narmonov licked his lips. "The Party," he said quietly, without inflection or emphasis, "is correct, because it is the Party and it holds paramount the interest of the people."

"And therefore . . ."

"Therefore, if the Party says I am a traitor and a rebel, then I must be a traitor and a rebel."

The interrogator nodded approvingly. "Good. Very good, comrade. We make progress."

Narmonov's face, which had momentarily been a window on passionate emotion, seemed to collapse before the eyes of the observers; all feeling and all sense of self vanished as if by the stroke of a draftsman's eraser.

"Very well, then," the interrogator continued when he thought Narmonov was ready. "Let us explore these disloyal remarks a bit further."

He paused again, as if offering Narmonov a new opportunity for protest.

"You spoke to newspaper people, and the television. Yes?"

"Yes." Narmonov's tone was neutral.

"Yes," the interrogator echoed. "But how did you get them to listen? I mean—you were not here, in the motherland, at the time."

"No."

"Where were you?"

"In Austria. Vienna."

"For what purpose?"

"It was a . . . goodwill tour. For cosmonauts and astronauts. A tour of Europe, to show—oh—international amity in space. That Americans and Russians can be friends."

"This tour, it went well?"

"Yes. Very well. We began in Denmark, continued through Holland, Belgium, then to France, the Germanies—"

"Both the Federal Republic and the GDR?"

"Yes."

"And then?"

"And then on into Czechoslovakia and Austria."

"And it was during this trip that you became friendly with the American spaceman. Carter?"

"Uh . . . yes. No!"

"You contradict yourself."

Narmonov's eyes clouded and his brow wrinkled, as though he were deep in thought.

"Yes," he said at length. "Yes. We became . . . friends. But no, we did not discover this just in Austria. In Vienna. We had talked from time to time, during the trip."

"You have much in common?"

"We have both gone into space."

"Aside from that."

"No. Not really."

"I think there may be something."

Narmonov shook his head. "No. I do not recall. . . ."

"You are both fathers."

This time, the cosmonaut seemed honestly surprised. "I . . . well, yes," he said. "No. I mean, yes, we both have had children. One son each. But . . ."

"But?"

"But his relationship with his son was not good. And this worried him."

"So you spoke of this?"

"Yes."

"Because your own relationship—with your son—was a good one. And he envied this?"

Again Narmonov paused, as if for thought. But when he answered, his tone was firm and assured. "Yes," he said. "Because Andrey and I, we had been close. So very close. Yes. I think he envied that."

The interrogator nodded, almost amiably. "Your son, Andrey, you are still on good terms with him?"

For a moment, Narmonov's face remained impassive. But then control was lost and it twisted into lines of anguish.

"No," he said in a barely audible voice. "No."

The interrogator seemed surprised. "No? And why not, comrade?"

"He is dead," Narmonov almost whispered.

"What? Speak up. I cannot hear."

"He is dead!" This time Narmonov uttered the words in a shout, and for a moment it almost seemed that he was about to leap across the table to tear at the interrogator's throat.

But then he subsided. Passion drained from his face as if an emotional plug had been pulled, and his control returned.

"Dead," he repeated, this time almost without inflection. "He died nearly a year ago."

"I see."

The interrogator glanced at the clipboard in his hand, then at the mirror, as if for new orders.

"Perfect!" In the room behind the mirror, the voice of the chief psychologist was at whisper level, but it filled the darkened space with his own sense of personal vindication. "The subject," he hissed, "truly believes what he is saying. This is obvious, is it not? It is as real to him as—"

"—as we are to each other," Tregorin supplied in a somewhat louder tone. "Yes, Comrade Doctor. Yes, yes! And you have our thanks and congratulations. But be kind. Allow this ignorant peasant, please, to hear the remainder of the interview."

Moscow, U.S.S.R.

Saturday, September 13
11:38 P.M.

Comrade General Viktor Tregorin, deputy commander of Strategic Rocket Forces, sat in a brown leather wing chair in his den. The door was closed, but Tchaikovsky's 1812 Overture boomed throughout the apartment. Tregorin didn't hear it. The music coming through his headphones was Count Basie's version of "Blow Top." Thirty years earlier he'd heard an American jazz band during its tour of the Soviet Union and had secretly loved the swinging rhythms ever since. He felt it would not be to his benefit if this were generally known, so he covered his musical transgressions with the more acceptable Tchaikovsky for the big ears of his GRU bodyguards in the apartment next door. Not bad stuff for a Russian composer, but it just didn't swing.

Tregorin's personal diary lay open in his lap. A ballpoint pen beat a regular rhythm on the leather-bound book. As the Basie band slid into "Taxi War Dance," Tregorin began writing. It had been a big day, beginning with his observation of the successful reconstruction of Yuri Narmonov early in the morning. The trip back from Gorky had been tiresome, but the news awaiting him upon his return had purged the weariness from his body. If everything went according to plan, tomorrow would be an even more important day.

> Temnota will move into Phase Four tomorrow. I finally received Petchukocov's cable from Iran today, saying all is well, and that he'll be returning tomorrow via Iran Air and Aeroflot. Of course, he'll not be on the Iran Air flight but will contact me next when he is safely in Israel.
>
> It has taken months, but he has been successful in converting one of the Iranian air traffic controllers to our view with a "gift" from the motherland. Petchukocov's most persuasive powers of speech convinced the man to direct this Iran Air jet over the position of U.S. warships patrolling the Persian Gulf. Our monetary gift made it possible for the passengers who will lose their lives on this flight to become martyrs instantly in the ongoing fight against the Great Satan that is the U.S.
>
> I eagerly await the developments of tomorrow. I only hope that Comrade Petchukocov has remembered to purchase a ticket for this flight in order to have his name placed on the passenger list. But I will not worry. Petchukocov is a smart and, so far, reliable coconspirator. And may Allah bless you, air traffic controller.

The cassette tape ended, but Viktor Tregorin flipped it over to listen to "Super Chief" one more time before he shut off the Tchaikovsky record and went to sleep.

Coronado, California

Sunday, September 14
5:22 P.M.

The water was rising around his neck now, and Rick found himself fighting off a minor attack of claustrophobia.

Give him an ocean to dive in, and he was happy; let him dive from the top of a tank like the one he would be entering as soon as this chamber was filled, and he had no problem at all. But using the air lock was something else.

The diving tank at the SEAL base was more than fifty feet tall. It was a swimming pool that had, in effect, been stood on end. Perfectly round, the pool was only about fifteen feet in diameter—hardly wide enough for a wading pool—but nobody was likely to do any wading because the water was forty-seven feet deep. The SEALs used it to train divers not to blow their cool.

Properly trained, the instructors said, no swimmer should need scuba equipment to reach the bottom of the pool and return. All he had to do was hold his breath, and one test that each SEAL had to pass sometime during training did, indeed, require such a dive. Rick had passed on his first try.

And he had passed the air-lock test, too, sitting in the lock until it was full of water and then passing through the hatch to the main tank where he made his way to the surface . . . still without the assistance of an artificial air supply.

But he had felt claustrophobic that time, waiting for the lock to fill with water, and he felt the same now—even though on this occasion he was wearing scuba gear. The fact that the apparatus was experimental had nothing whatever to do with his feelings.

"Let me dive the thing from the surface," he had said when Mac first proposed that he try the device, an odd-looking bit of work that he called the hemoglobin gill.

But Mac had been emphatic. "Kiwi and I have been using the thing for a while, and we've dived it from the top of the tank so many times that we know just exactly what it will and will not do. That's why we want you to do it this way."

Rick was nonplussed. "You've never taken it in through the lock at the bottom of the water tower?"

"Of course we have."

"Then . . ."

"Look—trust me on this, okay? I'll explain it all later. After you're done and have a chance to make your own evaluation. Without any input from either of us."

Rick agreed to it, but he didn't have to like it, and now as the last of the air disappeared from the very top of the lock, he admitted to himself that his attitude toward this particular maneuver was not likely to improve with familiarity. It was still just a little too much like being buried alive. . . .

Rick took a deep breath from the mouthpiece—and decided at once that whoever used the damn thing last must have had terminal halitosis. Trying the mouthpiece before getting into the airlock, he hadn't noticed anything unusual about it. But now it, and the air it was offering him, seemed somehow to taste of copper—heavily overlaid with something else. Something like spoiled meat.

He suppressed an urge to retch and moved quickly toward the hatch that would admit him to the main tank.

It opened without difficulty and he passed through, turning to close and dog the hatch again behind him so that the lock could be used again.

He looked at his wristwatch.

Five minutes into the evolution, as the SEALs had taught him to count time. All right. That meant he was supposed to spend at least three more minutes down here. Unless he found himself having some kind of problem.

The mouthpiece, and whatever was coming through it, still tasted like spoiled meat. But that probably wasn't the kind of problem they meant. He looked again at the watch.

Two minutes.

All right. Breathe as little as possible, then. No! That was wrong. The whole idea of having him down here was to evaluate the operation of the hemoglobin gill, so . . . wait a minute. Hemoglobin. Well, hell.

So far, he knew nothing about the operation of Mac's long-delayed development project, except that it was, in Captain Ward's phrase, "a whole new way of breathing underwater." But the name itself was all the clue he needed.

Hemoglobin—that was a component of blood, right? And if that was the name Mac used for this invention—the hemoglobin gill—then blood must have something to do with it. And stale blood. Was that what he was tasting here?

Well, then, okay. There were worse things. They could have called it the cow-dung lung or something. . . .

And that was a stupid thing to let himself think, because it made him want to laugh, and laughing was a no-no down here.

Do I have "rapture of the deep"—nitrogen narcosis? he thought. Though he'd never had the problem himself, he'd heard a lot about it and knew that one of the first signs was that you thought everything was screamingly, side-splittingly funny. Just like being high on grass. And his mind wasn't working just right. That was for sure.

One minute.

He realized, suddenly, that he had been looking at the dial of his watch for some time. The maker had guaranteed it waterproof to a depth of two hundred meters—as if anybody in his right mind was about to go that far down into the sea with that watch strapped to his arm, and still care what time it was. Go down two hundred meters, friend, and you could forget about coming up. Then he shuddered . . . and the convulsions started.

Suddenly, he was not alone, there at the bottom of the pool. Someone in a wet suit with regular scuba gear was beside him, tugging at his arm and jerking a thumb toward the surface.

Why?

Wasn't time yet.

Slowly, the dark edges of the world closed in until all he could see was the single, bright spark of light at the very top of the tank. He watched with detached interest as it glowed brightly for a long moment. And then winked out.

Imperial Beach, California

Sunday, September 14
5:51 P.M.

"Okay. The air tasted funny and I passed out on the way back to the surface. So what does that tell you?"

Rick, Mac, and Kiwi Kraus were in a booth at Barnacles, an Imperial Beach bar not known as a SEAL hangout. They headed there right after Rick got out of the hyperbaric chamber at the top of the tank.

"What it tells us," Mac said, answering Rick's question, "is that the reactions Kiwi and I were getting with our own tests were valid. You may have thought you got hit with some nitrogen narcosis, but it was really a touch of carbon-dioxide poisoning. No matter what the instruments say, the newfangled CO_2 scrubber we're using with the gill simply isn't scrubbing the carbon dioxide well enough. We can't do any deep diving with it if it can't even handle fifty feet."

Rick shook his head. "Sorry, gents, but you lost me way back there. About the time Mac said 'CO_2 scrubber.' "

Kiwi nodded solemnly. "Shouldn't wondah."

As usual, Rick found the down easter's tone irritating. "Shouldn't wonder what?" he said.

"Shouldn't wondah I'd have another beer . . . seein's you're buyin'."

Kiwi's face betrayed nothing, but Rick could feel the needle. The barrel-chested little clamdigger just never seemed to let up. What was it with him, anyway?

"I'll get a pitcher," Mac said, defusing the moment by standing up. "And when I get back, we'll talk about what happened. And why. Okay?"

Nobody said anything, so he walked to the bar, where the bartender was deep in conversation with the only other customer.

When Mac left, Rick and Kiwi glared at each other. Stupid thing for Mac to do, thought Rick, unless he wants to see me brawl with lobster-face. Or maybe he wants us to try to talk and work things out. If that's the case, he's a pretty sneaky bastard.

But Kiwi rose, breaking the tense silence, and said, "Gonna tap a kidney. Be right back." And he scuttled off, crablike, in the direction of the men's room.

Mac returned with the pitcher of beer. "Where's Kiwi?"

"In the head, taking a leak."

"Oh, okay."

"While he's gone, let me ask you something. What is his problem? Why's he constantly on my case?"

"Ah, he just likes you," Mac said, sipping some foam off the head of his beer, but avoiding Rick's glance.

"Got a funny way of showing it." Rick didn't figure Mac knew anyway. "And another thing, why am I even involved with . . . you know, your project?"

"If you must know, when Will Ward opened his big fat yap about it, the cat was out of the bag. We had to have you on the inside—and if you weren't interested, I don't know that you'd have been allowed to back out. But I'm glad you're in on it. Besides, you're a diver now."

"That's right," Kiwi said, returning. "I know that for sure because I am the one checked you out. Ever' Christly step of the way through training. . . ."

Rick grimaced. "Yeah, I remember." He paused, shifting gears. "So this is pretty hush-hush stuff, isn't it?"

"Damn straight," said Mac.

"So if we're going to talk about this—thing—of yours, shouldn't it at least be back at the base?"

Mac looked around the room. They were alone, except for the bartender and his friend.

"You see any spies lurking in the corners?" he inquired. "Or anyone at all, for that matter?"

"And that," Kiwi added, "is why we picked this place to come to. And do, most times after work. Because no one, not SEALs or much of anyone else, comes in here. At least to eat."

"I think they make their money," Mac said, "running a horse book in the back or something. I don't know. Or care. All I know is it beats the office they gave me, over at the amphibious base. After eight or ten hours, the walls there just get to looking too familiar. You know?"

Rick nodded. "What you're telling me, then," he said, "is that the Navy's still not really committed to your project. It just wants to make noises like it is."

"Maybe," Mac said.

"And maybe not," Kiwi said. "Could be some kind of budget problem. Maybe they's more money coming. Down the line a bit."

"Maybe," Mac repeated. "But the thing right now is, they were at least interested enough to let me go back to work on it myself—with a little help from my friends."

"Shouldn't wondah," Kiwi said, nodding.

"But that's the thing," Rick said. "Right there. The fact is, even though I tried the . . . uh . . . gill for you today, I still don't know anything about it. And you said you'd fill me in . . . afterward."

Mac grinned. "And I'll do it." He looked at his watch. "There is," he said, "a short form and a long form for all this. But the hour being what it is—"

"—and training gonna begin, right on schedule, at oh six hundred tomorrow," Kiwi said, "no matter what went on over the weekend—"

"—I'll stick to the short form. Okay?"

Rick nodded, mentally commenting that he probably wouldn't have understood the long form anyway.

"The whole thing," Mac said, "began as a kind of fluke. A pair of biochemists named Joseph and Celia Bonaventura were trying to determine exactly how hemoglobin works in the blood, and in the process noticed that fish—while using a liquid-to-liquid process to transfer dissolved oxygen—can inflate their swim bladders with gaseous oxygen at will."

"Whoa!"

Mac shook his head. "I always do that," he said. "Begin talking like a damn encyclopedia, when I really don't know my butt cheeks from my elbow. Look, the whole thing is, they figured, if a fish can get oxygen from seawater, divers should be able to also."

"And . . ."

"About fifteen years ago, they came across a porous type of polyurethane that could be impregnated with hemoglobin."

"That's the 'sponge' you were talking about?"

"That's it, and when water is pumped through that sponge, the hemoglobin extracts the oxygen that's dissolved in the water. The same thing happens in a fish's gills. But in this gill, when the sponge is given an electric shock, it gives up its oxygen, stores it in a tank, and then gets ready to extract some more oxygen from the next batch of seawater. You breathe the oxygen that the gill stores in that tank."

"Well, if the oxygen went through hemoglobin to get to me, then maybe that's why it tasted like raw liver," Rick interjected.

"Yeah," Mac said, grimacing. "I guess so. For a while, I thought it was my imagination. But if you tasted it, too, maybe it's really there."

"And it has got to go," Kiwi said.

"Yeah. Damn it. But what I was saying—the hemosponge attracts oxygen, but not quite as well as the human bloodstream does. Call it sixty to eighty percent as efficient."

"Which," Kiwi broke in, "is kind of too bad. Because it needs to do a lot better if it's going to give a working diver enough oxygen from the water around him."

"You mean . . . ?"

"I mean, with this thing, you don't really carry your oxygen supply down from the surface the way you do with any system now in use," Mac said. "The whole idea is to do what a fish does—utilize oxygen from the water itself."

"You mean, you're using your own, personal blood supply?" Rick demanded, thunderstruck.

Mac laughed, breaking the tension of the moment. "No, not that—though I admit the idea occurred to me at one point. What we use right now is something else. I'll come to that in a moment. But let me explain the main problem facing us first . . . which is the nature of seawater itself."

Rick could feel his eyes beginning to glaze.

"See, the thing about seawater," Mac said, "is it only contains about six to eight parts per million of oxygen. So a tremendous amount of water has got to be processed if a diver is going to get as much oxygen as he needs."

"How much water is that?"

"Well, at the surface, maybe he'd need a flow of around a hundred gallons a minute."

"A hundred gallons!"

"Of seawater. Yes. Through the sponge system. Anyway, that's what we're using as a base figure now. And the trouble is, our cycle isn't quite fast enough to do that."

"Cycle?"

"Yes, the cycle of absorb oxygen, electric shock, give up oxygen, store oxygen, and back to absorb oxygen again. It's just too slow. And that's why we started trying different forms of hemoglobin. Human, for one. Then from cattle. Or sheep—that looked good, gave up the oxygen more readily. But it was unstable and turned into an iron derivative."

"So . . . what was I using, there in the tank?"

"A kind of switch we discovered on something called cob-oglobin—which is what you get when you replace the iron in hemoglobin with cobalt. Much too expensive for general use in its original form, but I decided to . . . well . . . never mind about that. We're still working on it."

"I still don't see," Rick said, "why it wouldn't be simpler just to alter the lung of a human being."

Mac and Kiwi eyed him owlishly.

"A human?"

"Well—yeah. I mean, the whole idea is to take oxygen from the water the way a fish does, right? So why not just fill a human's lungs with seawater. And let him work it out for himself."

"Uh-huh."

"Well, why not?"

Mac looked away. But Kiwi favored Rick with one of his skeleton grins.

"Shit a gawddamn, boy," he said. "Sounds good to me! Seein's you lookin' to volunteah . . ."

All three broke up laughing.

Kibbutz Borohov, Israel

Monday, September 15
5:17 A.M.

The old man stirred, twitching his nose against the smell of thistle and onion, and rolled over, pulling the thin blanket over his shoulders to keep out the night damp.

Israel was supposed to be a warm place. So why was he cold and wet?

Growling in the subvocal range where old men hide their resentments, he closed his eyes and tried to go back to sleep. But sleep would not come. Sighing, moving slowly so as to avoid waking any of the others who slept in the common room reserved for unmarried men, he sat up and looked at the window.

It was getting light. Time to get up, then. Perhaps make points with the kibbutz leaders by going out to help with early chores. They hadn't been happy to see him come, an old man with no money and no muscles but with a piece of paper from a friend in Jerusalem, asking them to take him in.

Well, let them kvetch. They would be rid of him soon enough. Just a little while now—a little more waiting—and the next part of the charade could begin. Damn Tregorin!

Damn him for the too clever, too complicated mind that had conceived all this. A stroke of genius, yes. But infuriating for him, and personally humiliating, because of the part that he must play in it. Because to do it, he must become a Jew again after a lifetime.

For sixty years he had rejected that label. Turned his back upon it. Rejected the whole history of his mother's people and walked resolutely away from it to a life and a world where they did not exist. Where power came to those who had the wit and will to seize it.

And now he stood upon the soil of a Jew country and proclaimed his Jewishness to the Jews who ran it, in order to be permitted to hide in this Jew farming commune.

Quietly, determinedly ignoring the protest of muscles still

sore from the day before, the old man stood up and shuffled across the room, trying to remember where he had left his shoes.

Manama, Bahrain

Monday, September 15
5:31 A.M.

U.S. SHOOTS DOWN IRANIAN AIRLINER screamed the headlines of the American papers that were brought in weekly.

I can't believe this has happened again, thought Carter, recalling an almost identical incident three years earlier. His presence in Bahrain, in fact, was due to the recommendation of the congressional committee set up to review the facts of the earlier event. They wanted a high-profile man in the Middle East, and Carter was right for the job.

Carter threw down the newspaper in disgust and picked up a manila file folder.

But the only thing really wrong here, Adm. R. B. Carter told himself as he reread the findings of the official court of inquiry for the tenth time, was Petchukocov.

What in the hell had the old troublemaker been doing on that damned Iran Air flight? It made no sense at all.

And that, in turn, made gibberish of everything else. The court of inquiry was a gundeck job, intended for public consumption—a quick patch to lend credibility to the State Department's official apology and the President's official statement of sympathy. And it had all the expected elements. The *Akron*'s captain had his butt in a sling; no matter how you sliced it (and no matter how little he deserved it) his Navy career had just gone into the dumper.

Two other *Akron* officers, the ones in tactical control of antiaircraft weapons and target identification, were also prime candidates for the rank of civilian.

The United States would pay millions in "compensation" to families of the airliner's passengers and crew (despite the official position that the damn thing had no business being where it was) and that would be that.

And as area commander, he would come in for a little bit of the fallout—not enough, perhaps, to sink him, but surely enough to give someone in BuPers second thoughts about possible promotion and new assignments for Rear Adm. Carter, R. B., USN.

But no one had offered any credible explanation for the Iran Air jetliner's deviation from accepted civil air-traffic corridors (and from the flight plan filed just before takeoff from Tehran).

No one had been able to explain why any pilot in his right mind—even an Iranian one—would deliberately fly over a warship already hotly engaged in defending herself from surface attack. Hadn't they learned anything three years ago?

And . . . most of all . . . no one had even tried to explain Petchukocov. Damn him! Soviet officials, especially high-ranking members of the Politburo, did not . . . did absolutely not . . . travel outside the workers' paradise as paying passengers on commercial airlines. By KGB edict (and in line with the most elementary rules of security) they went from capital to capital on board one of the fleet of official jetliners held in readiness for such duty by Aeroflot. So . . . what the hell was going on there, anyway?

And why had there been no Kremlin reaction to the death of an old, and presumably valued, comrade?

True, Petchukocov had been demoted to minister of agriculture from the powerful position of defense minister. But it wasn't actually oblivion. There had been no "reassignment" as director of a power station in Siberia; no "retirement" to a one-room attic apartment in Gorky. The old boy had still been a player.

It didn't make sense. What he needed were more facts. Or at the very least, input from someone closer to the scene. Someone like . . . Yuri.

Sighing, tired but still not sleepy, Carter allowed himself to sink back into the padded recesses of the swivel chair at the desk in his off-duty office, closing his eyes against the light from the reading lamp.

He wished he could have just five minutes of quiet conversation with Yuri Narmonov. Five minutes of question-and-answer.

Right now.

Gorky, U.S.S.R.

Monday, September 15
5:40 A.M.

The interrogation was coming to an end, and in the room behind the mirror the doctor's gaunt features were animated by a large smile. Even Tregorin seemed unusually benign.

"He remembered it all." The doctor's whisper was ecstatic as he bent his head to the rocket general's ear. "All that he was told, just as he was told to remember it . . . and nothing else! No trace of the actual events or relationships. Do you know what this means, Comrade General?"

But Tregorin's expression had drifted back to neutral, and now he merely nodded, bringing the doctor back to earth with a thump.

"I know, Comrade Doctor," he said. "*Da . . .*"

But already, his mind was racing. Was it truly possible that Narmonov's mind had been so totally altered without disturbing the basic personality?

Was it really credible that he no longer remembered the true nature of his relationship with his son, or that the boy was still alive—albeit beyond his father's reach?

Tregorin mused, wrestling with the problem, while continuing to observe the scene in the interrogation room.

They were talking now about Narmonov's last journey into space as pilot of the Soviet shuttlecraft *Titov II.*

"The *Titov*'s on-board computers, then, actually bring the spacecraft back to earth?" the interrogator was saying.

"Yes. Assisted and seconded by the mainframe computers on earth."

"The computers on the ground, they are in communication with the space shuttle throughout this entry maneuver, then?"

Narmonov shook his head emphatically. "No, not all the way. They lose contact for a brief period, early in the procedure. Thermal conditions cause a break in reception. That is why we must have computers on board."

"Then the on-board computers normally manage the actual entry?"

"Yes."

"But on your last flight, they did not."

Narmonov was sweating again, and Tregorin found himself leaning toward the glass, straining to hear every nuance of the answer.

"No. On the last flight, I . . . took control of the craft myself."

The interrogator affected surprise. "You? But—is that not dangerous, comrade?"

Narmonov nodded slowly. "Yes," he said flatly. "It is. But I did it. And actually flew the shuttle myself all the way to touchdown."

The interrogator remained silent, waiting for Narmonov to go on.

"It was . . . an error," he said in the same neutral voice. "Ego. Even egomania, perhaps. I wanted to fly the shuttle, really fly it, myself. I was sure I could do it. And so I did so."

The interrogator nodded in what might have been an understanding way. "You prefer that? Like it better than permitting the computer on the ground to handle the landing for you?"

This time, Narmonov actually laughed. "Comrade psychologist," he said, "the next time you fly in an airliner, look at the faces of your fellow passengers just after landing. The ones that have a small sheen of moisture, whose lips seem to need licking or who seem excessively jolly with the false gaiety of the gallows . . . those are not the first-time passengers. Check the luggage of the ones with the sweat patches under the arms of their shirts, and you will find pilot's logbooks. No real pilot ever enjoys—or entirely trusts—anyone's flying but his own. Particularly the landing! It is a fact of life."

"But it was still a deviation from the shuttle flight plan," the interrogator said. "An act of arrogance . . . amounting to mutiny."

"I . . . yes." Narmonov blinked and swallowed, but his voice remained empty of emotion. "Yes. I accuse myself of this. I did it, and I alone am responsible."

The interrogator smiled, glancing in the direction of the presences unseen behind the mirror.

It was real, Viktor Tregorin told himself. It was real; they had done it. Narmonov now truly believed that his feat in landing the *Titov II*—and the press conference he had held in Vienna afterward—were both acts of unprovoked rebellion.

That he had assumed control of the shuttlecraft only when the on-board computers and those on the ground both failed; that his landing had been a miracle of airmanship; and that it had been the help of the then-astronaut Carter—brought in on emergency uplink from Houston with advice and limited computer assistance—that had enabled him even to attempt such a feat, all this was submerged. Lost. Forgotten as if it had never been.

Tregorin took a deep breath and expelled it silently in the semidarkness. Time was growing short. Narmonov's mission was already scheduled—the first hints dropped in *Pravda*. A few days, a week or so at most, and the gamble must be made. He forced his attention back to the lighted room where the interview was still in progress.

And Narmonov did the same.

Like Tregorin, Yuri had allowed his mind to wander while responding mechanically to the questions that had become so familiar now that they no longer required conscious thought. The years on earth, the years since his last space flight—had long since ceased to seem real or alive to him. They were dead years filled with the dead deeds of a dead man—deeds of a Yuri Narmonov he sometimes thought he did not even know.

But he knew the times and dates and places of the dead time. Knew them, in fact, better than he knew the years before. And he could recall the people, their faces and personalities, more clearly than those of his earlier life. Of his life before death.

One day he would hurt them. One day he would have his chance and when he did . . .

Mission Bay, California

Saturday, September 20
10:15 A.M.

Rick Tallman humped his back into a dive and used his arms to pull himself downward through the roiling clutter of sand, kelp, and bits of shell brought up by the surface swell. It was good to be free.

Weight belts and fins and all the other bits and pieces of high-tech diving were fine, but only in their way and in their place.

SEAL training had not been his first encounter with weight belts and flippers and diving gear in general. They had been a part of his life for as long as he could remember. But SEAL training had changed all that. Now they were a part of his profession. Tools. He knew them and understood them better than he had ever thought possible. Yet the emotional response had definitely changed. Swimming with them was business.

Swimming without them was fun.

Not that he didn't enjoy the SEAL swimming program. Or the continuing experimentation with Mac's gill. It was good to be on the leading edge again, out at the limit and beyond. It was similar to the way he had felt when he was flying fighters.

Today, however, was a chance to relax. It had begun with a telephone call from Captain Ward, who had bad news. The *Steel Albatross* was out of the water for maintenance and installation of upgraded gear. No more dives until next weekend at the earliest. Rick asked if there was anything he could do to help. But the captain said there wasn't, and when Rick mentioned the development to Mac, the ex-chief said he had a better idea anyway.

What they all needed, he declared, was a little R and R. "Let's get Sam and Billy the Goat," he said, "and some beer and Cokes and weird-tasting sandwiches, and make a day of it. At the beach."

Rick thought it over. "Maybe," he said, trying to be tactful, "Billy's mama has other plans."

Mac shook his head. "Sam's been hitting the ball a little too hard. Stretched right out to the limit. Just comes home at night to be with Billy, and then goes right back out before dawn the next day. So I just figured, what the hell . . . I mean, since the last time you were at the house, he's asked me about you a couple times."

"Yeah, sure." Rick grinned, remembering. "And I bet *she'll* be real tickled to see me!"

When he arrived, Sam was in the kitchen and dressed for the beach.

Samantha Deane in the uniform of a Navy two-striper was one thing; in a bathing suit she was . . . !!! Even The Eyes seemed larger and greener than he remembered. Clothes changed her. Uniformed and buttoned up in her workday persona, she seemed taller. And less approachable. But the sight of her in bathing suit and sandals, bending over a sandwich board making peanut butter and boysenberry jelly sandwiches, seemed to raise the temperature of the room twenty degrees.

"Looks like a helluva nice day—for September," Mac said, wandering in with the first beer of the day.

Instead of swimming trunks, Rick was wearing an old pair of jeans that had been converted (via trench-knife tailoring) into surfer jeans. They got an immediate vote of approval from Billy, followed by a demand that his own denims be similarly altered.

Sam didn't object, even when the boy wanted Rick to handle the scissor work instead of her. But his request for a can of beer like Uncle Mac's met stony silence. Mac mentioned that he'd been raised on the stuff himself, and he could even remember a can or two he'd shared with his little sister when she was about Billy's age.

"Our mother," Sam reminded him, "wasn't a doctor and never dissected half a dozen middle-aged rumpots after they'd finally died of cirrhosis!"

Mac drew himself up into a fair approximation of wounded dignity. "Middle-aged?" he said.

When the sandwiches were done, they piled into two cars (Billy riding with Rick) and drove to Mission Bay. Good surfing and ocean-swimming spots are plentiful around San Diego, but Billy the Goat wasn't really old enough for any of them, so Mac chose a quiet spot with just a gentle hint of wave action. Rick followed him there, parking alongside, and helped move blankets, cooler, and picnic basket close to the water, but not so close as to have to move when the tide turned. Then everyone but Billy sat down to relax.

The Goat had grabbed his Frisbee the second he spotted a golden retriever sniffing around the water's edge. An elderly couple sauntered along behind the dog.

"Billy!" Sam yelled before he could claim the shaggy pooch as his own. "Don't you think you should ask those people if you can play with their dog?"

Billy—not exactly a shy kid—ran right up to the white-haired gentleman holding the jangling leash. He was almost as glad to let Billy play with the dog as the dog was.

Mac started to open another beer, but glanced at Samantha and seemed to reconsider. He poured a cup of coffee and dug a semimashed sweet roll out of the food sack, eating while he stared at the gray eternity of the sea. "Beats an eleven-man boat drill with only seven men," he observed equably.

Rick, who'd been watching Billy hurl Frisbees at the willing retriever, suddenly uttered a loud lunatic shout and rushed headlong into the Pacific. Water closed over his head with a shock that left no doubt about the season. Fall had fallen, and the water was *cold!* He touched bottom, raking his hands through the seaweed and muck. A medium-size kelp plant came to hand and he seized it at the root to hold himself down. Odd sensation.

He relaxed his grip on the kelp and let himself drift upward, postponing his return to what he now identified as the "other world" of air and light. Let the body wait; let every damn thing wait. Down here I have no problems. Down here I have no duties. Down here, it is hard to imagine why the first amphibians ever went to all that trouble to slink ashore.

His head broke the surface, and he took a brief gasp of air before falling back.

Rick floated for a moment, savoring the piercing saltiness of the ocean-rim atmosphere, then struck out for shore, swimming strongly and catching a wave to give him a free ride for the last twenty feet of the journey.

A vagrant breeze wandered past just as he stood up, and the sudden difference in temperature was startling.

Screaming like a kamikaze pilot, he sprinted back up the beach and flung a towel across his shoulders. Samantha poured a cup of coffee and handed it to him. Mac shook his head. "Crazy," he declared.

Rick managed a grin while clenching his jaw against a spasm of chill. "Getting old," he taunted. "Can't hack ocean swimming anymore."

Mac snorted and tossed an ice cube from the chest at Rick. "Get smart, you should have better sense than to go into the water without a wet suit, this time of year."

"Fine, once you get under."

"And colder than a witch's tit the moment you get out," Mac said.

Sam turned and said tight-lipped, "Mac! Billy will hear you."

Mac ignored her and continued, "Jesus, Rick—don't you get enough of that during the week?"

Rick grinned at him. "Ask Kiwi Kraus," he suggested. "Now, there's an unprejudiced witness."

Mac sighed, then relaxed again in the sand, nursing the remains of his coffee.

"Kiwi Kraus," he said, "is a good officer, a first-rate instructor, and a decent enough guy. I know you're not his biggest admirer. You're not supposed to love the instructors while you're in training, and they're not supposed to love you. They're supposed to teach you. And you're supposed to learn. But I'd sure like to know what else there is between the two of you. Because there's sure as hell something."

Rick shrugged and avoided his friend's eyes, keeping his own gaze carefully focused on a sloop that had just gone into irons trying to tack out of the bay.

"Just chemistry, I guess," he said.

"Chemistry. Un-huh. And maybe the way you damn near broke his nose for him."

Samantha was helping Billy sort through the cooler and was

handing him a can of apple juice instead of the Coke he wanted. But now she looked up at Rick.

"You did . . . that?"

"Uh, well, it was kind of an accident. I sneezed—and his head sort of got in the way."

"Bull!" Mac had been chewing on another mangled sweet roll, but now he swallowed the last bite and wagged his head in a way that left no room for discussion. "You set him up and coldcocked him in order to protect one of the men in your platoon," he declared. "That's what happened, and everyone knows it. Including Kiwi. You treated him, Sam," Mac said, turning his head to look at her. "What'd he tell you about how he got hurt?"

"Nothing. I mean, he said he fell down."

"Aw, Sam . . ."

She favored her brother with a crooked smile. "Working with the SEALs," she said, "you find yourself getting used to things like that—and to taking them at face value unless you really have to know the truth in order to assess damage."

It sounded logical to Rick.

"Well, anyway," Mac said, "I'd sure like to know what's biting him. At first, I thought it was just my imagination. The training's supposed to be tough, and making it seem unfair is just another part of the treatment. Ideally, every recruit is supposed to get the idea somewhere along the line that he's been singled out for special persecution."

Rick groaned inwardly and added a silent affirmation, but did not interrupt.

"And if that makes him quit, toss in his flippers, and ring himself out of the program, well, better to find out he can't take the heat then than when somebody's life might depend on him. But the thing Kiwi pulled with Durant was strictly grudge-time. It surprised me."

"Durant?" Samantha prompted.

"Nice kid in Rick's platoon. He had some kind of problem, and Kiwi picked on him deliberately, trying to get Rick to bilge by throwing a punch at the instructor."

Samantha blinked.

"Kiwi . . . did that?" she said, aiming the question at Rick.

"Maybe. I couldn't swear to it. Hard to prove."

"And so you . . ."

"Sneezed. I sneezed, and my head came down hard and collided with his nose. Accidentally."

"Accidentally."

She looked at Mac and then back at Rick, and Rick looked at the sea, and suddenly everybody was laughing, roaring and spilling coffee and snorting. Billy the Goat thought they'd all suddenly lost their minds.

But the laughter finally quieted and the coffee cups were refilled and Billy found a dime in the sand and went off to hunt for more buried treasure, and the initial reserve of strangers on party manners was forgotten and replaced by the easy talk of old friends.

Billy returned after a few minutes with a nickel and a quarter and the determination, now that the sun had come out, to go swimming. Samantha wasn't so sure. While Billy was able to dog-paddle, he didn't like to put his head underwater because it always seemed to make him choke.

Rick remembered having the same trouble at that age, so he took over and led Billy to a part of the beach where the very gentlest swell was coming in. There he showed him, by example and in easy stages, how to keep the water out of his nose. When Billy found that it worked, he wanted to swim to Japan. But Rick managed to sell him on the ocean jetty to their left as a more realistic objective, and they made it (again, in easy stages) with Rick treading water and offering a stabilizing arm.

Walking back, Billy's pride in his newfound ability was distracted when he spotted a baby crab that he thought might interest his mother, so they picked it up. Samantha was suitably impressed, though Rick finally persuaded the boy that the little side-crawler would be happier back in the water.

And that was when Mac's beeper came to life.

He jogged across the sand to a phone booth in the parking lot.

Ten minutes later he was back, looking apologetic. "Gotta get back," he said. "Some kinda flap."

No one asked questions, and Samantha began to gather up blankets—but Mac had another idea.

"No reason to break up the party," he said, "just because I

have to leave. Rick's car's big enough to get everyone back to the house. And, hell, I might even be able to get back before the day's over."

Samantha started to object, but the morning clouds were gone now, the skies were clear and California bright, and Billy wasn't ready to leave. So after token resistance, things were arranged as suggested. Or maybe, Rick thought later, as Mac had planned from the beginning.

Rick walked his friend to the car, thinking there might be something that needed to be said out of earshot of the others. But Mac seemed unconcerned despite the apparent emergency nature of his call, and by the time his car had vanished into traffic Rick had filed any questions he might have wanted to ask under "The Navy Has Its Reasons," and he turned to trudge back to the surf line. He was not at all surprised to discover that he was pleased at the idea of spending the rest of the day with Samantha.

"Everything okay?" she inquired when he was back and seated on the blanket beside her.

"Yeah. I guess so. He didn't talk about it."

Samantha nodded. "He doesn't. About the gill project, I mean. And it feels a little spooky, you know, because he used to talk about it a lot—before the Navy changed its mind and decided to go ahead."

Rick nodded, understanding. "Security's always a lot of fun."

Samantha rubbed a handful of suntan lotion into Billy's tender hide, and he trotted off in the direction of the water, intent on repeating his newfound swimming skills. He waded in hip deep and then submerged, only to surface a moment later, sputtering and crowing with the delight of growing confidence.

"Something," Samantha said, keeping her eye on Billy, "has been eating that brother of mine ever since he got back out here. At first I thought it was just that he was uptight about going through SEAL training again at his age. But it's more than that. And now these calls . . ."

"These? There've been more than this one?"

"All this week. He'll get home at night, looking tired, and I can see from the wrinkles in his fingertips that he's been in the water for hours. And then the phone rings and he takes it on the extension in his own bedroom, says a few words, and then either goes around with his eyes blank for an hour afterward or leaves the house. I don't even hear him come in sometimes."

"I thought Kiwi was helping him. I know he's one of the guys Mac picked for the gill development team, soon as this SEAL class graduates."

"Yes. But Kiwi can only help on weekends—and I know you've started doing a little of the testing, too. So don't worry. I'm used to Navy security. Mac and I have lived with it all our lives. First with our father. Did you know he was a Navy helicopter pilot? Went all the way through Korea without a scratch and then bought it flying as an instructor, training MedEvac chopper pilots for Nam."

Rick nodded soberly. A lot of fan jocks had gone that way.

"And then Mac," Samantha continued. "I was in my first year of med school when he joined the SEALs, and he missed my graduation because he was off doing something he could never talk about, and I knew better than to ask, but I promised myself I'd never go near any service—the Navy especially—because I hated secrets."

"But . . ."

Her nose wrinkled. "Yeah," she said. "But! But later the Navy had a surgical residency I wanted, in orthopedics, so I put on the uniform and told myself it was just temporary, until the obligatory time had been served. And of course all that changed when I married a Navy pilot . . . and found out we could hardly talk to each other because of the subjects that had to be avoided: Restricted. Classified. Secret. Top secret. Q clearance only. I knew the rules and I lived by them.

"So then," she said, "when he was assigned to your almost-alma-mater, the Fighter Weapons School at Miramar—Top Gun—I'd had plenty of training on how to be a 'good Navy wife' so naturally I didn't ask any questions. Not even when the man with the very correct uniform and the very correct manner came to the door to tell me my husband had been killed.

"But the truth is," she went on with hardly a pause for the memory, "I still hate secrets, and this is one of those times, and I'm tired of being a 'good Naval officer' and I'm worried about my brother, because if anything happened to him, I think I'd really curl up and die. And I'm not even allowed to do that! Billy wouldn't like it. So I suppose I'm laying all this on you now, spewing it out like a drunk on a talking jag, because you're a friend of Mac's. And maybe, too, because your own father must have been full of secrets."

Had the admiral been full of secrets? It was a whole new idea for him, and he turned it over in his mind for a moment, amazed that he hadn't put the question to himself before.

The answer was yes. Chances were that old Fang Carter had lived a whole, human, inner life that his self-absorbed son had never known about. Which, he decided, either made the son a lot dumber kid than Samantha had been, or a lot less lonely. It also gave him a whole new view of her, and of the admiral. He was on the verge of telling her so when Billy ventured too deep into the water and Samantha was on her feet, galloping for the surf line, with him a pace behind.

The boy was having a fine time with the new trick of submergence Rick had shown him, and after an admonitory phrase or two Samantha decided to let him enjoy it without parental interference. They walked back up the beach to the blankets in companionable silence.

But soon Rick found himself speculating aloud—for the very first time—about a visit he'd had with his father just before he was selected for the space program, and how he hadn't said anything about having a chance to fly the shuttle into space, and he'd finally found out about it from his mother, because his father simply never discussed things like that.

Remembering it now, and talking to Samantha about it, seemed somehow to put the whole situation more in perspective, to take the curse off, and he found himself telling her other things—things he'd even avoided thinking about in the past. Like wondering how it was that his parents had come to marry in the first place, and why having his stepfather praise every single thing he did didn't matter, while the discovery that no accomplishment of his could ever win the full and unconditional approval of his real father crushed him.

He then found himself listening with interest and real sympathy as Samantha recalled the day Mac had come to her school, taken her out of class, bought a hot fudge sundae, and told her that their father was dead. And how she'd never been able to forget the way she'd gone ahead and finished the ice cream, even with tears running down her cheeks. And how she'd then decided she was some kind of freak, because to this day she'd never been able to weep for her husband.

It was a long afternoon, but they were still talking when they noticed that the sun was on the horizon and they were the last people left on the beach. Billy was asleep, wrapped tight in a couple of beach blankets.

So they packed up, checked the boy's sunburn and decided it wasn't serious, and helped him kick down the remaining walls of the sand castle he'd built (though not without a long explanation of why it couldn't be brought home with them). At Rick's suggestion, they went to a "family" restaurant that offered hot dogs and abalone on the same menu. Billy insisted Rick put the top down on the convertible.

When they got home, Rick carried Billy inside and stood awkwardly for a moment at the door. He turned down the offer of a beer, then finally initiated what they both intended as a strictly social thank-you-and-good-night kiss.

But halfway through it wasn't like that anymore, and suddenly Rick realized that it had been a long, long time since he'd been anywhere near a real woman, and this was a very special one, indeed. The kiss went on to the point where Rick would either have to come inside, or stop. He stopped, and grinning like an idiot, he walked to the Mustang with a bounce in his step.

It was all very confusing. She was Mac's sister, and—what the hell—also the doctor whose decisions had grounded him. Besides, he had always made it a firm rule never to become involved with a woman who had children, outranked him, or had more problems than he did.

Only none of that seemed to be as important as it had a few hours earlier, and Rick found himself driving around aimlessly for more than an hour before finally heading to his off-base quarters in Imperial Beach.

He parked, fumbled absently for the towel and sandals he'd

stowed in the backseat, and walked across the driveway down the path to his apartment—where he found Kiwi Kraus waiting for him.

The SEAL instructor didn't waste words. "Gonna muckle into you," Kiwi declared without preamble. "Y'want it here or back at the base?"

Rick stared at him, puzzled. "What's it all about?"

"Had me a dinner date with Sam Deane," Kiwi said. "Shouldn't wondah she f'got. Came by her house, later. Saw you."

Rick wasn't really in the mood for a fight. But this one had been coming on since the day he first reported to the SEALs. Mac had been right when he said Kiwi was a good officer—he'd had a chance to see the little lobster-grabber operate at close quarters, and personal animosities aside, the guy was really first rate. He was exactly the man Rick would want beside him on any job that turned out to be technically complicated or potentially dangerous . . . such as testing the hemoglobin gill. But that didn't make them friends.

What remained was to choose the proper arena. There were security patrols at the base, and neighbors (not to mention police) here in town. But the apartment complex was only a block from the beach, and they walked there in silence.

The beach was deserted when they arrived, and the moon was down, leaving just a thin sprinkling of light from the city to work by, but their eyes were already becoming accustomed to the gloom. They settled the terms of engagement as they shed encumbering clothing.

"Any restrictions?" Rick inquired.

"Well . . . I don't plan to kill you."

"Sounds reasonable. And no broken bones—nothing the Navy would have to pay the bills for—except by accident, of course."

Kiwi thought it over. "Accidents do happen, sneezing boy," he said, shucking off the civilian sneakers he was wearing.

"They do, for a fact," Rick said, grinning to himself. "Uh . . . maybe I better take my shoes off, too."

"Yeah. Maybe you better do that."

Kiwi moved back courteously to give Rick room, then immediately launched a murderous shin-kick to the crotch that would have disabled Rick on the spot if it had connected.

Rick had had months of hard, professional training to learn the game by Kiwi's rules. Kiwi, he knew, had seen his personnel records, and he would know Rick had been on the boxing team at Annapolis. So Kiwi might expect a straight pugilistic approach. And if Kiwi thought that, Rick thought, I might be at an advantage.

Kiwi was an experienced and expert streetfighter. The other instructors drilled recruits in basic moves, but any refinements—and demonstrations of virtuoso technique—were his personal preserve. So Rick knew what he could expect from Kiwi, but Kiwi might still have one or two things to learn about the admiral's little boy.

Kiwi's schooling, like that of several other SEAL officers, had been in the martial arts. Time and service had honed these skills, refined them under the tutelage of masters from other disciplines and turned them deadly in a way his first teachers might have contemplated with horror. But his style had been formed in those earliest years, and it was clear—at least to Rick—every time he led a class in unarmed combat.

Rick, on the other hand, had done only enough in those classes to demonstrate proficiency and keep the instructors satisfied.

So he thought there might be a good chance now that Kiwi Kraus would not know that one of his instructors at preflight training had been a Marine gunnery sergeant named Shigeo Matsunaga, who was a former national champion in full-contact karate. Sergeant Shig had thought enough of Rick's aptitude for the sport to accept him as a private pupil in the karate school he ran as a side business in Pensacola.

So instead of offering a direct response to Kiwi's initial kick, Rick stepped back out of the immediate danger zone and let his mind see *saika*—the mental state that prepares for action by erasing all distraction—while giving a fair imitation of surprise and alarm. Kiwi seemed to buy it.

Confident of his own ability, Kiwi came boring in with a boxer's feint that seemed to be aimed at Rick's jaw but was actually intended to set up a hook-kick to the ribs. Rick avoided that, and the follow-up blow that went with it, while contriving to stumble and fall backward . . . thus giving himself a chance to scoop up a handful of sand.

He rolled to the side to avoid Kiwi's feet. Kiwi landed hard, twisted adroitly to avoid showing Rick his back . . . and left his face wide open to the sudden, blinding arrival of the sand.

Kiwi hadn't expected it. And he didn't like it.

Rick had time to land a single, hard kick to the temple, followed by a blunt-lance blow that might have turned Kiwi's lights out for the evening if it had landed in the soft area just below his ribs. But it didn't land there, and by the time Rick was able to follow with a double-hook combination, Kiwi had rolled out of range and could see him again.

Moving with new caution and respect, Kiwi prowled seaward before diving straight at Rick's midsection, and it was only be Sergeant Shig's training that Rick was able to match the movement in time to bring his right foot up to assist Kiwi's motion and then continue his own back roll in order to bring himself back to his feet, on guard. He quickly sidestepped and deflected a second line-plunge that arrived a full second earlier than he would have believed possible.

Rick managed to land a single kick on Kiwi's backside as he thundered past, but it was too slow to be really effective.

No doubt about it, the bastard was really good.

An exchange of stance attacks—Kiwi's to the head and Rick's to the midsection—did absolutely nothing for either fighter, and a tentative switch to aikido (three *atemi* by Rick were well counterpunched by Kiwi) accomplished little except to prove that both men had undergone some training in the Harmonious Energy discipline.

And then the party got rough. Rick caught Kiwi fairly with a double blunt-lance to the *juka* (an organ meridian located just below the armpit) and had the pleasure of seeing the training officer wince, but missed the low-aimed follow-up that went with it. Kiwi answered with a full-body kick that would have crushed his ribs and perhaps even stopped his heart if he hadn't been backing away when it landed.

The world around Rick darkened and narrowed, like an old-fashioned movie dissolve, and before he was able to bring his hands back into any kind of defensive attitude, Kiwi was on him, hammering the points of his shoulders and the back of his head. Rick went to his knees and slumped forward.

A moment later Rick might have been facedown in the sand, telling his troubles to the king of dreamland, but the fingers of the hand he stretched out to ward off Kiwi's blows landed on Kiwi's inseam, and Rick grabbed Kiwi's family jewels so hard that he started laughing—thinking if he squeezed hard enough he could take the jewels to the bank and put 'em in the safe deposit box.

It was enough.

Kiwi yelled—an explosive and heartfelt "Sonofahawah!"—and wrenched himself free, cupping his brass balls with both hands.

Rick rolled again, paused for a moment to breathe, then launched his body in a desperate arc toward Kiwi. Both men went down, scrambling and thrashing for advantage. But the momentary lull had allowed Kiwi to recuperate, and Rick found himself wobbling as the point of Kiwi's elbow caught him just under the right edge of his chin.

Blocking the turn-and-strike that followed was not easy, but he managed it and hung on to Kiwi's belt, using it to lever his own feet under him while throwing himself sideways in the hope of catching the instructor off-balance. The move failed—but it gave Rick an opportunity to drop to the sand, twisting his legs through Kiwi's in order to snap-kick his opponent's ankles, bringing him down hard, beside him.

Rick rolled, pressing the advantage. His leg came up as they flipped over, ending with an "Ooof" from Kiwi as Rick's whole weight came to rest on a single knee-point at the center of his stomach. Now he had Kiwi right where he wanted him.

But Rick was unable to press his advantage. As the fight came to a stop, Rick realized how much Kraus had taken out of him. He rolled off Kiwi and flopped on his back in the sand. For a moment, the only sounds were the waves rolling in and the heavy breathing of the two exhausted combatants. Finally Rick spoke.

"You gonna say uncle, Kraus?" Rick croaked, motionless.

"Fuck you," Kiwi responded wearily.

"You get on my nerves, Kraus, you know that? Everything about you bugs me—your voice, your hair, your ugly lobster pop-eyes, your after-shave. The way you walk bugs me, your goddamn accent bugs me—I don't think you've ever even been to Maine! You're not even human. You're a fucking hard-headed . . . lobster!"

Kiwi sat upright, staring out at the ocean. Rick continued to lie on his back, focusing on the stars.

"And what the fuck is your problem? Why do you have it in for me? You started picking on me the second I met you. Are you jealous because my father's an admiral? You got some grudge against him? Join the club, so do I. I've never gotten along with The Admiral, and I don't need your shit because you don't either. Fuck him.

"Said you were gonna run me out during hell week. But I took your shit, and took and took, and I made it. I'm tough, Kraus. But I figured you'd lay off after I made it. You didn't. And when I started working on the gill with you, I expected more of your crap, but it wasn't there. You've almost been *nice* to me, and I just don't get it. You got a human twin running around somewhere testing gills?

Kiwi rose to his feet and started walking away.

"Hey, you can't leave yet! You hear me?" Rick got up to go after him. "You gonna talk? Or do you want to fight some more?"

Kiwi nodded no. "I may be hardheaded, but I'm not stupid."

Rick walked a few paces away, just in case Kiwi had been lying and was planning to rush him.

But the SEAL instructor stopped in his tracks. Rick paced around for a few minutes while Kiwi gathered his thoughts.

"Sit down, Tallman," Kiwi said. "I'm done for the night—don't wanna fight no more."

Rick sat warily in the sand about ten feet away.

"I gave my word that I wouldn't have this talk with you, but I didn't figger you'd know how to fight," Kiwi said.

"Gave your word?" Rick said. "To who? What are you talking about?"

Both men spoke in low, calm voices.

"Tallman, I'm gonna talk frankly now. Face it—you've been a fuckup. Not as a SEAL, but before you got here. Annapolis, Princeton, and even Top Gun. I don't give a shit that you were number one in your class at Top Gun. You pissed it all away with your motorcycle crash. Stupid, stupid thing to do, and totally unnecessary.

"Well, I'm not going to let you be a fuckup as a SEAL. It's my job. All right, you saw through my little speech the first day 'cause you've been through the wringer before. All new recruits get the same one. But I know you better than you think I do, and maybe better than you know yourself, in some ways.

"You're good. Plain and simple. You got talent. Once in a while, it shows through. You know when? When the pressure's on. When others shrivel up and die, you come through smelling like a rose."

Rick was really puzzled. This was the last thing he ever expected to hear coming from Kiwi's mouth.

"Reason I know you is, I know your type. Seen 'em before. Rarely—one every five years or so, if that. Most of the real good ones don't have the discipline, 'cause everything comes so easy to them. It's natural: the quick reflexes, the sharp eyesight, the intuitive knowledge to make the right decision.

"I tell you, boy, I used to get jealous of guys like that—like you. Didn't come natural to me, so I had to bust my tail—work twice as hard just to be average. And you know something, Tallman? It's paid off, 'cause now I'm good. Still got to work on my skills—diving, running, endurance. If I stop, I go flat. You could prob'ly fly an F-14 with your eyes closed right now, even though you haven't done it in a year.

"So you got to be pushed. Every goddamn step of the way. And I'm the pusher. If I don't get all over your ass—you'll pass the course anyway. But you'll only be puttin' out halfway and say to yourself, 'This is too easy.' You get bored. Then you gonna get in trouble. You get bored, then you gonna drop the program. Well, let me tell you, mister, you ain't gonna get a chance to get bored. If the only way to get you through the SEAL program is to keep it at a difficult level so you have to work at it, then it's my job to provide you with the hard stuff to keep you interested. I'll throw the toughest stuff I got at you, and make you do it perfectly, and then I'll make you do it again. And I'm talkin' 'bout stuff I wouldn't expect the other recruits to handle at all.

"You could be an admiral, too, Tallman. But it's not a hereditary title. You don't get to be one just 'cause your daddy is one. Me—I'll never be an admiral, and if you want to think jealousy is what's driving me, fine. Go right ahead."

They sat silently for a moment, listening to the waves crash on the shore. Finally, Rick spoke.

"Ahhh, don't give me your patriotic bullshit about making me into the best damn SEAL there ever was. You're no altruist. You just plain don't like me."

"Altruism's got nothing to do with it. Patriotism either. Personally, I don't care if you become a chicken farmer. But I don't suppose you ever heard of loyalty, did you? Or friendship?"

"Don't change the subject."

"Shut up. I'm not changing the subject. I'm doing this as a favor to someone. Old friend of mine. Fellow by the name of Will Ward."

"Shit, he's my godfather!"

"Boy, you sure can be dumb under all the smarts you got. I know that. Your father sent you out here hoping the captain would be a good influence on you. Help you straighten up and fly right, so to speak. Ward knew me, knew you were entering SEAL training, and asked me to lean on you. He knows you pretty well, too. So indirectly, I'm helping out the admiral. He might not have been there when you needed him growing up, but I've got to give the guy credit for trying, now."

"Goddammit!" Rick yelled. "I'm not a little kid. I don't need this shitty reverse psychology!"

"Mister, I'm not asking you to like me, or to thank me. Just do what I tell you during training. And don't think for one second that just because I've told you all this, I'm going to let up on you. But realize this—I've got nothing personally against you. Next year I get a new class of green, snot-nosed recruits. Go through the same program. Some good kids, some assholes. Some make it through, some don't. So at the end of training, and not one moment before, you're going to be leaving here for active duty, and if you're lucky, you'll never have to see my ugly mug again.

"Now get out of here and get some rest. Training resumes at oh six hundred." And with that, Kiwi Kraus wobbled off into the night.

Murmansk, U.S.S.R.

Monday, September 22
3:45 A.M.

The best thing would be to kill himself; Andrey was sure of it now. For weeks—ever since his first glimpse of the future that had been planned for him and other members of the Temnota training unit—he had been toying with the thought. But now the time for a decision had come. Surgery, the first step toward that grotesque future, was scheduled for this morning.

Just enough time left to steal quietly out of his bunk, make his way to the head, and hang himself in the shower. It would be easy. They were on the second floor of the old barracks, a relic of the Great Patriotic War, and nothing had been modernized. Their fire escape system still consisted of a length of rope, knotted at intervals and connected to the floor by a ringbolt. Simply untie it (he had checked, there were no metal fittings; the rope was attached to the ring by a bowline knot) and tie the thing around your own neck in a running noose. Then loop the other end around the shower spout and relax your legs to let the noose take your whole weight. A trooper with medical training had told him once that it was the easiest and surest way to die; you lost consciousness almost at once when the brain's blood supply was cut off, and the strangulation part didn't begin until later.

Or if you wanted it the quick way, just leave the rope tied to the bolt in the floor—and jump out the window with it knotted around your neck.

This wasn't the first time he had thought of suicide. The idea had occurred to him when he heard that his wonderful cosmonaut father whom everyone admired had turned against the Rodina and had been arrested for making propaganda against the government. He had been home from the technical school, spending a holiday at the dacha near Baikonur Cosmodrome, and his mother had tried to keep the news from him. He had intended to do the deed by swallowing a bottle of the blue pills his mother kept for insomnia. He had locked himself in the bathroom late that night and sat staring for hours at a handful of them, waiting for the moment to stuff them into his mouth and drink the water in the glass by his elbow.

But the right moment had never seemed to come, nor had it arrived a few weeks later when he was expelled from school and sent home to await conscription.

Still, there had always been something oddly comforting about the very idea of suicide. It was a trapdoor, an emergency exit. No matter how bad things became, you always had the means of escape. In SPETSNAZ training, it was as close as the knife you carried in your boot or the pistol at your belt or the top of the climbing tower—and he had actually thought of doing it that way, once. Dive off, headfirst. Fifteen meters to the ground. One crunch . . .

It was this safety valve—the assurance that he could control his own destiny—that enabled him to get through the worst of basic training and survive the rigors of SPETSNAZ conditioning.

But if he permitted himself to live for one more day, and undergo the first of the surgical alterations necessary to become an operational member of the Temnota unit, he and the world he lived in would be forever changed.

Of course, the officers in charge of indoctrination explained in detail that the surgery would be reversed when their tour of duty was finished. A squad of SPETSNAZ troopers who had completed their tour readily displayed the scars of the restorative surgery. These men had all seemed healthy enough. Normal enough.

But the officers were liars; that much he had learned in his first week here at the Temnota base. They had told him that men eliminated from the program, dropped by their own request or for medical reasons, were simply returned to regular duty or perhaps even to civilian life. And this was not true.

Temnota candidates took turns acting as clerks and orderlies at Temnota battalion headquarters; his own turn had come on the third day of training, and during the long night watch he had tried to keep himself awake by reading through the files on the duty officer's desk. One of the files was an action roster, with disposal endorsements concerning men who had lost their lives in training accidents.

He had recognized two of the names. They were former members of his squad—men who had been dropped from training because they were allergic to the antichill injections. And now the records said they were dead, "accidentally killed" in training here at the Murmansk base. But those men had never been here. And now he was sure they had never even left the base at Odessa—nor had any of the others who were, for one reason or another, eliminated from Temnota training.

They had been silenced, that was all. Dropped off the edge of the world to make sure that they told no one of the project to which they had been so briefly assigned.

So there was no going back.

Murmansk, U.S.S.R.

Saturday, September 27
9:30 P.M.

Well, it was done, and he was still alive.

Spit was collecting in the back of his throat, and Andrey Narmonov swallowed painfully. The pain would go away, they said. By tomorrow, or the next day at most, it would be gone and he would have other things to think about.

And after all, what did it amount to? A hole in his neck. The hole—a tracheostomy, they called it—robbed him of the power of speech and smell because the trachea had surgically been closed just above the opening; taking air through the neck rather than through the nose and mouth deprived him of the ability to tell the difference between garlic and roses.

And he could only taste sweet, sour, bitter, and salt. All the rest, they said, was really a matter of smell, no matter how it seemed to him.

Worse was yet to come; they made no secret of it. The other operations, the ones altering the lungs, would not begin until the hole in the neck was healed and working properly. Of course there was always the escape hatch. Suicide.

One of the candidates had already taken that option. Fifteen minutes after he awoke and discovered that he could no longer speak, he had gone into the washroom at the end of the barracks and cut his throat the hard way, using the blade from his safety razor.

PART VI

PLANNING

San Clemente Island

Saturday, October 11
9:21A.M.

Rick saw the helmetless diver swimming along effortlessly about a hundred feet off the *Steel Albatross*'s port beam the first time he glanced sideways wearing the snoopers—and decided at once not to tell anyone about it. For the very best of reasons. No matter what his eyes might tell him, that diver absolutely could not be there.

He'd taken the boat deeper than they'd ever ventured before—two thousand feet beneath the surface of the Pacific, probing the trench that runs between the coastline and California's offshore islands—with the dual purpose of checking out her reactions under extreme pressure, and of testing the brand-new underwater-light-enhancement device that Mac had adapted from standard night vision optics.

The boat had come through this day's tests as she had come through all the others—with flying colors.

The snooper glasses, however, were something else altogether. Mac, who was in the boat's backseat, had nearly gone blind wearing them when Rick unthinkingly switched on the *Albatross*'s forward light array without warning.

The snoopers, originally designed to gather and intensify starlight (enabling soldiers to see and fight at night), had seemed ideal for use in the depths where bioluminescence and extremely low levels of sunlight were the only nonartificial sources of illumination. If the *Steel Albatross* was to be a silent vessel, designed for stealth, it seemed only reasonable that her operators be able to examine their surroundings without using light visible to the unaided eye.

To that end, the sub was fitted out with an infrared illuminator, and the snoopers had been modified to be supersensitive to that range of frequencies.

Mac had worked out the adaptation while using the gill and had made the dive with Rick in order to test them at depths where even the brightest sunlight could not penetrate.

Below six hundred feet, they were entirely dependent upon bioluminescence. But that seemed to be enough for the snooper lenses, although they tended to give everything a greenish tint. They had been working perfectly until the lights overloaded Mac's eyes and put him temporarily out of action. So Rick had volunteered to wear the snoopers himself . . . with the boat's headlights off.

He had looked over his left shoulder and the diver was there . . . doing just fine, thank you. The diver wasn't wearing a tank or a mask, and he moved briskly along with a kind of easy flutter kick, pointing the way for himself with a little flashlight attached to the top of his head, as if he were just an ordinary fellow!

Just dumb luck, Rick told himself, that the swimmer hadn't turned the light in the direction of the *Albatross*—and left him as blind as Mac.

Grimly, Rick tried to force himself to concentrate on operating the controls of the *Steel Albatross*. The underwater sailplane was approaching the limit of its planned dive for the day; he was supposed to take her to 2,400 feet—400 fathoms—and then bring her up, slowly. The boat was still sinking at the 120-feet-per-minute rate he'd cranked into the computer before beginning the dive, with only about 300 feet to go. Time to level off.

He touched the screen.

SA-1
CONTROL OPTIONS

Descend	Ascend
Monitor	Cancel

Rick touched ASCEND and began to work his way through the checklist.

But it was no use. Within seconds, he found himself sneaking glances to port once more, and he couldn't decide whether he was happy or not when he didn't see the swimmer.

Of course, the swimmer had been on a course roughly parallel to that of the *Albatross*. But the *Albatross* had been descending. Rick raised the angle of his gaze.

The swimmer was there, moving along at the same depth and on the same course as before. Rick hadn't seen him at first because the boat was nearly fifty feet lower than it had been at the first contact. But this time there could be no doubt. Rick wondered why the man did not seem to be aware that he was being watched. Surely if Rick could see him, he could see something as big as the *Steel Albatross*. No, that didn't follow. Rick was wearing snoopers, and the swimmer wasn't.

"Mac . . ."

"Yo?"

"How're your eyes, now?"

"Still got big black spots in the center of the world, but the edges are beginning to melt. I can see you, and the CRT, if I look around the corners."

"But not good enough to try the snoopers yourself?"

"No. Why—don't they work?"

"Uh . . . yeah. Sure. Of course. They work just fine. I thought you might . . ."

"Well, I can't."

"Yeah. Sorry."

"Shit happens. How's the boat doing?"

"Uh . . . fine."

The word came out wrong, strangled and mangled. And Mac noticed.

"Something wrong, buddy?"

"No. Nothing. I'm gonna take her up a little. Lemme know when you think you're ready to try the snoops again, huh?"

"Okay."

Rick touched the panel a final time, adjusting their ascent rate to one hundred feet per minute, and tried to concentrate on the controls.

But he couldn't take his eyes off the man swimming just above and to the left. . . .

Station "O"

Saturday, October 11
8:57 P.M., Moscow Time

The operation had to be coordinated to the second. Orders from Murmansk had been very clear about that. The explosion on the sea bottom had to occur at exactly 2101 hours—9:01 P.M., Moscow time—or heads would roll.

Mikhail Putin humped his back between strokes and checked the glowing face of his digital wristwatch. The detonator switch was ready in his hand. Nothing could go wrong. He was swimming easily, moving away from the spot where the charges had been set. He would be far enough away when it was time to press the button.

. . . 2058:00 . . .

Putin humped and wriggled his hips again. In the habitat, in the strange home the scientists had designed for their peculiar needs, one could almost be comfortable. Sleeping on the ceiling and walking upside down took getting used to. But there were compensations—of which release from the age-old grip of gravity was only one.

. . . 2059:00 . . .

But always there was the cold.

Putin shook himself, yielding to the impulse that his daily injections were supposed to eliminate. Shaking was a symptom of HPNS, a muscular disorder known to afflict human beings working in the ocean depths. So this feeling of cold was an illusion.

But it was a damned good illusion.

. . . 2100:00 . . .

Putin looked to his left and to his right.

Darkness. But that was no guarantee that the others had carried out their orders and gotten out of the way.

He remembered the early lectures at the demolitions school they had all attended. "Any fool can make an explosion," the senior instructor had told them. "The thing we are concerned with is making sure that the explosion happens when you want it to, and that you are somewhere else at that time."

In another week, the submarine would bring a new crew down to relieve them. Seven more days, and he'd be able to breathe air again.

. . . 2100:45 . . . 2100:46 . . . 2100:47 . . .

His fingers tightened on the switch.

San Clemente Island

Saturday, October 11
10:02 A.M.

When the initial shock wave hit, the *Steel Albatross* violently skewed to port. Rick was still fighting for control when the main shock arrived, rotating the boat on all three axes simultaneously. The control screen display flickered, blacked out momentarily, and then gradually reassembled itself while Rick fought to bring the *Albatross* back to level. He made a mental note to have all control surfaces and linkages checked for damage when they got back to the *Berkone.*

The story told by the CRT was not comforting. The *Albatross* was about ten fathoms higher than it had been a few moments earlier and was rising at a rate in excess of a hundred feet per minute, but . . . proceeding in a direction he hadn't picked. He corrected both problems and was relieved to find the boat's controls responsive.

"Shit-a-mighty!" Mac said.

"I'll drink to that."

"Got any idea what it was?"

"Not a clue. You're the longtime underwater man . . . you remember running into anything like it before?"

There was a moment of silence.

"Uh . . . once or twice," Mac said slowly. "Yeah. But those times were both expected—major underwater explosions we'd set off ourselves."

"Then that's what it must have been."

"No way!"

"Why not?"

"Because we got laws about things like that—I mean right up the gazoo. You want to pop a cap in coastal waters, you let everyone in on the secret and deal with the objections beforehand. Not after."

"Well, maybe it was us—the SEALs, I mean—one of the Teams, training out here at the island?"

Mac shook his head again. "Teams, schmeams," he said. "Doesn't matter who or when: You give notice. So if it was an explosion, it wasn't anything that was on anybody's agenda."

But there were others . . . with agendas. Rick craned his neck, searching the sea around them as the *Steel Albatross* glided toward the surface.

Nothing there but good old familiar, green seawater. Yet he was haunted by the memory of seeing a man swimming without mask or other gear at a depth of 2,100 feet.

Mac hadn't seen the swimmer, though, and it seemed far too late to tell him about it. Rick pushed the thought of the swimming man firmly to one side and set himself to deal with more immediate concerns, touching a button labeled ELF for "extremely low frequency" radio, the Navy's special submarine communications system. ELF equipment was new on board, and Rick did not usually monitor its traffic; the *Albatross* was still not officially a Navy project, and the system had been installed for use only in emergency. But he had already decided the present situation showed every sign of being in the emergency category—regardless of the fact that the boat did not, for the moment, appear to be in immediate peril—and was psyching himself up to defend his use of the ELF frequency to contact the *Berkone*, when he discovered the decision had already been made. By others.

". . . *Albatross* . . . ," the radio squawked. "Sierra Alpha One, this is Berkone, do you read? Vessel Five to Sierra Alfa One, do you read? Over." Captain Ward sounded grim.

"Uh . . . Sierra Alpha One, Berkone. Read you five-square. Over."

"Sierra Alfa One, abort mission. Return to surface at once.

I say again, abort and return to surface. Do you copy? Over."

"Uh . . . roger, Berkone. Sierra Alfa One copies. Wilco. Surfacing in . . . uh . . . "—Rick ran through the depth-over-time equation—". . . in thirty-three minutes. Over."

"Sierra Alfa One, understand one zero four six ETA surface. Is this correct? Over."

"Uh . . . one zero four six is roger, Berkone. Sierra Alfa One, out."

The shock waves that had hammered the *Albatross*, Rick knew, could not have gone undetected on the surface. Captain Ward's use of ELF to contact them and his order to abort their dive could have been prompted by nothing else. But what the hell was going on?

Rick's fingers drummed impatiently on the stick and he forced himself to count off the numbers in sixes as they paraded across the depth indicator on the video screen, converting everything into fathoms, diverting his mind from speculation.

"Surface! Prepare to surface!"

Mac's vocal warning was almost smothered by the raucous bawling of a horn—a new warning device added by Captain Ward during the past week—and Rick swore under his breath.

"Sierra Alfa One, on the surface, one zero three niner," he said when they had reestablished communication with the *Berkone*. "Awaiting tow, over."

"R-Rog, Sierra Alfa One." Captain Ward's voice seemed oddly harsh on the cockpit speaker. Report your status, please. Over."

Rick glanced over his shoulder at Mac, who shrugged.

"Sierra Alfa One. Status normal," Rick said. "Mission aborted as ordered. Retrieval team in sight. Over."

There was a moment of hesitation before the captain responded, and when he finally spoke, it was with tension. "Thank God," the old man said. "For a minute there, I thought I'd killed the both of you."

On Board *Berkone*

Saturday, October 11
10:50 A.M.

The *Steel Albatross* had surfaced just abeam of the *Berkone*, and divers were in the water—attaching lines to the submarine in order to draw her back into her moon-pool berth—by the time Rick and Mac had cracked the hatch and collected their gear.

Stoically, the two aquanauts refrained from asking Captain Ward any questions over the radio. They didn't speak until all three were alone in the *Berkone*'s lounge-cum-wardroom.

"All right, then," Rick said. "The *Albatross* is fine. Mac and I are all right—see; not a scratch—and besides, we went down there to test the boat's escape system anyway, didn't we? So what the hell was all that about an emergency abort?"

"Not to mention how you thought you'd killed us?" Mac added.

Captain Ward just looked at them for a moment. "A test," he said in a lecturing tone, "is a scientific enterprise, fully controlled and with plenty of margin for error. If it doesn't work, you get to try again. But this thing . . ."

"You mean the—little surge?" Rick said.

"Little surge?" Ward said. "Little surge? Well, okay, you two don't know yet. All you felt was . . . tell me, what did you feel down there?"

Rick and Mac exchanged glances.

"Just what I told you," Rick said. "A surge. Like a sharp crosswind or a wind shear, in the air."

The captain nodded. "Nothing else? Anything at all . . ."

"No."

The captain looked at Mac, who shook his head, seconding Rick's negative.

"And nothing—odd—on the instruments?"

"We had a brief power outage but the standard display returned. And then the order to surface."

The captain thought it over for a moment, glancing out the

window toward San Clemente Island. Then he sighed and shook his head.

"Officially," he said, still not facing the two younger men, "this was a local oceanic disturbance. It'll be reported that way by Scripps and whoever else takes note of it. And Christ help us, I hope most people will really believe that's what it was."

"But it wasn't?"

"No."

The captain walked over to the coffee urn and poured himself a cup of hot, rich Navy-style brew.

"What happened," Captain Ward said, "originated somewhere north of here. But not far north. Probably off the coast of Las Olinas. You're both cleared to hear what I'm going to tell you now. And you have a need, not to mention a right, to know.

"We still don't know all the facts," Captain Ward went on, "but we can make some guesses. We think some kind of explosion occurred on the floor of the ocean. Now, that in itself wouldn't be any big thing. Not usual—I don't think anything like that's happened around here for a hell of a while, though I'll have to talk to someone back at Scripps to find out just when the last time was. But the point is, it's something that has happened before and can be expected to happen again because we're sitting on what's called the Pacific Ring of Fire."

Rick and Mac nodded almost simultaneously.

"Apparently the whole Pacific basin is rotating," Mac said. "Moving in a different direction from the continental tectonic plates. So this leaves faults in the earth that give us earthquakes—and volcanoes—along a line from Japan to the Aleutians to Alaska to California and so on south."

Rick nodded. "One of those faults," he said, "probably moved around today while we were down below, and we took a little surge from it. Nothing we couldn't handle. So . . . what's the big deal?"

"The big deal," Ward replied, "is that this time something happened that we didn't expect. Something we never thought a normal blowout—or even a man-made explosion that wasn't nuclear—could achieve. Tell me, have either of you ever heard of an event called an EMP?"

Mac hadn't, and his negative head-shake was almost automatic.

"Electromagnetic pulse," Rick said. "It's something we got lectures about at Top Gun. An EMP," he continued, "is a kind of electronic plasma-wave usually generated by high-altitude nuclear explosions."

Mac interrupted. "You mean—like the Bomb?"

"Yeah."

"Jesus!"

"And that, right there, is the whole thing," Captain Ward said. "Because originally we thought electromagnetic pulses were strictly a celestial oddity. We knew EMPs happened; they were measurable and we'd been recording them for years. But only on the face of the sun. Lots of EMPs there, see? Solar storms would raise hell with radio—and even wire communications—here on earth. Happened from time to time. All very natural."

"Only now, we can make them ourselves?"

"Uh . . . well, yeah. Sorta." The captain shook his head. "Damn it, I know enough nuclear physics to rate command of a modern submarine. But that doesn't make me a nuclear physicist, so the best I can come up with is to tell you we never had any idea that EMPs could happen anywhere except on the surface of a star until we started testing nuclear weapons."

"You mean . . . ?"

"Electromagnetic pulses," Ward said, "can be generated in a couple of ways: nuclear explosions, or high-power, narrow-beam krypton-fluoride laser equipment."

"Lasers?" Mac said, startled.

"Yes," the captain said. "But not the little lasers they use for surgery or to drill holes in dense matter. Or even the kind they have for limited-range communications. We're talking big here. The kind you aim into space to disable satellites. High-power lasers, especially in the orange part of the spectrum, release this electromagnetic plasma cloud as a kind of a by-product. Which is why you have to set up some kind of shielding around any computers you want to use in connection with laser installations.

"But we know the Soviets have been doing side-by-side studies, along with their nuclear-weapons research, which are directed at EMP production by nuclear and other means. They want to be able to produce an EMP strong enough to defeat any shielding currently in use. It makes me wonder if they've come up with a scheme to do just that on a large scale. If they have, and if this is a small-scale test of that scheme, then they could have the capability of sending an electromagnetic pulse across the U.S. at ground level, knocking out every electronic device we have."

"Which could include the command and control centers for all our computer-operated weapons systems."

"Yep. Now the question is, are we shielded well enough to counter this new threat?"

"Jesus Christ!"

"A defense nightmare," the captain agreed solemnly. "And the threat is very real. The answer, of course, is to protect the most important stuff, while making plans to operate at least temporarily without the aid of anything that isn't protected. And that's just exactly what a committee of the National Academy of Sciences urged the Defense Department to do as soon as the effect was analyzed and fully appreciated."

"So they did it?"

"Well, yeah. Or anyway, they did as well as they could under the circumstances. Like I said, you can't shield every damn thing in the whole country. Deciding what you can and can't do—or should or should not do—is a judgment call, every time."

"And sometimes, the judgment isn't so hot. Right?"

"It's a king-size pain in the butt," the captain admitted. "You'd never believe the kind of money it costs to make sure a really vital mainframe computer isn't going to show you a dead screen just when you need it most. Also, the shielding is cumbersome and takes a hell of a long time to install. And no one wants the responsibility for making all the decisions, so the first thing you do is appoint a committee—"

Mac and Rick made rude noises at the same moment and laughed grimly.

"—and then the committee sets up guidelines. Then it's nobody's responsibility."

"So of course the work goes even more slowly," Rick said.

"And some," Mac chimed in, "doesn't get done at all."

"How'd ya guess? Anyway, little by little—damn little, some years—it goes along, with weapons systems getting first attention. And then command centers. And after that, if there is an after that, they'll maybe start thinking about whatever is left over. And that, friends, is where we arrive at yet another way to generate an EMP . . . something a little easier to manage than a solar storm or a nuclear blast. Or even a real good laser beam. Because once you've got the electromagnetic shielding in place, the next step has to be . . ."

The captain paused, waiting for someone to supply the next word.

"Testing!" Rick said.

The captain grinned sourly and nodded at Rick. "No one wants to spend a couple of zillion bucks on guesswork," he said. "They'd never get a plug nickel without being able to prove the shielding works."

"So someone," Mac said, "figured out a way to generate a tame EMP. Something usable on a kind of laboratory basis."

This time the captain managed a laugh. "Tame," he said, "is a kind of relative term. But yeah. They figured out how to generate a wave small enough to test military hardware and software. Only trouble is, the equipment we use to generate a little bitty thing like that ain't small. In fact, last I heard it was a lot bigger than even the largest laser installation."

"Uh . . . how big is that?" Rick inquired.

"Well . . . big enough so you can't hide the damn thing, anyway," Captain Ward said. "The antenna array they use over at Kirtland Air Force Base, for instance, is big enough that when a magazine printed a picture of it being used to test the computer shielding on board a B-1 bomber, they had to put a line in the caption to tell you where the airplane was."

Mac whistled. "Not exactly a hip-pocket gadget."

"No. Or anyway, the first ones weren't. I understand they've got a much smaller model, now. Something you could camouflage anyway. But that's only scuttlebutt, really, because we've just about stopped making those tests."

"But why, for God's sake?"

"Someone didn't like them. And they filed a lawsuit . . . and that was that. In 1987, an organization called the Foundation on Economic Trends joined up with a bunch of environmental types—the Potomac River Association—and went to court with an argument that EMPs generated by the test equipment could hurt wildlife, or maybe screw up electronic equipment, outside the designated test areas."

"Well . . . does it?"

"Shit, no! Anyone with enough physics to get through high school could tell you that lightning would have a lot more effect on wildlife—or computers—than any side effect from an EMP generator. My God, you got to put something in the very center of the array at Kirtland to get enough effect to make the test valid!"

Mac sighed. "But the courts didn't see it that way."

"How'd you guess? In '88 the Defense Department caved in. Rather than go through all the hay and horseshit of a drawn-out legal action, they decided to negotiate the whole thing, and a federal judge signed a consent order that shut down just about everything until the government can come up with an 'environmental assessment' of the effects of the generators."

"Which could take months, or years."

"At least. And even then, if the environmental boys and girls don't like what the assessment says, they can go right back to court and tie you up again and keep doing it until hell freezes over."

There was a moment of silence while all hands pondered the strange and wonderful ways of democracy.

Rick asked finally, "Did they shut down every single one of the generators?"

"Well, no—not quite," the captain admitted. "The Army shut down its EMP simulators at Woodbridge, Virginia, at White Sands, New Mexico, and at the Redstone Arsenal in Alabama. And the Navy shut down its simulator at Patuxent River, Maryland, and another they called the Empress I on Chesapeake Bay. They even agreed not to operate a barge-towed simulator known as the Empress II that was built for testing whole warships.

"But the one I told you about at Kirtland is still up and running. It's the joint property of the Air Force and the Nuclear Defense Agency, and I guess the ecologists figured it was too far out in the boonies to do a helluva lot of harm . . . but a leader of one of the environmental groups said his people may go after it later."

"Okay, then," Rick said. "That's the testing devices. But let's get back to what happened today."

"Suits me," Captain Ward said. "What can I tell you that you don't already know?"

Rick grinned at him. "Well, the quick answer would be 'everything' because I'm still way behind the starting line, here. But for right now, maybe you could start by telling us exactly what it was that got everybody so uptight today. I mean—all right—I get the general idea that we've had an EMP hereabouts, and it wasn't generated in any of the ways we know about and are used to, but seems to have come in a kind of a package with a blowout on the ocean floor."

The captain nodded.

"I also get the impression," Rick continued, "that the EMP was a surprise because none of the previous ocean blowouts triggered any kind of electromagnetic whozis."

The captain nodded again.

"So . . . the bottom line is, how come this particular blowout—if that's what it was—caused an EMP when none of the others did?"

But Captain Ward only shrugged. "Wish I could help you, Ricky."

Rick blinked, looking at him.

"Like I told you," the captain said, "we had an EMP here that was apparently associated with an ocean-floor disturbance off Las Olinas. Now, the two events may have a cause-and-effect relationship. Or they could be connected some other way that we don't know about, yet."

"Yes, but—"

"—but, that's really all I know. Except, of course, that I also know I sure don't understand it. And I'm willing to bet no-one else does, either."

Mac, who had been listening in silence, spoke up. "You sure this was a natural occurrence?"

"Not for a damn moment," Ward said. "The idea that it was natural was just someone's first guess. They'll be double-checking everything and arguing about it for weeks. And even then they may not come up with anything definite."

"Oh. I just wondered if it could have been something else."

"No, absolutely not. The explosion wasn't nuclear in any sense."

"Just wondered."

"Just wondered"—the captain nodded—"if this could be a small-yield tactical nuke—to generate the EMP? That was my first guess, too."

"How can you be so sure, so soon?" Rick asked. "I mean—"

"No radiation. It's just that simple, Ricky. No radiation; no nuclear pollution of the waters around where the blast occurred."

"So what's left, far as we can see, is a perfectly natural occurrence. And that is where the whole thing turns a tad weird, because if the EMP was a natural result of a natural blowout, then why the hell haven't we detected it before?"

"And if, on the other hand, it wasn't natural," Mac finished the thought for him, "then we've got to find out whether either event—the blowout, or the EMP—was man-made."

"And if so, how," the captain said, nodding. "And why. And is it gonna happen again?"

"So," Rick butted in, "it's a scientific problem and a big surprise—but how come it was an emergency for the *Albatross*? We had a little frammis down there when the shock waves hit. Knocked us around. The boat wasn't damaged, and at that depth I think we'd have found out about it in a hurry. But it was still such a big emergency you got through to the Navy, had them to call us on the ELF transmitter so we'd abort at once . . . before you even checked with us to see if the boat was damaged?"

"Fact is," Ward said in a quiet voice, "if you hadn't answered the ELF message, we were ready to mount a full-scale deep-rescue effort without a moment's delay."

Both Rick and Mac looked blank. But the captain wasn't through.

"Think about that fancy-dan control system I was so proud of building into the SA-1. It's a computer, right? And it's in control of the boat; even decides whether it wants to let you crack the hatches or flood the control compartment in order to abandon ship."

The full implication of Ward's words hit Rick and Mac at the same moment, and their reaction came in unison.

"Christ!"

"And to top it all off," Captain Ward continued, "in all the hurry to get the thing built and tested, I had neglected one of the prime considerations of any kind of undersea engineering. I had forgotten all about redundancy. There was no backup. No manual override for a failed computer. Goddammit—don't just stand there taking up space. Get mad at me! I'm the son of a bitch who just risked both your lives unnecessarily!

"Whatever caused the EMP, if it had happened just a little tiny bit closer to here, you two could have been stuck on the bottom of the ocean in a disabled boat. Stranded, with no way in hell to bring her up, or even abandon ship."

Captain Ward and MacDougall exchanged glances.

Rick's eyes, however, never strayed from the linoleum beneath his feet. His mind was half a mile away—straight down. On balance, though, it seemed the wrong time to mention the swimmer he had seen churning along 2,100 feet beneath the surface of the ocean.

You had to be careful about reporting things like that.

Moscow, U.S.S.R.

Saturday, October 11
11:51 P.M.

Viktor Tregorin sat with a chunk of black bread generously smeared with sweet butter and strawberry jam. The butter and jam were items most of his countrymen couldn't afford even if the state-run supermarkets carried them. He chewed methodically as he made his diary entry for the day.

Though the red leather volume was not the official catalogue of the progress of Project Temnota, it contained his personal feelings and musings. The cold, hard facts were being recorded for posterity in the files in his Kremlin office. Someday—

soon—they would become important archival materials delineating the steps that changed Mother Russia's world standing.

> The test of Project Temnota was a success! At precisely 9:01 P.M., Moscow time, a small EMP, generated by the laser-enhanced explosion set by one of our Station "O" frogmen, was induced through the cable splice to the Las Olinas power station. In order to mask the actual source of the disturbance, a weak EMP signal was generated by the Cosmos 2300 satellite. It had no physical effect, but was strong enough to be detected. The effect of the explosion on the sea surface and their seismographs was noted, and the Americans thought that the blackout in Las Olinas was due to seismic activity under the sea. When they match the timing of the EMP with the pulse from the Cosmos 2300, they will point their fingers at our general secretary.
>
> It is not premature, I believe, to call Temnota a brilliant plan. The success of Temnota will culminate years of planning and will make a lifelong dream come true. When Temnota succeeds, our socialist state will be firmly in control of world affairs for centuries to come. I am afraid of but one thing. Without the United States, we will have only ourselves to blame if the ideal communist state is not achieved.

Tregorin shifted his position in his chair, moving the diary from one knee to the other.

> On a more somber note, I have arranged for the GRU's best marksman to be sent to Israel to carry out the apparent assassination attempt against Comrade Petchukocov. I am most sorry to do this to such an old and loyal friend, but it is for the good of the country. And it is vital to the success of Temnota.
>
> Of course, Petchukocov will not be killed. I need an excellent shot so that he is merely wounded—in the arm or leg, perhaps. But it must appear to be an attempt to silence a traitor. I feel like a magician sometimes, fooling the people with a flourish of one hand, while the other hand does the necessary work. I can hardly believe I hold the future of the Soviet Union in my hands. It is exciting to plan. And I am the mastermind who will have put all the pieces in their proper place.
>
> I am saddened that a talented and useful GRU assassin must be sacrificed for our cause. I have forwarded a detailed description of the man to an intermediary in Tel Aviv who will pass

the information on to Mossad. The moment the GRU assassin pulls the trigger, an Israeli hit man will silence him forever. He cannot be trusted to live with the knowledge he possesses.

Comrade P.'s wounding will give credence to his initial story that Temnota is under the sea. But Comrade P. believes this to be a lie. Naturally, when Israeli intelligence questions Comrade P., he will tell them, under great duress, that Temnota is in the sky. Petchukocov believes this to be the truth, and the only way he will reveal this is under torture. They will believe him!

Tregorin closed the book and returned it to its hiding place, propping up a leg of the wobbly table next to his bed. He went back to his bread and jam. Plotting gave him a good appetite.

Tel Aviv, Israel

Sunday, October 12
6:33 A.M.

The bastards certainly did not make themselves easy to find.

Carefully, not wishing to stumble, for the sidewalk was broken and uneven in this part of town, the old man made his way through the darkness to the door it had taken him nearly four hours to find.

Ah! This was it: 228B. The door.

Not much to look at; just a wooden door with nothing outside to identify it as the headquarters of an official security agency. A place of spies.

Taking a deep breath, and expelling it noisily through his hairy nostrils, the old man raised his knuckles and rapped—once, twice, three times—on the center panel of the door.

It was opened at once by a man whose face was obscured by the spill of dim light coming from somewhere behind him. "Yes?" he said in English.

"My name is Petchukocov," the old man said, also in English because that language came easily to him from his days at the United Nations, and because he really did not think the doorkeeper spoke Russian. "Dimitri Fedorovich Petchukocov. I am a fugitive, in fear for my life."

PART VII

INITIAL CONTACT

Las Olinas, California

Saturday, October 11
10:00 A.M.

"Mommy, how come we have to go to the mall?" Billy asked while Samantha tried to pay attention to Saturday-morning traffic.

"Because you're growing so fast you need a new pair of shoes already. And there's a sale on shoes at the mall."

"But I don't like shoes. What the hell is wrong with sneakers?" Billy grinned, knowing that his words would have an effect.

"If you keep talking like that, I'm not going to let Uncle Mac take you to the zoo anymore," Sam said as she coasted to a stop. The sign for the mall was now in sight, just a few traffic lights away.

"I don't care. I want to go with Uncle Rick."

"He's not your uncle, Billy. He's just Mac's friend."

"Don't you like him, Mommy? I think he's cool."

"Yes, I do like him. And tell me, how could a little boy like you get so smart?"

"Oh, Mommy. You forgot. I'm in kindergarten already." Billy bounced up and down on the seat, wishing he could see over the dashboard, wishing he could *drive*.

"Well, maybe Rick will come over again."

"Yeah!" Billy yelled.

"Maybe . . . if he's a good boy."

The light changed and Sam shifted the small hatchback into first. They made it halfway to the next light when all traffic came to a halt. Horns honked like a flock of angry geese, but no one moved. Sam stuck her head out the open window to see if there was an accident. But she hadn't heard the jarring crunch of metal against metal. Her flame-red hair swung in the morning sunlight as she looked behind her. Traffic was at a standstill in the opposite direction as well.

"Are we there yet?" Billy asked.

But Sam ignored him. She turned on the radio. All the stations were coming in fine, except the Las Olinas station. Strange, she thought. And then she looked at the traffic light. It had gone out. In fact, all the lights seemed to have gone out at the same time.

So this must be, she thought, what it was like in New York. This must be what happens when there's a blackout.

Station "O"

Tuesday, October 14
7:48 A.M., Moscow Time

Everyone on the relief team knew something had happened. Andrey was sure of it, and he knew the others felt the same.

Only five men had been at Station "O" when his six-man relief team arrived, and two of the five had to be assisted from the habitat to the submarine waiting to take them back to Murmansk.

But though the members of Andrey's team were the only ones who could actually go from the submarine to the habitat—and therefore the only ones able to carry out the evacuation—they were forbidden to use sign language or dot-and-dash code to ask the obvious questions of the trooper/frogmen they were relieving.

Yet he desperately wanted to ask questions, and get real answers, before the submarine closed its waterlock and turned toward home.

They would be here for six months—six months of such

isolation as no men, anywhere, had ever had to endure in the past. Not even in space. And to ask them to face such an ordeal in ignorance of whatever mishap had befallen their predecessors was simply beyond understanding. Were they slaves?

Angry, and for the first time in his life not unwilling to show it, Andrey crossed the dark space between the habitat and the submarine, passed through the waterlock, reattached the air-to-water throat hose, and sought out the warrant officer responsible for getting Temnota teams safely through the exchange.

The *michman* was busy and tried to put him off. But Andrey made signs demanding an explanation—and intimating that he would not return to the habitat until he was satisfied.

Writing slowly with a crayon on a special slate, and glancing repeatedly at Andrey from the corner of his eyes, the *michman* set down a minimal account of the mishap.

"An explosion . . . four men out of position . . . one was not seen again."

Andrey looked at the *michman*, hoping for something more. But the warrant officer had given up all the information he was going to give. Even that was better than nothing. But it still raised more questions than it answered.

What kind of explosion?

Had a search been made for the missing man?

But this time the *michman* was adamant. No more questions. No more answers. Return to your post at once. Or die.

Andrey read the words. At least he would have something to tell the others when he returned. Perhaps they could work out the rest for themselves, checking through the logs and other artifacts left behind by their predecessors.

Anyhow, it would be something to do. Something to keep from going crazy. Something to pass the time.

Coronado, California

Tuesday, October 14
8:44 P.M.

It was settling in to be a long night.

When Rick rode out to the drop point in his cocoon of wet suit and closed-circuit diving gear, the instructor mentioned the water temperature: forty-two degrees.

He had been cold before. While it wasn't his idea of fun, it was a little like hitting yourself over the head with a hammer. Felt wonderful when you stopped. The first shock of contact with the ocean when he and his dive buddy were dropped from the boat was far worse than anything he had imagined. It felt as if his body were freezing from the inside out. But countless hours of training paid off as Rick's legs scissored and thrusted, driving him downward as he "prepared himself for the evolution," which was how they put it in SEAL lingo. No sense wasting time.

Even with the illuminated compass-board before him, Rick's vision was only six inches in the inky water, and he found himself wishing he had the "snooper" goggles he had worn in the *Steel Albatross*. Even at the risk of seeing another scubaless frogman swimming nearby. Anything would be better than unrelieved darkness.

His dive buddy, Swenson—a fresh-faced brewery worker turned torpedo man from Milwaukee—was down there with him, acting as lookout and depth monitor as Rick guided them toward the target . . . a floating raft that they would theoretically demolish with limpet charges before swimming away to the assigned pickup point.

But the swim seemed to go on forever, and Rick found himself checking the radiant dial of his watch more than required for navigation purposes. He ordered himself to stop, and when he checked the dial again, he realized that only a single minute had passed since his last scan.

Combat swimming wasn't as easy as he'd expected it to be. It wasn't as bad as hell week, either. More and more he discovered that he tended to rate levels of difficulty on a scale arranged with hell week at the top with a ten—and everything else somewhere below. On that scale, swimming through black, 42-degree water with no guide but the compass board and a schedule memorized during briefing rated around a six. Seven at the most. Well . . . call it eight.

A squeeze on the arm from Swenson brought his concentration back to the mission. They were still on course and there had been no follow-up signal, so depth must still be okay. But Swenson didn't give signals for no reason.

Rick looked again at his wristwatch—and was startled to discover that he'd waited almost too long for an elapsed-time check. The watch dial said they had arrived.

If his estimate of their swimming speed—and his guess at the location of their drop point and the briefing officer's information about the probable direction and speed of the current and his underwater navigation with the compass board—was right on the money, then they should surface within easy striking distance of the target.

Rick was pleased to note a little glow of confidence as he led the way to the surface—and not at all surprised to find the target float just twenty yards astern. They had overshot, but not too badly after a three-mile underwater swim.

He touched Swenson's arm, making sure his swim buddy saw the target, too, then ducked under the surface again to "arm" the dummy explosive charge they had brought with them.

Together the two frogmen approached at a depth of a fathom, coming in on the float's up-current side and allowing the two-knot movement to drift them in for a perfectly soundless approach. So far, so good. Now to plant the charge . . . and clear the area before the timer said it had "exploded."

But self-congratulations were premature. Rick and Swenson were still drifting in, groping for the underwater hull of the target, when a disturbance in the water nearby told them they were not alone. Rick grimaced inside the mask and kicked himself mentally. This was supposed to be a combat simulation, and he should have expected at least minimal security measures. A team of instructors, assigned to roles as an opposing guard force, was in the water nearby. Rick touched

Swenson's arm, ready to signal immediate deep submergence—but never got the opportunity.

Another hand, not Swenson's, clamped down on his own wrist and would not be dislodged.

End of exercise, bozo.

Close . . . but no cigar.

Wearily, letting the instructor do most of the work, Rick permitted himself to be led to the surface and directed to the target float, where a nod of the head indicated that he was to go up the ladder to the deck. The instructor came aboard behind him, followed by Swenson and his own instructor captor. But the first words spoken when gear had been adjusted to allow voice communication were a surprise. "Mr. Tallman?"

The instructor nearest him was squinting, his eyes obviously not yet night adjusted.

"I'm Tallman," Rick said.

"Good. They thought you might be first in—and that saves us a long night's work."

Rick started to reply, then stopped, nonplussed. But the instructor wasn't trying to keep him in suspense.

"This isn't part of the evolution," the man said. "Sorry, Swenson. You'll have to swim the whole thing again tomorrow night. 'Cause we got to borrow your buddy."

The other instructor was at the far end of the float, speaking quietly into his walkie-talkie.

"Orders," the instructor not occupied with the radio contact said. "Relayed from the training office, sir. Via Mr. Kraus. They got a chopper laid on to take you back to the base to change your clothes."

Rick thought it over for a moment, then shook his head. "They give you any idea why they'd want me back there as bad as all that?"

"No, sir. Just find you and call the copter when we do. And tell you you're officially administrative status, as of now."

As opposed to operational. Navy talk for the distinction between active involvement in an evolution and passive observation. He was on the sidelines, until further notice.

But there was no sense trying to get anything more out of the instructors. Whatever might be going on, they certainly wouldn't have been told. And the one who'd passed The Word to him actually seemed a bit sympathetic.

"Jesus Christ, sir," he said quietly, "you musta really screwed the pooch this time."

Las Olinas, California

Tuesday, October 14
11:33 P.M.

The helicopter landed first at the SEAL base, pausing there just long enough for Rick to accept delivery of underwear, socks, shoes, and the fourth-best duty uniform that had been hanging in his locker at the training barracks. Then it took off again, leaving him to struggle out of his wet suit and into the clothing with help from the crewman, and second-class gunner's mate. By the time he was dressed, he could feel the chopper starting down, and he got his first hint of their destination.

Carefully, guided by the light-wands of a ground crewman, the helicopter settled and finally touched down in the landing circle of a parking lot marked LAS OLINAS COUNTY.

"Mr. Tallman?"

"That's me."

The ground crewman, who turned out to be wearing the uniform of a deputy sheriff (with AERO DETAIL engraved on the six-pointed badge), made a "windup" motion with one of the wands, and the chopper lifted away as he led Rick in the direction of a five-story office building featuring cracked and crumbling yellow stucco, rusty casement windows, and a truckbed-height loading dock above which the cryptic legend LAS O INAS C UN Y C RONER REC IVI G was just visible, spelled out in weathered block letters. They had landed at the Las Olinas County Morgue.

"This way, sir."

Rick climbed the steps to the loading dock, entered the building through weary-looking double doors installed sometime during the Truman administration, and found himself in a dimly lighted hallway—where a grim-faced Captain Ward stood deep in conversation with an equally somber Mac.

They stopped talking as Rick entered, but did not speak to him until the deputy had been greeted, assured that his services were deeply appreciated, and hustled back out of earshot. And even then, no time was wasted in preliminaries.

"Sam's here," Mac said. "In the next room." He nodded in the direction of a double door to his right.

Rick gulped. "You mean, she's . . . dead?"

"No, loverboy, she's okay, but we've got something to show you," Mac said.

"By the way, you had dinner?" Captain Ward inquired blandly.

"Or anything else to eat recently?" Mac added.

The questions seemed irrelevant, almost attempts at humor. But neither man was smiling, and both seemed to be waiting for an answer. Rick shook his head.

"Uh, no. But I could go for some—"

"Good!"

That closed the subject. Mac and the captain turned to usher him through the doors—and into a different temperature zone.

The overhead lighting in the room they entered was bright, almost painful to the eyes after the relative gloom of the corridor. But it was the chill of the air, even colder than the water he had just come from, Rick decided, that made the first strong impression.

"Through there," Mac said.

He nodded in the direction of another doorway, this one marked NO ADMITTANCE—MEDICAL PERSONNEL ONLY, and hurried Rick toward it. The cold room was a bare cube, featureless except for a set of oversize file drawers built into one wall.

In the next room lighting was less intense; a single overhead bulb of low wattage. But there was a bright light above a high, mechanical-looking table at the center of the room, where someone in a green gown was at work.

Rick squinted, adjusting his eyes for the second time in less than a minute, and wished that he were somewhere else. Not that he was squeamish; at Top Gun he had seen his share of crashes and helped clean up the aftermath and investigate their causes. Sudden, violent death was no stranger to him; it came with the territory.

The green-clad individual at the table was Samantha—though he would never have guessed if Mac and Captain Ward hadn't told him she was here. The bulky, discolored mass she was dissecting was a human being. Or had been.

"Dr. Deane . . . ?"

Absorbed in the work, Sam did not hear them enter the room, and Captain Ward's voice jarred her. She whirled, the scalpel in her hand held at a threatening angle, and froze for a moment before relaxing with a little laugh of relief.

"Sorry," she said.

Captain Ward shook his head. "My fault. This time of night, place like this, I ought to blow my horn or something if I'm going to come sneaking up on someone from behind. Especially in the . . . circumstances."

Sam turned to a side table, deposited the scalpel, and then moved to give the three men an unobstructed view of the table. She made no move to remove her gloves—or the strange-looking device similar to an oxygen mask that hung from a strap around her throat.

"Hi," she said, nodding in Rick's direction. "Thanks for coming. I know this interrupts your training schedule, and . . ."

"He knows," Mac said.

Samantha flashed her brother a weary half-smile and motioned for Rick to move closer to the autopsy table.

"Have you," she said, "ever seen this man—or anyone like him—before?"

At first glance, Rick was sure he hadn't. The face was black, suffused with blood as if by strangling, and the eyes were missing. Rick was sure, suddenly, that they had been gone before any pathologist went to work. And there was evidence of sea-creature depredations on the upper cheeks and nose.

But below the chin, dissection had been done by human hands. It was clinical; the inner secrets of the neck penetrated and curiously distorted as if for display in a medical textbook or in someone's notion of a late-night-drive-in-movie horror show. It was still identifiable as a neck, and it still connected the head to the shoulders, but that was all.

The chest and stomach cavities—where Samantha had been at work—were open in the double-Y configuration common to all autopsies. But the center of interest was plain. Of the body's original interior furnishings, only the lungs and heart remained. The rest seemed to have been taken away. Stored, perhaps, in one of the filing cabinets in the next room, or sent elsewhere for minute examination.

The heart itself appeared to be intact (though somewhat out of place, according to Rick's memory), and the left lung had been subjected only to superficial dissection. The right lung, though, was a hodgepodge of clamps and retractors.

Rick took a deep breath—and understood at once why Sam was wearing the mask. The man had been dead for a while.

"This dude and I," Rick said, forcing his eyes away from the gruesome exhibit, "could have gone through high school and college together, and I still wouldn't recognize him."

"We didn't think you'd been formally introduced," Captain Ward said sharply, cutting him off. "And if you wanta puke, the head's right down the hall. Use it."

"I'm okay."

"Then listen up! What we got here is a problem, and Mac thinks you might be able to help."

Rick looked quizzically at Mac, whose expression revealed nothing. Sam picked up a clipboard and read from the top sheet.

"The subject," she said, "appears to be a Caucasian male, twenty-five to thirty years of age, six feet one inch, one hundred eighty pounds, with dark brown hair and eye color unknown."

Rick looked at the remains on the table and tried to make himself believe that this had once been a living, breathing, functioning human being like himself. It was uphill work.

"Damaged, apparently by marine life, prior to retrieval. Body cavities appeared to be intact and there was no superficial evidence of gross trauma prior to death.

"Since the circumstances of the body's discovery," Samantha continued, "indicated a strong possibility of death due to drowning, initial gross examination was directed to the region of the throat and lungs."

"But they stopped work," Captain Ward interrupted, "and

called for help soon as they got their first close look inside the lungs. Even before they examined the neck. Because they found out that whatever killed this guy, it surer'n hell wasn't drowning. The sumbitch couldn't drown, because he was breathing water—had been breathing it for some time!"

There was a moment of silence after that. Rick looked from the captain to the remains on the autopsy table and back again, and began laughing.

But there was no trace of humor in the faces of the other three, and after a moment or two he found himself asking if he could get a cup of coffee somewhere. Sam said there was some—weak civilian stuff, but coffee all the same—on the next floor up. They adjourned without further discussion.

"Okay," Rick said when the coffee had been poured and the area checked for stray sets of ears. "He was . . . breathing water?"

Samantha tapped a finger on the clipboard, which she had brought with her. "The pathologist here in Las Olinas," she said, "didn't believe it any more than you do. But he knew something was fishy—uh, sorry—when he found clear fluid, which looked like water to him, in the lungs."

"Looked like water?"

Samantha nodded. "I was called in and we checked it out. Though the fluid was relatively clear and had other characteristics in common with water, it was actually some kind of emulsion—a fluorocarbon, we think; it's being analyzed—that had evidently been in the lungs for a lot longer than this guy's been dead."

"But—!"

"Let me go on, okay? I'll come back to anything that isn't clear when I'm done. Anyway, there was this liquid in the lungs. And then they found the hole in his throat. It wasn't a wound. This hole had been put there deliberately, by a surgeon, and then healed over. It was a tracheostomy, an opening in the neck intended to route air directly to the lungs instead of passing it through the nose or mouth. This one had been fitted with a little plastic tube—"

"Wait a minute! You said he wasn't breathing air."

"No. He wasn't. But he couldn't have breathed any kind of liquid, either, without that hole in his throat. The gag reflex, part of the pulmonary system's defensive equipment that keeps you from taking water down your windpipe, would have prevented that."

"This . . . tracheostomy . . . bypassed that?"

"Uh-huh. But we think there was something more to it."

"Such as?"

"Well, he was in the ocean and he was breathing a liquid. But the liquid wasn't seawater, and we were puzzled by that."

Rick shook his head emphatically. "Human beings," he said, "can't breathe water—seawater or anything else liquid—anyhow. Except in comic books and weird movies."

"Wanna bet?" Mac's voice was quiet, but very sure. "Human beings can breathe water—salt water, anyway—and have actually done so in controlled experiments: breathed the water in and out, extracting oxygen, using it for their bodily functions, and expelling carbon dioxide."

"You're shitting me."

"Nope. And no comic-book stuff, either, Rick. It's not even very new; the first known experiment happened more than twenty years ago, with a civilian volunteer, under U.S. Navy auspices at Bethesda. They filled one of his lungs with salt water through a tube down his nose, leaving the other full of air, as a kind of backup."

"He actually breathed seawater?"

"Normal saline. Sterile salt water, enriched with oxygen."

"Could he live that way? I mean, without help from the lung that was still filled with air?"

Mac shrugged. "Not really. The oxygen he got from the water, even enriched, wasn't really enough for his body's needs. It would have been if both lungs had been flooded but they didn't have a good way of getting rid of the carbon dioxide."

"So it didn't really work."

Mac grinned at him. "Hell, Rick, it worked as well as the doctor thought it would. Man, it was just a first step. All they were trying to do was see if the basic process was feasible. Turns out it was."

"Wait a minute, though—Samantha, you said this guy wasn't breathing seawater. . . ."

"Right," said Sam. "And that's when I decided to call my smart big brother for help. He had told me about that experiment years ago after it was declassified. He explained that someone had figured out that the liquid in the lungs didn't have to be salt water, or water at all."

"But if it's not going to be seawater . . . what's the point of breathing a liquid at all? God, what am I talking about!"

"Because number one, it completely eliminates inert-gas narcosis, no rapture of the deep to worry about; and number two, it completely eliminates all need for decompression. You go down and live like a fish, using your mouth only for eating, with no face mask or mouthpiece to get in the way, and you can come up as fast as you want because there is no inert gas in your body. The fluid in the lungs is superoxygenated, scrubbed and circulated by an exterior device. So you don't have to do a thing except let the gear breathe for you."

"Yeah," Rick agreed. "You could even miniaturize the circulating gear; get it down to a size that you could carry on your belt."

"Or even around your neck," Mac said. "Like on a choker necklace—which is what we figure this guy was wearing."

"There were marks on the neck of the deceased," said Sam. "But the fluid conditioning device was gone when the body washed up."

"So," Rick said, "the experiments are still going on. The Navy's still at it, and some poor swabbie—"

"No." This time it was Captain Ward's turn to interrupt. "The U.S. Navy," he said grimly, "has nothing at all to do with what you saw downstairs. The whole program was canceled after that first successful experiment. That's why Mac and I are here, instead of fifty gonzos from NIS and security and the SPs.

"I know, because I was personally involved in that deal, way back along."

"You?" Rick did not bother to conceal his surprise.

"Me. And a dozen like me. Undersea warfare weirdos."

"I thought you were a submariner."

"I was. And damn proud of it. For a while there, we were the tip of the arrow—working at what you fly-boys call the edge of the envelope. Nuclear boats were new, and the idea that they could carry long-range missiles was completely upending the strategic position and thinking of every military force on the face of the earth. Later, the concept of the hunter-killer sub was developed as a counter for the boomers. But there was always more to it than that, far as I was concerned.

"I took a sabbatical from subs in the sixties," Captain Ward said. "Like your old man did later, Rick, when he went off to fly in space for NASA. For me it was likely a bum career move if I ever wanted an admiral's flag. But that flag had never been a big dream of mine. For me the attraction of a service career was all the different and interesting things a man could do—at someone else's expense. So I went through the training and became a qualified diver."

Both Rick and Mac registered real astonishment.

"You . . . a SEAL?"

The captain shook his head. "Hell, no. Maybe I woulda been, if that was the only way I coulda become a diver. But by the time I decided to get on closer terms with the sea than you could in a submarine, the Navy had separated its specialties. UDT/SEAL frogs had also been qualified divers once upon a time, yeah. And there was still a lot of cross-training. But all I wanted to do was get me some hands-on experience with the world down yonder. So I got rated for every kind of diving there is . . . and got sucked into a couple of the experimental programs."

"Like the seawater-breathing experiment?"

"Things like that. Yeah. What happened in that case—a hopeful beginning that was never followed up because of decisions by higher authority—sent me back to the submarines, with my tail between my legs."

The captain paused again, and this time when he spoke, it was in a somewhat different voice. It sounded older, and chillier. "They deep-sixed the water-breather experiments and canceled the SEALAB program after a single accident, and in fact pretty much gave up on undersea research when it was beginning to seem hopeful. I could see the fun was over. I wasn't senior enough and I didn't have the political connections to make any kind of fight of it. So I transferred back to subs and, a hundred years later, retired. But I knew in my bones the research was going to go forward—with us or without us. And by God it did."

The captain and his audience sat for a moment in silence,

but Rick still had questions. "Okay," he said, "so somebody went ahead with the research. And that ex-dude on the table downstairs is an example of just how far the research went. That sort of explains what you and Mac are doing here. But . . . why me?"

Sam looked at Mac, who fidgeted with his dog tags. "You're here," she said, turning to Rick, "because Mac saw a diver—maybe that one, or his twin brother—swimming without a mask or tank or anything at all except some kind of box attached to his neck, about two thousand feet down the last time the two of you were down in the *Steel Albatross*. He didn't talk about it to anyone but me, because he was afraid they'd lock him up. So we wondered if you might have seen the same thing . . . and kept your own mouth shut for the same reason."

Langley, Virginia

Wednesday, October 15
3:11 A.M.

Sometimes Stan Leppard wished he had a normal job—one where you didn't get important calls at 3:00 A.M.

"Leppard, that you?" Adm. Fang Carter roared into the phone, as if he had to yell just because it was a long-distance call.

"Huh? Wha . . . ? Who is this?" mumbled Leppard.

"It's Carter, Admiral Carter. You told me to keep you posted if I got any more letters."

"Carter? Where are you? What time is it?"

"I'm in Bahrain! Where the hell do you think I am! And it's . . . oh, shit, it's three in the morning there, isn't it? You wake me, I wake you."

"Fair's fair, I guess," said Leppard, who was now fully awake. "Letters? Oh, you mean from Narmonov, the cosmonaut."

"Yeah, that's him."

"You guys have some kind of love affair going on?"

"Ha ha. Remind me to laugh later." Fang Carter was the only

person who could wake someone up with a three A.M. phone call, then get pissed off at him for making a joke.

"All right, all right. What's it say?" Leppard asked.

"Well, it's a short one. Not even a full page. He wants me to meet him in Vienna."

"Vienna's a big place. Anywhere in particular in Vienna?"

"Yeah, at a bar."

"Seems like an awfully long way to go just to grab a beer."

"Look," barked Carter, "that's all it says. I thought you'd like to know."

"Does he name which bar?"

"No. But it's a favorite place of ours."

"Oh. Wanna let me in on the secret?"

"Negative. I'll fax you the damn thing if you want. And you can go ahead and send it through cryptanalysis, not that it'll do any good. But I'll be damned if I'm gonna have a bunch of spooks follow me around and fuck the meeting up. I want to see the guy—as a friend, or 'comrade,' if you prefer the Soviet vernacular—and that's it. He's been through some rough times lately. Gorky ain't exactly Miami Beach, you know."

"Admiral, for your information, Miami Beach isn't even Miami Beach anymore."

"Well, anyway, I'll be there. Whether your people are there or not is up to you. You want to bug the bar, fine. Just don't tell me about it. And if you're going to pounce, pounce after Yuri and I say good-bye to each other."

The conversation ended with an abrupt click from the Bahrain end of the connection. Leppard jotted down all the particulars of the conversation on the pad next to the phone, right under the message to call Will Ward back during normal waking hours. Didn't Uncle Sam know a man's sleep was sacred?

Las Olinas, California

Wednesday, October 15
1:30 P.M.

"The whole thing," Captain Ward was telling the others as they sat waiting for the telephone to ring, "is that we stopped looking for answers down there at the bottom of the sea . . . and someone else didn't."

No one argued. They had moved to the deputy coroner's private office. Will Ward sat behind the desk with his hand on the telephone receiver, waiting for the operator to ring back on the call he had placed to an acquaintance at the Defense Intelligence Agency's Washington headquarters, after attempting to reach a friend who worked for the CIA.

Rick and Sam sat next to each other on an oversize leather love seat, while Mac was sprawled in an armchair in the corner. Rick figured it was not a good time to try the old put-your-arm-around-the-girl-in-the-movie-theater-yawn trick. Besides, his mind wouldn't let him concentrate on The Eyes.

Mac's admission that he had seen the frogman swimming without scuba gear during the last dive in the *Steel Albatross* had felt like a release from prison. Mac's impression had been a fleeting one—just a tantalizing glimpse through the snooper glasses before the glare from the *Albatross*'s headlights had blinded him. But it was enough to dispose of any doubts Rick might have had about his own sanity. Now he could speculate openly, for the others' benefit, about the possible cause of the frogman's death.

"I think it was the shock wave," he said. "Mac and I were protected by the *Albatross*'s pressure hull, and we were strapped into those special seats you designed, Skipper. Any impressions of the shock wave that we got were secondhand, filtered through several layers of protection. But what would it have been like for someone out there, with no shielding?"

Captain Ward thought it over for a moment. "I don't think the shock wave did the guy any great harm. Remember, he was down there without a mask or anything else. Wearing a wet suit, not a dry rig. If he could take that kind of pressure at all, I'd have to figure he could take a momentary increase and go right on swimming. Besides, I got a different idea."

"The fish?" Mac asked.

"Yeah," Captain Ward agreed. "I noticed you looking around after you came back aboard the barge, too. The shock wave that hit you down there was strong, all right. But not sharp enough to pose a danger to life."

"No fish floating belly up on the surface," Mac explained.

"And no other major disturbances, either. I told you at the time, I think, that the main danger from my point of view was that damn EMP—the pulse knocked out computers, they had a blackout here in Las Olinas . . . it was a big mess."

"So the shock wave didn't do the guy in," Rick said. "But something sure did."

"Something did, yes," Samantha agreed. Her eyes were tired, and she fumbled with a half-empty styrofoam cup of coffee, almost upsetting it. Rick wondered how long it had been since she'd been to bed, and he flashed on Sam in a short lace nightie.

"Okay, then," he said, finding it hard to keep his brains out of his crotch, "let's hear it."

"I think," Samantha said, "that everybody's initial guess, before they started examining him, was right. The man drowned. Not normally, but the way a fish does if you pull him out of the ocean and let him flop around on the ground."

"Oh . . . Christ!" Mac was the first to speak.

"Maybe I chose a bad image here. I don't really mean this guy actually got out of the water, or was forcibly removed from it and expired in the atmosphere."

"Then what?" Rick said.

"I think that he died from some kind of malfunction of the fluid-conditioning device he was wearing."

Captain Ward spoke up. "I thought that was all just speculation, about his wearing something like that."

"Well, look," Sam said, getting ready to explain. "The world is full of dangers for anyone who goes even a foot below the surface. And professional divers face additional hazards for every foot they descend.

"Many come under the heading of 'decompression sickness' or 'the bends' and involve gas bubbles in the blood. Little ones run from painful to paralyzing and big ones are fatal. You've all been through the training and know how easily that can happen.

"Another little beauty is aseptic bone necrosis. Nobody's sure why just yet, but working in a hyperbaric environment seems to cause deterioration of the long bones of the leg and the arm . . . the femur and the humerus."

Rick felt his own legs turn to jelly just at the mention of it.

"Since the regular nitrogen-oxygen mixture of air is no good for any but the shallowest diving," Sam continued, "we've long since substituted helium for nitrogen. But helium makes it very hard to retain body heat in the water. You get very cold very quick, and it can be deadly. That's called thermal-stress syndrome, but it's still not the worst. There's disseminated pseudomona, which is an infection that we're not even close to understanding, and good old cerebral infarction, which is the death of brain cells due to an obstruction in the blood vessels. And then there's high-pressure nervous syndrome—which is an uncontrollable shaking that makes it impossible to do any kind of useful work at depths below about seven hundred meters."

Sam got up and crossed the floor to the steaming coffeepot. Rick watched her movements intently, but found that her little lecture had killed his romantic thoughts completely.

"One of the main problems with deep diving," she said while waiting for the caffeine to hit, "is that we can't live without oxygen—but we can't live with it, either.

"People forget that oxygen is a member of the same chemical family as the corrosive halogens fluorine and chlorine. Hydrofluoric acid is an extremely high-powered corrosive, and it's that same quality in oxygen that makes iron get rusty or turns sliced apples brown if you leave them sitting around. Give a human body too little oxygen and it dies. But give it too much under pressure, and the results are just as fatal. It's very toxic indeed. So as pressure increases, we have to cut down on the amount of oxygen in your breathing mixture."

"Yeah, we know all this. It's our profession, you know," Mac said with a sly grin.

"I'll ignore my brother and continue," Sam said. "At the surface, you normally breathe a mixture of gases containing about twenty-one percent oxygen. By the time you've gone down a thousand feet, one or two percent oxygen in the mixture is about all your body needs."

"Or can tolerate," Mac added.

"Thank you. What was your depth when you first saw this man?"

"Over six hundred meters," Rick said. "Around two thousand feet."

"All right then," she went on, "It's complicated somewhat

by the fact that this man was a fluid breather, but even so, at two thousand feet the difference between deadly too much and deadly too little oxygen is very, I say again, very, small. And it's difficult to control within such fine limits.

"And that," Sam continued, looking directly at Rick and speaking more for his benefit than for the others, "is what probably did him in. I think he died because his oxygen-concentration controller failed to deliver enough oxygen to him. There is ample evidence in the body tissues of oxygen starvation—anoxia."

"Because he couldn't get enough oxygen out of the water?"

"No. Remember, he wasn't really getting oxygen directly from the ocean anyway. The recirculator we figure he was wearing was oxygenating and scrubbing the fluorocarbon fluid that filled his lungs. But the amount of oxygen had to be regulated—and his regulator failed. Maybe the surge had something to do with that. But that's the scary thing about anoxia. You have no inkling that it's happening. You just pass out, and if it goes on long enough, you die."

Rick exchanged sour grimaces with Mac. "Tell me about it," Rick said. "I went through the whole bit working with the gill."

"And I've been there, too," Captain Ward said. "And so has Mac. By jove, I think you've got it, Doctor."

Samantha grinned wearily. "We'll see," she said. "Still a lot more work to do, to nail down anything you could call a fact."

"But enough," the captain said, "to tell my friends back east—if we ever get to talk to one of them."

Rick shook his head, his mind on the dead frogman whose remains lay in the dissecting room downstairs.

"Poor bastard," he said. "Poor son of a bitch . . . he never knew what hit him!"

Moscow, U.S.S.R.

Wednesday, October 15
11:59 P.M.

As soon as General Viktor Tregorin's head touched the pillow and his mind began replaying the day's events, he muttered an expletive. He turned on his bedside lamp and reached down to slide his diary out from under the table leg. He grunted, found his reading glasses and pen, and began to write. How could he forget to make the day's entry?

> I received a double blow today. I was notified that the SPETSNAZ frogman who set the undersea explosion had been killed, presumably by the shock wave. Unfortunate, but the man knew that this was a dangerous mission. But when information came later that his body was recovered by the Amis, I had a hard time containing my anger. But rather than concentrating on events I cannot control, I forced myself to figure out what could be done to minimize this damage.
>
> Perhaps it is all for the best. Temnota's timetable was set up by strategists—scientific game-players thinking and programming against known values and hard projections. No wild cards.
>
> Please forgive me the American term. It is from their game of poker, and this useful phrase doesn't translate exactly into Russian. But I hold my own wild card, or ace in the hole if you will. After all, I make the first move and have the element of surprise on my side. The Amis can merely react to what I do.
>
> Despite all the elaborate war-gaming and crystal-ball gazing, perhaps it is now time to lay my cards on the table and rake in the chips.

Tregorin finished his final act of the troubling day and slid the diary back under the bed table's leg. He was asleep within minutes, but would toss and turn all night long.

PART VIII

RECONNAISSANCE IN FORCE

On Board the USS *Deyo*, Charleston, South Carolina

Saturday, October 18
1400 Zulu (Greenwich Mean Time)

Captain B. B. Lyons addressed his men on the deck of the *Deyo*, a Spruance-class destroyer. All leave had hastily been canceled the night before when the orders regarding Operation Deep Search had come through. The crew had, of course, grumbled, but at least now they would know why they couldn't tear up Charleston as they usually did. The *Deyo* carried a rowdy bunch of sailors, but they were all top-notch Navy men and women who put as much enthusiasm into their jobs as they did into their partying.

"All hands, this is the captain speaking," Lyons roared into the microphone, the echo rolling down the length of the ship. "I'm going to explain briefly what will be expected of us during the next week or two. You will receive a more detailed briefing when you report to your work stations." Lyons paused, waiting for the echoes to die down.

"Operation DeepSearch is a full-scale alert—both coasts—and we will be searching for what may prove to be a Soviet undersea installation. We have received conflicting intelligence reports from our sources. Some place this installation on the West Coast, some on the East Coast. One school of thought involves a killer satellite, but that obviously doesn't concern us." The men laughed at this, and Lyons took the opportunity to raise his hat and quickly pass his hand over his bald head. It was an unusually hot, sunny day, and Lyons needed to keep his hat on to keep his sun-sensitive scalp from getting burned. He also didn't want to give anyone the opportunity to make any "glare" jokes at his expense.

"Operation DeepSearch is at present a classified maneuver. The press has been told this is merely a 'readiness alert' ordered by the President. Since we're not even sure that this undersea installation exists, the Joint Chiefs felt there was no need to alarm the public. Therefore, should any of you be questioned by the media, civilians, or even family, a simple 'no comment' will suffice if you do not wish to say anything about the 'readiness alert exercises.' " What Lyons neglected to tell his men was that chances were mighty slim that anyone would be stepping ashore within the next fourteen days.

"As for the installation itself, it may be manned, it may be nuclear, and it may be resting on the bottom of the sea. That is, if it exists at all. The only thing we have to go on is the name for the thing—Temnota. So, wrapping up, if it's out there, you can bet that we'll find it. Dismissed."

As the men of the destroyer *Deyo* (hull number DD989) retreated to their quarters, similar speeches were being given up and down the East Coast on ships from the USS *McInerney* in Mayport, Florida, to the USS *Samuel B. Roberts* in Portland, Maine. It was going to be a long two weeks.

On Board *Sandpiper 4*

Tuesday, October 21
1851 Zulu

"Another two minutes. Then we head for the barn."

The Lockheed P-3C Orion's pilot nodded, acknowledging the tactical coordinator's dictum, and unwrapped another piece of gum. He'd given up smoking a week ago and was beginning to get pretty good at blowing bubbles. They were even starting to call him Bazooka Joe.

"Oh, for God's sake, Skipper—is it really as bad as all that?"

Lt. Comdr. Hal Pittersen looked owlishly at the younger man

occupying the right-hand pilot seat and allowed a large, pink bubble to form just below his nose.

"Yecch!" Lt. (j.g.) Nick Jones looked away in mock distress.

The bubble exploded and collapsed on Pittersen's chin.

Jones giggled—which was the point of it all. Anything to break the monotony of a standard electronic-search mission.

For four days now, Pittersen and his crew had been deployed over southern California waters, searching for something large, dangerous, and submerged somewhere between the coastal islands and the mainland.

A submarine, he guessed. Could be a giant squid for all he knew. They hadn't been told what to look for; only to report "any anomalous activity." Fat chance.

On Board USS *Anchorage*

Friday, October 24
1758 Zulu

"Got something, Mr. Forbes." Sonarman First Class David Drake was sitting up straight at the instrument table, eyes locked forward, fingertips pressed to the phones covering his ears.

Lt. Gene Forbes, halfway through his second back-to-back watch as sonar officer, looked up from the book he'd been reading and tried to focus on the job. But he was tired, and Drake had an irritating habit of calling you to listen to whales mating. Nonetheless, he put the book down and moved over to pick up the spare phones. Just sea noises.

"You still hearing it?"

"Uh . . . no, sir."

"Got any idea what it was?"

"No, sir."

"Well, call me if you hear it again; maybe together we can figure it out."

"Yes, sir."

Encourage them. Never criticize. Boring and fatiguing as standing an extra watch could be, the enlisted sonarman's job was infinitely worse.

Especially on wild-goose chases like this one: Operation DeepSearch. They were told this was a surprise emergency-deployment exercise intended to test unit readiness. But once at sea, they began ranging up and down the West Coast, looking for an undersea installation that might or might not be there. For all they knew, this was just a fleet test, but (as scuttlebutt had it) this could be the real thing, dressed up as maneuvers to keep the civilians from losing it.

They were searching for some kind of power plant, possibly nuclear, hidden down at the bottom of the sea. At least it was supposed to be somewhere near the coast. But how in God's name were they supposed to find it?

The *Anchorage* was a hunter, yes. But a hunter of other submarines, not of weird undersea spooks. A 688 Los Angeles–class attack sub, the *Anchorage* was equipped with passive and active sonar, the BQQ-5 system, as well as everything the Long Beach Naval Shipyard had been able to pack aboard before the emergency-deployment order was received. Forward, flank, and after arrays; passive range-determination array, circular array, active transducers—you name it, the *Anchorage* had it. Plus a brand-new computer to handle the data.

Yet the real work still came down to poor slobs like Drake, sitting there blank eyed, straining his brain to hear something he didn't recognize as a normal sea noise. The Navy did whatever they could to keep guys like Drake in the service, because without the kind of dedication and experience they brought to the job, there was no way in this world the job could be done.

"Uh . . . Mr. Forbes?"

"You got it again?"

"Uh . . . no, sir. I mean, yes. I got it, but I know what it is now."

"Not what we're looking for?"

"No, sir. Just a couple of dolphins telling each other there's a shark around somewhere."

Forbes grinned at the sonarman. "You can really tell what they're saying, Drake?"

"Well, yes, sir. I guess. Anyway, that's what it feels like to me. Maybe I'm just making it up."

Forbes shook his head, but knew better than to pursue the

subject. All sonarmen seemed to get like that after a while. Not really crazy, but a brick short of a load, as his grandfather used to say.

Hell's fire, the Russkies could have built a whole city at the bottom of the sea, and unless someone beat on something with a wrench, the *Anchorage* would never know a thing about it.

Their equipment was built to detect moving things; things that went whir or clank. Or chirped like the dolphins. And anyway, there was nothing down there in the first place.

Station "O"

Friday, October 24
9:01 P.M., Moscow Time

Andrey almost bumped into the intruder while making one of his regularly scheduled inspection tours on the perimeter of the place that was now his home. Although he'd never seen it before, he recognized it.

Heavy skeleton buoyed to land in an upright position, dumbbell protruberances arranged at the side of a big grid/dish antenna, aimed at the surface. Bulking almost as large as the home itself. It sat on the sea bottom just a few meters from the Temnota platform.

Any SPETSNAZ naval infantryman could have identified it as a sound-surveillance-system—SOSUS—listening device. It was one of the fixed-site sonars the Ami navy deployed along its own coast, on the bottom of harbor entrances, and at other choke points around the world. It detected submarines as well as other activities and transmitted the information via extreme-low-frequency radio.

Andrey had no idea why a SOSUS had suddenly turned up here, but he knew what to do about it. Moving in a series of leaps and bounds that would have been astounding on the surface, he turned back toward the habitat for equipment and assistance.

They would have to operate in full-stealth mode for an hour or two, but that was all right. It was a little break in the monotony. One of the first things they had learned was the proper sequence for disconnecting the low-frequency transmission antenna from equipment of this type. No trouble at all if you took your time and gave full attention to each point.

When this was done, however, he and the others would discuss the matter in the peculiar sign-language shorthand they had begun to develop and decide whether or not to tell Murmansk about their find.

They were under orders to use the radio as sparingly as possible. Andrey wondered if this was truly an emergency. Perhaps not. They did not know the circumstances; perhaps the SOSUS array had been dumped here by chance, or by accident. Such things were not unknown, even in the Soviet Navy.

Was it possible that someone on the surface was actually looking for their base?

Langley, Virginia

Friday, October 24
8:22 P.M.

"Yes, goddammit, of course it's important! And you can tell the admiral that I told you it was okay to wake him up," said Stan Leppard, grinning to himself. "It's only a few hours' time difference, isn't it?"

"Sir, it's eight hours ahead in Bahrain. Right now it's four twenty-two A.M."

"That a fact? Well, he'll have to be up at oh six hundred anyway."

"Sir, it's Saturday morning."

"I don't care. I'll wait." Now it's my turn, thought Leppard.

"What do you want, Lep?" said a groggy Admiral Carter.

"First of all, I'd rather you didn't call me Lep."

"I'll call you a lot worse if you don't get to the point and let me get back to sleep."

"All right. Just got out of an interesting conference with some National Security Council boys. I wanted to talk to you informally, you know, to keep you posted, get your opinion. Also, because your boy is involved."

The admiral groaned so loudly Leppard could have heard him from Bahrain without the telephone. "What's Ricky been up to this time? What's the damage, and how much will I have to pay her husband to keep it quiet?"

"What? Nothing bad has happened to him. He's involved with a project . . . wait, let me begin at the beginning. You know all about Operation DeepSearch, don't you? And Temnota?"

"Yeah, sure. The first letter from Yuri Narmonov told about Temnota. And when Petchukocov turned up in Israel, after he was supposed to be on the Iranian airliner we shot down, he confirmed Yuri's story. Except that Yuri thought the danger was from some killer satellite, and Petchukocov had Temnota as an undersea base."

"That's all you know?"

"I know we haven't found squat with Operation DeepSearch."

"That doesn't mean this undersea installation doesn't exist—only that we can't find it."

"Lep . . . uh, Leppard, I hope you didn't get my ass out of the hammock to tell me a lot of stuff I know already."

"No, sir. There have been some new developments. I spoke to Will Ward and—"

"That old son of a bitch! What line of crap has he been feeding you? Been mixed up in so many weird projects in his lifetime, it's amazing he can still tell reality from make-believe." The admiral laughed at his own joke, fondly remembering his best friend.

"This is plenty real, sir, and as weird as it gets." Leppard proceeded to tell Fang Carter about the discovery and autopsy of the water-breathing frogman, just as Ward had told him, including the Navy's experimental program in the 1960s.

"Because the dead frogman was wearing a Russian-made wet suit, and because of some other things, Ward believes the Russians have been doing some experimenting on their own. And gotten the jump on us once again, the way they did with *Sputnik*."

"You mentioned some 'other things,' " the admiral said. "Mind tellin' me what they are?"

"Well, this is where your boy Rick comes in." And Leppard

launched into the story of the *Steel Albatross*, and how Rick and Mac had seen the frogman swimming without a mask two thousand feet below the surface.

After Leppard finished his hardly believable tale, the line was so quiet you could hear the crackling and hissing of the telephone equipment. A long, low whistle escaped from the admiral's lips.

"So we think," began Carter slowly, "that Temnota is somewhere off the coast of Las Olinas?"

"Yes, sir."

"And Operation DeepSearch . . . ?"

"Is going to be canceled. Now we've got a place to concentrate on."

"And you're going to let Ward know this?"

"Hell, yes, if you'll pardon my French," Leppard exclaimed. "Maybe he'll even want to help."

"Thanks for keeping me posted, Stan."

"You're welcome, sir," said Leppard, but the admiral had already hung up.

San Clemente Island

Saturday, October 25
10:39 A.M.

Working with Kiwi on Mac's hemoglobin gill was a revelation, Rick decided as they leveled off at ten fathoms and took up a course for the *Berkone*.

During the week, the little ex-lobsterman was still pure poison. His determination to drive Rick out of SEAL training had not abated one whit. If anything, his campaign had intensified. Rick resigned himself to an all-or-nothing effort; let up for a single instant, and Kiwi would be there. Breathing down his neck and grinning like a half-starved shark. At least he knew why, but that didn't make it any easier.

But on weekends, all bets were off. Working with Mac and Rick—whenever he was free to help—the senior SEAL instructor was the soul of helpful professionalism, a person altogether different from the one who plotted to make Rick's life miserable the other five days of the week. And dives like this one were a perfect example.

Because Rick had the least experience with the gill (no longer called the "hemoglobin" gill now—the hemoglobin had been replaced with a more efficient synthetic), Mac had decided that he should be the "wingman," swimming back-cover and monitoring depth for Kiwi, who held the compass board and acted as navigator on this first seawater test of the device.

Depth assessments would come later, but for the moment it would be enough to make sure the gills could supply oxygen to both of them in sufficient quantity to avoid ill effects during the half hour or so of swimming that would take them from the western shore of San Clemente Island to the new position of the *Berkone*, where Mac would be waiting to debrief them and recheck both gills from top to bottom.

The gear was smaller now than the version he had first seen, mounted entirely on the chest for easy access. It had worked perfectly during the last few controlled-environment tests, in fresh water. Now if they could hold their own in the rough-and-tumble of the ocean . . .

Rick glanced in Kiwi's direction and then took a careful squint upward through the snooper goggles to the rippled silver ceiling that was the surface of the sea. The gill wasn't the only bit of new hardware being tested this weekend; one of the geniuses at Scripps had come up with a new wrinkle on the light-gathering snoopers that offered such clear vision in the light-starved undersea world.

Instead of the goggles he and Mac had worn on their last dive in the *Steel Albatross*, Scripps technicians had turned out a version that could be used like flip-down sunglasses. They wore regular goggles, with the flip-down snoopers over them. If there was a sudden flash, they could just flick the snoopers up. The new snoopers were curved on the sides, wraparound style, to improve the field of vision. There were still drawbacks, though. The snoopers sensitized the eyes to light, and it still took a while for the irises to adjust after taking off the snoopers in a normally lit area. And it was still possible to suffer the same temporary flash-blindness that had afflicted

Mac when Rick turned on the SA-1's headlights. Somehow, Rick told himself now, there had to be some kind of middle ground.

Suddenly, they changed course. But they were still at their assigned depth, so why the change? Rick moved up on Kiwi's seven to a point where the snoopers could give him a glance at the course. The lobster grabber must have been checking their path across the sea bottom (it was only a fathom or so below them) and come to the conclusion that they needed a heading change.

At least they were doing something.

At first, when it became clear that they were to have no part in the Operation DeepSearch exercise, Rick had thought he would go crazy from sheer frustration. He knew it was a cover for the effort to locate the source of the power failure and EMP that had raised such hell with Las Olinas fourteen days earlier.

Rick checked his depth gauge and watch strapped to his left wrist. Depth, okay. Time . . . lousy! They were already sixty seconds past the time when they should have had the *Berkone* in sight. Should he alert Kiwi? Tap him on the shoulder?

But the barrel-chested down easter was ahead of him. Stopped dead in the water, jerking his thumb upward to indicate the underwater portion of the *Berkone*'s twin hulls, just above their position. Kiwi's navigation had been flawless.

Point Loma, California

Friday, October 31
6:44 P.M.

Although SEAL training had ended early, Rick was still the last one to arrive. Mac had come straight from Scripps, but Rick wanted to go home and shower first—as if he hadn't already spent enough time in the water that day. He shaved closely, put on some after-shave, and then hunted around in the closet for some sharp clothes. As he'd been somewhat of a nomad lately (with clothing seemingly left at every port of call), the best he could come up with was a plaid shirt, a clean pair of blue jeans, an old leather flight jacket, and his blue suede shoes. He combed his wet hair back, looked in the mirror, said, "Eat your heart out, Elvis," and was out the door.

When he arrived at Mac's, he jumped right into the argument going on between Sam, Mac, and Billy. Sam wanted a smiling, happy jack-o'-lantern, while Mac liked the traditional sawtooth grin. Billy wanted a scary face and Rick agreed with him. With a Magic Marker, Rick drew a wicked-fanged, leering goblin that Billy thought was "really cool" on the side of the pumpkin.

Samantha, being the only doctor present, operated on the pumpkin head, plunging the knife in and cutting a circle in the top. Billy didn't want to see or touch "the pumpkin brains" inside, but when Rick grabbed a handful of orange guts and told Billy you could roast the seeds and eat them, he wasn't afraid anymore. With a loud "Yuck!" he helped spoon out the gloppy mess so they could get down to the business of carving.

Although Sam wouldn't let Billy carve with the sharp knife, she let him guide Rick's hand, and in a few minutes, they had one evil-looking pumpkin. Sam cut down a candle, placed it inside, and lit it, then put the top back on while Mac turned off the lights. Billy screamed with delight, and Sam and Mac applauded.

"Come on, Billy-goat," Uncle Mac said, "put your costume on. It's time for trick-or-treating."

"Okay!" he said, running to his room. "Mommy," he called out, "help me tie the strings."

Sam got up, turning the kitchen light back on, and followed him.

Mac looked at Rick once Sam was out of the room. "Look at you—are you going trick-or-treating as Beaver Cleaver?"

Rick didn't join in Mac's laughter. "Trick-or-treating? Man, I like Billy . . . great kid . . . but do I have to take him?"

"Well," Mac said, "I guess he just likes his uncle Rick better than he likes his uncle Mac." Mac paused, then said, "Hey, don't sweat it, I'll take the kid."

"Yeah?"

"Sure. I'll take him to every house in the neighborhood. And if it's still early, I'll take him to a few more neighborhoods. Expect us back around ten, if that's okay with you, sir. And it better be, or Sam will throw the both of us into the brig."

"No, that's excellent. Thanks a lot."

Finally, Billy emerged as . . . Batman. Rick wondered how many other Batmans would be out there tonight, receiving candy from the grateful multitude of Gotham City.

"You're sure it's okay?" Samantha asked Mac. "You really don't mind?"

"Hey," Mac said with a nose-wrinkling smile, "I was even thinking of using my old flippers and mask as a costume and seeing if anybody knew I was over ten years old. This will be the first time I've gone trick-or-treating since I took you—twenty years ago."

"Well, if Billy isn't safe with a Navy SEAL . . ."

"You mean if I'm not safe with Batman . . ."

Billy giggled. "I'll protect him, Mommy."

"All right. Have fun now, and listen to your uncle."

After they left, Rick carried the jack-o'-lantern into the living room and put it on the snack table near the window. "Gotta let the kids know they're welcome here," Rick explained. Sam got another snack table and placed it by the front door. Rick helped her set up the bowls containing the individually wrapped candy bars—as well as one with pennies, in case kids still collected boxes of money for UNICEF.

And suddenly, both realized, they were alone for the first time. Silently, they held hands and sat down on the sofa.

For the first hour the doorbell rang constantly. They both gave away candy and pennies to cute little ghosts, witches, Frankenstein monsters, ballerinas, cats, and both male and female Batmans. They watched a little TV and talked. Neither wanted to mention the SEALs, so they chitchatted idly as Rick kept glancing at his watch.

He jumped up after his last time check and went to the wall switch, turning off the living room lights. "Kids can see the pumpkin better if the background is dark," he said hoarsely. He turned off the TV, too.

In the dark house, sitting next to a wonderful, intelligent woman with beautiful green eyes and pumpkin-colored hair, all Rick could hear was his own heart beating. Their hands touched again, and Rick's knees began shaking. Omigod, he thought, I feel like I'm fifteen years old. This is crazy. They turned to each other—and kissed, faintly, barely touching each other's lips.

Rick's adrenaline was pumping; he was not the calm superpilot used to being completely in charge of himself. He was breathing so loudly he thought he sounded like an asthma patient. But Sam's breaths were coming at the same time, making Rick's seem louder than they really were.

The feather-light kisses grew more passionate as they brought their heads closer together. They shifted position, until they were lying side by side on the couch.

As Rick nibbled on Samantha's lower lip, their hands caressed each other—smoothly at first, then in a frenzy. When Rick began to pull the back of her blouse out of her pants, Sam said, "No . . ."

Shit, Rick thought. He traced the arch of her spine with his thumb, feeling a shoulder blade, her bra strap, the small of her back. . . . Again, he gave the blouse a tug, which was coming loose from all the squirming.

Again, Sam said, "No . . ."

Dummy! Rick thought. Go slowly! Don't treat this one like another fly-boy conquest.

Sam was breathing deeply. "Not here," she said.

Great. Now she's going to say I shouldn't even be here.

"Rick, let's . . ."

"Okay, okay," Rick said, sitting up. Let's not do this. Let's just be friends. Let's get something to eat. Let's discuss this. Rick expected her to say one of these things to him.

"Let's go to the bedroom."

Tel Aviv, Israel

Saturday, November 1
9:22 A.M.

The target was having breakfast.

Dimitri F. Petchukocov was in plain view, sitting at a table just inside the French doors that opened onto the balcony of his hotel suite. The shot would have been an easy one—except that the glass doors were still closed.

That did not make the shot impossible. The glass was not bulletproof; the Mossad men assigned to protect Petchukocov had not had time to make it so. They had moved him into the hotel two nights ago. One more night and they would move him again—and again three days after that. It was a standard security measure for Very Important Refugees—until the old man could be given a new and probe-proof identity in Israel or elsewhere.

To kill Petchukocov at this moment, the assassin was certain that all he had to do was make minor sight adjustment for the minor breeze that had just sprung up and the angle of deflection that could be expected from normal window glass. One touch on the trigger of the Marlin 600 (the KGB used rifles made in the motherland, but GRU specialists preferred the American product) and the target's head would explode into a hundred bloody fragments.

But he must merely wound—to make it look like an attempt on Petchukocov's life. So the assassin was content to wait. Comrade General Tregorin had been at pains to impress upon him the necessity of a single professional shot.

The bullet—and the message it embodied—must be delivered with maximum efficiency. A professional killer would mete out the inevitable fate of the traitor despite the formidable efforts of the Institute Mossad or Shin Bet.

The Israeli security agencies were getting too full of their own importance and invincibility. They needed another lesson, like the one they'd had when the Americans caught them spying.

Petchukocov couldn't stay inside forever. Not on such a day as this. To a Russian—to men like Petchukocov and the assassin, who had lived their lives far closer to the Arctic Circle than the Tropic of Cancer—this was a day to rejoice in fair skies and invigorating surroundings. The waterfront was only a block or two away; the beach less than half a mile distant.

Petchukocov would come out to sip a cup of coffee. To drink deeply of the morning air and congratulate himself on having found a fine and friendly place for the retirement that could have been far less comfortable in the Rodina. To let the assassin have his shot . . .

The target had relaxed.

Across the street from the assassin, concealed behind the metal louvers of a ventilator outlet at the top of the building where Petchukocov was lodged, a Shin Bet rifleman took a deep breath and expelled it with impatience. He was hot—damnable summer weather—and he would be here for another hour at least before his relief was due to arrive.

If only the son of a bitch over there would try the shot. It was frustrating to be so close, but still unable to make the shot. Orders: Don't create an international incident by firing first. Let the Russian make the first move. But before he did, Moshe Ben Zvi would get heatstroke and die, here on this stinking roof. Alone and unmourned. *Ausgespilt!*

Ben Zvi laughed at himself, blinked his eyes to rid them of double vision, and laughed again, hollowly.

For a day and a night he and his relief had been sitting here, six hours on and six hours off, waiting for the shotmaker in the other building to give them the opening they needed to kill him.

The shotmaker—what was his name? Benicov . . . Benicoff? At the shop they hadn't spelled it out for him, and it hadn't seemed important at the time. Nor was it, except as something to think about; something to distract the mind.

Yes, Benicov. Or was it Benes? Or Benito?

Bennett?

Beinfarb?

They had told him little more than they really had to this time. Told him that this was no mere run-of-the-mill Kremlin shotmaker but a real professional. Warned him to be careful, take no chances. Never go to sleep, never take your eye off him for a minute. And if he's gone from the window, from where you can see him, for more than thirty seconds . . . then be sure to guard your back.

This would have been impressive enough even if he hadn't known how the assassin had tracked the Russian defector Petchukocov all the way from Tel Aviv to Haifa to Herzliyya to Eilat to Jerusalem and finally back to Tel Aviv again. All the way around the hideout, safe-house course without being spotted until the last move, from Jerusalem to this place. He was good, no doubt about it. Every bit as professional as they'd said.

KGB? Or GRU? Certainly not The Company. Or even the Circus, sloppy and underfinanced as it had been since the near-wipeout over the Falklands.

Ben Zvi stiffened and brought the telescopic sight back hard against his right eye.

The target had opened his window. He was going to . . .

. . . make the shot. Right now! There was Petchukocov—the old fool was finally done with his breakfast, and now he was going to take the glass of orange juice out on the balcony.

The assassin pushed the casement window wide, out of his way, settled the Marlin on the sandbag rest, and focused the Jacobs scope on the edge of the balcony.

No wind.

Just come on out here, you old . . .

. . . son of a bitch. Petchukocov must have decided to come out onto the balcony.

All right.

Windage zero. A down shot—harder than flat or uphill, but no real problem—distance already cranked in. Don't think. Don't see anything but the target. Go for the . . .

. . . head shot. Through the frontal lobes and back to the ganglion; stop him in his tracks. But no. All they wanted was the hand.

One shot.

And then . . .

. . . out of here. Already he felt free; as though a load had been lifted from his shoulders.

Steady, now.

Take a deep breath. Let it out. Take another. Let half go, hold on to . . .

. . . the rest. No thoughts now but the target. No world but the target.

Hold it . . .

. . . hold it.

Hold it. . . .

The flat finality of the single rifle shot sent pigeons fluttering from the upper stories of both buildings, and it might have attracted attention below if the street had been less noisy or less occupied with its own affairs. Or if there had been more than one report.

On Board the *Steel Albatross*

Saturday, November 1
1:14 P.M.

At first, Rick thought they had been caught in an undersea earthquake. Nose-up and listing at least fifteen degrees to port, the *Steel Albatross* continued to vibrate with a clear, bell-like tone for several seconds after the initial shock. Ahead and slightly above, Rick saw at first glance what seemed to be an entire universe of rock and gravel.

"Shit!" Rick whispered.

"An' throw in a little bit extra for me," Kiwi's voice floated up from the backseat. "What the hell's going' on here?"

Rick opened his mouth to answer, but closed it silently over the words that had formed in his mind. This was Kiwi's first dive in the *Albatross*, and there was no need to hit the panic button until the situation had been fully evaluated. Rick took a deep breath.

Just a moment ago, they had been on their way to the surface after a highly successful test of the SA-1's new manual control system.

The initial dive—using the computerized control system—had been uneventful. They had "landed" on the bottom, at a depth of just over 1,100 feet, without incident and with hardly a bump. Even Kiwi had been complimentary.

"Sonofahawah!" he had said. "I got to admit, you sure c'n fly this crazy-lookin' thing!"

Once the boat was firmly in place and brought to a level attitude by her servos, Rick checked his watch, then cut the boat's switches. The instrument panel faded to black—and suddenly the world was extremely dark and extremely lonely.

Kiwi and Rick flipped their snooper glasses down. Then they began to "preflight" the boat, preparatory to leaving the bottom. Attitude controls seemed free, firm, and flexible; a mechanical Fathometer's luminous face showed a slightly greater depth than the one remembered from the computer readouts (be sure to check that when we get back to the surface); and other mechanicals (clinometer, vertical-speed indicator, etc.) all seemed in working order.

"Okay," Kiwi said, coming to the end of the checklist. "Lookin' good. Take her up when ready."

Grasping the stick lightly in his right hand, Rick dropped his left to the mechanical "ballast/exhaust" wheel now occupying the space where a fighter plane's thrust levers would ordinarily be, then turned it through one full rotation, counterclockwise.

The noise made by the pumps was louder than Rick remembered. Before, the sound had to compete with the hum of electronics. Now there was no sound to run interference. Worth mentioning in the dive report he would write about this.

Before he could note it on the pad strapped to his right leg, however, the *Albatross* lurched a little from side to side, then began to rise—slowly at first, then gathering momentum—toward the surface.

Rick tested the controls, waited for them to bite, then pointed the boat's nose in the direction of the *Berkone*. Blinking, but resisting the urge to rub his eyes, he looked out at the green-hued world ahead and was amazed by the clarity of the water at this depth. The snoopers were immensely better down here than any lighting array could possibly be.

And then the sky had fallen in. . . .

"Daylight, up ahead . . . I think," Kiwi offered, doing a little backseat driving. "Twelve o'clock, real low."

Rick craned his neck and saw what he meant.

Light and . . . what? Nothing, that's what! If they were indeed buried under a few tons of landslide as he'd thought, there should be a lot of rock in front of them as well as above. But if they weren't buried, just where the hell were they?

Rick turned his head to look again at the situation above. The rocks didn't seem as all-enveloping as they had at first glance, and on closer examination Rick could see spaces between them—spaces that shouldn't be there if the side of a canyon had really fallen in on them. But there seemed to be no rocks at all crowding in on the side. Since they were going up at the time, what the *Albatross* had run into was above, not in front—which would explain why light could be seen ahead of them.

The *Steel Albatross* had run into an overhanging cliff! And now it was bobbing against it like a balloon against a ballroom ceiling.

"Shit."

"An' two's eight," Kiwi agreed solemnly. "We . . . uh . . . still goin' home, Rick boy?" That, to Rick's Kiwi-sensitive ears, sounded like "rich boy."

"Shouldn't wondah," Rick said, needling him.

Carefully, Rick reached his left hand in the direction of the ballast control, then moved it slowly—clockwise—a full turn, flooding the ballast tanks.

When a full thirty seconds had elapsed with nothing happening, he turned the wheel an extra half-turn clockwise, waited for results, and was about to crank in still another quarter-turn . . . when the nose of the *Albatross* began to drop.

Rick moved the stick forward, as he would to keep an airplane from stalling, and gradually the boat began to move forward as well as downward.

Rick wondered if he should try to revive the electronics. But he decided to try to gut it out manually. After all, he was supposed to be running a test.

The *Albatross* settled into a nose-down attitude that Rick estimated gave her a twenty-to-one descent ratio. But this would have to change soon, as he wasn't planning to make another landing.

Delicately, moving with infinite care, Rick settled his hand back on the ballast control and began to turn it counterclockwise. Slowly, the *Albatross* began to lose momentum; the nose came up but then began to wander as the controls lost their bite. The ship was approaching a stall. Another half-turn counterclockwise.

Nothing happened for a moment (the boat seemed to respond in slow motion to the manual controls), but then the nose came up to what Rick thought was horizontal. He cranked in another half-turn of positive buoyancy to give him better control of the ship. The *Albatross* edged obliquely away from the side of the undersea canyon that his snooper-clad eyes could make out in the middle distance.

"Thought we'd bought the farm." Kiwi's voice was flat and matter-of-fact, but all the same Rick thought he could detect the barest hint of emotion in it. Something almost human. But the next words made him wonder. "And it pissed me off some," the SEAL instructor continued. "You wanna know how come?"

Rick didn't. But he was sure he was going to find out anyway.

"It pissed me," Kiwi said, "because I got to thinking, here we were, caught for fair in this little steel bubble when we didn't have to be. You know, Mac's gill," Kiwi continued, "the new version we tried last weekend? You remember how they were made? I mean—how they was all in front, nothing in back? Well, lemme ask you a dumb question, since you know this turtle better'n I do. Can you flood the cockpit of this little beast? Fill it with water, I mean, and then open the hatch?"

"Captain Ward says so. But we haven't tried it yet. He says all the instruments and controls—the electronic ones like the computer as well as the manuals—are watertight. There's even a separate pumping system to evacuate water from the cockpit if you want to get back inside again, later."

"Well, then, if we'd been wearing the gills—"

"—and the boat'd really been trapped down there instead of just stuck against a rock overhang, we could still have made it back to the surface. Right."

"Or," Kiwi said, continuing the thought, "in some non-emergency evolution, we could have gotten out and done some exploring on foot down there on the bottom, and then gotten back aboard for the return trip to the surface. Hell of an idea!"

"Hell of an idea," Rick echoed.

On Board *Berkone*

Saturday, November 1
2:39 P.M.

The sky had been overcast all day, the sea was building to state 3, and now the light was failing. Aboard the mother ship *Berkone*, west of San Clemente Island, Captain Ward cocked an eye at the lowering clouds and then turned his attention back to the water, where divers were struggling to get lines to the *Steel Albatross* so she could be drawn into the calm safety of the moon-pool.

He could see Rick grinning, and since he hadn't heard a peep out of Rick or Kiwi since the start of their dive, he assumed the grin—and the lack of communication—meant the new manual override controls must have worked as planned. Now the boys would be ready for a real celebration. The frogs in the water swore and called to one another as they fought the sea, but finally managed to maneuver the *Albatross* into the proper position. Lines were passed, and moments later she was once more safely nestled in the moon-pool amidships.

Captain Ward moved to meet the two younger men as they clambered up and out of the SA-1. "Good dive?" he inquired gruffly, expecting an easy affirmative.

Rick grinned crookedly. "Well, sir, if you mean, did the manual controls work, then the answer is yes. And if you mean is the computer system still in good shape, that's a yes, too."

"But . . . ," the captain said. "I hear a real loud 'but' in there.

Kiwi snorted. "Shouldn't wondah."

That called for an explanation, and after a moment Rick laid it out for him, doing his best to understate the danger they had encountered without minimizing the need for a thorough damage check of the boat's hatch and upper works.

"Jesus Christ!" the captain said when he was done.

Kiwi shrugged and spat. "But aside from that," he said, "you'd have to call the whole evolution a success. And I ain't so sure what happened was a total loss, anyway."

"That's right," Rick said, nodding. "Absolutely . . . because, look, now at least we know the boat can take one hell of a knock and still come home. Even on manual control. And besides, it gave us a couple of ideas—"

"—'bout how Mac's gill could be used along with the boat," Kiwi said, picking up the thread, "and how it could maybe be a big help if you got into real trouble, down there on the bottom."

"All of which," Rick continued, "we'll put in a formal report, of course. But we'd like to talk it through with you now." He bent to retrieve the clipboard strapped to his leg.

"Aside from that, though," Captain Ward persisted, still curious about the original purpose of the test dive, "the manual controls worked okay?"

Kiwi nodded. "Soon's we were sure the manual valves worked," he said, "we took her down deep."

"With the computer on? And working?"

"Computer fully functional, exactly as briefed. We took the boat first to about sixty feet, just trying the valves and making sure they all worked as well in the water as they did in the dry. And then we pulled the plug."

"Went down to eleven hundred feet like a lady," Rick said, handing over the clipboard. "And we leveled off there."

"No trouble with depth control, using the manuals?"

"Well . . . no."

"But it was harder work," the captain pursued.

Rick nodded reluctantly. "Yes, as expected. Operating under full computer control really spoils you. Gets you to thinking you're a genius—the way the new jet fighter control systems can make you think you're God's gift to airmanship. They keep you from doing anything really stupid. So you forget."

"But using manual control . . ."

"Using manual control, you get a real worm's-eye view of how much the computer's been helping, because you have to do it all for yourself. All the flooding and blowing and fine-tuning that you never noticed before." Rick grinned diffidently. "I felt like I did when I was a little kid, just learning to handle the controls of an airplane, and my father said let him know the next time we drifted through our assigned altitude!"

Rick's own smile vanished, and he reminded himself that

Captain Ward must have been under considerable pressure all the time they were underwater. "The *Albatross* worked fine," he said. "The manual controls do the job they were intended to do—and then some."

The captain nodded slowly. But his expression still did not lighten, and the two younger men misinterpreted his reaction.

"Come on, Skipper," Rick said. "There was a little frammis, yeah. But we came through okay and the boat's running like a Timex! It took a licking and it kept on ticking."

But the captain's expression remained bleak, and after a moment Rick's own spirits whipstalled and fell off into a flat spin.

"Got a little news for you," the captain said. "From the Navy department."

Something cold and hard that had been squeezing Rick's insides relaxed a little. Whatever the news was, it probably wasn't good; the captain looked like a thundercloud. But at least it was something professional, rather than personal.

"Stan Leppard, my friend from DIA, flew out from Scripps along with Mac this morning," Captain Ward said. "Got here just a minute or two after you left the surface. They'll both be interested to hear how it went. But Stan'll want to tell his own news himself." He led the way across the deck, with the two hydronauts (a commonly accepted name for submersible drivers)—still in wet suits—trailing behind.

The temperature in the lounge was at least twenty degrees warmer than outside, and they spent the first minute or so helping themselves to mugs of steaming coffee while exchanging social noises with their visitor and trying to get some kind of subliminal message from Mac. But the ex-chief sat silent and uncommunicative, eyes fixed on his own coffee cup, allowing Colonel Leppard to carry the ball.

"Got a message from an old friend of yours," Leppard told Rick. "Shavetail named Jinx Rafferty."

Rick grinned. "What's the old apple-knocker have to say?"

"Just that the next time you decide to start a war, include him out. And he doesn't want to play any more acey-deucy with you, either."

Rick laughed. "Can't say I blame him," he admitted. "On either count."

"You been hustlin' the Marines at acey-deucy again?" Captain Ward said. "Thought your daddy and me taught you better'n that."

"Hustling?" Rick said. "Who said hustling? I just play the game. A little."

"Yeah," the captain replied.

"The first thing that I came to tell you," Stan Leppard said when all were ready to listen, "is that the undersea search for Temnota has been suspended. As of now."

"You're crazy!" Rick said. "You mean just for the weekend, right? Begin fresh again on Monday . . ."

But Leppard shook his head. "Sorry," he said. "I wish it were that way, and I think a mistake's being made. But they're sure, now, that there's nothing to find. So the whole show's been scrubbed."

"But—damn it—it's got to be there!" Rick said. "I mean . . . according to everything we were told about it, this Temnota thing has got to be using some kind of nuclear power, right?"

"Also," Mac said, picking up the ball, "it just makes good sense to put a nuclear plant in deep water because pressures down there make everything safer. Accidents can happen because the radioactive coolant is under a lot of pressure that has to be dealt with the hard way—using a radiator of heavy-duty pipe inside a containment dome. Put it two or three thousand feet down in the ocean, and the danger of blowout is minimal because the pressure outside is about equal to the pressure you build up inside—and there's a perfect site right off Las Olinas. The Santa Ana Deeps: three thousand feet or more. You just couldn't ask for better!"

"Plus," Rick said, "you wouldn't even have to spend a lot of time designing a new system. The nuclear reactors that drive Soviet subs can put out enough power at peak demand to crank every car engine in Detroit, with enough juice left over for Toledo and Peoria!"

"To which," Mac concluded, "you add the physical evidence. Don't forget that."

Leppard looked at him. "Physical evidence?"

"Item one, An EMP right in Las Olinas . . . associated with a major blackout and some kind of underwater shock—which just has to be part of the same thing!"

"Especially," Captain Ward interjected, "since there was no seismic record of any quake at the time the three events took place."

"And item two," Mac went on, "the body. The one that's still in the coroner's office. The liquid-breathing frogman. The one Rick and I saw earlier, at two thousand feet . . ." He trailed off, and for a long moment there was silence in the room. And then Leppard sighed.

"You're right, of course," he said.

"Then . . . ?"

"The decision to call off the search wasn't mine," the Marine continued. "For whatever it may be worth to you, there isn't an argument you've presented here that I didn't use, trying to get the thing continued for even a little longer. Not a one! In the end, though, about all I did was raise the temperature of the air around me by a degree or two. The decision was made at the highest level."

"The highest?" Captain Ward said.

"Well—semihighest," Leppard temporized. "The Joint Chiefs, which usually is high enough. At least for me."

Captain Ward shrugged. "Well, I guess that tears it, then."

"Look, we could—" Mac began.

But the captain cut him off with a wave of the hand. "First thing I learned, fresh out of the Academy," he said, "is that you do not win arguments with the Joint Chiefs of Staff. Ever."

"Ever," Leppard repeated, nodding for further emphasis. "Amen! And anyway, there's something I haven't told you yet. You see, the chiefs' decision wasn't based—entirely—on the negative results of the search so far."

"If they'd give it even one more day," Mac mourned. "Just one more day to take a real look down in the Santa Ana Deeps."

"We did," Leppard said. "Sent a 688 boat, one of the Los Angeles–class attack submarines, down to check things out. Result—zip."

Captain Ward made a sour face. "Los Angeles–class attack boats can't go deep enough," he protested. "They've got an operational depth of . . . what? Maybe four hundred fifty meters; just less than fifteen hundred feet. Max depth, seven hundred fifty meters, which is about twenty-five hundred feet. And if this . . . Temnota . . . thing is there in the deeps, where

I really think it's got to be, then it's at least two hundred meters farther down."

"Checked the spot," Leppard said. "With sonar."

"And ran into a thermocline—a temperature gradient that reflects sonar waves just like a mirror," the captain retorted. "I saw the graphs myself."

"Maybe," Leppard admitted. "Maybe so, and I'm not saying you're wrong. But they also dropped a SOSUS listening device . . . and got back nothing at all. Not even a belch. Anyhow, as I say, the decision wasn't based just on the fact that the search hasn't turned up anything."

Leppard leaned back in his chair, sipping the coffee. "As you know, the whole search thing got started, before we even had any input from you boys and your liquid-breathing diver, on the basis of some information we—the DIA, I mean—got from our buddies in Israeli intelligence."

Captain Ward nodded. "Petchukocov," he said. "The old Politburo fugitive who walked in on them in Tel Aviv."

"The same. Talked his head off about Temnota and handed us what sounded at the time like a good idea of the location. On the floor of the ocean, within range of major population centers."

"Right," Captain Ward said. "And Las Olinas is a prime candidate, not only because the EMP happened here and the drowned Soviet frog was found here, but also because there's even a distribution cable from the Las Olinas power station that leads down into the bay en route to San Diego and L.A.—and that would be the best and easiest way of tapping into the power grid, right there."

Leppard looked at the old man with real interest. "How in the hell," he inquired, "do you know about that?"

The captain growled, "I got friends here and there, and they tell me things."

"Okay, then. So you also know divers have been checking the cable out inch by inch. And found zip. Right?"

"Wrong! They'd started to check. Nowhere near done with it; and there's places where it's too deep to have a real close look."

Leppard shrugged. "Anyway, your information, fitted in with Petchukocov's, just seemed to tie everything up in a neat bundle. But . . . now the whole tune's changed. Now he's claiming there was never anything under the sea—not in the Atlantic. And not in the Pacific, either."

"You mean, he's saying now there's no Temnota? At all?"

"Oh, no!" Leppard shook his head emphatically. "No. Petchukocov's still insisting that there's a Temnota, all right. Only now he says he was lying about the location."

"Lying?"

"Yep. Carrying out a deliberate attempt at disinformation; blowing smoke to keep us looking in the wrong direction."

"Bullshit!"

"Maybe," Leppard said. "Maybe so. But now he's telling the Israelis that the airliner he was supposed to be on was shot down not in an attempt to kill him as he said, but as part of the smoke screen. To make us believe him when he lied to us about Temnota's location. Told us it was under water."

"But damn it—it's down there! In the Santa Ana Deeps. I'd bet my life on it," Mac exploded. "The dead frogman, the EMP, the blackout; all of it points in just one direction."

"Which," Leppard said, "is just what Petchukocov says it was supposed to do. All to keep us interested in the ocean, while the real Temnota station is up above our heads. In orbit."

"And they . . . believe him?"

Leppard sighed. "They might not have," he said. "Might have figured it was just one more move in a long chess game. Except this time there was a real convincer."

Mac, Rick, Kiwi, and the Captain all looked at each other.

"Petchukocov changed his story," Leppard said, "after a second—and this time apparently very real—attempt on his life."

"Jee-zus!"

The Marine officer nodded appreciatively. "I'll drink to that," he said, waving the coffee mug in Rick's direction. "Because this time an Israeli Shin Bet agent iced a known professional hit man from GRU—Soviet military intelligence—just one split second after the guy had fired a single rifle bullet at Petchukocov's head . . . and missed!"

Vienna, Austria

Sunday, November 2
12:01 P.M.

He was a minute late—but this was Sunday.

The lobby of the Hotel Imperial on the Ringstrasse, across the square from the Opera, was almost deserted when a lanky man in an American-cut blue blazer and open-neck sport shirt entered and crossed quietly to a grand staircase.

Rear Adm. R. B. Carter, USN, had left uniform and perks behind in the Persian Gulf, traveling alone on an innocuous duplicate civilian passport. The State Department supplied them to senior officers whose duties might require them to move about the world without attracting attention.

So if anyone noticed a meeting between two old friends at the little two-stool bar on the mezzanine of the Imperial, he told himself, it would probably be only the CIA and KGB. No one had ever discovered a satisfactory way of avoiding them. And anyway, Yuri didn't seem to care.

Climbing the stairs, Carter wondered about that, remembering the multiple layerings of security and restraint that had inhibited their words and actions back in the days when they both had been active spacemen, exchanging visits to each other's country.

There was a special bond between Yuri and himself. Had they really achieved that elusive thing called friendship? Was it even possible?

"Carter . . . old friend."

The admiral halted and peered narrowly at the man who had spoken his name. But the gaunt and hollow-eyed fossil wearing a polo shirt and ill-cut sports jacket that hung limply from his shoulders was no one he had ever seen before in his life. He hesitated for a moment before grasping the hand outstretched toward him.

"Yuri . . . ?"

The apparition smiled, exposing a mouth almost devoid of teeth, and nodded eagerly.

"*Da!* Yes, old friend! It is Yuri. Old Yuri now—older than you can know. But Yuri. Yes!"

Carter tried to smile back, but wanted to weep. The Yuri he remembered, whose clandestine invitation to a Christmas reunion in Vienna he had accepted, had been a man dealing handsomely with the first mild harbingers of middle age. A few gray hairs. The barest hint of a paunch. Even little reading glasses that he insisted were needed only for the fine print. A sleepy Russian bear of a man. And always half-smiling. But above all confident: sure of himself and his world and of his place in it. That had been their great commonality. An identity of risks knowingly accepted and defied.

He did not know this man at all.

"Yuri." Richard Carter forced the lines of his face into a smile and moved forward, virtually forcing Yuri back onto the barstool where he had been sitting when Carter arrived.

"It's—it's good to see you."

"And I am looking well. Not?"

"Uh . . . yes."

"And you are as big a liar as ever, I think, my friend Carter. Ha!"

The sunken eyes flashed, and for a moment the Yuri of old looked out at his friend and laughed with him.

"I look," the Russian said, "like man who has been ill for hundred years, and unfed for twice as long. Old friend, they have mirrors, even in mother Russia. And I have looked into them."

Carter shook his head gently, unable to find words. But Narmonov spoke them for him.

"Not to lie," he said. "Not to dissemble and put on happy face for poor old man. Is enough we see each other again. I am glad you see me. Glad we talk. Now. Today."

The laughter was gone from the gaunt man's face, but the sense of identity lingered, and Carter was startled to find himself wishing that it might go away. And leave the memories of his friend undisturbed.

"Come, old friend. Now we drink—and then we talk. But not much, and not again soon, I think. No. Not again."

Narmonov's lips parted again, briefly, in the gap-toothed smile. He eased down from the stool and moved around behind the tiny bar where he poured two drinks—buffalo-grass-flavored vodka for himself, bourbon for Carter—and set them in place, totally ignoring the hotel barman, who seemed to be asleep in a corner niche.

"We drink now," the Russian said. "You to your great country, me to the motherland. And then . . ."

Abruptly, almost mechanically, Narmonov raised the vodka to his lips and swallowed it in three enormous gulps, smacking the glass down again when he was done and wiping his lips with the back of his hand.

"Good," he said, nodding. "Very good! Almost I had forgotten."

Carter sipped his own drink and looked at his friend with a curiosity he could not disguise. "You've been where drinks were few and far between," he said, making it a statement rather than a question.

Narmonov nodded. "Yes. But come, my friend. Let us talk. It goes well for you? You are happy?"

Carter nodded. "Yes, I would say so. I'm still able to fly—airplanes, not the shuttle; I'm out of the space program for good—and I've been promoted."

"I hear this," Narmonov said. "And I am glad for you."

"Thank you."

And then, quite suddenly, the amenities were over.

"The letter I send you," Narmonov said. "The one about Temnota."

"Uh . . . yes."

"You read this? You believe?"

"I . . . read it."

"And turn it over to your government. Your—what? Spooks? To decide whether old friend Yuri is senile or crazy or a traitor. Or merely plays tricks. Or perhaps, works for the KGB and writes letters dictated by them to old friends. You do this. Yes?"

Carter allowed himself a moment to wonder if their conversation was being monitored, then decided he didn't give a damn one way or the other. The question was an honest one and deserved an honest answer. "Of course I did," he said.

Yuri nodded. "Good. And they decided . . . what?"

"At first," Carter said, "they couldn't make up their minds.

But then when your Cosmos 2300 satellite started putting out EMP bursts when it wasn't supposed to—they decided it could be a danger."

"So?"

"So . . . our president protested to your general secretary."

"And . . ."

"And nothing. Your head man said it was all nonsense; the satellite was a simple reconnaissance bird. And that's where it was allowed to stand."

"Yes." Yuri nodded again and looked back at his empty glass, but seemed in no hurry to refill it. The barman continued to sleep soundly.

"But then," Carter continued, "something else happened."

"Something else?"

"Yes. A member of the Politburo—Dimitri Petchukocov—turned up in Israel, and—"

"I know about Petchukocov."

"You know?"

"I was told. Just before I left on this trip. They told me I might be asked about him."

"And they told you what to say?"

Narmonov's expression, already solemn, darkened perceptibly. "They tell me many things," he said. "But back to the letter. You still believe it? Even now?"

"No." Carter put his glass down, still half full, and faced the Russian. "I don't believe it. I don't think anyone has built a nuclear plant and sent it into space. Or if they have, I still don't think it's powerful enough to do major damage on earth."

"And you are right, old friend Carter!" Narmonov's ruined mouth was smiling again, but there was no smile in his eyes. "Right to doubt old Yuri," he said. "Right to think he wrote lies. It is true. Or . . . not true. There is no atom plant up in the space. No laser beam coming down to earth to cut off electric power. I wrote that, all that," Narmonov said, "because . . . you have a son. Do you not?"

Carter nodded. "Yes, Ricky. He's a naval officer now."

"You must be very proud of him."

"He doesn't . . ."

"What?"

"Ricky's mother and I broke up, were divorced, when the

boy was small," Carter explained. "She married again and her new husband adopted him. He doesn't have my last name and very few people, even in the service, know that he's my son."

Narmonov nodded understandingly. "But you love him."

Carter smiled thinly. "Yes," he said. "I do."

"And you are proud, thinking of him?"

"Yes."

The Russian nodded again, his eyes distant. And then he seemed to pull himself together again, with a shudder.

"I too," he said, "have a son."

"I remember. He is a grown man now."

"*Da*. Grown. And in the service, too. But not like your son."

"No?"

"No. He is in SPETSNAZ—that is a special force, like your Green Berets or SEALs."

Carter was startled. "SPETSNAZ? That's funny. My boy started out to be a naval aviator, like his old man. But . . . things went wrong. And now he's in the SEALs. In training."

Narmonov's expression was unreadable. "Yes, curious. But let me go on. I asked you about your son, Ricky, because I wished you to understand why I did . . . what I did."

"Yuri . . ."

"Let me go on. My son was eighteen years old when I began to speak out against the craziness that was going on at Baikonur. At the Cosmodrome. Eighteen—and he saw his father arrested. Called a traitor. Sent to madhouse." The pain in the gaunt man's face was plain now. But his voice remained calm.

"And then," he said, "they threatened me. By threatening him. He was conscripted into the service, sent to the SPETSNAZ, and I was told to write the letter to you or things would . . . be done to him."

"Good God!"

"God? I do not know about this God, who lets such things be. But I know about the men who rule the motherland, yes. So I wrote lies to you."

"And even this," Yuri continued, "was not enough. In the madhouse where they sent me, in Gorky, they showed me picture—of my Andrey. His graduation picture, in SPETSNAZ. And then they showed me another picture. A terrible picture . . ." Narmonov's breath was coming in gasps now.

"A picture of a human being with strange device connected to his throat and his nose stitched shut," he went on as if there had been no interruption. "The little thing on his neck was oxygen recycler, and this . . . thing, I cannot call it a man . . . this thing that wore it was breathing liquid instead of air. You believe this?"

"I . . ."

"No. Of course not! Nor did I. But they showed me other pictures. Many others . . . of the operations they performed to make a man into such a thing, into something that they told me can live under water. And they said this would be done to my little boy. To Andrey!"

Yuri went behind the bar again, but this time he did not bother with the glass. Uncapping the bottle of vodka, he tipped it to his lips and drank thirstily.

"And then they . . . took him away from me! Carter, do you know what a null tank is? What you call sensory-deprivation chamber?"

Carter nodded slowly. "They put you—into that?"

"And kept me there, who knows how long? A minute? A year? A century? In there, Carter, they took it all away from me. All my memories of the life before. Everything. And gave me back part of them, all mixed with lies that they had made up for me to believe."

Carter shook his head.

"They told me," Yuri said, "crazy things. You would never believe. But understand just this much: They took my Andrey away from me. *They told me he had died. Had not lived long enough to join SPETSNAZ. That he was* gone. And by that, I knew he was dead. Or about to be so."

Suddenly, Carter was sick. "Yuri, I am so sorry."

"Yes," Narmonov said. "Thank you."

"How did you survive, Yuri? I don't know much about these sensory-deprivation things, but from what I hear, they scramble you up pretty permanently."

"I don't really know. I suppose my love for my son kept me sane, and anger and hatred toward the people doing this to me kept me alive. Perhaps I am just blessed with a very strong personality—one tempered in the fire of being a cosmonaut. Many hours spent in training under all types of extreme conditions force you to be able to focus your concentration. Maybe I was just lucky. But—that is not why I wished to meet you here today."

"No?"

"Today, I wish to talk to you, face-to-face as you say, to make you know that I am not liar. That I do not use my friend to spread lies. And to tell you, now, the truth."

"Temnota," Narmonov said, "exists. It is. And is atomic—a nuclear power plant, intended to produce terrible blast of electric energy. Just once."

"But . . . why? For what reason?"

"To make America start a war," Narmonov replied, "that she cannot win, because she will not have the capability to fire her nuclear missiles."

"Impossible."

"Listen to Yuri, old friend. This is not something plotted and planned by my government, but by a few madmen. Madmen in positions of power, who know that the General Secretary will never allow a nuclear strike to be launched unless the Rodina is herself under attack."

"And you think my government can be tricked, made to do that?"

"I think they will have no choice. For here is what will happen. Suddenly West Coast of your country will be blacked out. A massive electricity failure—the entire coast without power. Think of it! Then add to that a massive electromagnetic pulse, such as happens when atom bomb goes off, only many times more powerful."

Carter nodded slowly. "Computers, all of them. They would . . . !"

"Would die. Be deprogrammed. Yes. Which would mean total failure of communications."

"But . . . amateur radios . . ."

"Would also be out. Some deprogrammed, some without electric power to make a signal—and those that are still on the air being so confused that no important message can be sent or received."

"It . . . might work."

"It would work! And your president, the only one able to

release nuclear weapons, he will be in middle of this devastation."

"It—Temnota, I mean—it's on the East Coast? Near Washington?"

Narmonov's head wagged emphatically. "*Nyet!*" he said. "It is in west, at the bottom of the sea in a deep canyon just off southern California. Near former president's home out there. His farm. What they call Little White House."

"Christ!"

"Since your president enjoys close ties with predecessor and visits Little White House often," Narmonov continued, "it would be easy to isolate president. But your vice president would not be isolated, and he would be led to believe that power failure and all the rest were from attack by space satellites—the one you were led to believe caused the first, small blackout. *Da?* So he would try to knock it out. Destroy it."

"And your General Secretary would think his country was under attack! It would be considered an act of war."

Narmonov sighed. "Just so. And then he would retaliate—probably with atom weapons. And then—"

"—and then it would be over, almost before it started," Carter finished the sentence for him. "Christ, Yuri! I think it would work."

"Yes," Narmonov said. "I think it might, too. But . . . not now." He smiled, keeping his lips together this time, and reached again for the vodka bottle. "You will warn them? Tell them this time old Yuri does not lie?"

"I'll tell them . . ."

"But?"

"But sometimes it's not so easy to make people believe. You understand?"

Yuri smiled again, gently. "Oh, yes," he said. "But this time, all the same, I think they believe. For it is, what you call, deathbed statement."

"Yuri . . . ?"

"I am a dead man."

"You are ill?"

"In mind, in the heart. Yes. But no, not body. Still, I am to die."

He drank again from the bottle and stirred the sleeping barman with the toe of his shoe. The barman, off balance now, tumbled out of the niche and onto the floor, where he lay motionless.

"GRU," Narmonov said almost happily. "Military Intelligence. Detailed to replace the regular barman here and watch us when we met. Make sure I said nothing I should not say."

"He's dead?"

"Oh, yes. I killed him—single blow to temple. If you know the right place, it is quite easy—a minute or so before you arrived." He tilted the bottle again. Drank deeply, then put it down on the bar. "Good-bye, friend Carter," he said, smiling. "Warn them. The deathbed statement—make them believe! And go to your son. Speak to him. Tell him that you are his father. That you love him."

The GRU man had been armed with a 5.45mm PSM automatic, standard issue for security forces of the Soviet Union and Warsaw Pact nations, and it was in Narmonov's hand now, with the hammer back in firing position.

"Yuri—no!"

Trained reflexes brought Richard Carter leaping halfway across the bar in a sudden, maximum effort. But the cosmonaut had the advantage of surprise, and determination.

Before the admiral could reach him, Narmonov had turned the barrel of the weapon toward himself, took it into his mouth, and tightened his finger on the trigger.

Las Olinas, California

Sunday, November 2
6:14 A.M.

The smokestacks of the power plant, right down on the beach, made it easy to get a fix offshore. Just line them up with the water tower. After that it was a piece of cake. And there was no real need for the boat to stooge around waiting for him. He was less than a mile out. If he missed the boat at the end of the dive, he could make it in by himself. Coastal charts showed that the shelf dropped off sharply into the depths here. Temnota had to be using the Las Olinas plant's underwater cable to transmit the EMP to the surface, so it was just a matter of following that down . . . and up again when he was ready.

The only real problem, therefore, was going deep enough. And for that, he had his gill.

The *Steel Albatross* would have been a far better way to get down to the Soviet plant, of course. But it was out of the question. She was miles away in *Berkone*'s moon-pool off San Clemente Island, surrounded by government security types.

All he had to do was to get down there, to where it was all happening.

"Okay. We're in position."

The skipper of the charter boat throttled back. The morning wind hadn't begun to ruffle the water as yet, and the deck remained steady underfoot.

"You know," the skipper said, "that I think this whole thing is crazier'n hell?"

The charter skipper was a heavy man with sad eyes that concealed the soul of a riverboat gambler. Which made him an ideal choice for this morning's work; he would state his objections, but only once—and then get on with the job.

"I'll wait for you," he said after he helped Mac over the side.

"Don't bother. I don't know how long I'll be down. And I might not even come up right here."

The sad eyes got even sadder. "I'll wait," the skipper said, but Mac wasn't listening.

Mouthpiece. Knife. Buoyancy compensator. Belt. Face mask . . . and make sure you've got the snooper goggles clipped to the belt. Wouldn't do to get down there and find out you can't see. The HPNS injections . . .

That was the weak point, because the shots that the Scripps scientists had developed to combat high-pressure nervous syndrome were really still in the experimental stage. And anyway he didn't know the exact dosage for where he was going. And of course he couldn't ask.

Well, so what? It wouldn't be the first time.

La Jolla, California

Sunday, November 2
6:45 A.M.

Captain Will Ward was only half-awake when Stan Leppard finally talked a Scripps operator into putting him through to the old man's cubbyhole bedroom adjoining the *Steel Albatross* laboratory. The DIA man's first words brought him bolt upright on his cot. "The hell you say!" Ward thundered.

"Look," Leppard said, "your old buddy Fang fucking Carter always had a wild talent for finding trouble. But this time he's sort of outdone himself."

"But why'd Narmonov kill the GRU man and then himself? Was he nuts?"

"Far from it, at least according to the admiral. He says the poor bastard did it in order to warn us that the Temnota station is located under the sea, right off the coast here, and not in space. That a letter he sent about the deal a few weeks back was a lie . . . dictated by the GRU."

The captain took a deep breath and massaged his eyes. "Well," he said, "I guess you could say the message got delivered."

"Loud and clear," Leppard said. "Apparently Carter got through to DIA as soon as the Austrian cops let him make a call. But you know the way things are on a weekend in Washington. The guy who talked to him was a junior officer with an IQ that matches his hat size, who decided to protect his ass with paper . . . and forwarded everything through channels."

Captain Ward groaned. "In that case, how come we didn't hear about it sometime next spring?"

"Because the guy the j.o. bucked it to decided to come in and do a little paperwork in the morning. When he spotted the note and listened to the tape of the conversation, he had the guts to disturb his own boss—not to mention people at CIA and the Joint Chiefs—at their weekend revels.

"I owe him a bottle of Scotch, because he even remembered

ol' Stanley, way out here in Injun country, and tracked me down to my motel to give me The Word."

"It's a fucking miracle," Captain Ward snarled. He put his feet on the floor, groped for his reading glasses, then opened a drawer in the nightstand where he kept a supply of paper and sharpened pencils.

"All right, then," he said when he had found everything. "You didn't call to let me gloat over having been right all along. What do you want, and how long do we have to do it?"

Leppard told him—stressing the need to attract as little attention as possible. He slid over the fact that none of this had been approved, or even considered, by anyone empowered to authorize such movements.

But the captain didn't want to wait, either. "All right, then," Leppard said when they were done. "I'll start making my calls right now. Or maybe you'd like to get your lazy ass out of bed and give me a hand?"

"You got it!" The captain thumbed through his bedside book. "Okay," he roared, "then for starters, you get hold of Rick Tallman—I'll give you the number at his place in Imperial Beach—and I'll call Mac. Okay?"

Leppard put the phone down, looking for a pencil and paper of his own, but was back in a second and copied down the number the captain dictated. "Right," he said when he was done. "I'll make the call right now. No sweat. Fact is, I was going to have to phone the guy today anyway."

"What the hell for?"

"To give him a message from the admiral. Kind of personal, too, about how he'll be seeing him in person, just as soon as he can. You make anything of that?"

Captain Ward snorted. "Only that it takes some people longer to grow up than it does others."

"Huh?"

"Never mind. Just make your call."

The captain hung up, then lifted the receiver again to punch out Mac's home number.

Point Loma, California

Sunday, November 2
7:02 A.M.

Samantha Deane was off duty for the weekend. She was still asleep when her phone rang. Captain Ward asked her if she would mind putting her brother on the line. Her first impulse was to say that she would indeed mind. And her second was to smash the receiver against the wall. But her Navy discipline rose to the surface, and after a moment or two she managed to force herself to sit up and say that she would call him.

Yawning and wincing from the strong sunlight pouring through the living room windows, she crossed to the other side of the house and knocked on Mac's bedroom door.

But Mac wasn't there.

PART IX

OPERATIONAL MODE

Station “O”

Monday, November 3
10:51 A.M., Moscow Time

Though it was not yet time for his midday meal, according to the schedule for the Temnota frogmen, Andrey had completed his tasks early and found himself hungry. Eating in Station “O” was not the pleasurable experience it was for the rest of humanity, but it kept them alive. The frogmen couldn’t smell the food, so it had no taste. It was probably just as well.

Andrey opened a cabinet in the control room and removed a long, narrow foil pouch. He cut the top off with a pair of scissors, and began to work the food toward the open end with his fingers. This meal was beef and soy mix—all ground together and formed into a substance somewhat like baby food. Andrey tried to expel all the salt water from his mouth after he took the first mouthful of the bland, unattractive meal, but, as always, a little seawater flavored every bite. Station “O” ’s water purification plant gave them fresh water to drink, but every sip of fresh water was tainted with the salt water that was everywhere.

Andrey was almost used to the food now, but every once in a while he’d think about eating a normal meal—chicken, some bread and butter, and some sweet cake for dessert. He tried to keep these thoughts from his mind. At least, he rationalized, it’s easy to go to the bathroom.

As Andrey finished eating, a message came from Murmansk. The orders were entirely specific:

Activate the nuclear pile, take the generators to peak power, charge the potential storage vessel, and prepare to discharge the massive electric charge—at a signal to be relayed by radio.

Station "O" had been moved to operational status.

On Board *Berkone*

Monday, November 3
1:31 A.M.

"Way he went at it," Kiwi Kraus was saying, "I shouldn't wondah he made it all the way down there."

"But he couldn't get back up again?"

"Not alive. No."

The *Berkone*, with the *Steel Albatross* tucked snugly into a padded cradle amidships, was under way from San Clemente Island to the location just off Las Olinas beach where her crew hoped to have her anchored—and at work again—before dawn. They would set up shop where Mac was believed to have made his dive.

Not that anyone had the slightest hope of finding him alive. The dive-boat charter captain who had taken him out to the drop point had made a full report as soon as he was sure his client hadn't made it back to shore on his own.

"Told him it was a nutty thing to do," he said. "But I known ol' Mac since he was a pup, and he always seemed to know what he was doing. So this time, I guess I shoulda said no and stuck to it."

"Known Mac for a while now, myself," Captain Ward said. "And if you hadn't taken him out, he'd just have found someone else. Or rented a boat and gone alone."

"Or stolen one, if he couldn't rent it. Yeah, I know! But still . . ."

Samantha's reactions worried all of them. Dry eyed, she had been a model of efficiency throughout the day's air/sea search for her brother, parking Billy with a friendly neighbor and tending to the details that such a widespread effort generates.

Later, when the search was abandoned and all hope had vanished, she still didn't cry—or even speak of her loss—and the others began to worry. Rick remembered what she'd said about her inability to mourn the death of her husband properly and tried to get her to open up to him. But it was no use, and after one or two efforts he gave it up, afraid that she'd stop talking to him altogether.

She was aboard the *Berkone* now as medical officer, having assigned herself to the position after learning that Rick and Kiwi planned to dive the *Albatross* to the 3,000-foot level. That's where Mac had thought the Soviet Temnota installation would be.

Kiwi was self-assigned as well. "Thing is," the down easter said, explaining his determination to join the clandestine—and highly illegal—expedition, "Rick knows more'n anybody, 'cept of course for the skippah here, about the *Steel Albatross*. He can get it down there to where we got to go. And get us back."

"And so can I!" Captain Ward insisted loudly. "I was diving that damn thing before either one of you ever set foot aboard her!"

"True." Kiwi nodded, though no one believed he meant it. "True as a mama shark always goes for the balls. But you nevah been checked out on the gill—and you need to be trained on the Christless thing if you lookin' to do any good once you get down there."

"I could learn it all. In an hour!"

"Shouldn't wondah," Kiwi said. "But we don't have an hour to spare. And Rick has already made a whole bunch of dives with it, so he already knows enough about it not to kill his fool self halfway to the target."

"And besides," Samantha added, "I'd never authorize the dive with you in the boat."

"Authorize, my ass!" the captain screamed, a vein in his neck bulging.

"My prerogative, as medical officer. And I can assure you, sir, that if you set one foot on that boat without my say-so—I will not only resign, but inform the Navy, the Coast Guard, the Central Intelligence Agency, and anyone else I can think of that you've stolen government property for the purpose of making an unauthorized assault on a foreign military base, a breach of international law tantamount to treason, piracy, and an act of war!"

"Sweet . . . shit."

But Samantha didn't back up an inch.

Station "O"

Monday, November 3
11:37 A.M., Moscow Time

The Amis were definitely hunting them. First, the SOSUS rig. Then the sound of a submarine screw—with active sonar pinging—overhead. And then the diver, which was the real terror. . . .

In training at Murmansk, they had been told that the Amis were twenty years behind in undersea technology and there was no need to keep up their combat skills, since no one would be coming down to fight with them. That there was nothing to fear but the sea itself.

And now this. The diver had been dead when they found him. But not from a malfunction of his underwater breathing apparatus. He had most surely been alive on arrival at the base.

And he'd been able to accomplish a good amount of work before death claimed him. Somehow, the man had not only found their base but understood its purpose, and worked intelligently to neutralize it, sabotaging some of the heavy electrical connections and even trying to open one of the hatches. Perhaps he was planning to attack the residents of the habitat with his bare hands, for they had found no weapons.

Wire cutters, yes. And a complete underwater workman's tool belt with even a fascinating mini–welding rig (that the *starshina* had appropriated for his own). But no weapons, and no kind of artificial lighting equipment, either . . . which was a major puzzlement. Certainly no one could see at this depth without artificial light.

And the diver had not even been wearing a mask or goggles when they discovered his body, resting on the steel work-platform below the intake manifolds.

Andrey believed that the man had used some chemical means—as he and his companions did—to eliminate high-pressure nervous syndrome. And somehow he had gotten the dosage wrong. It was easy enough to do. Andrey had seen two or three cases of adverse reaction, triggered either by forgetting to renew the injections on schedule, or by overdose. And either could kill you, especially if one was diving alone, and there was no one around to help—which was the other thing about the diver that remained a mystery.

Immediately after finding the body, the entire squad had turned out to search the platform and its immediate area for the man's diving partner. But no partner had been found. Why would any sane man—and there was much about this diver to indicate that he was no lunatic—dive this deep alone?

It made no sense at all.

On Board *Berkone*

Monday, November 3
5:00 A.M.

Mooring the *Berkone* close inshore, and rigging the *Steel Albatross* for the next dive, were accomplished before dawn. But there was still much to be done before the dive could begin.

"I'm as much for making this dive as you," Captain Ward told Stan Leppard, who stood beside him in the lee of the main deckhouse. "But you haven't told any of us why your balls are on fire to get it done today."

Leppard tried to shrug the query off. "Just antsy, I guess. Like to get it done before someone finds out we . . . uh . . . borrowed your little bathtub toy."

"That's a load of whale shit," the captain said.

"Well . . . ," the Marine admitted.

"So . . . if you'd just let me in on it, it might be something I know how to fix, and maybe I can help. If it isn't, well, anyway I'll know what's going to hit the fan."

But Stan Leppard still had reservations. "Knowing about this," he declared, "could earn you an extra ten years in Portsmouth if anything goes wrong."

The captain managed a laugh. "Hell, boy," he said, "at my age, any sentence at all would turn out to be life."

"All right then. Here's the poop—but just keep it to yourself for the time being. Okay?"

"Loose lips won't sink this ship," the captain said.

"Well, when I talked to the guys back in Washington, the way they spelled the situation out to me, the dudes who thought up this hairy little plot—Politburo mavericks, or whatever they are—are a pretty good bet to be going operational with the damn thing in the next day or so."

"You're shittin' me."

"No, sir. Look, the whole idea is to cut the President off from the rest of the country for a while, isolate him and keep him from using the codes that can unlock the country's nuclear arsenal. To do that, they need to act at a time when he's out here. And he's visiting the former president and first lady. Staying at what they refer to as the Little White House. The Farm."

"Hot, wet, flying shit." The captain thought about it for a moment. "He's there now," he said, "at the farm."

"And it's no secret."

"So, now they'll go ahead?"

"The guys back at DIA—and CIA, too—think so."

"When?"

"Sometime in the next day or so. Which is why we have to destroy the installation now, before they can put their plan into action."

"Jesus-on-a-stick!"

"My sentiments exactly."

"But if the spooks know all this, why in the ever-loving, piss-eyed world don't they just scoop him up and move him out of the danger zone?"

The DIA man sighed profoundly. "You've never had to deal with our chief executive on a personal, one-to-one basis, have you? Remember, this is the man who won't allow broccoli in the White House."

On Board *Berkone* (off Las Olinas)

Monday, November 3
5:20 A.M.

Samantha wasn't happy about being unable to fine-tune the saturation statistics on the two men, but there was no equipment aboard the barge for a proper workup, and she had to be content with the saturation stats she had developed a week earlier for use in the gill's testing program.

Physical conditioning for maximum effort—the edge-of-the-envelope descent they would be making today—was a different matter entirely, and she trotted them through tests and chemical preparation with care and sensitivity, all the while subjecting them to a wide-ranging medical/technical refresher on problems they might expect to encounter . . . and measures for countering same.

". . . calculations in atmospheres absolute," she said, slipping a clip over Kiwi's nostrils and shoving a mouthpiece between his teeth, "which is the commonest procedure for measuring exotic gas atmospheres, though in fact you could probably tolerate the normal helium-oxygen mixes at pressures up to forty atmospheres or more, but below that the gill is programmed to start adding hydrogen to the gas—you'll be on tri-mix. Big breath, now. Good! Exhale." Kiwi bore it all with silent fortitude.

Not Rick, however. He was ordered to strip (he had a hard time believing he was actually taking his clothes off in front of Sam with Kiwi watching) and lie full length on the lounge conference table in order to receive a massive chemotherapeutic dose. The Scripps technicians had decided this was necessary to control the high-pressure nervous syndrome, counteract the effect of the rapid compression they would experience—and avoid hypothermia they would otherwise encounter.

"It's . . . cold," Rick objected.

But Samantha offered no sympathy. "Not as cold as where you're going. Now, move! No—not that way. On your back. Facing up. Okay."

"Ow!"

Samantha had inserted needles in both his arms. But the one she stabbed into his leg, uncomfortably close to the groin, struck him as an insult.

"What in the blue-balled hell was that?" he demanded.

"I told you that this dose of anti-HPNS serum would be larger—and more pervasive—than the injections you've had earlier," she told him. "And it's got something new in it, too; something to keep your nerves nice and steady while you're down there, without adversely affecting judgment or making you drowsy."

"Thanks, Mom!"

"Don't mention it. Now shut up. The gill has been tested satisfactorily to thirty-seven hundred feet, and experiments indicate that it will only increase in functional efficiency the farther down you go."

"Yes, dear."

"As currently conceived, it is entirely self-monitoring. . . ."

But by this time, Rick was beginning to lose interest. The needle attached to his upper leg was in wrong. He was sure of it. The whole day was beginning to shape up as a real loser. Formal complaint, however, would have to wait.

The *Berkone* had no chaplain on board.

6:15 A.M.

The *Steel Albatross* was ready: equipment and explosives loaded, batteries fully charged, all systems go. Checked and rechecked. They would never be in better condition. Time to begin the dive.

"I'm coming back from this," Rick told Captain Ward as he pulled on his cowl and prepared to climb down into the forward seat. "I'm not the suicide-mission type."

"And neither am I," said Kiwi, already in the aft seat and strapped down.

"Gee, I thought you were," said Rick, grinning at Kiwi.

"I know you're not," the captain said.

"But," Rick continued, "my mother—you know how she is—she might not know that. Might not understand. She always did think I was a little too fond of the hairy action. So . . ."

"I'll tell her. If it comes to that."

They paused awkwardly, trying not to look at each other.

Rick had something he wanted to say to Samantha. Not a good-bye. Just a joke for Billy about a bear and some ants. But she seemed suddenly to have made herself scarce, and remembering what she had been through in the past few days, he didn't pursue her.

"One other thing," Rick said. "About my father . . ."

"That reminds me, Ricky," the captain said. "He wired me care of Scripps. It was passed on by radio, but—damn me—it slipped my mind until right now."

"That's okay, sir."

"The hell it is! But anyhow, he's on his way here. Wanted you to know that."

Rick smiled reminiscently, then grinned. "You know, back in the Gulf, when he sent me off to the SEALs, I was really pissed."

Kiwi grinned at him. "Well, you coulda fooled me. I thought you were tickled pink to be here."

"I was ready to have a cow. And when the plane stopped over in Washington, I damn near got off and took a hike over to BuPers to see about a change of orders. Or maybe even turning in my resignation."

"You didn't, though," the captain said.

"No. But all the same I kept the idea in mind. Never totally ruled it out. And I have to tell you, I still haven't made up my mind."

Captain Ward nodded. "I know, Ricky, I know."

On Board the *Steel Albatross*

Monday, November 3
6:36 A.M.

Ten minutes into the dive, Rick and Kiwi knew they were on the right track.

The descent had been swift. With Captain Ward's grudging consent Rick had programmed the *Steel Albatross* for a descent rate of 170 feet per minute, gambling that nothing of interest would be found above the 1,500-foot level that still marked the upper boundary of the sonar-reflective thermocline recorded during the earlier sonar searches.

Rick used the SA-1's headlight array to check the water ahead. But when ambient light was totally gone as they passed over the edge of the continental shelf and began their plunge into the Santa Ana Deeps, he shut off the lights and they flipped down the light-enhancing snooper glasses.

The effect was, as ever, eerie. And briefly disorienting; Rick experienced a moment of vertigo—vaguely reminiscent of his first peep over the edge of the Grand Canyon—as his senses struggled to adjust themselves to the altered world around the boat.

Ocean water is murky near the surface when you remain close to shore, polluted by the atmosphere and by the beings who lived their lives in that gaseous environment. Even in those parts of the sea least touched by man and his artifacts, the actions of tide and wave can fill the area with light-scattering grains of dirt and sand that dazzle the eye and frustrate sight-dependent exploration of all kinds. But deeper water is different. Surface agitations are left behind along with sunlight, and the undersea world has its own unique sources of illumination, many of which are normally below the threshold of human perception.

The snooper lenses Rick and Kiwi wore had been designed to gather the meager radiance of marine bioluminescence—light emitted by certain fungi and deep-sea fishes—enhance it, and transmit the result to the eye, where it was registered as a green-tinted world of sharply etched realities related to, but vaguely different from, the world of the surface.

The two hydronaut/aquanauts had seen the undersea world revealed by these snoopers before and accepted it as they accepted the upper world into which they had been born, on a basis of trust, combined with equal parts of caution and curiosity. And it was on such a basis now that they rode the SA-1 into the depths.

Rick found his fighter pilot's instincts challenged by the

work of keeping the *Steel Albatross* within sight of the eastern wall of the undersea canyon.

Terrain here (they were now at 1,800 feet, and still descending at 170 feet per minute) was entirely unexplored and unmapped; outcrops of rock and sudden folds in the seabed posed very immediate hazards given the slow reaction time of their undersea glider. But Rick was at pains to keep the wall in sight nonetheless, because it was there that he hoped to find concrete evidence that a nuclear power-generating station lay in the abyss below.

He blinked, straining behind the high-tech goggles for any evidence of man's handiwork. Something square in the world of irregular randomness. Something rectangular. Any straight—or near-straight—line.

But it was Kiwi who finally spotted the telltale sign. "There!"

Rick drew a sharp breath as he craned to check Kiwi's observation with his own.

"Two o'clock. Low."

Rick looked down and to his right.

"There on the canyon. The big, thick, round something. See? It runs from somewhere up there on the surface almost straight down to . . . nowhere!"

Give the barrel-shaped clamdigger credit—his eyes were sharp. That was the Las Olinas County Water and Power Company cable Colonel Leppard had speculated the Soviets might have tapped into, down in the Santa Ana Deeps.

"Mac must've seen it, too," Kiwi said, thinking out loud.

Rick nodded somberly. Slightly increasing the nose-down angle, he maneuvered the *Steel Albatross* even closer to the side of the canyon, inspecting the heavily insulated power cable, trying to see how it was tethered, and toying briefly with the idea of reporting their find to the surface via ELF radio.

But the Navy would be monitoring all traffic, and a transmission from the *Steel Albatross* would set off alarms all the way to the Pentagon.

"There's our Yellow Brick Road," Rick said, turning the boat around in a figure eight.

"Lions 'n' tigers 'n' bears, oh my!" Kiwi replied.

Startled by the entirely un-Kiwi-like comment, Rick threw

a glance over his shoulder—and was surprised to find the senior SEAL instructor grinning at him. Why, that little turkey liked the hairy action as much as he did!

"Wish't we could use the headlights," Kiwi said. "Just for a minute, maybe."

"So do I. Like to get a better look at that cable. At least we know where it goes. It's tied in to San Diego and Los Angeles, so electricity can be shifted around during peak use periods."

Kiwi grunted. As an observer, undistracted by any need to control the *Albatross*, he was free to keep an eye on the armored electric cable.

The nuclear-powered generator that they figured the Soviets had on the bottom had to have some way of transmitting the power to the surface if it was to be used there—and everything they had heard about Temnota pointed clearly to such a conclusion. So there had to be a splice in the cable that was attached to the power station.

All sense of the ocean's surface had been lost now, and Rick concentrated on the nuts-and-bolts work of easing the *Albatross* downward while keeping the cable in sight . . . following its downward path along the near-vertical side of the submerged canyon, and being very, very careful to stay out of the way of potentially disastrous overhangs.

There was something odd about the cable's angle; it turned sharply to the north as if in response to water currents down here. He banked to port, trying to scan the area without losing sight of the main attraction.

The computer screen, even adjusted to minimal brightness, remained a distraction, and a real danger. At a level that would be entirely dark to the unaided eye, the blasted thing was a center of blinding intensity when amplified by the snooper lenses. But cutting it off entirely was out of the question.

Here, he thought, was something to take up with Captain Ward when they surfaced. Snoopers and computer screens could turn out to be mutually exclusive luxuries unless some way could be developed to make it visible to the unsnoopered eye, while not overwhelming to a man equipped with the special lenses. Meanwhile, the best thing was to keep his eyes front, away from the screen, risking just a glance now and then to check their progress. Maybe snooper bifocals? Or polarization?

. . . 2,319 feet . . . They were going down more slowly now. Rick had adjusted the descent rate to 120 feet per minute, which made a noticeable difference in the *Albatross*'s handling qualities. Accustomed to the firmly positive feel of the controls in fast-descent mode, he was irritated to find himself thrown off-balance by the boat's slower responses.

. . . 2,660 . . . "There," Kiwi commented. "Think it—yeah—goes back the other way. To starboard."

Rick brought the *Albatross* around in a wide turn and saw that Kiwi was right. The thick cable was attached to the steep side of the canyon, where it branched into two cables. The marine-life-encrusted cable angled back to the south, and the spliced-in cable plunged downward. He held the turn for more than 180 degrees and then overcorrected in an effort to keep clear of the wall of unadorned rock. Damned mushy controls.

. . . 2,766 . . . Straining snooper-assisted eyes into the darkness ahead, Rick followed the descending cable on its northward zig, down into the depths. He moved his left hand to increase their descent rate, but stopped short. They were going down fast enough already. Bottom couldn't be too far below. The boat was equipped with an extremely accurate Fathometer, and side-looking sonar that could have established their position to within a few inches—but he had turned them off before the dive and stuck tape over the controls to avoid any possibility of turning them on by accident. No sense setting off bells and whistles to let anyone down below know they were coming.

Still, it might be time to level off. Take just a moment to have one more look at the coastal chart—check out the depth of the little sunken valley where they had decided the Temnota base might be. But he restrained himself.

. . . 2,809 . . . "Bottom coming up. Twelve o'clock . . . Jeezus!"

Kiwi's last word echoed in the cockpit, defining its limits and emphasizing the tightness of the fit. Rick remembered his own initial reaction to the sight of a human being—at ease in the depths without an air tank—moving and obviously quite at home, like the man he could see kneeling on the bottom now, a little more than a hundred feet ahead. And looking straight at them. . . .

Santa Ana Deeps

Monday, November 3
5:41 P.M., Moscow Time

Kornilov knew he should not be outside without a partner. But it was only for a moment, and everyone else had been busy when a small water-processing intake was blocked. So he had slipped out to handle the chore by himself and the hell with them.

Too much had been made of the discovery of the Ami diver's body. He had been dead, but not because of anything they had done. The sea itself had claimed him, because the Amis could not match Soviet undersea technology. They just didn't work hard enough at it.

The object that had been obstructing the water intake finally came free in his hand, and he held it up curiously for inspection.

Eyeglasses? Or some kind of . . . goggles? Unlike anything he had ever seen before in his life; certainly not made in Mother Russia. And not a part of the equipment issued and approved by SPETSNAZ for the Temnota units. Perhaps he should bring them back to the *starshina*.

But first, why not take an extra moment to check out the electric connections in this same service pocket? No sense doing things by halves.

Santa Ana Deeps

Monday, November 3
6:52 A.M.

"I don't think he can see us," Kiwi said.

The Soviet frog hadn't offered the slightest response to their arrival. He was just kneeling there on the sea bottom, face turned in their direction but obviously oblivious to their presence, examining something in the beam of his helmet-mounted light.

"The eyes," Kiwi said. "Someone should have thought to check out the eyes of that dead one they found—see if they'd been altered for better vision in darkness or . . . showed signs of prolonged pressure from wearing goggles."

Rick agreed. "Yeah. But the eyes were gone by the time the body was recovered. Anyway, I think we got all the answers we need, now. See that miner's lamp he's wearing on his head? I think there's a chance they can't see . . . at all . . . without it. Can't see anything not in the direct beam of the headlamp."

The *Steel Albatross* had landed, softly and evenly, on a flat part of the bottom. Rick paused for a moment to check their depth (they were at 2,907 feet) before turning the screen's brightness control sharply to the left, leaving the cockpit in total darkness as he turned his snooper-assisted eyes back in the direction of the Soviet frog.

The snoopers gave them a real edge on the Russkies. They could see without being seen.

"Spooky mother," Rick muttered.

"Wondah why he didn't hear us coming, even if he couldn't see us. Water's a good conductor. He ought to have noticed."

"Maybe," Rick said. "But remember, sound travels so fast in water, he's getting no directionality, so if he heard anything, he probably thought it came from his own habitat. Depends, also, on what kind of shape his eardrums are in—after all they've done to him—and how much interference there was."

"Interference?"

"Ambient sea-noises. Clicking shrimp; things like that. You can hear 'em now, if you . . . fuck!"

The enemy frog had shifted position for a moment, and a flash of blinding intensity struck the canopy of the *Steel Albatross*.

"Wooo," Kiwi said. "Kind of bright with the snoopers on."

"Fuck," Rick repeated.

"Some other time perhaps. But that light can be used as a weapon against us. Okay? Hey, looky there what he's doing. The thing in the little box—I make it a volt-ohm meter, like you could buy for a few bucks in a hardware store. Little hand-held gizmo."

"And he's using it, down here?"

"Seems to be. Might be running a checklist against someone punching the buttons in the . . . control room or something."

There was a moment of silence, broken, finally, by Kiwi. "So—what's your pleasure? Take the bastid now, or wait and let him lead us to . . . wherever."

Kiwi's question had more than one answer, and the very fact that he had asked it instead of making the decision himself as senior officer present was unsettling. Certainly out of character. Rick might nominally be in the position of authority so long as he was piloting the *Steel Albatross* and Kiwi was a passenger on board. But they were stationary now, ready to exit their delivery vehicle, and that put the senior officer back in command. Especially since he had far more experience with the gill they would be using to stay alive as soon as they began the EVA (extravehicular activity)—went outside the boat.

"Well, before we decide what to do about our Russkie friend out there," Rick said at last, "I think we better find out what happens when we flood the boat."

"Was afraid you'd say that."

Preparations for leaving the *Steel Albatross* were not simple. Rick and Kiwi were both wearing wet suits and weight belts. But fins would have been uncomfortable and unhandy during the descent, so they had to struggle into these after they were on the bottom. And the fins were only the first problem; weapons and explosives were outside, strapped to the hull of the *Albatross*. Other equipment (that had to be mounted on their chests and backs) had been stowed under the instrument panel, and in other nooks and crannies.

The weapons and explosives could wait until they went EVA, but they had to be wearing the rest before the cockpit was flooded.

Rick and Mac had gone through the evolution together on a dry-run basis a few times in order to become familiar with the various problems presented. But Kiwi had been through the routine only once, with the *Albatross* in its cradle on the barge during the trip from San Clemente Island to Las Olinas, and now Rick found himself trying to get into his own gear while keeping an eye on the other man and worrying about his reactions to things that a surface exercise couldn't teach.

"Turn," Rick said.

Kiwi, bent double in an effort to get the equipment pack in place on his back, shot a baleful glance in Rick's direction, then understood what was intended. He squirmed himself into a kneeling position in the seat while Rick adjusted the straps. Then he wriggled around to face front again and went to work on Rick, returning the favor.

After that came the fins. "Like this," Rick said. "Make like a yogi."

Kiwi watched unhappily while Rick eased his right leg out of the cockpit well and brought his knee even with his ear—holding his foot in the only remaining space while he forced the toes into the flipper, then eased the heel band in place.

Then Kiwi tried it himself. And got stuck. The carbon-dioxide-scrubber unit for the gill was positioned in the center of his chest, and Kiwi couldn't seem to get his leg past it, no matter how far he forced himself into the corner of the rear cockpit.

"Loosen the straps," Rick said, pointing to the ones on his own chest and moving to ease Kiwi's when he was in position to do so.

"Didn't the Marx Brothers start this way?" Kiwi grunted as his right foot finally came within range of the waiting fin.

"This," Rick declared, "is the stateroom scene from *A Night at the Opera*. All four Marx Brothers: Groucho, Harpo, Chico, and Karl."

"Hey, you forgot Zeppo."

"And two hard-boiled eggs, honk, honk."

"You're a sick man, Tallman."

"I had a good instructor, sir!"

The last pieces of equipment they put on were their new goggles, automatically pressure-regulated by small air tubes connected to the gill. They couldn't wear standard face masks, which would be too bulky to fit under the flip-down snoopers. And at these pressures, regular goggles would be driven straight into their eye sockets as you can't regulate the pressure inside the goggles. But the people at Scripps had come through in the clutch.

They were fully suited up now, and facing front in the seats.

"Prepare to exit the boat?"

"R-Rog," said Rick.

"Then . . . take a big breath."

It was a standing joke, one hoary with age among SEALs (and probably thought up by their UDT forebears). But it had always seemed to get a smile, until now.

The on-board computer system of the SA-1 was hermetically sealed, and Captain Ward said it was pressure-tested to four thousand feet. Rick shut down the electronic system and used the auxiliary manual system to flood the cockpit anyway. He was careful to keep the rate slow and steady.

These Soviet frogs, Rick mused as the water began to rise, have to be the most dedicated and selflessly devoted servants that Mother Russia has anywhere in the world. He ran off in his mind the almost endless list of self-imposed deprivations they endured: no normal communication by voice with anyone, no normal eating, no normal sleeping in a bed with covers, no sunshine, no blue sky or clouds, no normal body functions of any kind (having a machine doing their breathing for them), not even any air for chrissake. He found himself hoping they had some form of diversion, like movies or music or something, to keep them from going any crazier than they already were.

"Keep an eye on our guy outside there," Rick said as the water level approached the top of the instrument panel. "Sea noises or no sea noises, the Russkie could hear our air escaping and get curious. If he does, we'll have to do something about it." He looked over his shoulder and saw Kiwi grinning at him.

"What'd you have in mind, buddy?" Kiwi said.

Rick grinned back.

But the Soviet frogman continued his work oblivious to the SA-1, and ninety seconds later the cockpit was full, pressures equalized. Rick cracked the hatch.

Conversation was impossible now, but it wasn't needed. Rick was first out, allowing Kiwi to push the front seat forward, giving him room to make his own exit. Rick used the time to ease himself upward, checking his own buoyancy to make sure there was enough weight on the belt to give his feet traction, but not so much as to make swimming an effort. It seemed just right. Still, something seemed amiss.

Briefly panicked, Rick craned his head for another look at the Soviet diver, still a hundred feet away. Had the man moved closer? No. The man was where he had been, doing what he had been doing. But Rick's depth perception was altered, now that the snoopers were functioning in a liquid environment rather than a gaseous one.

Something else was weird though, and if it wasn't that . . . the temperature. It was normal; even a little bit warm. And that was contrary to everything he knew of the sea. Ocean water was not warm—not at this depth, anyway. But this time the water had seemed warm as it seeped into the boat, crept up his legs, around his neck, and over his head. Even without reference to the boat's built-in sensory system, he knew the readings at this depth would be low.

It had to be the shots, the conditioning injections developed by Scripps for reducing decompression times, staving off the cold, and controlling HPNS. They were working as advertised.

He dismissed it all from his mind and looked around to see Kiwi. All right, then, time to arm themselves.

This was Kiwi's field of expertise. He had drawn up the list of devices to be used for the mission, and now he acted as armorer, loading Rick with specially designed limpet mines and clamshells intended to do specific damage to steel hulls or armor plate (with minimal disturbance of the near environment), topping it off with a pair of Taglin-A spear pistols.

"Tag spears," Kiwi had said, leading Rick through the list of armaments before the dive, "are the best thing if we have to snap assholes with any of those jeezly water-breathers before we get down to business."

"I thought," Rick had said, surprised, "that you were a knife man. Liked the quiet."

Kiwi shrugged. "I am. And if we're in a place where a knife, or a garrote wire, can be used instead of the spears, well and good. They don't make noise; the spears do. If it's a matter of a pitched fight in the open, well, then the Tag spear's your weapon of choice, but you don't want to be too close to the target when it hits. It makes one hell of a bang. The explosive charge is a lot more powerful than the old spears that mounted a shotgun shell on the end. Even this one-hand pistol-type will knock a hole through a brick wall!"

The explosives were heavy, more than Rick could have carried on land. They were lighter here in the depths, but they were unhandy. If the Soviet frogman was to be their first target, then it might be better to dispose of him first, before encumbering themselves with the bulky ordnance.

He was going to try communicating this to Kiwi. But Kiwi was gone. Rick had the impulse to swear and started to drop the limpet mines he was carrying. But he stopped with the weapons still in his hands as the snoopers picked up something moving in the middle distance to his right.

Squinting, Rick was able to discern the flat outline of a man swimming. Evidently Kiwi had decided to take their man from behind—silently, without using a spear—in expectation that Rick would do his own part without coaching.

So go, bro! Let's get it on!

Kiwi was going for it now, his movements almost invisible even with the snoopers, but Rick didn't need to see him to know that he would be turning to port, beginning the flank run that would put him in striking position if the quarry was distracted at just the right moment. For Kiwi and he had the double advantages of surprise and superior vision; advantages that should count mightily in their favor.

Rick moved forward cautiously, like a man walking on tacks, carrying the load of explosives with his left arm. Take it easy. Move in on the guy, but don't get him all stirred up until Kiwi's in position.

And then he saw the second Soviet frog.

Rick's first reaction was a rush of intense anger directed at himself. From the very beginning of SEAL training they'd been drilling the doctrine into his thick skull: You Do Not Swim Without Your Buddy! SEALs come in two-man units. And for the very damned best of reasons: because two is the minimum number of swimmers needed to assure survival. One to do the work, and the other to guard the worker's butt. One to hold the compass course, one to watch for obstacles. One to get in trouble, one to get him out of it. So if it works for the SEALs, why not for the Russians?

Of course they would be down here in two-man teams, and of course a man working outside would have his swim buddy with him. To do part of the work, and to get him out of any trouble he got himself into.

Rick had frozen in position the moment the second Soviet swimmer appeared. But now he knew he must move.

Rick's knife was in his free right hand and he was moving forward, even as his left dumped the explosives. Allowing for the odd flattening effect of the snoopers, he was able to time his rush to the movements of the enemy frog. One step. Two. Three. And then the man was within reach.

Underwater combat is unlike fighting on the surface. It's slower, and the moves are different. But some holds—the ones that clamp and strangle—remain deadly, no matter where they are employed. And a knife can do its work anywhere.

Rick arrived in position behind the second enemy frog with his left arm already snaking forward to clamp over the head, baring the neck to a single stroke of the knife. But some instinct seemed to alert the man at the final moment.

The Soviet diver tensed, moving his head and shoulders as if to look behind him and shifting his body into a defensive semicrouch . . . which was just enough to spoil Rick's attack.

The intended face-clamp missed entirely, and Rick jinked sideways to avoid the inevitable counter.

The Russkie would try to bring his antagonist around to the front where he could get a look at him. The movement of light and shadow would surely attract the attention of the first frogman—which would overload the odds.

But the counterattack did not come. Wondering why, Rick was astonished to see the Russian standing entirely still, bent into a pose of defense, with something thick and green beginning to issue from his body obscuring Rick's view in the water nearby.

For a moment, Rick thought that they had all been mistaken—Sam, the pathologist at Las Olinas, Mac, the captain, and himself. They were dealing with true aliens; beings from some other world, where people lived underwater, and had green blood.

It was a thought to inspire awe, a replay of all the science fiction movies he had seen as a child. But a moment later he knew the truth.

The green ooze was really red. Its color had been shifted by the snoopers. This was the blood of a human being, one altered surgically to be able to breathe liquid. And sure enough, just as Sam had predicted, the guy was wearing a little flat box—the oxygen recycler—on a choker strap around his neck. And this was the first man Rick had ever killed.

The enemy frog's sudden movement had saved him from getting his throat cut. But it had not saved him from the knife. Instead of slicing through the arteries of the neck as intended, the razorlike blade had penetrated the lungs and heart.

Rick suddenly fought an urge to vomit and closed his eyes for a moment. But when they opened again, the world seemed much the same as the one in which he had always lived.

Suddenly Kiwi was behind the first frogman, and then it was over. Kiwi's arm went around the head in textbook fashion, clamping on the mouth, forcing the jawline up and backward to expose the neck. The second frog's blood flowed as green as his companion's.

But Kiwi didn't seem to notice. Before Rick could reach his side, Kraus was cleaning up the scene: towing his victim aside, looking for some place to stow the body where it would not immediately attract the attention of other enemy frogs who might pass by. Rick immediately began his own disposal routine.

Kiwi was in the lead, heading back to their landing site. If the Soviet frogs ever spotted the *Steel Albatross* squatting on their turf, it wouldn't matter what else they saw—the shit would hit the fan.

But when Kiwi started to wedge the body of his victim under the bulging side of the SA-1, something on the bottom seemed to distract him, and he began exploring the vicinity by touch.

Curious, Rick did the same. On emergence from the boat, he had found their landing surface agreeably hard and level underfoot, but he had hardly noted it at the time. Now, however, he examined the site more closely, and discovered that it seemed to be a steel grid—a hard, regular grille. Construction matting.

They were standing on a broad, artificial platform that must have been installed before anything else. Perhaps the terrain here was too unstable—or too rugged—for use without some kind of engineering adjustment. Or maybe this was simply a convenience. Electric cable could be rigged beneath the platform and serviced through access ports, like the one where the first Soviet frogman had been working when they initially saw him.

Kiwi was already making use of their discovery, using bungee cords to bind the dead enemy's body in place. Rick followed suit at once, discovering that whatever distaste he had felt for handling the body had evaporated in the heat of the need to get on with the job.

When they were done, the two aquanauts retrieved the tools of their trade. Limpet mines and other demolitions gear were where they had left them, but the rest of the load wasn't as easy to find. The construction mat was covered with a layer of silt that concealed any small object dropped onto it. Only the tip of a spare Taglin spear, protruding from the muck, offered a clue—and everything else had to be recovered by touch.

When their armament had been reassembled, Rick glanced at the luminous dial of his watch and was astonished to discover that less than five minutes had elapsed since they'd left the *Steel Albatross*.

Now nothing else was visible in the vicinity, even with the snoopers, so they would have to make a search. But it mustn't take too long. This called for a decision. Separately, they could examine twice as much territory, but separation would make them twice as vulnerable should either happen across the path of another water-breather.

Rick thought it over, then glanced at Kiwi, whose expression was unreadable behind snoopers and mouthpiece. Rick quirked his head to the right and stabbed a thumb at himself, then pointed left and looked at Kiwi—who hesitated only a moment before nodding agreement. They would search separately.

It was a violation of sacrosanct SEAL doctrine—you do *not* lose contact with your dive buddy—and also of the basic military caution against dividing one's forces in the face of superior (or undetermined) hostile forces.

But the decision was made. Leave the arguments to the debriefing they would undergo afterward. If there was an afterward.

Cautiously, scanning a 270-degree arc before each step (and glancing occasionally behind him as well), Rick moved away from the place where the two Soviet frogmen had died.

In addition to the explosives, he was carrying one of the compass boards they had brought along to keep themselves oriented when outside the *Albatross*. The course he had selected was north, so he could be fairly sure of finding Kiwi again along a reciprocal line if he found what they were looking for. But it was edgy work all the same, and more than once he found himself on the ragged edge of hyperventilation.

Then something touched him on the right shoulder. Rick's reaction was immediate—a twisting turn of 180 degrees that scattered equipment and ordnance in all directions and left him facing the way he had come with knife in hand.

But it was only Kiwi, who simply stepped back out of range of any countermove Rick might make and waited for him to settle down. Rick swallowed painfully and allowed himself a long moment to think unkind thoughts. Had Mrs. Kraus borne any children who lived? And was that little son of a bitch grinning behind the mouthpiece? He struggled to reassemble his demolition gear for the second time in five minutes. Kiwi's return could only mean that he had found what they were looking for, so when Rick was ready, they moved out smartly, with Kiwi in the lead.

Together, they had spent hours studying photographs and blueprints for various Soviet submarine types during the trip up the coast from the San Clemente Island anchorage. But they had concentrated on old "Yankee"-class boats, the Soviets' first modern nuclear-powered subs, which seemed the most likely choice for use in a program such as Temnota.

Thirty-four Yankee units had been turned out at the Komsomolsk and Severodvinsk shipyards between 1967 and 1974, apparently based on stolen plans for the USS *Benjamin Franklin*. Each was powered by a pair of pressurized water-cooled reactors providing heat to steam generators, and several were known to have been deactivated in compliance with SALT agreements in the early 1980s. It was Captain Ward's theory—

strongly seconded by Stan Leppard—that two or more of these "deactivated" nuclear submarines (SSBNs) were now lying on the bottom, with their nuclear reactors still active and ready to provide muscle for a surge that could black out electric power from Seattle to Tijuana, while deprogramming computers over a slightly smaller area.

The Yankee profile, with its blunt, asymmetrical nose and peculiar ellipsoidal cross section, was uppermost in his mind as he scanned his side of the Soviet work platform. But Rick did not recognize the first submarine that he encountered.

They were approaching her bow from an angle, and the portion that first became visible was high above their heads—a conventional boat-beak intended to cleave the surface rather than ride below it as did most modern submarines. He stopped in his tracks, looking at it and running the full Soviet nuclear-fleet list through his mind, but came up empty and turned questioningly to Kiwi, who was holding his hands in a T shape.

Tee?

Tango . . . ?

Vaguely, Rick recalled that the very top of the profile-book list they had studied had a section reserved for diesel types still believed to be in service with the Soviet fleet. He had paid little attention to that part of the list. They were looking for nuclear boats. All the same, he remembered that one of the diesel-powered types included was designated the Tango class.

But the last of those had been built sometime in the early 1970s. And anyway, the whole object of the exercise was to find something parked down here that would be capable of generating large amounts of power. He remembered reading that the last Soviet diesel subs had been highly advanced types, able to stay down running on batteries for a week or more. But they were power consumers, not power generators. Diesel engines do not operate under this much water (unless the Russkies had found some way of building 3,000-foot snorkel tubes), and besides, old boats like these could not possibly have withstood the pressure. Unless they were flooded?!

Kiwi seemed to understand Rick's thoughts. He shook his head, raised his shoulders in an elaborate shrug . . . and moved out again, gesturing for Rick to follow.

Something had been done to the side of the old diesel boat. High up, above the bulge of the ballast tanks, a through-hull fitting had been welded into place to accommodate a number of electric power cables.

These cables were strapped tightly together, assembled in a large umbilical—only slightly smaller than the main they had followed to get here—that angled off into the darkness ahead.

Once again, Rick and Kiwi exchanged glances.

But this time no shrug was necessary. Together, still carrying their demolitions gear and weapons, they moved to follow the cables—and almost immediately encountered a second diesel submarine. Another Tango, sited parallel to the first and connected to it by the bundled cables, which entered via another fitting welded into the hull.

Impossible as it might seem, these old diesel relics had been hooked together in a way that left no doubt about their functions. Somehow, these boats had been fitted with new power units—nuclear, presumably—and then dispatched to this place, where they were sunk and put to work providing the humongous helpings of power required for the Temnota plan. Here was the weapon they had to find, and destroy.

But the problem was complicated by their unfamiliarity with the type of submarine being used. Working with photographs and blueprints of the boats they had expected to find here, they had worked out what appeared to be the most effective points at which to set their explosive charges. All this, however, was now wasted effort.

Thinking it through, trying to work out the details in his mind, Rick found himself unable to guess what kind of nuclear reactor might have been installed in the old diesel subs—or even in what part of the ship the plant might be located. He hadn't studied any schematic drawings for diesels and wasn't even sure of the engine room's position in the hull, never mind the point at which it might be most vulnerable.

Rick checked his watch again. A lot of bottom time had been used up just finding their way around. Time to go to work.

Kiwi was on the move again, and Rick spotted him in the distance, just before he passed out of sight, going around the nose of the second Tango sub, apparently tracing yet another bundle of power cables.

Moving as swiftly as possible over the grating, Rick gained enough ground to be almost up with the SEAL instructor when they arrived at a third boat—which differed subtly from the two submarines they had seen before. It was a bit wider at the beam, and perhaps a little shorter, too.

Rick wished he could talk to Kiwi and ask some questions. But the damn mouthpiece simply made voice communication as impossible for them as the hole in the throat made it for the Soviet frogs.

Mac had been working on that and had actually tested one device similar to the sonovox used by cancer victims whose vocal cords had been removed. You didn't really talk, just subvocalized, and the electronics did the rest, transmitting the result by radio to a receiver plugged into your companion's ear. But it hadn't been operational by the time Mac . . .

Rick tried to stop his mind from wandering and forced himself to concentrate. The third submarine didn't resemble any of the Soviet nuclear configurations they had studied either, yet the builders of Temnota must have had some reason for using a different kind of boat. The engineering that had gone into this place and the technology supporting it were both first rate. Destroying it might be an even bigger job than they had expected.

Kiwi was standing still now, just looking at the side of the third sub. Rick came alongside to see what it was that his partner found so interesting.

The trail, the cables—and the work platform itself—ended here. Just ten feet or so from the far side of the third boat, the world seemed to drop off into infinity. Actually, the true sea bottom was only a few feet down. The builders had selected a reasonably level part of the drowned valley for a building site. No sense making more trouble for yourself than necessary. So the work floor on which they were standing was probably a convenience, something to make it easier for the original construction crew.

Kiwi touched Rick's arm and pointed. Time for the wrecking crew to get with it. The first limpet mines would buckle the hull of this boat while cutting the cable connections to the others. Rick nodded, assuring Kiwi that he understood, and dropped the load, keeping only two mines with him.

Moving aft, Rick tried to remember the positions of hatches shown on the submarine profiles he had studied. Nuclear boats—and even the more modern diesel types—seemed to be designed almost entirely for underwater operation. Even the "sail" area that corresponded to the conning tower of World War II subs had been altered. Hatches were located at the top of the sail on modern submarines, but this high vantage point was intended for command use only during docking and brief surface maneuvers. Otherwise, access was restricted to deck hatches forward and abaft the sail, with an extra hatch nearer the stern. The Temnota crew would probably have a ladder to that hatch.

As he had hoped, metal rungs had been welded to the bulging side of the boat, at a position closer to the screw and control surfaces of the tail assembly than to the sail.

But then another alteration claimed his attention. A new opening had been cut in the side of the boat. The job looked professional, like something that might have been done at a naval shipyard. Looking at the rectangular opening, with its rounded edges, he recognized a standard watertight door, a fitting common to most Navy surface ships. Carefully, cautiously, he checked and rechecked the area against the possibility of unwanted company, then moved closer to get a better look at the hatch itself.

Like most doors of its type, this one was secured by rods, or dogs, intended to pass through a flange at the rim of the hatch and into slots set into the jamb, somewhat after the fashion of the much heavier bolt system used on bank vaults. These rods were activated—driven into the jamb or pulled out—by a wheel that was fitted into the middle of the door. The hatch was shut and dogged.

For a moment, Rick considered the possibility of running a Taglin spear through the spokes of the wheel, to make sure it wouldn't be turned unexpectedly from the inside. But in the end he resisted the urge. No matter what he did to that door, there would still be the access hatches in the deck and sail. And the noise of jamming the wheel would be sure to alert someone.

He swam to the weather deck and begin moving forward again.

Sure enough, he was able to count five hatches aft of the sail and three more forward; the Russkies seemed to believe in easy access.

The through-hull fitting for the electric cables was directly below, and Rick couldn't see how he was going to reach it after all. For some reason, it seemed to have been placed out of reach, both from below and above. Slowly, taking elaborate precautions against the smallest contact of metal on metal, Rick put down the mines, spread himself prone on the deck—and discovered that he was just able to touch the cable fitting. It was closer than he had thought. Once again he had been misled by the snoopers.

He pushed himself back into a kneeling position and picked up one of the limpet mines. The object was to cut the electric cables, and the mine would do the job. But . . . just barely, and then only if it was placed just right.

What he really needed was plastique—something that could be properly shaped to the job at hand. Working with any one of a number of plastic explosives, the job would have been a cinch for less than half the actual effort. But they hadn't brought plastique, and that was that.

As cautiously as before, but this time using only one hand to move himself while holding the limpet mine in the other, Rick dropped back into his former facedown position on the foredeck of the submarine and began the ticklish work of maneuvering the explosive. Stubbornly, repeatedly, the mine went down to the proper position but slipped upward again before it could be clamped into place on the hull. Rick wanted to swear, wanted to call someone for advice, but denied either alternative, took a break to think things over after the third unsuccessful try.

Irritably, feeling as though he should be wiping sweat from his face, he peered over the side for another look at the fitting. Some kind of tube (or a bolt or a sensor, who could guess?) was in the way—right in the place he wanted to put the charge—just above the point where the cables were routed inside the outer hull. Rick looked at the offending object and considered ways and means.

Best and easiest, he decided, would be to simply get rid of the thing. Saw it off or bang it flat with a sledgehammer. But that would have made too much noise even if he'd had the tools. The only way to go at it was from the other side—the reciprocal of the position he had originally intended, but still aimed at the nexus of hull and cable.

Slowly, wriggling instead of actually coming to his knees again, he moved a foot forward and allowed his upper body to sag limply over the side, bringing the mine to the exact position desired . . . and setting it silently in place.

The timer fuse was armed, and Rick checked his watch, noting that he was already behind schedule. By agreement, all fuses were set, just before they left the surface, for detonation at the same moment—about 180 minutes after their exit from the *Steel Albatross*—and he would have to hustle.

Any damn fool can make an explosion. The important part's not to be there when it happens.

The combat-demolitions instructor's voice came, unbidden, to his ear as he moved back aft along the deck, pausing to set the second charge in the spot where he guessed the nuclear plant would be located.

One more, right at the side of that nice, new door. Ought to be the weakest point on the hull if they cut the hole down here. Try a clamshell this time; clean their clocks for sure.

On Board the *Steel Albatross*

Monday, November 3
7:21 A.M.

Getting back aboard the *Steel Albatross* presented no problem. But getting off the bottom did.

Submarines achieve positive buoyancy—become lighter than the surrounding water—by blowing air into their ballast tanks in order to force the water out, and this becomes more and more difficult with each foot of descent into the depths of the ocean. Water pressure near the surface is relatively low, so the quantity and pressure of air needed to empty the ballast tanks are minimal. But evacuating the tanks at 2,900 feet was another matter entirely. Nearly ten minutes—and a lot of air—

had been expended before they felt the first stirrings of life from the boat.

Rick checked his watch again and tried a few tentative motions with the stick. It moved loosely. But nothing else happened.

That was as expected—difficulties in blowing the tanks at extreme depth had been discussed and evaluated before the dive—and he forced himself to let go of the control stick, relaxing his body part by part to reduce the hazard of hyperventilation.

Slow and easy . . . the fuses on the explosives were set with plenty of time to let them get back to the surface and even get the boat out of the water before the explosions began. So take it easy. Air's coming in, water's going out.

It would have been comforting to talk to Kiwi, in the aft seat. But that would remain impossible until enough air had been pumped into the cockpit to force the water down below mouth level.

Rick's hand moved tentatively toward the stick again, but he forced it back into a relaxed position. Time enough to try the controls when the boat actually began to move. Not that it would be controllable then. An ascent rate of at least a hundred feet per minute was necessary for control, and they would probably have gone two or three hundred feet toward the surface before they were moving that fast.

Besides, he might have to guess at everything—including their vertical speed—because although Captain Ward had assured them the electronics were watertight, this was the first time the cockpit had been flooded at that depth, and one or more of the sensors might not have made it. In which case, they'd be back to manual operation.

Suddenly, the boat lurched to starboard. Rick and Kiwi were strapped down, but the sudden motion forced a yawp of surprise from both men—followed by an invocation of the Fighter Pilot's Blessing by Rick. At last the water level in the cockpit had passed their chins.

"Shit!"

"Second the motion," Kiwi growled. "What'n the pluperfect hell's goin' on?"

For a moment, the *Steel Albatross* had settled back on her

landing gear. But now the left side of the boat (still expelling water) was lifted clear of the construction mat and the boat was canted to the right.

Rick remembered an incident early with the SA-1. They had landed on a plain of deep ooze off San Clemente Island, and Captain Ward had showed him how to break the boat free of the bottom by rocking it.

Then he remembered. No mud or ooze here. They were on a construction platform. Rick craned his neck to look over the side—and then marched his memory around the boat. Nothing forward. Nothing to port. Nothing aft. And nothing starboard, except . . .

"The damn bodies," Rick growled over his shoulder to Kiwi. "I think somehow one of the Russkie frogs has gone afoul of the boat's landing gear."

"That's it," Kiwi said. "So . . . what we gotta do? Flood the boat and go out there again?"

A second EVA was feasible. Still plenty of time. But—dammit—he didn't want to do that if he didn't have to.

"Hold your left nut," Rick said. "And try not to think about what's happening outside."

"Don't follow you."

"Good!"

The *Steel Albatross* was equipped with attitude jets fore and aft, and he used them now to start the boat rocking.

Nose up . . .

Stern up . . .

Nose up . . .

Stern up . . .

The pumps were still surging away, making the SA-1 lighter and lighter, and the angle reached by the nose was gradually increasing with each try.

Nose up . . .

Stern up . . .

Nose up . . .

And suddenly, with a jolt, they were free of the bottom.

"What . . . gave?" Kiwi asked.

"You don't want to know," Rick replied.

Breathing more easily now, and trying to blot their grisly

departure from his mind, Rick struggled to bring the *Albatross* back on an even keel.

Water level in the cockpit was down below the instrument panel now. The control surfaces were getting a good bite on the water, and he was able to bring the ascent under control. The *Steel Albatross* headed for the surface at a steeper angle than he had allowed on descent, but that was okay. It was good to be going up instead of down. Good to know the worst was over.

It had all seemed so easy. Planting the remainder of their explosive charges around the Soviet power station had gone like clockwork—less than forty minutes elapsed time—and all without seeing another enemy frog. There had to be more than just a two-man crew aboard this complex.

That was the part that bothered Rick. Not that he was in any hurry to meet another of the weird liquid-breathers. The swimmers they had killed must have been missed by now. . . .

The stick was trying to move under Rick's hand. But it was still too early, he thought, to switch on the computer. He sorely missed the information he might have had from the screen. Flying by the seat of the pants, without reference to horizon or instruments, was no easier down here than in an airplane. That was how pilots got the Order of the Wooden Cross.

If anything was wrong with the computer, he didn't want it overriding his manual controls to smash them into the side of the canyon or take them back to the bottom out of control.

The magnetic compass was functional, and he used it to set a heading of 180 degrees—about 15 degrees west of due south, since he wasn't trying to compensate and make good a true heading as yet. That would take them away from the coast, toward the open sea.

This was not the tactic discussed during final briefing before the dive. At that time, Captain Ward had advised them to try to make their ascent as close to the path of descent as possible, with the object of surfacing in the vicinity of the barge, ready for immediate pickup. And he had agreed.

But at that time, no one had guessed how much time it would take to achieve positive buoyancy, or that they would encounter other problems in getting away from the target.

They were entirely out of visual contact with the side of the canyon, and the course he was holding was one that he hoped would keep them in one piece.

Rick now strained his snooper-enhanced eyes for the first glimpse of the opposite canyon wall. It was a lazy pilot's version of old-time "fisherman's navigation," which might not allow for a positive position-fix at all times, but never got you completely lost: "When approaching a major land mass, instead of trying to hit your checkpoint dead center, aim to miss it far enough to port or starboard that you'll be sure of which way to turn when the shoreline comes in view."

Sparing a split second to glance again at his watch for a check on their elapsed time, Rick noted that almost all the water had now been forced out of the cockpit. Another minute or two, and it would be time to try the computer.

But before he could pursue the thought, his eyes had locked onto something solid in the water ahead of them.

"Ten o'clock!" The flat terseness of Kiwi's tone from the backseat was startling.

Ahead and to starboard, the first vague outlines of the canyon's western wall were becoming hazily discernible. Rick applied aileron and rudder to put the *Albatross* into a banked right turn, then nursed it gently into a heading of ninety degrees.

"Fire up the computer?"

"Sounds good to me."

The water was gone, though the cockpit was still wet enough to give someone a terrific shock if there was a short anywhere in the system after its high-pressure immersion. But it would never be dry enough to be perfectly safe, and any danger was fully balanced by the need to know their true depth and rate of ascent.

Rick checked his course against the compass one more time, took the stick in his left hand, and began pressing the switches in order. Basic hardware first. Then the software program: load and run.

And then wait, trying not to hold your breath while dividing attention between the dark green of the world outside and the gradually growing light of the cathode-ray tube.

TIMER RESET
Counting 00:00:00

Auto   Manual

The numbers began to run backward on their own, but Rick stopped the clock, touching the MANUAL command and then inputting 07:37:00 from his own wristwatch. It wasn't absolutely accurate, but good enough for their purposes right now. Rick worked about thirty seconds ahead and waited on HOLD for the hack, then pressed the GO command.

The clock began running again, then jumped to its normal position in the extreme upper-right side of the tube.

SA-1 COMMAND MENU
Do you require assistance?

Yes   No   Cancel

Progress through the various levels of procedure was steady but irritatingly slow, and Rick wished that he could rewrite the software. Build in some kind of jump-ahead option instead of working through the basic steps. Reduce the frustration factor. Or at least provide some kind of emergency override.

They were still a long way down; 1,900 feet according to the on-screen display, and ascending at a rate of 150 feet per minute. His watch said they still had more than an hour before the explosions began.

Rick decided to try the radio. Captain Ward—and Stan Leppard, too—had warned him to monitor ELF on the way down and as soon as possible while ascending.

Just a precaution, the captain had said. No actual plans to use the low-frequency underwater radio system on this dive, which was, after all, technically illegal. Any contact through ELF would give the show away, so it would be used only in direst emergency. But it should still be monitored.

Switching the computer screen to communications mode, he waited for the menu, selected ELF, and then waited a moment while the computer did the rest of the work, switching to the low-frequency band and automatically punching in the numbers for the calling frequency. At first nothing seemed to be happening.

Rick brought the screen back to control mode and checked their depth: 1,600 feet and still climbing; heading 120 true, speed six knots.

Still nothing from the radio—which was ridiculous. How could the calling frequency be as dead as all that?

But the ELF calling frequency wasn't dead; the failure was in his own memory. Calling frequencies were set up as defaults in the computer. Some of them—especially the scrambled, secure ones that carried messages not intended for the ears of civilians or other outsiders—had to be changed on a regular schedule. And ELF was like that; it changed on the second day of each month. Promptly at 2400, Zulu.

They had been listening in the wrong place. And he didn't even know which one was right. Muttering, really annoyed with himself this time, Rick switched the screen back to communications and ordered it to run a search of the ELF spectrum, looking for any kind of traffic.

Not that he really thought anybody was trying to get in touch with them. God forbid. Because that could only mean trouble, and thus far everything was going like silk. Piece of cake.

"Pelican. Sierra Alfa One, Pelican! Pelican! Pelican . . ."

Routed through the cockpit speaker, the message came through with a clarity that was startlingly loud in contrast with the silence. But it was not the sound that caused Rick to stiffen and sit bolt upright, while eliciting a "Shit a goddamn" from the seat behind him.

"Sierra Alfa One, Pelican! Pelican!"

That was the mother ship, *Berkone*. Calling them in the clear with no attempt at concealment except for the single-word code message, which they were bound to obey without question:

"Pelican."

Just one word, but a full message in itself. A mandatory-abort signal, agreed upon just before the dive—to be used only in case of major emergency.

PART X

MAXIMUM EFFORT

Las Olinas, California

Monday, November 3
7:52 A.M.

"So the reactors are hot and on-line," Stan Leppard was saying. "Unless there's been some change of plan—something Petchukocov didn't know about—then they're running at maximum."

The *Steel Albatross* had surfaced about a mile from the *Berkone*, but her hatch was dogged down, interior still pressurized, and communication was by radio.

Captain Ward had decided to meet the *Albatross* at sea, instead of bringing her all the way back to the mother ship, in order to cut turnaround time to a minimum, and support divers labored in the water to ready the sub for another dive.

The message that had been passed to the Defense Intelligence Agency from Mossad—and swiftly relayed to Leppard aboard *Berkone*—could not be doubted: Direct assault on the Temnota power station was out of the question because the nuclear reactors were already activated, which they hadn't known at the time of the dive. Any mishap involving them would trigger a disaster hundreds of times more devastating than any previous nuclear incident . . . including the catastrophe at Chernobyl.

Rick and Kiwi listened to Leppard's explanation. But they did not entirely understand, so Captain Ward took over, in his capacity as a former commander of nuclear-powered vessels, to offer a capsule explanation.

"Reactors of the 'light water' kind that we think they installed in the boats you saw down there," he said, "are pressurized to about twenty-eight hundred pounds per square inch, which raises the boiling point of the water they use to cool the nuclear core to around nine hundred degrees Celsius. But this coolant water is dangerously radioactive as the result of the fission that's going on inside the reactor.

"The reaction is controlled by the position of the control rods. Fully inserted, the rods shut the core down, preventing any reaction at all. Fully retracted, on the other hand, they would permit a runaway reaction, leading to meltdown.

"So we have two major dangers. One—and it's the worst—you get a runaway, the 'China syndrome' where the core melts right out of the vessel and into the ocean, en route to the bowels of the earth, releasing massive radioactivity.

"Or two, you get some kind of break in the reactor vessel, which releases the coolant water—and also releases massive radioactivity into the ocean."

"And that," Leppard added, "is not just bad. It is as bad as it gets."

"No," Ward said. "That's not 'as bad as it gets.' It's far worse, believe me!"

"Why worse?" Kiwi asked.

"Because it happens in the sea, instead of the atmosphere," Captain Ward said. "Vent radioactivity into the air, and it's bad. Look at Three Mile Island. Or Chernobyl. But at least in air the main damage is done in the first few hours; after that, diffusion and dispersion of the hot stuff reduces its effectiveness to a point where it can be tolerated.

"But in the sea, the diffusion/dispersion process is slower—you'll be dealing with dangerously radioactive water up and down the coast for a long, long time—and meanwhile, you got to expect it to wipe out marine life, including undersea vegetation, over who knows how wide an area."

Rick and Kiwi exchanged glances. "Sounds bad," Rick agreed. "But wouldn't the damage to sea life at least be better than killing human beings, the way it would if it happened on shore?"

"No," Ward said. "You'd still kill human beings. Radiation reaching the surface would pass into the atmosphere and drift ashore with the morning breeze or fall as radioactive rain. There's more—but I think you get the picture."

"Sonofahawah," Kiwi said.

And that seemed to say it for all of them.

On Board the *Steel Albatross*
Santa Ana Deeps
Monday, November 3
8:25 A.M.

At 1,300 feet, Rick increased their rate of descent to 250 feet per minute and felt the controls stiffen accordingly.

Descending at their present rate—which was already too fast for safety—they would reach the bottom at about 0833. Detonation was set for 0956. Which left them a little more than an hour to deactivate all the mines they had set—to shut down the reactor units—even if they didn't run into trouble with more of the water-breathing Soviet frogmen.

"Leave the cable-cutting charges in place?" Kiwi said.

"Leave 'em," Rick said, nodding. "So even if we have to leave the reactors in working order, they won't be able to use the power plant to go through with the Temnota plan."

"Right."

There were pros and cons—for instance, the possibility that the cable-cutting mines might also damage the reactor containment domes—but Rick could see no point in discussing them now.

The *Albatross* was going down in a series of figure-eight turns, once again allowing the thick cable to lead them to their objective. The swifter descent had increased the boat's speed to nearly eight knots, and even with their snoopers, the work of keeping the cable in sight while avoiding the wall of the underwater canyon was proving harder than Rick had expected.

But the timers on the explosive charges weren't the only clocks running backward toward zero. Others were running inside his body and Kiwi's. The injections they had been given to ward off HPNS and the cold would be losing effectiveness in another hour. And Samantha said they couldn't be repeated—or even boosted—for at least seventy-two hours without risking severe kidney and brain damage.

Rick had never experienced high-pressure nervous syndrome himself. But Mac, Kiwi, and Captain Ward all said they had, and they assured him that it was a bone-rattler. If it hit him during a dive, they said, he would find it impossible to maintain control of the *Albatross*—or even of his own body. So he and Kiwi would have to be back on the surface, or very near it, by the time the shots wore off.

In addition, the technical crew warned them that their ballast tanks were going to be harder to clear this time. Because the SA-1 was intended as an experimental craft rather than an operational one, Captain Ward had not designed her air tanks for quick recharging. The topside support divers had done their best while the boat was surfaced, but it had been impossible to complete the task in the time allotted. But there was still enough liquefied gas on board to bring them up. More than enough, in fact.

Remembering how much extra time had been required to restore positive buoyancy even when the tanks were at full charge, however, Rick had wondered how much longer the process might take this time.

Two thousand feet. Nine hundred feet—around four minutes and a second or two at their present descent rate—until they would be on the bottom again.

Maneuvering the SA-1 through yet another turn, Rick checked the computer screen, noted that they were approaching the 2,600-foot level, and cut their descent rate accordingly. Make the landing as soft and easy as possible. And as silent. And as near the original touchdown site as you can, bro—because that's where you left the missile weapons.

They had brought the explosive-tipped Taglin spears and pistol-speargun back to the *Albatross* after carrying them during the process of mining the Temnota installation, and he had intended to replace them in their external brackets on the side of the boat. But it had slipped his mind, and by the time he remembered the spears again, he and Kiwi were back in the cockpit with the hatch secured, and retrieving them just hadn't seemed important enough to warrant the extra time it would have cost.

Stupid, sloppy work. And potentially disastrous to the operation. What if one of the Russkies had found the damn things? True, they didn't make much of a pile on the platform, and the Soviet frogs hadn't seemed able to see much of anything anyhow. Not likely they'd be able to spot a few discarded underwater small-arms.

"Bottom coming up!"

Kiwi's voice jolted him, and he touched the screen once again, adjusting their descent rate to zero just in time to avoid a bone-rattling landing on the platform.

But it wasn't the soft touchdown he'd hoped for, and Rick found himself on the verge of hyperventilation again as he stuffed the mouthpiece of the gill into place, adjusted the flow, switched off the computer, opened the manual valve to flood the cockpit . . . and then had to fight off an attack of hilarity.

Biting down hard on the mouthpiece and forcing himself to concentrate on the step-by-step process of exiting the SA-1, he managed to avoid the craziness that he could feel bubbling up inside him. Laugh now, idiot, and you could actually choke on your own air supply!

For a second, Rick thought he was succumbing to the raptures of the deep. But it was far worse than that. For the truth—the dirty little truth that he had always been at such pains to conceal from himself and from everyone else, all his life, was that some vital thing or other had simply been omitted from the character of Lt. (j.g.) Richard Biddle Tallman, USN.

The situation into which he and Kiwi had projected themselves here was life-threatening. More, it posed a threat to all life, on land and in the sea, from Canada to Mexico City. Dealing with the Temnota installation and living to tell about it was a long-odds bet that no respectable gambler would have touched, even with someone else's money.

And he was having a ball.

Rick Tallman, noted Top Gun dropout and SEAL trainee, was back in the fun zone.

Silently, suppressing his lunatic jubilation, Rick forced himself to sit still in the seat while the water rose around him and finally closed over his head.

Station "O"

Monday, November 3
7:35 P.M., Moscow Time

One thing, at least, had gone right. The *Steel Albatross* had come to rest within a foot or two of her original position on the Temnota platform, and no one seemed to have heard the noisy landing.

Rick and Kiwi were out of the boat, armed and moving as quickly as possible to do the job they had come to do.

Something was wrong, though, and they both felt it. It wasn't the sight of the mangled remains of the two Soviet frogs, still tethered to the construction matting. The bodies, in fact, helped them locate the weapons they had left behind.

But one of the Taglin spearguns was missing, was not with the other three guns and reload spears they had dropped on the grating. But that was almost predictable. The great surprise was that they had been able to find and retrieve the others so easily.

It was, Rick finally decided, just an extension of the sense of unreality he had experienced earlier, while returning to the surface after the first descent. A feeling that it had all gone a little too well.

The first submarine, the one closest to their landing site, was in view now, and Rick's first instinct was to head for it. Go after those mines first, then move along to the next boat. But he resisted the urge, staying close to Kiwi and following the SEAL instructor's lead into the greenish void that stretched ahead. Before diving, they had agreed to begin at the far end of the installation and work back, in order to be in position to reboard the *Steel Albatross* as soon as they were done. And this time, they would not be separated.

One man doing the work; the other guarding his back. They had disregarded that rule once in the interest of speed, and there was even more need for haste this time. But the situation had changed. By now, the two frogmen they had killed must have been missed, and there was every reason to expect that someone had stumbled upon one or more of the demolition charges, or the bodies, or some other indication of their visit. Now they would be much more alert to danger.

Nonetheless, their progress toward the far side of the Temnota platform was unimpeded. They reached the third submarine without incident and went to work at once. Rick found the clamshell mine that he had affixed to the watertight door just where he had left it, and he moved impulsively to remove the timer—but was restrained by Kiwi, who grabbed his hand with a hard negative shake of the head.

Hadn't he learned anything in the combat-demo training course? Timers could be removed from the limpet mines and satchel charges; they were designed to allow it. But the time/detonators used for clamshells were an entirely different proposition, fitted with a little time-delay fuse wire that was broken on insertion. Leave it alone, and the fuse would blow the main charge at whatever time you had set. Try to remove it, or even bump the mechanism too hard, and it would go off at once.

Carefully, sweating a little inside his wet suit, Rick pried the clamshell away from the jamb of the watertight door, carried it to the edge of the steel grid platform, and started to put it over the side. Let it tear up the ocean floor. But the drop, slow as it would be in the watery environment, might still be enough to touch the damn thing off.

All right, then, at least put it at the edge of the grid. Out of the way. Where it wasn't likely to damage whatever was inside the sub. The limpet mine on the nose—the one intended to cut the bundled electric cables—would serve the purpose of putting the plant out of business for as long as it took to mount a real neutralization effort. Holding the clamshell mine carefully before him like a waiter in a café, he knelt at the edge of the platform and attached the device to the metal grid.

Settling the mine in place with a final, gentle push, Rick stood up and turned back toward the third submarine . . . where he saw Kiwi, just five feet away, locked in close combat with another of the Soviet frogs.

Ivan Kamarov and his partner had spotted the interloper at the same moment.

Darkness on the platform was total; the man had been almost

on top of them when their struggles with the cable shunt mechanisms forced them to change position, and the unknown diver had stood highlighted in the beam of their work light.

The intruder took a step to his left, perhaps intending to feint and bring one of them off-balance before dealing with the other. But Kamarov stood his ground while his partner launched himself at the enemy and managed to close his arms around the interloper's chest.

They fell—not heavily, because of the water—and Kamarov's next thought was to come to his partner's aid. But training doctrine was still fresh in his mind, so he resisted the notion, moving a pace closer to the side of the old Tango submarine and climbing a few rungs up the ladder they had welded to her side, where he unclipped a knife and his own hand light from his belt and stood waiting with them ready in his hand.

Perhaps, like SPETSNAZ swimmers, these divers came in pairs. . . .

Like SEALs, the Soviet frogmen seemed to come in pairs. . . .

Rick took two steps forward, intending to help Kiwi. But the down easter seemed to be doing well enough on his own, so he hesitated an extra moment before moving in—which was just long enough to save his life.

A sudden flash of brilliance from above struck his snooper-adjusted eyes like a physical blow. A second Russian frog—this one holding a knife—was above him, descending through the water with knife at the ready.

Moving instinctively forward and to his right in order to intercept the enemy diver at what he hoped would be the best angle, Rick fought to control the momentary disorientation produced by dazzlement. His attacker's helmet light was off, but he was carrying some kind of work light that was hideously brilliant when its beam was enhanced by the snoopers. Rick closed his eyes and moved into a counterpuncher's stance, trying to clear his mind of distractions and achieve the state of openness that can allow the other senses to replace sight in the perception of danger.

His shift to the side and rear had, as hoped, disrupted the initial attack. The knife that had been aimed at his chest missed entirely and stabbed the water behind him. But the light was still there. It blazed like the sun on the other side of his clenched eyelids—effectively neutralizing his most potent advantage, and even turning it against him. So long as that light was on, he couldn't even risk a peek.

Yet he found he was able to judge the general position of his adversary by the waxing and waning of the brightness, while the stirring of the water could give advance warning of hostile movement.

A sudden rush of water to his left told him the enemy frog had found footing on the platform and was resuming the attack. Rick backpedaled, twisting again to the right, bending suddenly at knee and hip to take his torso out of range—and then sprang forward, directly toward the light.

It was a move of desperation, and it worked. Surprised, the enemy frog responded too late. Rick's head caught him amidships—in the solar plexus—and he was driven backward, going down suddenly with the American on top of him.

Rick felt a sudden searing pain in his right thigh. The knife had been in the Soviet frog's right hand, and he had withdrawn it quickly after inflicting the stab wound. It was descending now, on Rick's unprotected left side. Following his man down in watery slow motion, Rick rolled and squirmed to his right while maintaining a left-handed death grip on the other man's throat.

Continuing his move, Rick relaxed his left hand while his forefinger found the neckband of the man's oxygen recycler. Reaction on both sides was immediate and violent.

Rick's hand ripped at the recycler, wresting it free from the necklace, and then from the plastic tube leading to the hole in the man's neck. It was over before the victim could complete any effective countermove.

Suddenly the light that had been so blindingly close to his eyes wasn't there anymore. Steeling himself against the possibility of a ruse, Rick opened his lids a fraction of a millimeter . . . and found himself staring directly into the bulging eyes of the Soviet frog. They were pale, almost colorless in the green-shifted spectrum of the snoopers, and Rick figured they were probably blue in the real world above.

Rick's left hand was still clamped around the recycling device, and all the Russian's efforts were centered on that single spot, trying to retrieve it. The Soviet diver was strong; Rick could feel the massive, big-animal movement of the shoulder muscles as he brought both arms up in an effort to pry the recycler from the hand that had stolen it. It was a poor tactic. Rick would have attacked the opposite diver's own air supply, the gill so vulnerably attached to his chest. But Rick could see that the other man had panicked and dropped both his knife and his hand light. Rick was now free to use both his own hands instead of reserving one to ward off a renewed knife assault. And that was all the edge he needed.

Almost lazily, Rick brought his right leg up, and his opponent, thinking Rick meant to knee him in the groin, moved away. But Rick just wanted to seize the knife he carried strapped to his calf. The enemy frog had just time enough to realize his error before the razor sharpness of Rick's blade sliced into his throat, severing both arteries just below the mutilated trachea.

Rick released the corpse, dodging the vision-obscuring green blood, and turned to help Kiwi. But the SEAL instructor's man was dead, too. Both Russians had died by knife cuts to the throat. Was that going to be a standard attack-mode—one for the tactical books issued by the Navy Department?

The thought was grotesque, but the idea of some future manual with a title like "Liquid-Breathing Soviet Special Forces: Applied Combat Doctrine (Restricted)" struck him in his most vulnerable spot. Rick was barely able to strangle the shout of laughter that threatened to displace his mouthpiece, despite the pain from the new hole in his leg.

Tallman, he thought, you are one sick puppy.

This time they made no attempt to get rid of the bodies. The two Americans simply plowed through the floating bloodstains in order to get on about their business.

A sudden tap on the shoulder sent Rick into violent motion, twisting and turning to avoid whatever was moving in on him. But it was only Kiwi, trying to get his attention, and Rick turned to see what the senior SEAL wanted. For an instant, Kiwi's face seemed cockeyed, one eye dark, the other light, with a dark eye above it. But then he understood. Kiwi had bent the metal frame of the snooper flip-downs so the right lens rested on his forehead.

He could still use his snooper-covered left eye to see here in the depths, but the enemy frogs could no longer blind him with their work lights because he could use the unassisted right eye for those situations. Without hesitation, Rick bent his frame, moving his right lens up to his forehead, and endured a brief attack of dizziness.

The left eye, still covered by a snooper lens, continued to give him a clear picture of his immediate surroundings. Vision was more limited—about 60 percent of the side-to-side range he'd had with two eyes, he guessed. And depth perception, which had already been impaired by the snoopers, was almost totally lost. He would have to be very, very careful where he put his feet.

It looked promising though. Sight would be a bit disjointed—but maybe they could figure out something better when they were back on the surface. If . . .

Meanwhile, time for a little search-and-destroy. The frogs that attacked them hadn't materialized from thin air. So where was the nest? The Soviet frogs had to have some place to roost; some secure habitat for eating and sleeping. The third boat was as good a place to start as any. They couldn't go on with the cleanup until they were free from the threat of hostile action.

At the side of the submarine, Kiwi hesitated and then turned to look for a moment in Rick's direction, pointing first at himself and then at the ladder. Rick nodded agreement. Kiwi would go topside and see about entering the boat from one of the deck hatches, while Rick stayed by the watertight door in the hull, awaiting the signal to go in. Fair enough. If the enemy frogs were in there, they would find themselves attacked from two different directions. Rick watched as the SEAL instructor climbed the ladder, disappearing behind the bulge of the side and reappearing a few seconds later as a disembodied head—and a hand with five fingers extended. Rick looked up at him and nodded again, ready to begin the countdown:

Five fingers . . . four fingers . . . three fingers . . . The hand disappeared, but Rick continued the count at the pace already established. Two fingers . . . one finger . . .

Zero.

Hands already locked tight upon the rim of the door's securing mechanism, Rick threw his whole body into the effort of turning the wheel counterclockwise, to remove the bolts from the jamb. He was rewarded with immediate action . . . accompanied by the great-grandfather of all rusty, rasping metallic groans.

Son of a bitch! Quickly and easily, despite the noise of the operation, the bolts retreated from the jamb and the wheel came to a stop. The door was built to open inward—so Rick gave it a kick and entered in a rush, Taglin spear at the ready.

But there was no target. Rick's left eye was able to discern the bare outline of a narrow passageway stretching off to vagueness in either direction. Rick paused, trying to decide which way to go.

Above his head, the thud of a deck hatch being thrown open told him Kiwi was also inside the boat. And moving aft as fast as he could go.

Rick turned to his left and put himself in motion, but it was very dark. The only light he had was bioluminescence coming through the hatch he had left open behind him. A few feet down the passage, he found himself blind. Tracing the bulkhead with the tip of his right forefinger, his left hand collided with something solid, directly in front of him. The corridor ended here.

Quietly, trying to avoid a repetition of the noise that had heralded his initial entry, he located another watertight door and turned the wheel to open it.

A shaft of light dazzled him. He closed his left eye and opened the other—which offered him the blurred image of a room beyond the door where lights were burning.

Rick's first instinct was to throw the door open and enter the lighted place. It was almost an irresistible temptation. His right foot was already lifted to pass through the door when he hesitated and decided to do it by the book. Braced, Taglin speargun at the ready, and standing aside from the jamb, he kicked the door open (a flash of bright pain from the right thigh) and waited.

Nothing. Which did not, of course, prove the room was empty. Assuming that the Soviet swimmers assigned to this station had been through some kind of combat training, the possibility remained that someone was waiting inside the room to give him an unpleasant surprise.

But he would never find out by standing around outside, and one way or another the threshold had to be crossed. Rick dropped to the deck, clutching his spear, and risked a peek over the bottom of the portal—which showed him a bare room, stark under what looked like a common industrial lighting fixture. And a man: black wet suit; breathing gear strapped to back and chest; Taglin spear handgun aimed at the door. One eye was almost black, the other more or less eye-color, making him look lopsided. A real nightmare. Rick waved a hand at Kiwi, who hesitated for a moment and then waved back.

On his feet once more, Rick stepped through the door, reached back to close it, and secured it behind him before turning to face his partner.

There was still no way they could talk, but communication in this instance was no real problem. Kiwi pointed to the corridor from which Rick had come, and Rick shook his head. No one and nothing of note back there; he jerked a thumb in the direction of the upper passage Kiwi had traversed. Another shake of the head.

All right, then. Time to explore. Rick looked around the room, dissatisfied with the poor vision afforded by his unaided eye. Shapes and forms were easy enough to identify, but details remained a problem. Coping with it in the only way he could for the moment, he began a trip around the bulkheads, exploring each with his hand and bringing his right eye close in an effort to identify any irregularities.

He decided the bay had formerly contained some kind of office equipment or machinery. Probably machinery: plugged bolt-holes in bulkheads and the deck left him with that impression. No reason to anchor desks that firmly. But what kind of machinery remained a mystery, and by the time he had covered three sides of the room his interest had cooled. Time was wasting.

Kiwi, who had been exploring the overhead (where a major penetration seemed to have been plugged) came to the same conclusion. They must move on.

There were only two doors to this bay, and the one through

which he had entered led nowhere. He pointed at the other—the one Kiwi had used—and his partner merely shrugged. The clamdigger hadn't been impressed with the possibilities there, either. But it was the only remaining egress, and Kiwi followed readily enough when Rick moved in that direction.

Outside was another corridor, also lighted, and there was no argument about the direction to be taken.

The hatch Kiwi had used to board the drowned submarine was forward. So they moved aft, following the lighted companionway toward what had originally been the engineering compartments. Steam turbines and electric motors. Reduction gears. And maybe stern torpedo tubes if the Russian boats were anything like their Western counterparts.

Despite the brightness of the lighting, the end of the corridor was out of sight beyond the watery limit imposed by the naked eye. But more watertight doors offered egress in two directions.

Rick glanced at his watch, holding the dial close to be sure of the reading. Bad news. If the Soviet frogs were in here, waiting for them somewhere, he wished they would show themselves and get it over with. He and Kiwi now had exactly twenty-two minutes in which to disarm the mines, shut down the reactor, and clear the area. Or die.

Together, the two aquanauts moved to enter the bay to their right. This door was not fully secured; whoever had passed through it last had turned the wheel only enough to put the tips of the bolts through the slots in the jamb. Kiwi turned the wheel and moved back, giving the door a little shove while Rick waited to lay down cross fire with his speargun. But nothing happened.

They entered the room, Kiwi in the lead, and stood for a moment trying to adjust their eyes to an even higher level of illumination.

The corridor and the first lighted room had seemed bright enough to begin with, but that was only in contrast to the inky darkness of the surroundings. But the Americans now realized that the lighting there had been moderate—like the lighting in a comfortable living room, contrasted with that of an operating theater. This was a room where work was done.

But the exact kind of work was not immediately clear. From

deck to overhead, the far bulkhead and the ones to right and left were banked with glass panels, through which could be seen an array of dials and gauges marked in Cyrillic characters. Okay, the machinery was Russian. Big surprise. But what the hell was it supposed to do?

Rick looked at Kiwi, who seemed absorbed in one panel that appeared to have been fitted with waterproof switches. Looking at them was like finding an old friend in a crowd of strangers; these were the same kind of Japanese-made waterproofs he had learned to use in SEAL training. Kiwi recognized them, too. And suddenly Rick found himself smiling, despite the interference of the mouthpiece.

It had irked him to discover that certain kinds of equipment had to be purchased overseas in order to obtain quality in accordance with service specifications. It must have been much more galling for some purchasing agent in the workers' paradise to discover that Tokyo was the only source for the kind and quality of switches he needed for such exacting work.

If this was, indeed, the control room of a Soviet nuclear submarine, Rick decided he and Kiwi were certainly in deep shit because he didn't recognize a single thing.

None of the controls he had studied seemed to be included in the panel facing him, and he had a feeling none of the other panels was going to be much more informative. And there didn't seem to be anything a man standing here could actually use to manipulate the machinery. Strictly a monitoring station.

He nudged Kiwi, who broke off his own inspection to look at him, but offered only a shrug in response to his interrogative gestures. He poked Kiwi again and turned back to the door, but Kiwi seemed to have other ideas. There was some kind of hatch directly beneath the switch-panel. Kneeling, Kiwi first pushed at it, then turned to use his heel in the best kick he could manage against the resistance of the water. It was enough. The inspection panel gave way.

Kiwi ducked down to see what was on the other side—and came up almost at once, propelling himself in the direction of the hatch through which they had entered. Rick followed the SEAL instructor down the corridor to the right. The next opening was considerably larger than any of the hatchways they had encountered thus far. On it was a double-wheel arrangement of a type he had never seen before, with hinges on both sides.

Kiwi seemed to recognize it. He bent at once to turn the nearer wheel, but made violent signs of objection when Rick tried to help by turning the other. The one Kiwi was turning merely withdrew the jamb bolts, allowing the big door to be opened like the smaller ones they had already seen. The one Rick had tried to turn was connected to the hinges. This door was designed to be opened either to the right or to the left—or to be removed entirely if desired. And this was explained when the door was finally opened.

Here—in the room Kiwi had glimpsed through the inspection port—was the very heart of the Temnota installation. Unlike the other two rooms they had just explored, this one was unlighted, but even the dim illumination filtering in from the corridor was sufficient to identify the oversize objects nearest the door.

Nuclear power plants, of whatever kind, looked nothing at all like this. But he remembered something that did. As a boy, Rick Tallman had never been much of a tinkerer—no taking apart the alarm clock and putting it back together for him. But he had survived the basic electronics courses required at the Naval Academy, and again at Pensacola. So he was able to recognize the objects nearest the door as some form of condenser or capacitor, intended for collection and storage of major electrical potential.

The nuclear generators—he assumed there were two, one for each of the other subs—might have, as he had been told, "enough power to run every car in Detroit." But not enough for the EMP; not enough to create that free plasma wave that was supposed to knock out computers all over the West. But this lashup, this storage facility, might offer the potential for one utterly devastating effort.

Destroy this component, and you cripple the installation—without risking nuclear disaster.

He turned to Kiwi, trying to imagine a series of gestures that would communicate his conclusion. But Kiwi was ahead of him. The SEAL instructor had turned back and was proceeding at flank speed down the corridor the way they had come, with Rick close behind.

They had to destroy the capacitor/condenser equipment. Explosives. Something to make a bang underwater. And the best place to get them was from the hulls of the other two submarines. Retrieve the charges as planned. Then use them to knock out the centerpiece of the whole crazy plan.

Nice, neat, and complete: a textbook SEAL maneuver. No loose ends. And all they needed to make it real was twice as much time as they had . . . and enough luck to make a lottery winner look disadvantaged.

They were alone, now, in the control room. The others would not be back. He knew it, and so did Ullanov; he could see it in the senior SPETSNAZ trooper's face. Alexei Ullanov was near panic, and there was nothing Andrey Narmonov could do about it except stand his watch at the main panel and wait for whatever would come.

If they could shut down the cores—ease the rods back to the minimal output level where they had been when they arrived here on Station "O"—they might be able to do something. Take some action to deal with the situation. But their orders forbade that.

Every bit of their training, from the day they had been assigned to the Temnota unit, had revolved about the necessity of absolute obedience. Once a plan was set in motion, the officers and petty officers said, any deviation could be fatal. To them. To the Rodina. Who knew . . . perhaps to the whole world?

Dealing with nuclear power was no game for the faint-hearted. One slip, one switch turned the wrong way or one reading misinterpreted, could bring calamity. Especially here at the bottom of the sea. Poison the ocean, and you bring the whole future of mankind into question.

Andrey tried to think of something else, but he could not. First Kornilov, sneaking outside on some errand in disobedience to orders. Then the *starshina* going after him, both never to return.

Ullanov had stood it as long as he could. But the necessity

of manually throwing the switches that would shunt power to the surface on command, combined with anxiety about the two missing men, had finally been too much for him. He had cracked and sent Kamarov and Poliski out to remove the pins from the switches and move them to active position. Now there were only the two of them left here.

There was still the radio. Not the regular VHF set that needed its 1,200-meter antenna unreeled all the way to the surface. That required a trip outside. But they had the ultra-low-frequency transmitter, sitting unused with its "War Emergency" seal unbroken. That needed no long antenna. And if ever a unit of SPETSNAZ naval infantry faced an emergency, it was the one now on duty in this place.

He glanced at Ullanov. The man had simply come to a stop, floating there on the ceiling and staring at nothing. Was he still conscious? The eyes seemed to move from time to time, not looking at anything in particular, but jerking left and right. And still wide open.

Andrey shivered. Soon it would be time for their injections; perhaps that would be a good time to try to make Ullanov see what they must do. They must either use the underwater radio or shut down the reactors. They could do it all from here; that was why the control room in the middle boat was always locked. It was strictly an auxiliary. Both units were controlled from the spot where he was standing now. It would be so easy to shut the reactors down, or let them run away and melt down. End it all. Burn them all—and their world—to radioactive ash.

Together, working as quietly as possible, Rick and Kiwi removed both of the clamshells and all three of the limpet mines that they had planted on the middle submarine, leaving only the satchel charge in place, with an eye to blowing the electric cable fittings to make sure the unit was entirely disabled.

Then they lugged the mines across the grating platform to the third boat, where they reattached the explosives in a pattern calculated to shatter the room where they had found the huge capacitor.

When all but one was in place, though, Rick found himself vaguely dissatisfied. No sense doing a job half-assed, and the only way to be sure was to go inside. Plant just one bomb in the middle of the capacitor bay. But when he picked up the final limpet mine and started for the access door, Kiwi stopped him with a single imperative gesture—holding the dial of his wristwatch in front of Rick's face and pointing at the dial.

Only fourteen minutes to go. Fourteen minutes from now, the timer fuses would explode the mines they had set everywhere on the Temnota platform. The ones they had moved and the ones they had left in place.

Any damn fool can make an explosion. The important part is to be somewhere else when it happens.

And they were not going to be "somewhere else." No way, José. There were simply not enough minutes left to do the job and get away. Especially when it was going to take so much longer to blow the ballast tanks a second time without having completely filled the air tanks after the first dive.

Captain Ward might have designed his SA-1 to descend to these depths, but no one could have anticipated the kind of abuse she had already endured. They were exceeding the basic capabilities of the equipment.

And their body clocks were running out, too. Mac's gill might have been designed to operate for prolonged periods at depths well below those normally attempted by men in wet suits. But nobody could tell what effect the pressure at three thousand feet might have on the chemical reactions—or on the hardware itself. And even if the gills held up, high-pressure nervous syndrome was lurking out there in the darkness, waiting to pounce as soon as the Scripps injections wore off. Which could be anytime now. It was already getting cold.

Thirteen minutes. They were clear of the middle submarine now, moving quickly but warily toward the boat nearest the landing site of the Steel Albatross. No enemy frogs in sight. And no blinding lights.

Kiwi headed for the weather-deck hatch and Rick headed for the nearest of the explosive charges. He computed the amount of time needed to remove all the explosives they had set—and came out with a negative number every time.

Rick looked at his watch . . . twelve minutes . . . and then understood what Kiwi was going to do. And hated it. But he followed in the down easter's wake anyway, arriving on deck just as Kiwi was opening the hatch, preparing to make a speargun-first descent into the interior.

Rick had to admit that it made sense, knowing he had no real alternative. They simply didn't have enough time to disarm all the charges they had set earlier. The nuclear reactor, they had been told, was hot and operating on-line. Kiwi was going to shut it down or die trying, before the clamshells went off. And it was with this thought in mind that Rick followed him into the bowels of the old Russian boat.

Ullanov began to scream when the first frogman entered the room.

You could tell that was what he was doing: the mouth opened and the cords stood out on the senior trooper's neck, though of course there was no sound. But the intruder didn't see him.

He was carrying some kind of weapon, a speargun with an explosive charge on its tip, which he pointed at Andrey. He didn't see Ullanov, who was still on the ceiling.

Andrey was frightened, not for himself, but for the reactors and what might happen if he stepped away from the safeties—the emergency cooling control, and the scram lever. The reaction could run away. He looked at the armed frogman and shook his head, as if to say, "Don't disturb me. Can't you see how dangerous this is?"

The intruder stared at him, and it was only then that Andrey noticed the strangeness. The man was wearing heavy-looking equipment on his chest, and there was a breathing mouthpiece between his teeth. But his left eye was closed in a huge, comical wink—as though he and the intruder shared some insane secret. How very strange.

And then Ullanov sprang down from the ceiling. Like everything else that happened underwater, it occurred in slow motion. But the intruder was taken completely by surprise, losing his grip on the speargun and tumbling backward out of the control room into the passageway. Ullanov—his face a mask of mad terror—rolled to his left, kicking first against the downed frogman's chest and then against the metal frame of the doorway before vanishing into the warren of corridors.

Andrey stood perfectly still, his hands motionless on the controls.

The intruder was back on his feet now and had retrieved his weapon. But he no longer pointed it at Andrey, and for a moment they simply stood there inspecting each other. Andrey noticed that the man was wounded. A thin trail of blood was oozing from a slash in his right leg. The man didn't seem to be paying any attention to it.

Strange as he knew he must look to someone accustomed to life on the surface, Andrey told himself the man facing him looked even stranger. The wet suit he wore—was it one piece or two pieces? Hard to tell, but the fins and all the rest were familiar. Andrey had learned to use gear similar to that during basic SPETSNAZ training. Was this man some kind of special trooper as well?

One of the British Royal Marine Commandos, or the Ami Special Forces? If he was a diver, and an American, he would be in their own crack Navy unit called the SEALs.

Andrey was about to try a few common gestures that might make sense to the stranger, but before he could make the effort the intruder was joined by another frog, also armed with a speargun. Had this one seen Ullanov? Killed him, perhaps? No. Probably not—he had heard nothing that sounded like an explosion.

Suddenly the newcomer moved toward him, easing down at the assistant's station in front of the panel and staring as if fascinated at the gauges. He looked at Andrey, then back at the panel, and brought his hand up in an unmistakable gesture across the throat.

Cut. For a moment, Andrey thought the man was threatening to cut his throat. But then he understood. The frogman wanted him to shut the reactors down.

Andrey stood still, hands steady over the controls. Of course, this was why they had come. Americans! Somehow they had discovered a way of entering the deep-sea universe that SPETSNAZ had thought its own domain.

And now they meant to disrupt Temnota! Well, they had much to learn. Standing where he was, with his hands in this position, they were at his mercy, not he at theirs.

One twist of that dial there, and the control rods would leap free of the core; the Amis would have just time enough to see the pointers climbing into the red zones, and understand what it meant for them—and for the whole sunlit world above them. . . .

For a long moment, Rick wasn't sure what the enemy frog would decide to do. The man's hands were on the controls. And his expression was unreadable.

Kiwi's gesture had needed no explanation; its meaning was clear, and he was sure the Russian understood it. But the man still didn't move, and the longer he hesitated the more Rick wondered if they might not be better off to yank him away from the control panel and have a go at twisting dials and shoving levers themselves.

Stan Leppard had speculated that this base was manned by specially trained SPETSNAZ naval infantry troopers. A Russian version of the SEALs. So perhaps their thought processes would not be entirely dissimilar. What was this guy thinking?

Now his hand was moving, reaching toward the long lever on his immediate right. He grasped it, closed his fingers around it . . . and slammed it down. Rick stopped breathing and fixed his whole attention on the gauges.

One by one, the pointers began to unwind, sagging down the numbers until they rested on the zero pins. The Russian had scrammed the reactors, activating the emergency control-rod insertion system, killing the reaction and turning the core cold. In a little while it would be stone dead. Meanwhile, it was time to leave. Eight minutes . . .

The Russian removed his hands from the controls and stood for a moment with his mouth open, as if trying to say something—perhaps to offer an explanation. Maybe even an apology?

But then he moved with a suddenness Rick didn't think possible, leaping toward Kiwi, snatching the SEAL instructor's Taglin spear-pistol from his hand, and executing a perfect tuck to land on his feet with the business end of the weapon swinging toward Kiwi's head.

But before he could fire, Rick's own weapon was up and aimed at the Russian's chest. He pulled the trigger . . . and was hurled back against the bulkhead by the force of the recoil.

Confined to the little control room, the explosion was deafening. And almost blinding, as well; Rick had allowed his snooper-eye to open a crack, and the flash of the exploding spear-point turned the world around him dark for a moment.

But when sight and hearing returned, it showed the Russian down—hands empty and chest torn open—against the far wall.

Kiwi, safe but showing signs of shock, was sprawled nearby.

The Russian's eyes were open; he was looking at Rick, and he wagged his head feebly, curling the edges of his mouth into a smile.

I tried; could you have done better, Yankee?

And then the eyes closed and the muscles of the face went slack as the last of life departed.

Slowly, Kiwi levered himself to his feet and moved over to look closely into the face of the dead man—the enemy frog who had saved all their lives, and then tried to kill him.

Hell of a man. Human enough to want the world to survive, to deny himself the act of vengeance that could have destroyed it. But still soldier enough to do his duty: try to kill the enemies of his country, no matter what.

Rick looked at his watch again. Six minutes . . .

A final check of the panel; the markings were in Cyrillic, but the gauges whose calibration seemed to be in degrees centigrade were still dropping.

So were the ones with numbers that might have been p.s.i. or something like that. Most others were already down to zip.

Nothing to be done about the coolant water. It was radioactive, and when its containment system let go (which it would, sooner or later), the result would barely be worth a nod compared to the cataclysm that had been averted by the Russian frog's final act. Hell of a man, for sure. But time to move along; save the bouquets for them as can use 'em.

All right then: bug-out time! Drop everything you don't have to carry, and let's get the hell out of here. Swimming now—moving swiftly and freely without thought of stealth or caution—the two Americans kick-turned into the corridor, crossed an unlighted reception bay, climbed a ladder touching only one or two rungs, and fumbled in darkness for the hatch.

It was closed. But the wheel had not been turned to lock it in place, and Rick had set his heel on the ladder for leverage to throw it open again when memory caused him to hesitate. Hatch closed? How? He had followed Kiwi into the boat. It had not occurred to him to close the hatch before they split up to look for the control bay—nor would he have done so if he'd thought of it, because he knew they were going to be in an even bigger hurry to get out.

Five minutes . . . Kiwi was beside him now, misunderstanding the situation and trying to help him crack the hatch. Rick wanted to scream in sheer frustration. The other Soviet frog he had found in the control bay—the one who had knocked him down and gotten away before Kiwi arrived—must have closed the hatch.

Even money the son of a bitch was waiting for them to come out. But there was no time to assess the situation or consider alternatives, even if he'd somehow been able to communicate it to Kiwi. Four minutes . . .

Bracing a shoulder against the locking wheel and thrusting hard with both legs, Rick catapulted himself out the opening head foremost . . . and was immediately hurled backward and sideways. At first he thought the demolition charges had exploded prematurely. Then the image of the fourth Taglin spear-pistol swam and drifted in his mind. Somehow the fugitive Soviet frog had found it and turned it against them, and missed.

He and Kiwi had left their own spearguns in the control bay, along with everything else that might slow them down. But he still had his knife. Rick drew it in the same motion that propelled him out of the boat.

Quickly he squinted the right eye closed and opened the left—to find Soviet frogmen directly in front of him, only a foot or two out of reach. Rick dodged to his left, bringing the knife up to a guard position, but the Russian did not react.

Perhaps he was stunned by the blast from the Taglin spear, too. Or maybe blind out here, unable to see without artificial light. But there was no time to find out.

Rick's attack was immediate and double-pronged—right hand driving the knife to the center of the torso, striking deep and ripping upward into the hollow beneath the ribs, while the left clamped firmly around the recycling device attached to the neck and tore it free.

The enemy frog died in a single massive convulsion, and this time Rick released the body without a second glance.

Two minutes . . . Where the hell was Kiwi? The SEAL instructor had been right behind him when they cracked the hatch. So why couldn't he find him now?

The dead Russian's chest was leaking, blanketing the area with a green cloud. Rick hardly noticed as he whirled, kicked back to the yawning darkness of the hatch opening, and dived in.

To hell with the Russkies and to hell with Temnota and to hell with Limpet mines. To hell with 'em all, and tell 'em Rick Tallman said so. And tell them he said they could all go piss into a headwind with his sincerest compliments, because he and the clamdigger are getting out of here together, or nobody goes anywhere.

One minute. For chrissake where . . . Ah! There you are, you little lobster-grabber. Gotcha! Now what the hell's the matter here? Hey, Kiwi, what's going on? Come on, dude, wake up and give your favorite SEAL candidate a hand. . . . Rick and his partner had done their jobs well, and the clock ran out on all of the mines they had set to explode at exactly the same moment.

Right on the hack.

On board *Berkone*

Monday, November 3
9:56 A.M.

The explosions were too deep in the ocean to make much of a noise on the surface. But the hydrophones Captain Ward had lowered from the *Berkone* picked up the sound. A few minutes later the ocean half a mile away suddenly boiled with an upsurge that dotted the surface with flotsam and assorted sea life.

Sam Deane, watching, shivered once in the winter chill, then glanced at her watch. The HPNS injections I gave them," she said, "the shots, will be wearing off soon."

Stan Leppard and the captain exchanged glances, but

avoided looking at her, or at the still-unshaven man who stood silently with them near the after railing of the *Berkone*.

"If they were on their way up," Admiral Richard Carter said finally, "that surge could have knocked the hell out of them."

Captain Ward nodded. "But the *Albatross* can take it," he declared. "And they'd be strapped down in the seats—not rattling around the way they would be in a regular submarine."

The admiral nodded, looking out to sea.

Santa Ana Deeps

Monday, November 3
10:02 A.M.

The first thing Rick Tallman noticed when he recovered consciousness was that he couldn't hear.

Vaguely, he recalled stories of near-death experiences where people stood outside their bodies, watching other people move around them, without being able to comment or interfere. But he couldn't recall whether or not they could hear what the people around them were saying.

Coughing, sputtering seawater into his mouthpiece and then fighting to clear an airway in order to get a decent breath, he opened both eyes and discovered he was blind as well as deaf.

Something—an oval of greenish light, dim and distant, was floating above his head. He reached for it, but his right hand didn't seem to want to follow orders.

He gave his hand explicit directions to move, thinking it needed some convincing. Finally, he realized his hand didn't work because it was locked onto the weight belt of his dive buddy, Lt. K. W. Kraus, USN, the well-known clamdigger. And Kiwi was not moving at all.

Rick's legs flexed and kicked (intense pain shot through his right leg), bringing the oval of greenish light closer, while he maintained his grip on Kiwi. He wasn't entirely sure about where they were. If only he could get to where the light was . . . but it was taking forever. And then the hatch was open and he levered himself out, dragging Kiwi after him. He paused for a moment, trying to reassess the situation.

Rick was, indeed, alive. Kiwi's chest was still moving and his breathing apparatus was still in place. But Kiwi's eyes remained closed, without even a flicker of the lids.

Something was wrong with the landscape around Rick; the *Albatross* wasn't in sight, and nothing looked familiar. Then he remembered the explosion. He and Kiwi had been responsible for it. The demolition charges had gone off right on schedule.

They were alive, though a little scuffed around the edges. But better than they should have been since they had violated the first rule of demolitions: *The important part is not to be there when it happens.*

So flunk me, Rick thought. Flunk us both.

Slowly, Rick began a 360-degree scan of their immediate area—and spotted the *Steel Albatross* just as he was passing through 180 degrees. There it was, about fifty or sixty feet beyond where the nose of the submarine used to be.

Demolition charges attached to the stern section near the nuclear reactor had cut the submarine in two, turning the broken pieces at angles to their original position, separated by a gulf of green water. But the bay they had just left seemed to have come through the explosion more or less intact, its bulkheads strong enough to weather the violence.

Breathing more naturally after a few moments of rest, Rick turned back to check his swim partner's vital signs again. Pulse slow but strong, respiration deep and regular. Kiwi must be out cold. Had he hit his head on something?

The Soviet frog had tried to ice them with their misplaced speargun. But Rick had been lucky enough to get only a little reflected blast effect. Kiwi had been behind him—so maybe the thing had gone off right in his face.

He peered narrowly at the SEAL instructor. Kiwi didn't seem to be leaking (though a green haze seeped from his own leg wound). The best thing would be to get him back to the *Albatross*.

He slipped an arm around his partner's chest and began towing—pushing off from the second sub's deck and bringing them to a relatively soft landing on the Temnota platform.

The metal grating under his feet was tilted now, loose from the force of the explosions. Suddenly, the side of the SA-1 was directly ahead of them, and Rick gave one more hard kick with his good leg to bring them to her side.

No damage visible. But that didn't mean a thing. The real test would be when they tried to get her back to the surface.

A tiny fingertip of chill touched the very center of his back, and Rick tried to dismiss it as a reaction to the place and their situation. But he knew he was kidding himself.

Kiwi's swim fins were still attached to his feet, and Rick struggled to get them off before trying to reinsert his dive partner in the aft seat. Even with the hatch fully open, it was heavy work. Not to mention a bad fit.

He backed off and tried again. This time, Kiwi's feet and legs went where they were supposed to, but the instrument panel kept trying to poke the SEAL instructor in the face. The canopy wanted to snag the breathing equipment, now unshipped from Kiwi's back.

Break some part of the gill now, dammit, and the rest of the evolution would be purely academic, Rick thought.

Finally, Kiwi's limp body sagged against the seat and Rick bent over the side to strap him in. Then he turned to the more familiar business of getting himself into the forward position. Accomplishing it was more difficult than he remembered; his fingers did not offer perfect cooperation. When he, too, was strapped down, another chill crystallized in the middle of his back.

He checked his watch—10:14.

Samantha had warned them that they needed to be back on the surface not later than 9:45 A.M. That was when their HPNS injections would wear off. It was the Cinderella factor, and their coach was starting to turn back into a pumpkin. After Rick closed the canopy and locked it down, the chill came again—harder, accompanied by the first tremors—and he groped for the auxiliary cockpit-drain switch.

Fighting back the sudden surge of adrenaline that was the leading edge of real panic, Rick forced his mind to assume conscious control of his extremities and begin working through his checklist.

Bubbles began to rise to the top of the canopy; soon he would be able to remove his mouthpiece. And Kiwi's.

He tried to look back over his shoulder to make sure Kiwi

was still breathing, but the effort was more than he could handle. His head just wouldn't turn that far. And trying touched off another chill.

It passed, but the trembling remained. There was no doubting it now, the Shakes were upon him, but not as bad as they would be. For the moment he still had control of his extremities.

Rick stole another look at his watch: 10:21. It was taking one hell of a long time to get the water out of the boat's cockpit and ballast tanks, and the boat was still a long way from achieving positive buoyancy. The *Albatross* was as near total exhaustion as her crew.

Another major tremor, the strongest yet, seized his shoulders and shook him like a dog, effectively amputating the thought that had been forming a moment earlier. Rick sat it out and tried to concentrate again when the spasm was done.

If it turns out that the SA-1 can't get loose from the bottom, Rick thought, you're still not out of choices. You could:

—Reopen the canopy and try to make it to the surface with Kiwi in tow, using the gill, or

—Reopen the canopy and try to make it to the surface by yourself.

But going back without Kiwi was out. He knew he'd never be able to live with having abandoned someone on the bottom of the sea in order to save his own skin. That wasn't the way the Teams operated.

Even if they dropped everything else except the breathing gear and recyclers, they would still be dead meat.

There had to be an alternative. Rick was sure he was forgetting something else. Something he'd almost had hold of a little while ago. Something important.

Another shiver took him.

The bubbles stopped coming from under the seats. The deballasting tanks were empty. They weren't going home.

Precious minutes passed.

Slumped in the front seat of the *Steel Albatross*, Rick tried to control the shaking that now racked his entire body. His mental processes had become more and more erratic; thoughts erupted into his consciousness, then slipped away before he could grasp them. It was like being drunk or in the grip of nitrogen narcosis—rapture of the deep—but without the euphoria. It was a bad trip. Very bad.

Something important was trying to break through into Rick's chaotic mind where a spark of conscious, logical thought lingered. With an effort of will, he managed to center his efforts on a point at the middle of his back. And . . . push. Not physically; no muscular exertion was involved. But push was the nearest metaphor for the mental effort involved.

A picture of the *Steel Albatross* formed and lodged among the mental seaweed that now filled his brain. But not a picture of the dark-painted boat he and Kiwi were trapped in. This *Steel Albatross*, the one he was thinking of, was bright and shiny. A vehicle formed and polished and controlled by radio in . . . in . . . in . . .

The image in his mind shimmered, shifted, changed shape, and became a silver goldfish he had as a child. His stepfather had bought him a king-size aquarium, complete with air pump, living weeds, and a little drowned castle. That fish had lived there for three years before an alteration of the chemicals in the Palm Beach water supply made it float on the top. And soon he would be just as dead, but on the bottom.

No, not the silver goldfish. The *Steel Albatross*. The original *Steel Albatross*. The one the captain had had in his laboratory at Scripps. The stainless steel model. The keel on that boat.

What about it? It was just a keel. A piece of shaped steel attached to the bottom of that model to keep it upright in the water. Was that all, though? No—something else. But what? Well, the goldfish didn't have a keel like that.

The hell with the goldfish! The keel! Something had happened about the keel, in the lab at Scripps. Something important. Visualize it. Remember, goddammit!

The captain had done something with the keel. A picture started to form, fractured and formed again, and then came clear: Captain Ward with the shiny model of the *Steel Albatross* in his hand, shaking it. To get the water out. The damn thing leaked and had an irritating habit of sinking to the bottom of the tank after a dive or two. Just like the full-size boat.

But when the model did things like this, the solution was a

breeze. Just take a long stick and fish for the thing. Wish someone had a long stick like that now. Or . . . Captain Ward could just punch a button on the control panel and—presto! The little boat would drop its . . .

Oh, Christ Jesus, yes! Yes! The keel of the model boat would come off and stay on the bottom of the tank while the rest of the boat, deprived of the weight, would just pop right back up to the surface.

The tiny flicker of hope brought Rick's head erect and enabled him to focus his eyes briefly on the dark and useless rectangle of the computer screen. No help there, of course. The name of this game was Manual Control—subheading: keel jettison handle.

It had never actually been used, not even in testing after Captain Ward had installed the manual system. Impossible to get the keel back if you left it down on the bottom of the sea. But he'd shown Rick where it was, of course, and it had been dry-tested a couple of times, aboard the *Berkone*.

The thought of the *Berkone* set Rick's mind adrift again, jittering and skittering out of control just like his body.

Got to focus on the keel. Keel jettison handle. On the deck. Under my feet, and back out of harm's way near the seat pedestal. Tucked away there and guarded to keep it from being pulled by mistake. This time, the release would be on purpose. If it happened at all.

Rick tried to move his right hand down to where he could grasp the jettison handle, and discovered that he could not even release his fingers from the control stick. A major effort of will would be required to make his tightly clamped hand relax. A major effort that he was entirely unable to mount.

Damn it! Concentrate, Tallman. Get it all together and aim it right at the hand. At the stick, aim the thoughts there and tell the fingers to let go of the damn stick and relax. Straighten out the fingers. Point them out from the palm of the hand and then move the arm back from the . . . from the . . . ah! There! Got you now, you son of a bitch.

Rick's right arm, freed suddenly from the stick, began to vibrate fingers and palm dancing before his eyes.

Cautiously, still fighting for conscious control, Rick bent his body forward, spreading his knees to allow the arm to fall between them. So far so good. Now to get it down to where the keel release handle was.

By long-established habit, he had fastened the seat belt as part of the act of sitting down in the cockpit. But now the shoulder harness was keeping him from bending as far forward as he needed, in order to reach the keel release handle. Release the sissy straps first, then go for the keel toggle. But the right hand was in no position to do the work, down there between his knees.

Numbly, blinking his snoopered left eye, he forced his chin inch by inch to the left. At last he was able to register the fact that his left hand was simply hanging by his side. It was twitching and shaking like the right, but at least it wasn't tied to anything.

Switching concentration from the right side of his body to the left, he took charge of the shaking hand and brought it up to the shoulder-harness release. His finger found the button. And pushed. But the hand just wasn't paying attention. Try as he would, he could not press hard enough on the release button.

Son of a bitch! Abandoning the fingers, he concentrated instead on the knuckles. The one just under the thumb . . . into the release button. Hard. Harder . . .

Suddenly the harness was loose, freeing his upper torso, which fell forward, banging his head on the side of the dead computer screen.

It hurt, but he hardly noticed. He turned his efforts back to the keel jettison handle.

Groping, the fingers of his right hand made brief contact with the deck at the base of the seat. Rick was able to identify the release before his fingers danced away.

He had to find a way to control his fingers just for a second or two. Rick bent more to let his shoulder ride free. His whole hand was in contact with the release handle, now. He had to make the fingers go in and under the handle.

For just a moment his hand had been in the right place. But before the order could be given to his hand to tighten and pull, the moment was past.

Rick knew he had to do the whole thing again. And again

and again and again as long as life endured and consciousness lasted.

Fingers down, under the handle. Curled around under it and tighten the fist. Harder.

Please, God, just this once let me hold on and not let go because every damn part of my body is going to go into this pull.

Squeezing his eyelids shut, Rick stiffened his back and turned his shoulders suddenly counterclockwise in a single, ultimate effort.

A lurch to port and a sudden blow to the back of his head shattered Rick's reality and sent it spinning for the second time in less than an hour. The handle was still in his hand. But it was limp; unconnected to the boat. Just a piece of metal. He had failed. And the boat had failed, too. Come apart just when he needed it to work the way it was designed to do.

Well, fuck it. The handle was released by the renewed twitching of his fingers, and it fell free. It struck his right thigh and just lay there, as he was lying on his left side in the seat of the SA-1.

He had an odd sense of lying on the floor of an elevator.

EPILOGUE

Moscow, U.S.S.R.

Tuesday, November 4
2:00 A.M.

They came for the old man long before dawn, pulling up to his house on Kutuzovsky Prospekt in a convoy of black Zil sedans. Bursting through the door, they found the body of Comrade Gen. V. I. Tregorin, deputy commander of Strategic Rocket Forces and voting member of the Politburo, sitting ramrod straight in a brown leather wing chair facing the front window and staring sightlessly into the night.

An extra yellow pill was in his left hand. But he hadn't needed it. The KGB officer who led the party sniffed near the mouth and caught the last lingering scent of burnt almonds.

No oral valedictory was picked up by any of the room's several listening devices. But there was a red leather-bound book in his right hand. A piece of paper on which he had written two words in English marked the place of the final diary entry:

"Wild card."

Although several of the security policemen could read English, and one or two even recognized the American poker term, nothing was made of it. But inside the diary was a letter.

The first rule of a good patriot is "Be prepared to die for your country." And I, General Viktor I. Tregorin, have lived like a patriot, for I believe that the motherland is sacred above all else, especially the individual. As one who loves the U.S.S.R., I feel I owe it to her future to explain my actions and detail my plans, in the hope that subsequent generations of patriots may learn from my mistakes.

My plan was called Temnota. The goal—to free our country from the threat of foreign presence on our soil. Historically, there is much to fear, for though Napoleon and Hitler both tried and failed to conquer us, never before has our internal political situation been as threatening as the external forces. I did not fear invading armies as in the past, but the encroachment of democracy. Communist countries that have buffered our borders since the end of the Great Patriotic War began turning toward the West. Czechoslovakia, Hungary, Poland, East Germany, the Baltics, and the Balkans have all denounced our way of governing and living in favor of Western European and American ways. Soon, there would be a McDonald's in Red Square, and a Pepsi-Cola billboard in front of Lenin's tomb. And I blame our present general secretary.

Though it is difficult to imagine (considering his life prior to gaining his present position), our general secretary has presented a world image as a man of peace, a man of reform, a man of reason. He is unwilling to face the consequences of war. He is letting slip away the hard-fought victories of the last fifty years.

The Americans like him because they see him as similar to themselves. For once, I agree with them. I find him as foolish and as weak as the Americans are. However, this is not a world made for weaklings and fools.

Though the General Secretary would never make an initial move in a military sense against the West, he would have to respond to an attack. If the Amis were to attack property of the U.S.S.R.—to commit an act of war—he would retaliate.

For their part, the Americans would probably not initiate a military attack against us either, though they are certainly unstable and unpredictable in such matters. Therefore, they must be provoked into an attack.

I had to come up with a plan where I could delicately pull all the strings, as a master puppeteer handles a complex marionette. I therefore devised a masterpiece of timing and misdirection, a two-pronged attack I christened Temnota. First, a new communications satellite was launched, the Cosmos

2300. Ami intelligence followed the launch and monitored the satellite's orbit closely, as a matter of routine.

Meanwhile, an undersea nuclear power station was nearing completion off the coast of the town of Las Olinas, California. It met the requirements of Temnota by being off the western coast of the United States, being near a major power station, and being in a deep underwater trench close to the shore. This installation, known as Station "O," sat on the sea bottom almost nine hundred meters below the surface. Its construction tested the limits of the finest technology the U.S.S.R. has to offer. It even required new technology, with men specially trained to use it. The intimate details of Station "O" are in clearly marked files in my Kremlin office.

It was necessary to test the EMP technology to make sure it worked. And therefore it was necessary to mask the source of the EMP during the test. A simple undersea explosion was touched off at the moment the small EMP generator on Station "O" sent a power surge up the Las Olinas cable. Simultaneously, the Cosmos 2300 satellite sent out a weak EMP from its krypton-fluoride laser. This EMP was not strong enough to harm anything.

Since the Cosmos 2300 was assumed to be a spy satellite, it was being tracked by the U.S.'s tracking network. Nobody actually sits at a desk watching a screen. The monitoring is all automatic, and the weak EMP would have set off an alarm. The officials would be able to check tapes and printouts and would see an anomaly. It would probably show up as a type of static. They would know they were measuring something, but they wouldn't be quite sure what it was, in the same way that if you tell someone with an AM radio to monitor the FM band, they would not be able to report any occurrence of FM signals. The FM signals exist, of course, but not to a person with a radio that cannot pick them up. And the Amis certainly wouldn't be looking for EMPs from the Cosmos 2300.

Eventually the Amis would figure out that the EMP came from the satellite, and figure that the undersea explosion was a by-product of the power surge. Then the two events would have been associated by the Pentagon. The generals would tell this to the new, untried Ami president. They would tell him we attacked his country from space.

Of course, nothing would happen yet. But it was necessary that the President and the General Secretary begin to argue, to accuse, to distrust each other. It was imperative that mutual suspicion should grow between them.

Despite all the intricate planning, the rigid training of the men recruited from SPETSNAZ, and the attention paid to the most minute details, Project Temnota was vulnerable to the unforeseen. The American poker term "wild card" has no parallel in the game of chess that so fascinates our countrymen And it was this wild card that we could not adjust to. Perhaps our society is a more controlled, more structured, and more rigid one than that of the Americans, and we are not as able to improvise and handle matters when the unexpected happens.

It would have worked. Many men gave their lives for Temnota—Comrade Petchukocov, many SPETSNAZ frogmen, Yuri Narmonov, and now myself. My greatest regret is that I shall not live to see Mother Russia, the Rodina, become the on world power; safe, strong, and secure—forever.

General Viktor I. Tregor

On Board *Berkone*

Monday, November 3
2:11 P.M.

All things considered, being dead wasn't so bad. Except f the headache. And that got Rick pissed off. You aren't su posed to get headaches when you're dead.

"I think he's awake."

Rick took a deep, yawning breath. And almost gagged. Wh the hell was wrong with the air in this place? Burned his thro Like French-kissing a can of Drano.

Irritated—he opened his right eye, only to find another e staring back at him from close range. But the eye staring ba at him was out of focus. And the light here wasn't right, eith Not green enough.

"Take a deep breath, sir."

"Fuck it," a second voice said.

"Deep breath . . . good! Again," the first voice said.

His chest hurt and his throat hurt, and if he didn't do som thing soon, it was going to get worse.

"Leave me alone!" the second voice said, sounding strangely familiar to Rick. Parts of him seemed to be operating well enough, but someone had forgotten to cut the brain into the command loop. That second voice was his. He'd have to speak to someone about that. Complain to the management.

Suddenly, a hand clamped down on his forehead. A pair of fingers gently parted the lids of the eye he had opened earlier.

"Can you see, sir?"

Rick started to answer, but thought better of it. Tough question. He couldn't bring the world around him into focus. And he couldn't understand why all the colors were so bright.

"Do you hear me, Mr. Tallman? Can you see me? I'm trying to find out if you can see."

The eye that had been so close before was farther back now, and Rick was able to make out the face around it. Mustache. Nose. Mouth.

"Do you hear me?"

"I hear you."

"Can you see me?"

"I . . . uh, it's blurry. Where . . .?"

"In the chamber. On the barge; we're recompressing you."

"Huh?"

"Taking you back down to twenty-nine hundred feet and bringing you up again a little bit at a time—on table seventeen alpha. You fellows, uh, came up kinda sudden a while ago."

"Oh."

"No! Don't go back to sleep on me yet!"

Rough hands seized Rick's arm, and he felt the sudden sting of a needle. The world under his head tilted downward, and something painful was done to his chest.

But at length the darkness receded. The paramedic seemed satisfied and broke off the rest of the torture routine.

"Look at me."

Rick really didn't want to play the eye game anymore.

"Look at me!"

Rick winched his eyelids open.

"Better. Much better."

Rick was beginning to get used to the surface light, when he remembered.

"My dive buddy?" Rick said.

"What about him?"

"Is he . . . ?"

"He's fine. Sleepy, like you. But the doc got him awake."

"The doc?"

"Ms. Deane. I'm a Coast Guard paramedic. Mr. Kraus seemed to be having some really serious problems, so she's in the chamber with us."

Sam's face, strained but cheerful, appeared beside the Coast Guard paramedic and flashed Rick The Eyes.

"Kiwi's going to be fine," she said. "And he said you did good."

Rick grinned at her. "I can't wait till he wakes up, so he can say it all over again, to me."

Samantha went on smiling. "Congratulations, Rick."

"Thanks, Sam. For everything. I . . ."

"Not now, Rick. When we're out of the chamber, we'll talk. There's a lot I have to say."

Then the loudspeaker crackled. "Back with us again?" Captain Ward's voice. But tinny; like a recording.

"Where are you?"

"Outside. Talking on the intercom. I'm looking through the window."

Rick craned his neck and pushed with his right leg, trying to see behind himself.

"Ow! Shit—!"

Samantha settled him back onto the cot where he had been lying.

"Take it easy," the captain's voice said. "You got kind of a mean-looking stab wound there."

"Tell me about it."

"What the hell'd you and Kiwi do down there—take on the whole damn Russian Navy?"

"Tell you all about it sometime," Rick promised. "Even let you read the whole report. In triplicate."

"No report." Another voice. Also sounding tinny.

"No report—what's that supposed to mean?" Rick inquired.

"Just what I said," Stan Leppard replied. "Not from you. Not from Kiwi. Not from Captain Ward. Not from anybody."

"You want to sort that out for me?" Rick asked.

"Sure. Situation's as follows: None of today ever happened.

No nuclear-reactor base down under the sea. No liquid-breathing frogmen. No plot to knock out every computer on the coast. No Temnota. Nothing!"

"Wanna bet?" Rick said.

"Yeah. How does this trifecta grab you: the Department of the Navy, the Joint Chiefs of Staff, and the President of the United States."

"Jee-zus!"

"Him, too," Leppard said with a snort. "For whatever it's worth, the President got on the horn to Moscow and laid the whole thing on his buddy the General Secretary—and I think there's gonna be a hot time in the old Kremlin tonight. And I'd bet real money on that.

"Anyway, don't go buying a new uniform for any Navy Cross ceremony."

"So since it never happened," Rick agreed, "I guess I'm not really here."

There was a pause, and for a moment Rick thought they had all gone away. But then another voice took over.

"Richard?"

"Dad . . . ? Are you here, on the ship?"

"Yes, Richard."

"I'm . . . glad to hear your voice.

"And I'm damn glad to hear yours."

"Yes, sir . . ."

There was an awkward pause. But before it could become too embarrassing, the admiral was speaking again.

"Dr. Deane told me a couple of things while you were unconscious."

Oh, no, thought Rick. What did she do!

"The first was that your SEAL class is going to graduate without you, because you're officially on medical rollback. As of now."

"Shit! That's not fair!"

"You could still finish, of course," the admiral continued. "The next class should be open about the time the wound in your leg is healed."

"Great . . . and what was the other message?"

"She also said she's changed her mind, now, about your arm."

"Changed her mind?"

"She'll operate, if that's what you want. Says she'll personally supervise your follow-up therapy, to make sure you complete it."

Rick found himself smiling a little. But not as widely as he'd thought he would at that kind of news. "Will she, now?" he said.

"Yes. Seems very dedicated." The admiral paused. "You'd be able to fly fighters again," he ventured.

"Yep," Rick said.

Another pause. Longer this time. But the admiral hadn't lost interest or gone away.

"I . . . uh . . . talked to an old friend in Vienna a few days ago," he said. "I wish you could have met him. I think you two would have liked each other. He made some suggestions to me. Good ones, I think."

"Yeah?" Rick said, wondering what his father was babbling about.

"We'll . . . uh . . . talk about them later. Um . . . there's a telephone call I'd like you to make. Someone who wants to talk to you . . . as soon as you get out of there, I mean." Suddenly, the admiral shifted gears. "Did Colonel Leppard tell you that everything about your . . . expedition . . . today is classified?"

"Yes, sir. He said it never happened."

"Well, I don't know how, but your mother has the damnedest way of hearing about things."

"You mean, she—?"

"Actually phoned the ship! Spoke to Will Ward and demanded to talk to you. On an open-frequency radiophone, by God!"

Rick wanted to shout with laughter. That was his mama, for sure. He wondered what they'd had to promise her to get her off the horn.

"So now," the admiral went on, "she's home in Palm Beach. Call her, will you? And let her know you're all right."

"Okay."

"And Richard . . ."

"Yes, sir?"

"I'm proud of you, son."

"Thanks."

There was a pause while the admiral shooed away Will Ward. "And whether you know it or not, I love you, Ricky." Then he left.

Rick yawned hugely and tried to sort it all out. It was a marvelous jumble—Mama's spy system, the SEALs, Kiwi, the *Albatross*, international conspiracies that never happened, the chance to fly fighters again—and his father's approval.

Nobody else tried to talk to Rick, and after a minute or two his eyes drifted shut again. This time the paramedic let him sleep.